David Rollins was born in Sydney in 1958 and grew up in a household where politics was consumed at dinner along with lamb chops, peas and mash. David has worked as a journalist and advertising copywriter. His first novel *Rogue Element* was published in 2003. He lives in Sydney with his family.

Also by David Rollins

ROGUE ELEMENT
SWORD OF ALLAH
THE DEATH TRUST
A KNIFE EDGE
HARD RAIN

THE ZERO OPTION

DAVID ROLLINS

MACMILLAN
Pan Macmillan Australia

First published 2009 in Macmillan by Pan Macmillan Australia Pty Limited
1 Market Street, Sydney

National Library of Australia
Cataloguing-in-Publication data:

Rollins, David A.
The zero option / David Rollins.
9781405039178 (pbk.)

A823.4

Typeset in 11/15 pt Birka by Post Pre-press Group
Printed in Australia by McPherson's Printing Group

Papers used by Pan Macmillan Australia Pty Ltd are natural, recyclable
products made from wood grown in sustainable forests. The manufacturing
processes conform to the environmental regulations of the country of origin.

For the 269

A lie which is half a truth is ever the blackest of lies.
—Alfred Lord Tennyson, 'The Grandmother'

Prologue

September 1, 2011

Wakkanai, Hokkaido, Japan. Curtis Foxx removed his shoes one at a time, balanced on one leg and then the other as he peeled off his socks. It was late afternoon and the black sand between his toes felt cold but not unpleasant; the violent winter that would eventually sweep down from Siberia was still months away.

The man he'd come to meet was already down by the water's edge, quietly chanting a prayer to his gods. It had been on a boat off this stretch of sand, exactly one year after the terrible event, that a bond was forged between them. He watched as the man threw his hands high in the air, tossing chrysanthemums into the waves rolling in from La Pérouse Strait, the bleak stretch of water that separated this far northern tip of the Japanese island of Hokkaido from Russia's Sakhalin Island.

The chill breeze carried with it a few words of the Shinto prayer. More flowers were thrown into the waves, which immediately tossed them right back as if the man's prayer had been rejected, the stems eddying around his ankles. Curtis walked to the water's edge and into the man's peripheral vision.

'Yuudai-san,' Curtis said, his voice a coarse whisper.

'Shh . . . let me finish my goodbye,' Yuudai Suzuki replied.

Curtis took half a step back. He'd stopped believing in any kind of god long ago. He folded his arms in an attempt to capture some warmth. Theirs was an odd friendship, bound by a secret. The day was September 1, the anniversary of the crash that had simultaneously joined their lives and changed them forever.

'How long have the doctors given you?' Curtis asked when his Japanese friend had finished.

'Long enough. Four months. Perhaps more, perhaps less.'

The ravages of cancer were easy for Curtis to see. Yuudai's face was bony, the cords in his neck plainly visible. Several bandaids covered sores on his forearms where his paper-thin skin had torn. The clothes he wore hung off him as if they were borrowed from a much larger person. Indeed, when they first met, Yuudai Suzuki had been a big man and his friends had called him Sumo.

'And you, Curtis?'

'Less.'

'You look okay. They might be mistaken.'

'Perhaps.'

When Curtis happened to catch his reflection in the mirror, what he saw was a virtual cadaver—yellow, gaunt and dying. With a shot liver and no hope of a transplant, there wasn't much of anything the doctors could do for him. Still, nothing would have stopped him from making this journey.

'You having second thoughts about going through with it?' he asked.

'No. We agreed and it is time,' Yuudai said. 'You?'

'No.'

'Is your son ready?'

Curtis shrugged. 'How do you get anyone ready for this?'

'It's a big responsibility. The knowledge will be a burden.'

'I know his mother. She'll have brought him up right. He'll figure out what to do.' Curtis pulled the zipper up tighter under his neck. 'No way is this secret going to die with us.'

Yuudai had no children and had never married. As an only child, his line would finish with his death. His private shame was that he had no one to pass anything on to—good or bad.

'What about the girl?' Curtis asked. 'You still stalking her?'

'I moved out of her building six months ago. Watching over someone is not stalking.'

'You haven't changed your mind about her?'

'I got to know her quite well. She has inner strength, as well as every book ever written on the subject. Yes, together, Akiko and your son are our best chance.'

Curtis, like Yuudai, had signed secrecy agreements. He had sworn to honor them. But on his death, that pact of silence would expire.

'The nightmares are getting worse,' said Yuudai, changing the subject.

'It's just your medication.'

'No, I don't think so.'

The sun was setting, the temperature dropping with it. Neither man spoke as the stiffening late afternoon breeze sliced through their clothes. A wavelet rolled over Curtis's feet, the sudden cold snap-freezing his blood. It numbed his toes but focused his mind. The event that had brought them together had happened twenty-eight years ago today. He still remembered it with piercing clarity. On that day, also, his son had been born, making it the very best and the very worst day of his life. In time, Curtis thought, perhaps the man his son had become would understand. He hoped so.

'Did you bring it with you?' he asked.

Yuudai dug an envelope out of his pocket and passed it to Curtis, who broke the gum seal and peered inside. There it was: twenty-eight minutes and six seconds of tape. Only two men in the world knew for certain of its existence. Soon, his son and Yuudai's protégée would take possession of it, but not before Curtis and Yuudai were gone from this world.

BOOK ONE

THE TIMES
October 5, 1981

Soviets Shoot Down President's Plan

Washington DC—The Soviet Union announced today that it has formally rejected the 'Zero Option' plan proposed by United States President Ronald Reagan to limit the proliferation of nuclear intermediate-range ballistic missiles (IRBM) on the European continent.

In broad outline, the plan called for the scrapping of US IRBM Pershing II and ground-launched cruise missiles (GLCM) in exchange for the Soviet elimination of the SS-4, SS-5 and SS-20 intermediate-range missiles.

Pentagon sources say the Soviet Union has completed the deployment of more than 330 of the new mobile SS-20 missiles, each with three independently targeted warheads, aimed at population centres as well as military sites and storage facilities across Western Europe.

In response to the Soviet rejection, NATO has announced that it will bring forward the modernization of its intermediate-range nuclear forces (INF), deploying 108 single-warhead Pershing II missiles throughout West Germany and 464 of the single-warhead GLCMs in Great Britain and in Sicily.

Missile deployment is scheduled for December 1983, despite European fears that introducing the new missiles will make the continent a nuclear battleground.

THE NEW YORK TIMES
March 5, 1983

Protest Blocks US Army Base

Neu-Ulm, West Germany—Medium-range Pershing II missiles are set to be deployed in West Germany, but the several thousand protesters who blocked the main entrance gate at the Neu-Ulm US Army Base today were determined to prevent that from coming to pass.

A further series of protests is scheduled to take place this month, culminating in an attempt to ring the base with a human chain of interlocked arms. This would symbolize unity and defiance, said a spokesman for the anti-missile movement. He added that more than 150,000 people were expected to take part, dwarfing even the massive demonstrations organized by British anti-nuclear protesters at Greenham Common recently. The spokesman said 30 special trains and 800 chartered buses would transport the demonstrators to the base, people from all walks of life, and from all over West Germany.

Today's protest started peacefully, but the mood deteriorated later in the day when a convoy of army trucks arrived at the base and the police riot squad was called in to clear the road of protesters. The US Army is responding with indifference to the public show of disquiet, maintaining a facade of business as usual. When asked if the new missiles would arrive on schedule later in the year, a US Army colonel who asked not to be identified said it was not the American military's habit to pass out delivery dates, nor was it policy to either confirm or deny the presence of nuclear weapons.

March 4, 1983

US Army Base, Neu-Ulm, Bavaria, West Germany. It was a fine early spring day, but noisy as hell. The uproar from the besieging hordes beyond the wire was so loud that National Security Agency analyst Roy Garret could feel the vibration through the soles of his boots. He took a deep breath then started heading off the base through a secondary gate. He was joined almost immediately by a spook who'd introduced himself earlier as Hank.

'Mind if I tag along?' Hank asked.

Garret shrugged.

The two men gave the army sentries a nod as they passed beneath the boom towards the barbed wire coiled across the road. A group of demonstrators spotted them leaving and identified them as the enemy.

'He! He sie . . . !' they called out.

Garret and Hank ignored them, and once off the base were enveloped by the chanting, dancing, swirling crowd, becoming just another couple of guys among those with 'Ban the Bomb' patches on the pockets of their jackets and hand-rolled cigarettes drooping from their lips. Teachers, doctors, merchants, clerks—the middle-aged mainstream—had all been drawn into the protest. Garret observed that many had even brought their kids. This wasn't just a bunch of hippies, although they were also here in numbers. This was a ground-swell, just as he'd predicted.

They continued to push their way through into a more conventional peacenik sideshow dominated by incense, patchouli oil and body odor. Garret smelled marijuana. Sinewy hippie types were dancing to Janis Joplin. Other demonstrators painted like skeletons towered over the crowd on stilts. A man dressed as Uncle Sam darted here and there, thrusting his palms smeared with fake blood into people's faces. Costumed Grim Reapers with scythes prowled among cardboard coffins lying on the ground.

Placards were everywhere, ranging from the unimaginative 'Missiles Out' and 'Down with the USA' to the more inventive 'Smoke the Weed, Not the Ground' and 'USAssholes Out!' A large banner had been painted with 'USA' and 'USSR' combined to make crosses in a graveyard.

Above the commotion Hank shouted, 'These people have no idea.'

Garret agreed. They didn't realize that the only barrier between them and a few thousand Soviet T80 tanks rolling across their deluded pacifist asses was the determination of the United States to stop Ivan dead in his tracks. And yes, okay, with nukes. The protesters only saw the mushroom clouds. They didn't see that the bombs were far more potent just sitting around, *deterring*.

At the main gate, the crowd was more condensed and more determined. There was no carnival atmosphere here and the front lines of the protest advanced with arms interlocked.

'It's like those Vietnam demonstrations, the ones in DC,' Hank shouted. 'All those pissed moms and dads, remember?'

Garret remembered. Disenchanted moms and dads made politicians nervous.

'You know,' said Hank, 'I was at Greenham, and this ain't no isolated event. What we've got here is a trend. And a trend, my friend, is hard to defend.'

This Hank guy was getting on his nerves. Garret stopped, the protesters whirling around them. 'You're CIA, aren't you?'

Hank turned. 'Nope, State,' he said with a grin. 'And you? NSA, right?'

'Peace Corps.'

'We're both professionals, then,' said Hank.

Garret took a moment to give the spook the once-over. He was five eleven, average build. Maybe 180 pounds. A narrow, pinched face with brown hair, brown eyes, skin grafts on one side of his neck, a deep scar on the other. A 'Nam vet, probably.

'Who sent you to spy on me?' Garret asked, walking toward a patch of less crowded higher ground.

'You're paranoid.'

'You flew in last night,' said Garret. 'A C-130 with no tail markings. I'm guessing it's a Company plane.'

'Okay, you got me. Think of me as your security.'

Hank craned his neck to look over the heads of the protesters and watched the crowd flow back and forth like compacted trash in a rolling swell. A water cannon had arrived, along with five buses, all painted black. The bus doors opened and a riot squad surged out.

'Spy, security—same thing. You're what, early thirties?'

'Close enough,' said Hank.

'So your pay grade is probably O-4 and therefore too senior to be muscle. And I'm bigger than you, anyway. I could be *your* security.'

Hank grinned. 'Don't flatter yourself, pilgrim.'

The Polizei, all in black with clear shields and brandishing long riot sticks, advanced in lock-step toward the protesters, escorting the water cannon. A roar went up from the crowd as a convoy of US Army semi-trailers appeared further down the road, heading for the base at a crawl. The riot police were there to clear a path. People passed around the word: '*Raketen*'. It swept through the crowd like the wind. '*Raketen*', '*Raketen!*'

'Rockets,' Hank yelled over the noise and the chanting. 'The Krauts think those trucks are carrying fucking missiles. Don't these morons know we'll be *flying* them in? Probably just truckloads of pizza and ice-cream down there.'

Hundreds of demonstrators turned away from the base, swarmed onto the road and lay down in front of the trucks. In the rush, Garret saw two of the skeletons on stilts fall and become trampled by the swirling masses.

11

A hover of helicopters arrived to film the action for the evening news. The riot squad cut off the main body of demonstrators while the water cannon went to work on the human speedbumps. The truck convoy inched forward.

'Let's cut the crap, Hank. Are you going to tell me why you're looking over my shoulder, or do I have to make a formal complaint?'

'No need to be a fuckwit, Garret. I'm just doing what I've been paid to do, which in this case is to keep you out of trouble. I'm not here to wipe your ass or be your whipping boy, so bottom line . . . keep a leash on your attitude, okay?'

'You still haven't answered my question. I want to know who sent you here and why.'

'You have friends in the administration.'

Garret snorted in disbelief.

The riot squad were hammering away with their truncheons, raising the heavy sticks high over their heads, way back behind their shoulders, and then swinging them down like pickaxes. Several demonstrators, faces covered in blood, were hauled from the mob by their fellow protesters. The crowd retaliated, swallowing a couple of police officers on the outer end of the line. The uniformed men disappeared beneath a torrent of fists and boots as another water cannon truck knocked down people before sluicing them away with powerful water jets.

'You wrote a discussion paper,' Hank said.

Garret blinked. The paper he'd written was an internal one. As far as he was aware, it had gone no further than his section head.

'Roy, frankly I'm surprised. Being such a bright spark, I thought you'd have figured it out by now. I work for the office of the National Security Advisor.'

Garret was stunned. 'You work for Clark?'

'No, I work for the guy who works for Clark.'

Hank paused as a unit of riot police sprinted past them and tackled a Grim Reaper to the ground for poking at another cop with a scythe, which was a cardboard blade, taped to a roll of cardboard. 'So when you're done here, that unmarked plane you saw will whisk you Stateside.'

'What for?'

'You're wanted back in Washington. Whatever it was you wrote in that paper, pilgrim, some hombres with some serious fucking weight want a word with you about it.'

January 2, 2012

The Florida Keys, Florida, United States. Ben Harbor propped himself up on an elbow in the sand and admired the woman as she tied the bikini string on her hip.

'I used to think leopard-skin print only looked good on leopards,' he said, grinning, lying naked beside her on a large beach towel.

'You want me to take it off?' she asked.

'No, put it on. I'd like the opportunity to take it off you again. Just give me a little while to get my second wind.'

'What's a little while?'

'Ten minutes.'

'I'll give you five.'

Ben grinned. 'You're a tough negotiator.'

'Growing up in New York will do that to a girl.'

The girl in this instance was twenty-three, tall, blonde, and maybe a thirty-four B cup. Her name was Joan, and Ben had met her only yesterday. Joan's parents had booked an island discovery flight with Ben; her old man was keen to see a few of the best marlin and wahoo spots from the air before hitting them in a Riviera. It was the wrong time of year, but it didn't matter. The guy was loaded. Joan said nothing the entire flight, just gazed out the window, her oversized white-framed sunglasses obscuring most of her face from view—either hiding or way too cool to communicate. Ben had also noted, when she walked down the dock, that she wore no underwear beneath her blue cotton sunprint dress. He hadn't expected to see her or hear from her again, but she surprised him by calling first thing the following morning to book a joy flight. Ben wasn't sure which of them was getting the most joy out of it, but so far the scores seemed about equal.

'Have you been to New York?' she asked over her shoulder as she stood up and tiptoed into the water lapping at the coral sand.

'Nope. One day, maybe.'

'A guy like you could have a lot of fun in New York.'

'What's a guy like me?'

Joan porpoised under the water and came up smoothing her hair back. She trotted up the sand, tan breasts bobbing. 'Okay, let's see. Six two, six-pack, and *way* more than six inches. The blonde surfer-dude hair and green eyes wouldn't hurt your chances, either.' She regarded Ben in a detached way, as if appreciating a sculpture. 'Good short-term prospects.'

'Short term?'

'Not a lot of seaplanes in New York. Actually, come to think of it, there aren't any.'

'There's more to me than seaplanes.'

'Yeah, you've got the cutest buns I've seen in a long time.'

'Didn't I tell you? I split atoms in my spare time.'

'Sure,' she said, giving him a sympathetic smile. 'Hey, no offense, right?' She knelt beside him and kissed him, her cold wet hair falling over his sunburned shoulders. 'How're we doing here?' she whispered. 'Your five minutes are nearly up, buddy boy.' She took him in her wet hand. 'Hmm . . . looks like we'll be going into extra time.'

'Are all New York girls as pushy as you?'

'It's a tough town. Push comes with the territory. *You'd* get eaten alive.'

'If it's so tough, why don't you get out?'

She laughed. 'Get out? Look, after you've lived in New York, everywhere else is a trailer park. Besides, it's not that tough for me.'

'What do you do? What's your day job?'

'I was an art history major, which qualifies me to answer the boss's phone. Junior PAs don't earn a lot of money. But my daddy's rich, as you know. He pays off my credit cards. And he takes me on amazing holidays once a year, like this one, though I'm sure he didn't see *this* in the brochure.' She leaned sideways, fondled Ben's testicles and kissed his half erection. 'And then, when the time is right, I'll marry one of the men I know who has as much money as Daddy and then I suppose I'll spend the next twenty years doing what everyone else does—charity work and fucking the hired help.'

'And you think *I'm* aimless?'

She sat up on her knees. 'Say, have you got anything to eat or drink in that plane?'

'Depends on what you want. I've got sandwiches, ice water, energy drinks . . . ' Ben started to push himself up.

'No, I'll go,' Joan insisted. 'You relax. Save your strength.'

She walked down to the water's edge and then cut left, heading for the blue and white De Havilland Otter nosed onto the beach. Stepping up onto the float, she opened the door and bent over. A bitch with a real nice ass, Ben thought. A moment later, she held up two bottles of water and gave them a waggle. He answered her with a wave.

'Is this yours? Or does it belong to . . . Key West Seaplanes?' Joan called out, reading the name on the side of the plane's fuselage.

'Mine. And the bank's,' he said when she trotted up the beach toward him.

'Well, that's something. I'm impressed.' She gently pitched a bottle underarm at him. 'What would you do if you didn't have it? Get a job with the airlines?'

'Those guys don't fly, they manage systems. And they wear dumb uniforms.'

'I love a uniform.'

'Why am I not surprised.'

'Hey, there was a chopper lifting off back at Key West. I've never been in one. Can you fly those, too?'

'Yeah. Back to what-ifs . . . What if your daddy ran off with the maid and took all his money? What would *you* do?'

Joan laughed. 'She's Mexican. She was also born when T-Rexes walked the earth. Come to think of it, she even looks like one.'

'Then maybe his private fitness instructor? Does he have one of those?'

'Hmm, yeah. Monica. She's kinda cute . . . And I'm assuming in this "what-if" scenario that Mom didn't manage to clean him out with the divorce settlement—which would happen by the way.'

'Whatever, canceled credit cards for you, baby.'

'Well, New York's expensive. I guess I'd probably do what most girls my age do who don't earn enough.'

'What's that?'

'Have six or more boyfriends.'

'For sex?'

'Hey, it's not always about sex, you know. Most New York girls spend their money on rent and clothes. Boyfriends are necessary if you want to *eat*. You can diet on the weekend so one for each night of the working week is best. Nothing elaborate, just something hot and served by a waiter, with a glass of wine.'

'Maybe I'll give New York a miss.'

Joan snuggled into Ben's arms. A couple of pelicans soared overhead on a course for Key West, while high above them a jet drew a furrow like a speedboat across a pink lake. New York was a long way away.

'You wouldn't have to worry,' she said. 'I'd look after you as long as you looked after me, if you know what I mean . . . '

Ben reached around from behind and cupped a breast, which had the effect of making Joan coo and wriggle her ass against his erection.

'Happy New Year,' he said.

She giggled. 'It's starting to shape up nicely. I was beginning to think you were all talk.'

His fingers picked at the spaghetti strap on her hip, the knot dissolved and her bikini bottom peeled off as she rolled onto her back. Ben admired her lithe, shaved, waxed, plucked and tan body. No doubt about it, Joan was one spectacular—and spectacularly spoilt—creature.

'You love your job, don't you?' she said with a smirk, watching him watching her.

Ben grinned shamelessly.

'Someone's gotta do it, right? So can you hurry up and *do* me? The sun's going down. We have to go and I'm getting impatient.'

Ben scooped her in his arms and stood up.

'Hey . . . what are we doing?' she squealed.

He carried her to the water's edge, the setting afternoon sun having turned the sea into a pond the color of orange juice.

'This time, Joan, we're gonna do it like fish.'

She wrapped her arms tighter around his neck and said, 'Um, Ben . . . the name's Jane.'

Half an hour later, the Otter was approaching the landing pattern dictated by the winds. Ben banked hard over Key West until he could make out the windsock waving at the end of the dock.

'Are you showing off? You're making me sick.'

Ben reassured her with a gentle squeeze of her bare brown knee. On this approach, when the sea breeze was rising over the spine of the key, the air could get lumpy. He glanced in the direction of the sun, a glowing rind vanishing below the horizon. The night was half an hour away. Time to deposit Jane on the dock and move on to the next adventure. Captain Tony's Saloon was calling.

'Is that where we're landing?' Jane asked. The inlet off the wingtip looked no bigger than a bathtub in the growing dusk.

'Yeah.'

Minutes later, the aircraft flared a couple of feet above the water and then the floats kissed the wavelets. With their speed washed off, Ben tweaked the rudder pedals and taxied to the dock.

'That was fun,' said Jane over the engine noise and propwash, her calm returned.

'No, *you* were fun,' Ben replied.

'I'm here another couple days. Shall we, you know, get together again?'

'Sure, key in your number.' He took his cell from a door pocket and handed it to her, his mind already running through the after-landing checks.

The water around the berth was dark and smooth. Ben closed the throttle, pulled the mixture and the engine died. The prop came to a stop with a *chug* and the Otter slid silently sideways, toward the pontoon. He opened the door, jumped out of his seat and hopped down onto the float, all in one fluid motion. Cecilia, the owner of Key West Seaplanes, was waiting on the pontoon.

'Yo, Cecil!' he called out.

'How was it?' she asked as Ben passed her the rope to tie off.

'Flying won on the day,' said Ben as he jumped onto the pontoon.

Jane's door opened and she tentatively stretched a toe down toward the float, nervous about falling into the black water.

Ben came around and gave her a hand across.

'Where do I pay?' Jane asked Cecilia.

'Up at the office—where you came in. Good flight?'

'Amazing,' she said, giving Ben a sly glance.

'You go on up and I'll be there in a minute, honey,' Cecilia told her. 'Help yourself to a soda.'

'Thanks.'

Jane climbed up onto the dock and then strolled toward the shore in a sarong split to the top of her thigh.

'Free sodas? There must be something wrong,' Ben observed.

'Where'd you go?'

'The tide was low, so over to N313.'

'That little island's a pretty public spot. Lots of fishermen call in there. You should watch yourself. One day you and a customer might find yourselves providing free, R-rated entertainment on YouTube.'

Ben flashed her a grin and passed over a bag of trash.

'I had a call from a lawyer in Miami—a guy by the name of Kayson Bourdain. You know him?'

Ben shook his head. 'Nope, never heard of him.'

'He wants you to give him a call.'

'And why's that?'

'It's about your father.'

Ben stopped what he was doing and closed the log. 'My father? What about him?'

'He died.'

Something caught in his chest. 'What!? Frank's—'

'No, not Frank. Your *other* father.'

March 5, 1983

The Old Executive Building, Washington DC. There was no name-plate on the heavy oak door, which Garret figured meant that if you didn't know whose office this was you probably weren't meant to open it.

Hank paused, hand resting on the brass knob. 'You set?'

Garret swapped the briefcase from one damp palm to the other and nodded. Hank opened the door. Behind it sat a thin middle-aged secretary. Her powdered face was accentuated by hair dyed fire-engine red. A purple vein wriggled in her temple. A cigarette smoldering in an ashtray on the desk curled smoke into shapes like bent wire. She glanced up from an IBM typewriter. With a voice dry as old sawdust she said, 'Go straight on in, Hank. They're expecting you.'

'You're a doll, Deirdre.'

Hank moved to another oak door opposite, knocked, and opened it. A conversation on the other side stopped mid-sentence as they walked into the sprawling sunlit office.

'Hank. Always good to see you,' said a man in his mid-fifties with red suspenders, a ruddy face and several chins. He was leaning back on a comfortable couch that hugged the floor, hands clasped behind his head. Garret recognized him instantly. Ed Meese III. He knew him by reputation: a lawyer and a Lutheran, the President's best friend and chief counselor, a member of the President's cabinet. Meese had been responsible for calling in the National Guard to quell the People's Park Protest at Berkeley back in '69—one dead student, many wounded. He had a seat on the National Security Council.

'You must be our author,' Meese said, unclasping his hands and holding one forth for Garret to shake. 'Thanks for coming in on a Saturday.'

'No problem at all, sir,' Garret replied as they shook. 'Glad to meet you.'

'And this is William Clark,' Hank said behind him.

Garret turned. The National Security Advisor sat behind a broad, simple wood desk. With his dark, neatly combed hair, lined face and conservative suit, Garret thought he looked like a history teacher at exam time, an impression strengthened by the neat stacks of paper and folders organized in front of him. Four phones, each a different color, were arranged in a semicircle on the desk's right-hand side.

'Some analysis you've written here, Roy,' Clark said, picking up a sheaf of paper from one of those stacks. 'Congratulations on some great work.'

'Thank you, sir,' Garret said as Clark's CV ran through his mind. Clark was the President's most trusted aide and former justice of the California Supreme Court—indeed, his nickname was 'the Judge'. He was also a former army counterintelligence officer, a former Catholic seminary student, and known to be deeply religious. Up on the wall behind him hung a framed square of calligraphed parchment—a law degree—and a photo of a smiling Ronald Reagan haloed by the seal of the President of the United States. Dominating the wall, and in line with Clark's deeply held beliefs, was a large porcelain Christ nailed to a cross, purple blood welling from a bleeding heart and his many wounds.

A man in an expensive tailored suit occupied a chair in front of the National Security Advisor's desk. Garret didn't know him.

'And this is Des Bilson,' said Hank, filling the gaps. 'Des, meet Roy Garret.'

'*The* Roy Garret,' said Bilson with the hint of a smile. 'I've heard a lot about you.'

Bilson's tan face and blond perm reminded Garret of a porn star, except that the man's eyes were the color of ice build-up on a fridge freezer—cold on top, colder below. He was mid-thirties, Garret guessed, and a narcissist.

'Des is my go-to guy,' said Clark.

'For the last six months, the Judge has been heading up a working committee looking at ways to turn around public opinion on these missiles,' said Meese. 'And then out of the blue your paper comes along and blows our thinking clean out of the water.' There was a chuckle mixed with gravel in his voice. 'Sit down, Roy, and take a load off.'

'Thank you, sir,' said Garret, moving to the couch opposite Meese. He caught the view out the window: the south gardens of the White House and the tips of the pencil pines screening the President's swimming pool.

'Are you a God-fearing man, Garret?' Clark asked.

'Yes, sir. I go to church regularly,' he replied.

'Then how do you think He feels about the Soviet empire?'

Garret had never thought about the USSR in religious terms. 'He probably doesn't like it, sir, I'd say.'

'And I'd say you're right. We're dealing with what the President likes to call the Evil Empire: 280 million atheists covering a huge swath of His earth, led by a regime hellbent on world domination. We believe that God has given us the mandate to once and for all rid the planet of the Soviet menace.' Clark pounded his fist into his palm. 'Ed and I think your paper provides us with a potential strategy to do just that. Or, at the very least, give the Soviets a heck of a shake.'

'There are big plans afoot, Roy,' said Meese, sitting forward, his elbows propped on his knees. 'The President is not a fan of détente.'

Garret had heard that.

'The Soviets are envious of our wealth, our technological edge. It's making them increasingly nervous. Right now, with their SS-20 intermediate-range missiles on mobile launchers roaming the East German countryside, they enjoy a window of superiority. The United States is vulnerable. They know it, we know it. And I'm sure you know it. As long as they have that window, we believe they might do the unthinkable.'

Meese leaned further forward. 'General Secretary Yuri Andropov has forced the KGB and the main intelligence directorate of the Soviet Armed Forces, the GRU, to cooperate in a worldwide intelligence operation codenamed RYAN. That's an acronym for *Raketno-Yadernoe Napadenie*, which means "Nuclear Missile Attack".'

'Right now,' Clark interjected, 'RYAN has the KGB out hunting for the remotest confirmation that we're about to go to war. They're even checking our blood banks to see if they're paying more for donations. They want to know if we're stockpiling supplies to meet wartime demand. They're looking at our religious leaders, taping their speeches and sermons, analyzing them for signs that Washington has brought the church into our warfighting loop. Andropov thinks that because we believe they're about to push the button, we're going to push it first and go for a pre-emptive nuclear strike.'

Garret knew the Politburo had mobilized its agents in an urgent renewed drive to infiltrate the west, but he hadn't known why.

'We need to get our Pershings into Western Europe and restore that balance, offset those SS-20s, and we need to do it fast,' Clark continued. 'But as you know, the anti-war movement over there is strong and growing stronger by the day. It is now *the* most important tool of propaganda and disinformation in the Soviet arsenal.'

'Those damn hippies are even poisoning the minds of the United States Congress,' Meese added.

'Roy,' said Clark, 'we need bills approved for the manufacture and deployment of the new Peacemaker missiles—'

'I know you like that name, Judge—Peacemaker—but I don't think it'll fly,' Meese chuckled. 'The President wants to call MX the Peace*keeper*.'

'Just as long as it does the job.' Clark stood, walked around his desk and sat on the corner. 'As I was saying, Roy, what's hanging in the balance is the development and deployment of America's defenses into the future. Congress is baulking at the funds required for the new Bigeye binary gas weapon. And we need money to arm the Contras so they can help us stop the spread of communism in Central America. But those peaceniks in Europe are convincing everyone, even the folks at home, that Moscow's evil intent is a figment of this administration's imagination. People seem to have forgotten about Stalin, the Red Army's push through Europe, the Cuban missile crisis. *We're* being blamed for the arms race. But you understand that, Roy. From what you've written here, your analysis of the European peace movement, you see it with a clarity that has eluded even a lot of the folks Americans have elected to protect them.'

The National Security Advisor flicked through the paper in his hand. 'Ah yes, here it is . . . You wrote in your analysis that we need "a unifying calamity to regalvanize international antipathy toward the Soviet menace". Beautiful. In one sentence you've managed to clarify and focus months of internal National Security Council confusion. "A unifying calamity",' he repeated, nodding and smiling.

'There's a lot at stake,' said Meese. 'No less than security, peace, freedom. Recently, at a meeting of the full National Security Council, President Reagan gave us a vision to work toward—a missile shield encircling America and her allies. We think it will capture the nation's imagination—a purely defensive shield to protect our loved ones against incoming missiles. It'll be called the Strategic Defense Initiative—SDI. But if it's to work, we're going to need the Russians to take their intermediate-range missiles out of the Warsaw Pact countries. Those damn things fly too fast. An intercontinental ballistic missile gives you roughly thirty minutes from launch to warhead detonation, but, depending on the target, it's down to a handful of minutes with intermediate-range missiles—too quick for any shield. The only way we'll get Moscow to take their missiles *out* is if we get our missiles *in*. And the peace movement is our biggest impediment to making that happen.

'Now, as you know, our Pershing II IRBMs are scheduled for deployment on West German soil in December. With the level of disquiet out there, we have no confidence that the deployment will go forward as scheduled. We've had a number of back channel conversations with our NATO allies and the whole deal is looking shaky.'

'Your paper helps us formulate a clear campaign to achieve the President's dream—a world at peace,' said Clark. 'The question for us now is *how* to put your strategy into practice. You don't make any suggestions. I see in your record that back in the navy you were counterintelligence. Do you have any thoughts of a more *practical* nature that you chose not to commit to paper?'

Garret's heart was racing. As an analyst at the NSA, he was party to secret information, but mostly he had no idea how the fragments fitted into the overall picture. It was just information. But what he was hearing now encompassed the world. These guys sat on top of the mountain with an unobstructed view over the whole.

'No, sir, I haven't,' he replied, then hurriedly added, 'but whatever the incident, it would have to engender public outrage, even horror.'

'Go on,' said Clark, who had left the corner of his desk and was moving about his office, arms folded.

'Something like an attack on the USS *Maddox* in the Gulf of Tonkin wouldn't do it.' Despite what he'd said, Garret had in fact given the notion of 'a unifying calamity' a lot of thought. The pretext under which the United States had committed itself heart and soul to the Vietnam War wouldn't be enough in this instance. 'A nuclear warhead accident might do the trick. *That* would outrage the world, but the Soviets are too careful to let that happen. As I'm sure you know, they're actually a very conservative leadership . . .'

'We agree with you wholeheartedly,' said Clark, massaging his chin thoughtfully. He walked slowly into an adjoining room and around an antique Civil War-era conference table, before coming back and picking up where he had left off. 'I'm even more confident now that we're in complete accord. How about you, Ed?'

'Yes, I think we've found our guy,' agreed the counselor.

'"Take now your son, your only son, whom you love . . . and go to the land of Moriah, and offer him there as a burnt offering on one of the mountains of which I will tell you." Does that quote mean anything to you, Roy?' asked the National Security Advisor.

'Genesis 22:2, sir. It's God commanding Abraham. It's about sacrifice.'

'Do you think the nation would be prepared to make a sacrifice?' asked Clark.

Before Garret could answer, there was a soft knock on the door. It opened and a bald head ringed with a thatch of white hair filled the gap. Garret had only seen this face on a wall in Langley. It was William Casey, director of the CIA.

'How we doing here?' Casey asked.

'Come on in, Bill, and meet Roy Garret. He penned that analysis on the peace movement you read earlier.'

'Really?' said Casey, stepping into the room. 'Let me shake your hand, son.'

Garret stood and they shook.

'NSA, huh?' said the CIA director, looking Garret up and down. 'If you ever want a *real* job, Roy, there's always room in the Company for a bright young man with big ideas.'

'Thank you, sir,' said Garret.

'Well,' said Casey, addressing Meese and Clark. 'You two old soldiers ready? We've got a meeting with the President in ten. Time to hustle.'

Ed Meese got up off the couch and reached for his suit jacket, plucking it from the coat stand. Clark's was hanging off a hook on the back of the door.

'It's been great to meet you, Roy,' said Clark as another round of handshaking ensued. 'We'll speak again soon.'

'Looking forward to it, sir,' said Garret.

'Take care of this man for us, Hank. He's valuable government property,' said Meese.

'Yes, sir,' replied Hank.

'Oh, and Roy,' said Clark, pausing mid-stride, 'why don't you stay around for a while longer. I'd like you to have a word or two with Des. He has a few thoughts he's going to take you through.'

'Yes, sir,' said Garret.

The National Security Advisor gave a final wave as he closed the door behind Meese.

'Please . . .' said Bilson, stepping into the vacuum left by Clark's and Meese's departure and motioning at Garret to retake his seat on the couch. 'So tell me, Roy, what do you know about commercial aviation?'

January 3, 2012

Sapporo, Hokkaido, Japan. Yuudai Suzuki lay dying, monitors beeping metronomically to the rhythm of his last moments. His body was light, consumed by cancer, yet he felt heavy, so heavy. His long bony fingers were like sticks of dried bamboo. They held a letter—stamped and addressed—which had been written three weeks ago when he still had the strength to guide a pen. In it was everything he had agreed on with Curtis, everything that needed to be said.

Ah, Curtis, you beat me to it, he thought. Warm the sake. I will be with you soon.

A nurse entered the room. She inspected the equipment, read the chart and departed. She never acknowledged Yuudai. He was a DNR and therefore her relationship was solely with the machinery, not the patient. It was the machinery that governed her responses. If the beeping became a continuous drone, she would simply turn off the machines and pull the sheet over his sightless eyes. This is what happens, Yuudai told himself, when your line ends with you; when you are all that is left.

He gathered his strength, lifted his head from the pillow and raised his hand, the one holding an old, creased newspaper clipping, yellowed like his skin. His fingers shook, the clipping fluttering like a frightened bird. He managed to smooth it on the bedclothes without tearing it, and slide it into the envelope. He knew the article by heart. It had been cut from the *Hokkaido Shimbun*, the local newspaper, in September 1983—a follow-up on the crash of the airliner, a human interest piece. The headline read, 'The Tragic Survivors'. The article discussed the plight of husbands who had lost wives, wives who had lost husbands, of brothers separated from their sisters by death, and best friends who would never meet again. Mostly, though, it focused on a girl, little Akiko, whose mother had been one of the passengers. The story included a photo taken at Anchorage airport shortly before the flight boarded. It showed Akiko asleep in the arms of her mother with the husband standing beside her. Both parents were smiling. It was a photo that belonged in a private album, or on the fridge, or even in a wallet. Instead it was on the front page of a newspaper, highlighting the anguish of loss.

Yuudai closed his eyes and that awful night came to life. The blips on the screen. The panic in the radar room; the horror that came with the realization that the blip was a 747, a civilian plane, 200 miles inside Soviet airspace, heading toward Sakhalin Island and its hornet's nest of fighter planes.

'I could do nothing,' he whispered.

The machines beeped.

Yuudai squeezed shut his eyes so tightly that they burned, but the pictures and the sounds remained in his head as he saw the 747 once again dive from 35,000 feet. What must it have been like inside that plane, rushing toward the sea, death accelerating toward them, the airframe screaming?

The machines beeped.

The blip flickered. And then it disappeared. It was on his screen and then it wasn't.

'Airman Suzuki. Airman!'

Yuudai was suddenly aware that he was being spoken to. He turned and announced, 'They're going to make it. They've got a chance.'

'We don't know that,' said a lieutenant colonel, an American.

'Yes, we do. Didn't you see?'

'I didn't see anything,' the colonel insisted.

28

The metronomic beep was now a continuous tone, triggering a silent alarm at the nurses' station. Yuudai's last breath leaked away like a slow puncture.

The nurse walked into the room, her efficient steps squeaking on the linoleum. She checked Yuudai's pulse, switched off the machinery and noted the time of death on his chart. As she pulled the sheet over his face, a letter slipped out of the folds and dropped onto the floor.

June 7, 1983

Sheraton Hotel, Seventh Avenue, New York City, New York. Roy Garret was taking a breather, looking down on pedestrians from a fifth-story window, having a smoke. This wasn't the hotel that Korean Air Lines used for flight crews, and neither did any other carrier, which was just the way he wanted it. Most important, it was central, comfortable and discreet.

He drew back on his cigarette, cheeks hollowed, as he watched a woman with three children and an armful of shopping bags brave the afternoon traffic snarl. They made a run for it across Seventh Avenue. A cab screeched to a halt, but not before it hit one of the kids and knocked him to the road. A horn blared, distant, beyond the double glazing. Garret raised an eyebrow. The fact that the sound reached him at all way up here was surprising.

He glanced over his shoulder. The air in the suite's dining room was thick with smoke. Korean Air Lines 747 captain Chun Byung-in had started to pace. First Officer Sohn Dong-hwin and Flight Engineer Kim Eui-dong sat hunched over the dining room table holding their heads in their hands. Kim was making an odd humming noise, like catgut before it snaps.

In the adjoining lounge room, a couple of spooks from the Korean Central Intelligence Agency were sitting on the couch, chain-smoking and flipping through magazines on the coffee table in front of them. The one named Pak was fat. The other, Lee, was rake thin. Both had faces flat as ironing boards.

The mission lead, Colonel Eric Hamilton—a retired USAF full colonel now working for the CIA—sat at a writing desk in one corner of the dining room reviewing his notes, the overhead light bouncing off his polished bald head.

Suddenly, there was an unexpected knock at the door. Everyone froze. The KCIA agent Pak, the fat one, slid his hand to the pistol in his shoulder holster. A 'Do Not Disturb' sign had been placed on the external door handle. Calls had been made to reception and housekeeping to make sure it was heeded. Watergate was still fresh in everyone's mind and there were parallels: they were in a hotel room; they were talking conspiracy; the trail led to the highest levels of government. Garret went to the door, tensing for whatever was behind it, and threw it open.

'Jesus Christ, Hank,' he said, breathing hard.

'Who were you expecting? Miss February?'

The KCIA guy with the trigger finger shrugged and said something to his compatriot. They shared a laugh followed by a pack of Lucky Sevens, each plucking out a cigarette.

Garret led Hank to the privacy of a connecting suite for a hurried conference.

'What the fuck are you doing here?' he whispered.

'Always good to see you, too. How's it going?'

'It's going well, all things considered.'

'Considering what?'

'Considering what we're asking them to do.'

'Which group do we have here?' Hank enquired.

'Group Delta—I think these are the guys we want.'

'Are they putting up any resistance?'

'Some.'

'But they know they have to do it, right?'

Garret nodded. As citizens of the Republic of Korea, what choice did they have? The Soviet empire was close, hanging over them like smog. North Korea was next door. And over *their* back fence were the millions of commies in the People's Liberation Army itching to help the North have another crack at moving in. No doubt about it, the ROK was in the middle of a pretty crummy neighborhood. If you could relocate, you would. So of course Chun Byung-in and his crew would do it, but that didn't mean they wouldn't have to be convinced.

Hank followed Garret back into the dining room. He chose a chair next to Hamilton, spun it around and straddled it.

There were no handouts, just slides, and they'd be destroyed at the conclusion of the briefing. A map of the mission area was projected onto one wall. Clearly identified were the landmasses of Alaska, Japan, the Korean Peninsula, and the Soviet territories of Kamchatka and Sakhalin Island. Threading them all neatly in international airspace was Romeo 20, one of the five commercial aviation routes connecting South East Asia with Alaska. The normal course taken by aircraft flying from Anchorage to Seoul along Romeo 20 was marked. A dotted line indicated another course, one that diverged from Romeo 20 and over-flew the USSR on a course roughly parallel to Romeo 20.

'I have thought about it—we all have—and there are serious concerns,' said Captain Chun, loosening his tie.

'I'd be surprised to hear otherwise,' said Garret.

'Why do you think the communists will believe us?'

Hamilton fielded the question. 'You won't need to explain anything to Soviet air traffic controllers because you'll be observing selective radio silence—when they call you, you won't answer. Also, your transponder will be switched off so you won't be broadcasting your call sign, altitude, heading or carrier details. If they pick you up at all, they won't know who or what you are. At first, they might even think you're one of theirs.'

'We will have to explain these things to the US and Japanese air traffic authorities afterwards. What will we tell them?'

'Everything will be put down to a combination of human error and malfunction, each compounding the other,' Hamilton said.

'Human error?' First Officer Sohn appeared bewildered, like a kid lost in a crowd.

'Human error is not plausible,' said Captain Chun, speaking slowly, his

English near perfect. 'Let us begin with the divergence from Romeo 20. I am not sure which aircraft you flew, Mr Hamilton, but our 747-200B uses three inertial navigation system computers to get it from point to point. After I cross-reference the flightplan with an independent en-route chart, as the captain I would then enter into a keyboard the aircraft's gate position at the airport in latitude and longitude, followed by the waypoint coordinates. These coordinates are immediately displayed on two other panels for the first officer and flight engineer to cross-check. And then each INS checks the other for errors. With respect,' Captain Chun shook his head, 'human error? No, I don't think so.'

First Officer Sohn and Flight Engineer Kim nodded.

'We will be asked why we didn't spot these errors,' the captain continued, 'why we were so far off course. There's no acceptable answer.'

'This will ruin our careers,' said Sohn.

'No, it won't,' interrupted Pak, the fat KCIA agent. 'We have influence with your management.'

'There's also the precedent of Korean Air Lines Flight 902,' Garret said, tag-teaming with Hamilton.

The flight engineer grunted. 'Right, the 707 back in '78 that departed from Paris heading for Seoul and somehow ended up in Russia.'

'The crew didn't suffer for their mistakes,' Garret said. 'I believe the captain went on to command 747s.'

'Yes, I know him. And you're right, he did,' Chun agreed. 'But only because demoting him would have been an admission of fault by the company administration.'

Garret had studied every facet of KAL Flight 902. In fact, he was using it as a template for the mission now on the table. In the 902 incident, the flight crew had executed an inexplicable 180-degree turn above the North Pole, passing over the Soviet submarine base at Severomorsk, Murmansk.

'The Russians shot it down,' said Kim.

'They *forced* it down,' Hamilton countered. 'The plane landed safely on a frozen lake.'

'Passengers were killed,' Kim grumbled.

'902 was flying into the heart of the USSR,' Garret reminded him.

'You'll be skirting the edges. In and out.'

'And then back in again,' said Sohn. 'Was 902 also on a mission?'

'No, it was not,' Garret lied. 'Look, don't be concerned about how to explain your flightpath once you've landed. We will be controlling the flow of information and verification. When it comes to substantiating your actions, the relevant information will either become lost, we'll fog it up, or the tough questions just won't get asked.'

More silence.

'The point is, you won't be doing this on your own. We'll be with you every step of the way. When you land in Seoul, no one will know what happened, not exactly. And the facts that are released will be done so judiciously, and by us.'

'The course you want us to fly will have us deviating to the north almost immediately we depart Anchorage airport,' said Chun.

'Yes,' said Hamilton.

'But this deviation will be noted by air traffic controllers before we leave the Alaskan coastline,' Chun continued. 'The Regional Operations Control Centre in Anchorage will see our radar track. They will know instantly that we are way off course and ask us to correct it.'

'That facility is at Elmendorf Air Force Base and we can therefore control it,' Garret informed him. 'In fact, that issue has already been taken care of. We also intend to decommission the Anchorage navigation beacon—put it offline for routine maintenance. The civilian controllers you report to will simply assume that you'll correct your position at Bethel, the first mandatory reporting waypoint along Romeo 20.'

'You have reminded me,' said Sohn, lighting a cigarette with trembling fingers. 'As we deviate further north, we will eventually fly beyond the range of our VHF radio. We will not be able to make any of the mandatory reports along Romeo 20—at NABIE, NEEVA, NIPPI and so on. The authorities will have to investigate.'

'You can use your HF radio, which has more range, and we'll give you a relay,' said Garret.

'A relay?' asked First Officer Sohn, confused.

Captain Chun nodded. 'He means another KAL flight. We often fly the route with a KAL aircraft either just ahead or just behind us. This plane can relay our position reports. And if it flies behind and varies its speed, there's a chance it could even be mistaken for us. The confusion would help.'

'This is madness,' said Flight Engineer Kim.

Captain Chun said nothing, his face a mask of calm.

'What about the Shemya radar facility?' the first officer murmured.

'It won't be a problem,' Hamilton assured him.

'Why not? It is company policy to take a fix on Shemya,' Sohn said.

Garret was aware of the procedure. Korean Air Lines required its flight crews transiting Romeo 20 to get a fix on a type of radio navigational aid called VOR/DME, which was located on Shemya, an island at the end of the Aleutians chain jutting into the Bering Sea. The aid enabled an aircraft to verify its position relative to the NEEVA waypoint adjacent of Shemya. Obviously, if the aircraft was 200 nautical miles to the north when it was supposed to be passing within a mile or two of NEEVA, this procedure would alert the flight crew to the fact that they were way off course. And the flight crew would then take steps to get back on course. At least, that's what an *innocent* flight crew would do.

'You will make your report at NEEVA as usual,' said Hamilton. 'And if you are out of range of the Shemya beacon, the relay aircraft will simply pass on your transmission.'

'Yes, exactly,' said the flight engineer. 'But the reality is that we'll be in one place while we're claiming to be somewhere else. Surely you are forgetting the huge radar facility also on Shemya Island—Cobra Dane. It will detect our location, and our lie.'

Garret lit a Chesterfield off the embers of another. 'You're very well-informed, my friend,' he said, drawing deeply.

'I have to be.'

Garret had to admit, these were excellent questions—just what you'd expect from an experienced, top-class 747 crew. He exhaled smoke through his nostrils. Cobra Dane, the giant phased-array radar on Shemya Island, kept a constant eye on Soviet military movements across the Sea of Okhotsk. With it you could count the maggots on a carcass 2000 miles away.

'Cobra Dane has two modes—surveillance and tracking,' he said, carefully considering what he could say that wouldn't compromise national security. 'The facility is shared with a number of federal agencies and organizations. I can guarantee you that on the night of the mission, Cobra Dane will be in tracking mode, searching the skies for Soviet and other foreign satellites on behalf of the North American Aerospace Defense Command—NORAD.'

'So, you have told us what you want us to do but not *why* you want us to do it,' said Captain Chun, who'd begun pacing again.

Garret glanced at the others. After interviews with three alternative crews, Hamilton and the KCIA spooks knew the drill. They got up and filed out of the room.

'I think I'll stay,' Hank said.

Garret wasn't going to argue about it in front of the flight crew. He waited until the door closed and said, 'Drink?'

Captain Chun and First Officer Sohn said no. Hank shook his head.

'Scotch,' Flight Engineer Kim replied.

Garret fetched a brace of Johnnie Walkers from the minibar and poured them into a couple of glasses. He opened the fridge. 'Rocks?'

'Please.'

'Let me just remind you of the secrecy agreement you signed before this briefing,' said Garret, as he handed Kim his drink.

The flight crew nodded almost imperceptibly.

'President Reagan believes that Moscow is planning something. Their anti-aircraft defenses are being bolstered in and around the Petropavlovsk-Kamchatsky Naval Base, home of the Soviet Pacific submarine fleet, as well as the defenses at Sakhalin Island. Without a doubt, this activity is all related. And we don't like the picture when we connect the dots. In the event of war, the President's concern is that Moscow will undoubtedly target South Korea with its new SS-20 medium-range nukes. The proximity of the ROK to the launch sites on Kamchatka Peninsula means your country would have barely minutes to react.'

'Moscow may even use the Korean Peninsula as an example,' Hank interrupted. 'Burn it to a crisp just to let everyone see that they mean business.'

Garret glared at Hank, then continued. 'Frankly, we need to know what's going on down there. If we send a military plane into Soviet airspace, it'll get shot down.'

'What makes you think that won't happen to us?' asked Kim.

'You've accidentally strayed off course. You're a civilian aircraft.'

'If we're darkened and not showing cabin or navigation lights, with no transponder transmitting, they will know we are trying to hide from them,' said First Officer Sohn. 'They will fire on us, just like they did on 902.'

'Obviously, we don't think it will come to that. We estimate you'll be flying over the Kamchatka Peninsula for approximately thirty-three minutes. We believe you'll be back in international airspace before Soviet air defenses can react.'

'Thirty-three minutes is a long time. How do you know they won't shoot first and ask questions later?' Sohn asked.

'The Russians are inquisitive. They'll want to know what's flying around in their airspace. They'll launch interceptors to have a closer look at you. And then they'll see that you're a civilian passenger plane.'

'That's if they ever get the interceptors up,' Hank said. 'Our intelligence leads us to believe that the Soviets are a spent force, a rusted-out hulk. Most of the peasants out on those Far East bases are drinking the glycol out of their air-con units 'cause they've already drunk their month's supply of vodka. Their pilots are damn lucky if they can *find* their planes, let alone fly them straight.'

Garret regretted not pushing Hank out of the room when Hamilton and the others had left. He took a breath and continued. 'Thanks to your mission and the interrogation you'll receive from the Soviet air defense network, our signals-gathering assets will collect a rich harvest, vital intelligence that will enable us to prevent the enemy's first strike— at least from the Far East at the ROK. You'll be helping to secure the peace and prosperity of your country and the world.'

'What about Sakhalin Island?' Chun stood and approached the

projected map on the wall, still unconvinced. The islands of Japan rippled across the back of his shirt. 'The defenses on Kamchatka will be able to call ahead. They will know we are coming. They will wait. How long will we be over Sakhalin?'

'Approximately thirteen minutes,' Garret said. 'Just thirteen minutes.'

'You'll be gone before they know it,' Hank added.

'Ultimately, your defense is the truth—you *are* a civilian plane that wandered out of the commercial lanes,' Garret reminded them.

'Yes, intentionally,' said Sohn. He turned to speak with Chun and Kim. 'It will seem as if we took off from Anchorage, put our feet up on our instruments and went to sleep.'

'The world will know we have lied,' said Kim. 'No one will be fooled. It will look like a spy mission and they will point the finger at you—the CIA.'

From his seat, Sohn followed the intended course across the map on the wall. Far out over the Sea of Japan to the southwest of Sakhalin Island, they were to alter course abruptly, turning forty degrees to the southeast, and announce to Tokyo Radio that they had suffered unspecified navigation and equipment failures. 'At least you're not asking us to overfly Vladivostok.'

'This is an intelligence sortie, gentlemen, not a suicide mission,' Garret said as he polished off the Johnnie in his glass, avoiding eye contact. Vladivostok was the home of the Soviet Pacific fleet, one of the USSR's most secret cities and closed to all foreigners. It was also ringed with air defenses.

'This is something we all have to think about,' said Captain Chun. 'Korean Air Lines has many crews. Why have you chosen us?'

'Your government says you're the best men for the job,' Garret replied, neglecting to inform them that CIA shrinks had also earmarked three other crews for the same mission. 'You've all flown high-stress military sorties for your country, in addition to which there are well over 20,000 hours of flying time between you, much of it on 747s. You have all flown this route many times. You're also patriots, and right now your country needs you.'

'When would this mission take place?' Kim asked.

'Very soon,' Garret said, fetching his suit coat. 'Gentlemen, I know this is a lot to take in. Why don't we break for half an hour or so? Feel free to talk it over without us looking over your shoulders—no one's expecting you to agree to this right now.'

'Thank you,' said Chun.

Sohn and Kim came to their feet and exchanged wan smiles and slight bows with Garret and Hank.

'I'm assuming this area's clean,' said Hank, scoping the hallway as he followed Garret to the elevator.

'Swept every hour, random pattern. The elevators and shafts as well as floors four through seven. Standard practice.'

'Do you think they've figured out what we're really asking them to do?'

'The real objective? No, but those boys aren't stupid. We have to be careful what we say to them.'

'What about the media?'

'We'll have plausible deniability,' said Garret. 'We can also play the national security card if the questions get hot.'

'What if the mission doesn't go to plan?'

'You really need to ask? If this goes in the shitter, our Washington buddies will be looking for fall guys. I've already bought my one-way ticket to a small South American dictatorship. I'd do the same if I were you.'

The elevator arrived with a chime.

'Where are we going?' Hank asked as they stepped inside the empty car.

'Sixth floor.'

Hank pressed the button. 'What about compartmentalization?'

'The only person who knows everything is me,' said Garret. 'Next on the list is you.'

'What about Hamilton and those KCIA gooks?'

'Watch your mouth, Hank,' Garret warned.

'Oh, don't be such a fucking hypocrite, Roy. I see the way you look at them.'

'Then do what I do and keep it to yourself. Those "gooks" are our allies. As for Hamilton, he's retired but totally committed to the cause. The mission profile is his baby. And your KCIA pals have the highest clearance.'

'They're still weak links.'

'What are you suggesting, Hank?'

The elevator pinged and the doors slid open. Garret got out and stopped, patting down his jacket.

'Not what you think I'm thinking, Roy. Times have changed. Can't throw people out of helicopters any more,' Hank said with a grin. 'The more people have got to lose, the more they'll do to keep it. Hamilton will find himself getting some lucrative contract work, maybe even a board position with a major military contractor. He might even wake up chairman. And we'll make sure the Koreans go home to corner offices.'

'And what are they going to do for me? Give me Des's job—make me the apple of the Judge's eye?'

'Pull this thing off and Ronny himself will bend over and let you fuck him.'

Garret's lungs hurt. He took out a pack of Chesterfields and searched for a light.

A metallic 'clink' sounded and a flame appeared. Hank held the lighter.

'Thanks,' Garret said, sucking the fire into the cigarette. Hot kerosene fumes filled his nostrils. The tobacco crackled. He offered the pack to Hank, who pulled one free and then lit up, a hand cupped around the flame.

'You get that in 'Nam?' Garret enquired, indicating the zippo.

'Yeah.'

'Mind if I take a look?'

Hank gave it to him.

He turned the lighter over a couple of times. The zippo's brass edges were worn smooth from years of use. On one side was a black horse's head and a diagonal stripe inside a yellow triangle. On the other, an inscription.

'First Cav,' said Hank. 'I was a gunner on Hueys.'

Garret turned the lighter over again and read the inscription. *Killing is my business and business has been good.*

'A mamma-san gave us twenty of those for ten bucks, pre-inscribed. For an extra two she'd blow you.'

'Those were the days,' Garret said, handing it back.

'They certainly were,' sighed Hank as he pocketed the lighter.

Garret led the way, turning to his left. He stopped at a door, pulled out a key, and opened it. The room on the other side was identical to the one directly below, where the briefing had been held. There was, however, one big difference. In this room, the KCIA men were seated with headsets at a bank of black boxes with flickering lights and the needles of sound-level meters.

'No one looking over your shoulder, eh?' Hank said with admiration.

Hamilton appeared from the washroom.

'How are they doing?' Garret asked him.

'Chun is undecided, Kim is against, and Sohn is waiting on Chun. Whichever way Chun jumps, Sohn will follow. Kim won't want to be left outside on his own.'

The skinny KCIA man, Agent Lee, slid back his headset and addressed Garret. 'Sir, they're talking about fuel loads, insurance policies . . .'

'That's a good sign,' said Hamilton.

'Flight Engineer Kim is still not convinced,' Lee said, adjusting one of the headset cups over his ear. 'He could be trouble . . . wait . . . Kim is talking about the Soviets, reminding the others that they have many surface-to-air missiles, fighter jets and other defenses in the area. Many radars, too. He says it is one of the most heavily defended areas on earth.'

'And he'd be right,' Hank said.

'Should I put them on speaker?' enquired Special Agent Lee.

Garret gave him a nod.

Voices came through, speaking Korean. Lee translated.

'No one will believe it. And I don't believe them. Saving our careers? We will never fly again.'

'Who was that?' asked Hank.

'Kim, I think,' Garret said.

'Look, this is dangerous, but we live in dangerous times. Our country is surrounded by enemies. Every Korean is still part of the fight . . .'

'That was the captain,' said Hamilton, with nods from Garret and Hank.

'We should go somewhere else to talk about this. They will be listening for sure.'

'Kim again,' said Hamilton.

'That guy has seen too many movies,' Hank added.

'What does it matter if they are?'

'Sohn,' Hamilton said, Garret agreeing.

Silence for a long period.

'So you really think we should do this?' said the flight engineer, suddenly speaking English.

'Do we have any choice?' Sohn replied.

'How about those names: Chun Byung-in, Sohn Dong-hwin and Kim Eui-dong. Sounds like someone dropped a xylophone, don't it?' Hank said, grinning, extinguishing his cigarette with a hiss in a half-empty coffee cup.

Garret and Hamilton glanced anxiously at the KCIA agents but got nothing from their eyes.

'What's the usual ethnic make-up of the passenger list on the intended route?' Hank continued. 'I got asked that this morning. I'm going to get asked it again.'

'KAL's 747-200s are configured for more than 300 passengers,' Hamilton said. 'For the flight between Anchorage and Seoul-Kimpo, we can expect roughly two-thirds to be Korean, one-third American.'

'That many Americans?'

'Anchorage is a US airport. You were hoping for Canadians?' said Garret.

'What about a passenger manifest?'

'Not yet. We're too far out.'

Hank extracted his Marlboros and pulled one out with his teeth. 'So you got a mission date in mind, Roy? We're running out of time.'

'A couple of options in mind, but the odds on the early morning of September 1 are firming. That's a Thursday.'

'What's the flight number, so I can be sure to miss it?'

'007.'

Hank grinned. 'And here I was thinking you had no grasp of irony.'

January 4, 2012

Miami, Florida. 'Coffee?'

'No, thanks,' Ben replied.

'Please make yourself comfortable, sir. Mr Bourdain won't be long.'

The receptionist was sleek, her skin the color of milk chocolate, and she resumed doing what Ben's arrival had interrupted, her fingers caressing a slim Apple keyboard. He glanced around the room, which was dominated by the high-altitude panorama of downtown Miami and the beach beyond. The furnishings were stark and modern, and on the wall behind the receptionist was a striking painting of colorful squares and triangles that he vaguely recognized from a book. Ben gave the letterhead in his hand another examination. *McBride, Sweeney, Sweetman & Bourdain LLP.* Wealthy respectability certainly wasn't what he'd associated with his estranged father, but from the address, the hot receptionist, the artwork and the minimalist décor, this was clearly a high-end firm.

He took a chair beside a middle-aged, silver-haired man in an expensive suit who was sipping a cappuccino and reading the *Wall Street Journal.* There were no other clients in the room. Ben picked up a *Time* magazine and began to flip through it.

An African-American man walked out from behind the wall of

modern art. 'Ben,' the man said, walking toward him, hand outstretched. 'Kayson Bourdain.'

Ben stood. They shook.

'Let's go into my office.'

The fifty-something year old attorney led the way. He swiped a card and a glass security door slid open.

'Nice office,' said Ben.

'We like it.'

'The receptionist come with the lease?'

Bourdain smiled over his shoulder.

They continued past a buzzing open-plan office populated by young lawyers and legal secretaries before entering a corner office. The view was the same as the one in reception. Bourdain closed the door behind them. Ben noted a couple of tall bookshelves containing various green and red leather-bound volumes. The mushroom-colored walls were hung with framed degrees, diplomas and awards.

Bourdain motioned at Ben to take a seat on the sofa, a collection of interlocking black leather shapes. 'You look like him.'

'Look like who?' Ben asked.

'Your old man.'

'I wouldn't know.'

'You've never seen a photo of him?'

'They were thrown out when I was a kid.'

'We served together in the air force, y'know.'

'How nice for you.'

Bourdain picked up a stack of folders from his desk and sat opposite Ben in a matching armchair version of the sofa. 'Do you know much about your father's military career?' he asked, placing the folders on a low frosted-glass coffee table between them.

'No,' Ben replied. 'I've been going out of my way to give the guy no thought whatsoever.'

'Curtis was one of the best pilots in the air force. I met him at Offutt Air Force Base—in Nebraska, just outside of Omaha. I was a maintenance engineer back then, a ground pounder. Then Curtis got assigned to Eielson AFB in Alaska.'

'Gee, that's great,' said Ben, glancing around distractedly. 'Is there something you wanted to see me about?'

Bourdain cleared his throat and said, 'Well, I guess we should dive straight into it then.' He opened one of his folders, sat a pair of gold-rimmed bifocals on his nose, and picked up a sheet of paper. '"I, Curtis Eugene Foxx,"' he read, '"am making this will in the presence of witnesses. My son, Benjamin Curtis Harbor, is my sole beneficiary. To him I leave all my possessions to do with as he pleases. Inclusive is the total of all money in any bank accounts, minus any debts I may have. I ask only that my remains be cremated and scattered over Chena Lake, Fairbanks, Alaska. I want no headstone, no memorial, no religious service. I leave to my son, Ben, my service dress, which I want him to preserve for only as long as he wishes. Ben, I am proud of you and I will be prouder still if you embrace the truth. Yours sincerely, Curtis Foxx."'

Two words stuck firmly in Ben's craw: *My son* . . . And then the final paragraph, the change in tense: *I will be prouder still if you embrace the truth.* It sounded weird, like the man was actually in the room. 'Is that a legal document?' he enquired, rattled.

'You asking because there's no Hollywood baloney about being of sound mind and body and so forth?'

'I guess.'

'Curtis drafted this will in my presence with Jim Sweetman, my partner here, as witness. It's a legal and binding document.' Bourdain opened another folder. It contained an unsealed envelope, which he handed across. 'This is yours.'

The envelope was weighty, thick with paper. 'For Ben' was written on the front, neat and precise.

'Curtis prepared the package himself,' Bourdain said as Ben examined it.

'So he knew he was going to die?'

'Yes.'

Ben opened the envelope, removed the contents and sifted through them. The first item that caught his attention was a photo, an old washed-out Kodak color print. He flipped it over. On the back, '1983' was penciled in the bottom right-hand corner. The picture showed five young men from waist to shoulder, the nose of a large aircraft behind them. The men were all in flight suits, smiling, enjoying the sunshine. Bourdain was right. The guy at the far left could have been Ben's twin, except for the whitewall haircut.

'Who are these others?' he asked.

'His crew.'

Ben put the photo on the table and looked at another item—a postcard. 'Relax at Chena Lake' was written in the top left-hand corner. It showed a man, his back to the photographer, standing waist-deep in clear green water, whipping a trout fly out over the lake. The postcard was hand-colored, the blues, greens and purples pushed beyond reality.

'What's this about?' Ben asked.

'I wouldn't know, but he wanted you to have it. The place was important to him. He wants his ashes scattered there.'

Ben frowned and put it down. There was also the man's birth certificate, his medical discharge from the United States Air Force, an official copy of his death certificate and a copy of the medical autopsy performed on his remains at the Northside Hospital mortuary in Atlanta, Georgia.

'Is that where he lived, Atlanta?'

'No. As far as I know, Curtis had no fixed address.'

'Why not?'

'I don't know.'

Ben examined the birth certificate: Curtis Eugene Foxx, born San Antonio, TX, July 19, 1950, at 7:42 a.m. in Wilford Hall Hospital, Lackland AFB. His mom and Curtis had met each other in San Antonio, he knew that much. What had his mom told him? That they'd both grown up in San Antonio but had gone to different schools. Nikki had met her future husband when she'd gone back to visit her parents, a PhD in English Literature from Louisiana State University in her suitcase. She was thrown together with Curtis at a mutual friend's pool party and they had something in common: Curtis was heading to a new assignment at Offutt AFB and Nikki was also going to Omaha, to take up a posting as an assistant professor of English Literature at Creighton University. Four years later, they were married.

Ben picked up the autopsy report. Here was something new. 'It says he died of acute liver failure, cirrhosis. Was he a drunk?' Ben asked.

'For a while,' Bourdain said. 'But Curtis eventually pulled out of it. The cirrhosis stemmed from a blood transfusion that came with a dose of hep C.'

'Why'd he need a transfusion in the first place?'

'He got mugged.'

'You seem to know a lot about the guy.'

'Curtis would drop me a line from time to time.'

'More than I got.'

The lawyer made no comment.

Ben flicked through to the medical discharge. 'How'd you get to be his lawyer?'

'I left the air force, went back to school. A couple of years down the road, he looked me up.'

Ben went back to the photo. 'What did he fly?'

'RC-135s.'

'What kind of plane is that?'

'Reconnaisance—spy planes. Basically a Boeing 707.'

'If he was such a hot shit pilot, why'd they kick him out?'

'Curtis had some problems he couldn't deal with. I believe he suffered from severe post-traumatic stress syndrome, back when no one knew what that was.'

Bourdain pulled a second envelope from the folder and slid it across the table. 'And this is also yours.'

Ben took the envelope. It was unsigned and unsealed. A weight inside it was causing the envelope to bend. He tipped it up and a key dropped into the palm of his hand. There was a number on it.

'007. Is that a joke?'

'Yeah, license to open. Ha!' Bourdain said, amusing himself. 'He left you a safe deposit box.'

'What's in it?'

'Wouldn't have a clue. Not my business to know.'

'Where is it?'

'At a branch of the Bank of America, up in Orlando. The address is on the back of a sheet of paper in the envelope.'

Ben dropped the envelope back on the table with an air of indifference.

'I really think you should have a look for that sheet of paper,' Bourdain advised. 'Make sure it's there.' The attorney leaned back in his chair and interlocked his fingers on his stomach, a smile tugging at the corners of his mouth.

Ben picked up the envelope again, held it upside down and gave it a shake. The sheet fluttered into his lap. There were figures on it, and when he saw the amount in bold at the bottom of the right-hand column, his jaw swung open.

'The tax accountant here has completed the reconciliation and we're holding the balance in escrow. Just email me your bank details and I'll make an EFT.'

'For . . .' Ben examined the amount again, '$96,112.90?'

'You'll have to pay his burial expenses out of it,' the lawyer told him with an apologetic shrug. 'But my fee was taken care of in advance.'

'Curtis had money?' Ben asked, stunned.

'Yes, he had a small armed forces pension, a casual job here and there. I guess he saved.'

'Jesus. We never saw a cent.'

'Never too late to make things right.'

'Ya think?'

'Well, that's up to you, I guess.'

Bourdain sat back again and regarded Ben. 'You're a pilot, too, aren't you? Just like Curtis.'

'No, nothing like Curtis,' he said, his anger flaring.

After a few moments of silence, Bourdain said, 'The burial. What would you like to do?'

Ben shook his head slowly. He felt trapped by the sudden responsibility for a man he'd only ever resented. 'I've never had to bury anyone before.'

'It's easy. Choose a crematorium and let them know the body's at the Northside Hospital mortuary in Atlanta. I've taken care of the obituary and all the legals. The crematorium will look after everything else.'

'What if I just leave the bastard where he is?'

'If you like, I'll get my assistant to handle it.'

'Works for me.'

'Obviously, a lot of this has come as a shock,' Bourdain said. 'That's understandable. You know, despite your experience with Curtis—or should I say, lack of it—he was a good man. Troubled, yes, but decent.'

Ben flipped back and forth through the documents as Bourdain got up and walked behind him.

'There's one more thing he wanted you to have.'

Ben glanced over his shoulder. Hanging on the door was a pressed blue USAF coat, encased in clear plastic. He caught a glimpse of a major's gold oak leaf clusters on the epaulets. He put the key and all the documents back in the envelope and then stood up. Bourdain lifted the uniform off the hook and gave it to him with some reverence. The uniform was heavy.

'Those ribbons on the blouse tell you a lot about his military career,' Bourdain said.

'Blouse?'

'The jacket—the Air Force calls it a blouse.'

'Mr Bourdain—'

'Call me Kayson.'

'Do you have any idea what he might have meant when he said he'd be prouder if I embraced the truth?'

'I'm a lawyer,' Bourdain grinned. 'What the hell would I know about truth?'

Ben worked the keyboard. His own image shrank to one corner of the laptop's screen as a woman's face filled it. She was in her early fifties, her skin still smooth and remarkably line-free. A handful of light freckles sprinkled her small straight nose. She smoothed her hair, hooking a tawny lock behind her ears. A dead leaf hung from her fringe, which she hadn't noticed. Nikki had been gardening.

'Hey, Mom,' said Ben.

'Hi, Benny. You okay, honey?'

'Yeah, why wouldn't I be?'

'Oh, you know . . .'

'Hey, Ben,' a man interrupted, his face suddenly crowding the frame. 'How they hangin', pal?'

'Like Sweet Chariot's, Dad.'

'What's the weather doing down there?' Frank asked.

'The usual perfection. I heard it's raining in Norfolk.'

'I'm not complaining. It's good for the garden,' Nikki said, reclaiming the computer. 'Now go away, Frank.'

Frank disappeared.

'So, what happened? How'd the reading go?'

Ben began with the money, which elicited genuine astonishment, then followed with a run-down of the documents and the uniform. 'It's weird. I feel like he's trying to communicate with me. You know, make up for lost time. I found out more about him in one hour than I've known over the last twenty-eight years. Like, I didn't know he drank.'

'Yes, he drank,' his mother said flatly.

'That's because he was a *loo*-ser,' Frank called out from somewhere in the room.

'*Shoosh*, Frank. Curtis had a breakdown,' Nikki told Ben. 'He went through some kind of hell—real or imagined, I don't know—but the point is, he changed.'

'Into a jerk!' Frank interjected.

'Frank!'

'The kid should know!' shouted Frank. 'It's time. He's twenty-eight, for Christ's sake.'

'Don't make it out to be more than it was,' said Nikki.

'And what was it, Mom?' Ben asked.

'He came back from a mission rotation. And he was damaged.'

'So he had a bad day at the office,' Frank said. 'That's no excuse.'

'Do you want to tell it, Frank, or shall I?'

Silence.

'Thank you.' Nikki fumed, looking off screen, and then to Ben she said, 'At first I thought he might have been having an affair, but it wasn't that—it was something worse, if that's possible. He'd seen or done something he just couldn't come to terms with. He wouldn't talk about it, so he just ended up in this downward spiral. What did the lawyer say about it?'

'The same, pretty much.'

'Booze amplified the problem. He refused to fly. The Air Force psychs back then weren't what they are today. They couldn't help him. One day, Curtis and I had a fight. Every couple has them, but we'd become dysfunctional. It was over his drinking, the lack of emotional support he was providing you—and me. I pushed him. And he hit me.'

'He *hit* you?' Ben said, shocked.

'It wasn't hard, but that's not the point, right? Curtis was deeply depressed and distracted in ways I can't begin to understand, even now. Something *happened* to him. But when he hit me, we both knew he'd stepped over the line. It wasn't the beginning of the end, it was the full stop. He just walked out. I never saw him again. I took you to my parents' place here, met Frank—'

'The man of her dreams,' Frank called out, walking back in the room.

'And you know the rest,' she said.

Ben had heard bits and pieces of this story over the years, but not all of it. He wondered what else he'd never been told.

'This photo was with the documents,' he said, holding up the shot of Curtis as a pilot with his buddies.

Nikki peered at the photo. 'Amazing . . . I'd forgotten how much you look like him.' She gave a heavy sigh. 'Such a waste. Nearly everyone in that photo is dead.'

'What happened?'

'They were in a transport plane that went down.'

'There was a survivor?'

'Tex Mitchell, the guy on the end. He was on vacation at the time. Tex was Curtis's navigator.'

'Do you know where he is these days?'

'Why?'

'I might want to talk to him.'

'About what?'

'I don't know.'

'I doubt you'll get anything out of Tex.'

'Because . . .'

'Because he signed the same secrecy agreement that Curtis signed. And those guys stick to the agreement.'

'Mom . . .'

With a sigh Nikki conceded. 'Tex used to own the Radio Shack in Homestead. I don't know if he still does. Listen, you don't owe Curtis anything.'

'He just gave me a whole bunch of money.'

'He owed you that and a lot more. If I were you, I'd consider the account closed.'

'Hey, I almost forgot,' said Ben. 'There was also this.' He held up the postcard.

'Oh . . .' said Nikki, bringing her hand across her mouth.

'What?' Ben asked. It had obviously moved her.

'Brings back memories—the summer of '83. I was pregnant with you. Curtis was stationed at Eielson, Alaska. We were living in Fairbanks and it'd been raining, sleeting, snowing, drizzling—every kind of falling wetness you can imagine—for eight long months. Everyone was going nuts. And then suddenly the sun came out for a whole month. We couldn't believe it. Curtis took leave. We spent three weeks at Chena Lake. It was our favorite place—so beautiful. We swam a lot. Curtis fished. It was often just like that postcard—heaven.'

'He wants his ashes scattered there. It's in the will.'

'Really?' Nikki seemed disturbed by the news.

'Are you okay?' Ben asked.

'Yes.'

'So he gave this to *me* to remind *you* that it wasn't all bad?'

Nikki frowned. 'Yeah, maybe . . . I don't know.'

'You want me to mail this to you?'

'No. No, thanks.'

June 21, 1983

The Old Executive Office Building, Washington DC. Hank could feel the sweat seeping into his shirt collar. He hooked a finger inside it and pulled the fabric away from his skin. It had to be 100 degrees outside and the air in the government Chrysler wasn't working.

'Des is expecting you,' said a young woman who looked the part of Des Bilson's personal assistant—young, pert, long fingernails painted red, a St Moritz smoker. He walked past her into the office.

'Hey, Hank,' said Bilson. 'Close the door and take a load off.'

Des looked cool, the knot of his blue and yellow designer silk tie hard up against his shirt button. Hank found himself wondering if the guy actually had sweat glands. His skin had taken on an odd waxy quality.

'Jesus, it's hot out there,' Hank observed, slipping out of his suit coat and laying it beside him across the chair arm.

'So, my man . . .' said Bilson. 'How's our business coming along? Where are we, exactly?'

'The crew we wanted is on board. Eric Hamilton has had several briefing sessions with them.'

'I like Hamilton,' Bilson said. 'Solid guy. What about Garret?'

'There's a lot to put in place. Garret's working through most of that.'

'What I mean is, do you think he's the right man for the job?'

'Garret's a fast learner.'

'I get that from his report,' said Bilson. 'But when it comes to the hard decisions, can he make them? I'm not convinced. We need to make absolutely certain that we end up with the result we're after, and we're not 100 percent sure we're there yet.'

'Is that the royal we, Des?'

'It is what it is, Hank. We'd like to introduce some certainty into the mission profile.'

'How?'

The phone on the desk rang. 'Excuse me,' said Bilson, answering it. 'Yes, send him in.'

The door opened and Eric Hamilton entered. Hank was surprised to see him. Hamilton was at the tactical end of the mission, the dirty end, and sometimes the dirt stuck. And that usually made people in this building nervous. If the plan didn't work and he was seen in these corridors, deniability would be a stretch.

Bilson motioned Hamilton toward the chair beside Hank, the ceiling lights reflecting little squares on the colonel's glossy head.

'As I was saying, Hank,' Bilson continued, 'one of our colleagues—who will remain nameless—had a few thoughts that we've been kicking around. Colonel, would you mind outlining for Hank what we discussed earlier?'

'Yes, sir.' Hamilton was a little on edge, aware that he'd been put in a difficult position. He half turned toward Hank. 'We don't know *how* the Soviets will respond to the overflight, so we need a worm on the hook.'

'I'm not sure I understand.'

'We might need to help the Russians take the bait.'

'What kind of worm are you talking about?'

'An RC-135, flying in close formation at the appropriate time.'

'I see,' said Hank.

'We've got RCs—Cobra Balls—stationed at Eielson and staging out of Shemya. They're a gift. They spend all day every day flying right up to Soviet airspace—sometimes even penetrating it. Makes the Russians

55

crazy. Play it right and the Soviets will believe—because they're paranoid and they'll *want* to believe—that there's a spy plane rather than a 747 on their screens heading for Kamchatka.'

'What about Chun and his crew?' Hank asked.

Hamilton shrugged. 'As far as they're concerned, the RC-135 will be employed as a decoy to lure Russian defense assets *away* from them.'

Hank nodded. 'Sounds good to me,' he said truthfully, though he was concerned about what Garret would think.

'Why don't you put this RC business to Roy? Feel him out,' said Bilson with a perfect smile. He reminded Hank of an Armani mannequin. 'Do you think he'll have a problem?'

'And if he does?' Hank replied.

'Then you're not doing your job right, Hank.'

June 23, 1983

Norfolk, Virginia. 'Excuse me, sir,' said the waitress, her slight wrists straining under the weight of the platter she was holding.

Garret took his elbows off the table, clearing the way. She lowered a massive lobster with claws as big as Muhammad Ali's fists between his knife and fork.

'Something to drink, sir?'

The offer conjured up a scotch, but this was lunch—wrong time of day. 'Think I'll stick with water for the moment.'

'Oh-kay,' she said, making a note on a small pad and walking away.

Garret took in the view beyond the balcony: a marina with million-dollar yachts and cruisers bobbing at their moorings. The air smelled of diesel oil and salt.

Hank swaggered through the door dressed in light green slacks, a green knitted shirt, white shoes.

'Straight from the golf course?' Garret asked as Hank approached the table.

'The driving range. Golf's too hard. I like to hit balls without having to give a shit where they go.'

'That could be your motto, Hank.'

The CIA agent grinned.

'Why'd you suggest this place?' Garret asked.

The waitress appeared.

'I'll have the same,' Hank said, pointing to the prostrate lobster on Garret's plate. 'And a bottle of . . . let me see . . .' He flicked through the wine list and read out the name of a Napa Valley chardonnay. The waitress departed. 'Where was I? Yeah, this place. Hard to find, wasn't it?'

'Very,' said Garret.

'So that's why, pilgrim. You know what it's like around DC. CIA seen out to lunch with NSA, people speculate. This place is out of the way. No one comes here.' He gestured at the vacant tables. 'Not on a Thursday, at least.'

Garret pointed a bread knife at a cruiser piloted by a young man whose wife and young child had just gone below, its exhausts snarling as it maneuvered slowly through the narrow channel. 'See that boat?'

'What of it?'

'Can you read her name from here?'

Hank stretched his neck. '*Barnestormer*.'

'It belongs to New Hampshire Democratic Senator Barnesdale. And that's his son up there on the bridge—Trent Barnesdale.'

Hank's humor evaporated. 'Shit, that CNN fucker? Did he see us?'

'I don't think so. The point I'm trying to make here, Hank, is that there's no such thing as an out-of-the-way place, especially this close to Washington. Now, why are we here?'

'How's our flight crew?' Hank said.

'They've taken the mission to heart. They believe they're striking a blow for the free world. Hamilton has won their trust.'

'Eric's a good man.'

'Why do I get the sense that you're stalling?'

'Something's come up.'

'Really.'

Hank's lobster arrived on its stainless-steel oval plate. The waitress struggled to set it down, and returned a moment later with the wine and two glasses. There was the usual bottle-opening and tasting ritual, during which Garret stared out impatiently at the marina.

'They want insurance,' Hank said finally.

'Who's "they", Hank?'

'Bilson, the Judge, Meese . . . I don't know. Maybe the President.'

'What kind of insurance?'

'Some suggestions were kicked around with Hamilton.'

'Thanks for telling me.'

'I'm telling you now.'

'Get on with it, Hank,' said Garret with naked anger.

'They want an RC to rendezvous with the Koreans in the buffer zone, on the edge of Soviet radar. They want to confuse the issue.'

Garret digested the implications of this. He didn't like them. 'Getting a Cobra Ball involved, bringing the Air Force into the loop. That's a mistake.'

'It's not a suggestion, Roy.'

'I'll think about it.'

Hank shrugged and took another look at the marina.

'While we're here there's something I want to talk to you about, Hank.' Garret bent down and picked a folder out of the briefcase by his foot, then placed it beside his plate. 'At the NSA, we're wizards when it comes to electronics. It's what we do. People can erase and shred all they like, but if someone somewhere makes any kind of digital record, we can get at it. That's the power of computers, and right now we're on the cusp of an information revolution. You know anything about computers, Hank?'

'Do I look like I would?'

Garret smiled. 'The day will come when all information as we know it will be committed to hard drives.'

'What's a hard drive?'

'The NSA is about to leave the CIA and the FBI in the dust. Advancements in technology mean we're on the verge of becoming the most powerful and invasive agency the world has ever known.' Garret flipped open the file. 'I'm telling you this because, Staff Sergeant (E-6) Henry Louis Buck, RA 3215684, former Green Beret, didn't you say you were in the First Cavalry, a gunner? It says here you were trained as a sniper—and you were quite a good one apparently.'

'My service record is classified,' Hank said, agitated.

Garret enjoyed the moment, lifting his eyes from the file to watch Hank squirm. 'It was supposed to have been destroyed, right? Like I said, computers are about to change the world. Let's talk about Project Phoenix.'

'Phoenix was a long time ago.'

'Only twelve years. The way time flies, it probably seems like only yesterday, right? Project Phoenix: the sanctioned assassination of suspected Viet Cong and North Vietnamese sympathizers operating in South Vietnam. Nice idea in theory, only some people went a little . . . overboard. Like you, for instance. July 12, 1971. Quang Tri. Ring a bell? A certain plantation owner and his wife and kids, remember? You know, stuff like this doesn't look good in your employment history.'

'We found tunnels,' Hank said, lowering his voice. 'The plantation owner was French. His operation had been left alone by the enemy for a reason. We found out he was harboring a high-ranking Viet Cong cadre.'

'That's what *you* reported, only it was well known that you wanted to screw the guy's wife. You assaulted her. She filed a formal complaint with the US Military Assistance Command. Two weeks later the husband was found murdered, his throat slit. The wife was raped and murdered and the children—eight-year-old twins—were shot and left for dead. One of them survived.'

'I was in another part of the country.'

'Your alibi was cooked up. The kid picked your photo out of a book from her hospital bed. The following morning the hospital was bombed. A lot of people—our own people—died along with the witness.'

'Wounded Viet Cong prisoners were being treated there. We'd turned a couple of them. Their comrades found out and got even.'

'Maybe someone told them.'

'I was never implicated.'

'That's not what it says here,' Garret said, tapping the folder lightly with an index finger.

Hank stared at the vanilla-colored article. 'Are you thinking of holding that over me, Roy?' He looked at Garret, unblinking. 'You think the people I work for now give a shit? Look at what's on the table with our Korean friends. What you've got there is nothing more than a further recommendation.'

'This is not about blackmail, Hank. You just need to know what you're dealing with. I know more about you than you know about me, which makes me unpredictable.' Garret took one of the lobster's massive claws and wound it in a circle until the shell cracked. He ripped it from the body. 'Keep that in mind next time you have a meeting with Des behind my back, *pilgrim*.'

September 1, 1983

Anchorage International Airport, Alaska. 'It's 2:35 in the morning, what did you expect?' Hatsuto Sato said to his wife, Nami. 'She's not going to wake up and say goodbye.' Their daughter, Akiko, lay asleep in his arms, eyelashes like little caterpillars.

Nami brushed the hair from Akiko's forehead, kissed her and smelled her skin, fragrant with youth. 'I will see you in a week, little Kimba,' she whispered, missing her daughter already, nuzzling the child. 'And I will bring you a present from your great-grandmother.'

'I know you don't want to think about it,' Hatsuto said, 'but your grandmother could be annoying her ancestors in person before you get there, which would make this trip a waste of time and money.'

'I know, so please . . . I feel guilty enough already. But what can I do? I am all the family she has. If Grandmother dies alone, I will never forgive myself.'

'Maybe she's not sick at all,' said Hatsuto. 'This could just be a plan to get you away from me. She never liked me.'

'It's not her fault that she's old and ill.' Nami kissed Hatsuto on the cheek. 'And of course she likes you.'

'We did better than that in the hotel last night,' he complained.

'Shhh.' Nami glanced around, embarrassed.

'Hey, there's only us and the potted plants, and they won't blush.'

'Akiko might hear us.'

'Nonsense. Kiss my lips, woman, and this time give me a little tongue.'

Nami giggled and gave Hatsuto a kiss more like the one he was expecting.

Akiko stirred in his arms, snuggling deeper into his chest. 'What's your flight number again? KAL 007 or 015?' Hatsuto asked, shuffling sideways across the airport carpet. He leaned around the corner to get a better view of the departures board in the main area of the hall. Two Korean Air Lines flights were scheduled to depart within fourteen minutes of each other.

'It's the one leaving at 3 a.m.'

'KAL 007. Your gate is 2N and the flight has been delayed, though the "now boarding" sign is lit. I'm sure they'll make up the time en route, but even if you arrive as scheduled, you won't have much time in Seoul to make the Sapporo connection,' he said. 'You'll have to hurry when you land.'

'I know. I'm still not sure whether I have a seat. It hasn't been confirmed.'

'You might just end up waiting around in Kimpo.'

'This was the earliest flight I could get. If I waited till morning, I might be too late. Please let's not go through all this again. *You* could be coming with *me*.'

Hatsuto sighed. 'Time to go. You have to clear immigration.'

'There's still time,' said Nami.

'For what?'

'A photo. For Grandmother. The three of us together. I don't have one to give her.'

'That's because you don't really care about her.'

'Stop it.' Nami grinned and pulled the Nikon from her carry-on bag.

'Maybe you can get one of the potted plants to take it,' teased Hatsuto.

Just then a couple of Korean businessmen came around the corner.

'Look, they've come to life,' he said in mock astonishment.

Nami went off to intercept the businessmen with the camera. Hatsuto watched them nod and smile with body language that said, 'Of course, no trouble. No trouble at all.'

Nami showed them how to work the camera and then she rushed to Hatsuto, put her arms around him and smiled.

Flash!

'One more, please?' Nami took Akiko from Hatsuto's arms. Hatsuto stood behind them and smiled.

Flash!

There was a sudden commotion nearby. A crowd of Americans appeared around the corner, moving in a hurry. The crowd was noisy, and it was closing in on them. She heard someone mention KAL 015. Whoever they were, she thought, they were on the other plane leaving just after hers.

Hatsuto glanced at his wristwatch: 2:56 a.m. 'Come on, Nami. Don't let them get in front of you. You'll get held up. I'll see you at home at the end of the week. Give my regards to the old witch.'

They kissed again, hurriedly this time. The Americans swept Nami along with them toward the immigration section. Akiko rolled in Hatsuto's arms, disturbed by the activity invading her sleep. He lifted his free hand, realizing that in the confusion he'd been left holding the camera.

Hatsuto looked for his wife, but she was gone.

Nami joined the queue shuffling along the airbridge toward the door of the 747. Once in the departure lounge, the passengers had been told that the flight was delayed again, and now probably wouldn't leave till 3:50 a.m. Nami wished she'd taken more time to say goodbye to Hatsuto and Akiko instead of dashing off in such a hurry. Somehow the camera had been left behind with her husband and now there was no photo to give her grandmother.

The flight attendant, a young Korean woman, gestured to see Nami's boarding pass and then directed her to the next aisle. Before moving forward, she glanced at the staircase that led up to the first-class cabin.

A couple of flight attendants appeared to be fussing over one of the passengers coming down, offering him a drink from a selection on a silver tray.

'Them politicians sure know how to travel,' commented an old man wearing a cowboy hat coming up behind her. 'Especially when they're funded by the taxpayer, right?' The man made a clucking sound with his tongue and shook his head. 'US Congressman Larry McDonald,' the man said when Nami turned to look at him. 'I talked to him back at JFK. Not a bad fella—for a Democrat.'

Nami gave him a polite smile and made her way up the aisle, pulling her overnight bag behind her. Seat 52A was midway between the wing and the very back of the plane. Working her way down the aisle, she saw that many people were already asleep—passengers who'd boarded in New York around seven hours ago and hadn't disembarked during the stopover to stretch their legs. The warm air smelled close and a little stale, of dusty blankets and the acrid tang of old cigarette smoke.

Nami found her seat beside a window. She watched the man with the cowboy hat open the overhead locker and stow his bag. There were plenty of empty rows. The two seats beside hers were vacant and she hoped they'd remain that way. Directly across the aisle, a heavy middle-aged European man was draped across his seat and the one beside him, snoring loudly, his mouth open and his tongue out, drooling onto his collar.

Nami sighed. It was going to be a long flight.

January 5, 2012

Shibuya, Tokyo, Japan. Akiko Sato pulled the mail from her mailbox and headed for the elevator. The doors opened and a young couple stepped out of the tiny, mirrored box. Akiko knew them, or knew *of* them. They lived down the hall, two of the many residents jammed together in this small apartment building on the busiest street in Shibuya. Outside, a car revved its engine, a gathering crescendo of aggression that ended in wild tire-screeching. Akiko winced until the noise mercifully faded into the general traffic thrum.

She and the odd couple from down the hall exchanged small bland smiles. The girlish boy wore dark eye make-up and one side of his blue-black hair was dyed white with a pink stripe down the middle—white, pink, white, black. He was extremely thin, tight jeans accentuating skinny legs. His companion was dressed in a short baby-doll outfit. She looked like a cute ten-year-old slut. On their way to a nightclub, Akiko thought, where they would fit right in, dancing and popping whatever drug was on the menu that night.

The girl glanced at her as they squeezed past each other, surveying her up and down. Yes, this is what a schoolteacher looks like, Akiko thought, reading the girl's mind, particularly if she's exhausted and lives alone with a cat. Akiko opened the door to her apartment and a large Siamese charged her.

'Komainu, Komainu,' she sang. 'Home at last.' The animal leaned into her shins and coiled its tail around her kneecap, meowing and purring loudly. 'Late today, I'm sorry. Are you hungry? You're not going clubbing tonight, are you? I hope not. I have papers to grade. You have to hang around here and keep me company.'

With Komainu dodging between her feet, Akiko dumped her mail and satchel onto a small wooden dining table and went to the kitchen, a galley off the compact one-room apartment. She lifted a tin from the top of the stack in a cupboard.

'You had teriyaki beef last night, didn't you?' The cat purred, circled. 'Yes, I know you like that. Well, tonight it's gourmet Atlantic salmon with lemon and rice,' she said, reading the label. 'You eat better than me!'

She peeled back the lid and forked the beautifully presented fish into the cat's bowl. Komainu unfurled himself from her legs and attacked the bowl before it reached the floor.

Akiko washed her hands, threw some instant noodles in the microwave, and spooned some rice from the refrigerator into a white porcelain dish. She carried it to the altar, a narrow wooden shelf attached to the living room wall beside the entrance to the kitchen. On it rested two old color photos of her *kami*—her chosen spirits—as well as two small, carved *komainu*, the guardian lions protecting them, and a rice offering.

Exchanging the old rice for the new, Akiko bowed and then prayed to the *kami*, asking that they guide her and look out for her. The prayer was the one she always said. In fact, she hardly heard the words any more and nor did she really see the photos perched on the altar, even though she spoke to them every single day. Indeed, Akiko often had to remind herself that these two *kami* were her parents, Hatsuto and Nami. Hatsuto, her father, had died recently. He wasn't particularly old—his heart had just given out. The photo was taken a couple of years ago, before he went into a final decline. Nami, on the other hand, was just thirty-two when her photo was shot, shortly before she'd perished all those years ago—the same age Akiko was now.

Akiko lifted Nami's photo off the shelf and took it into the kitchenette to wipe the glass. She studied her mother's features. They were almost identical to hers: the same full mouth and pronounced cheekbones; the same thick black hair, a gentle wave sweeping the ends in a soft layered curve to the right. Akiko had looked in the mirror six months ago and seen Nami staring back. At that moment she'd made a decision. It was time to stop asking what had happened. There were no answers, only questions. Nami's life had been cut short in the Korean Air Lines disaster when Akiko was just four years old. Suddenly seeing her mother's face in the mirror had made Akiko realize that it was time to pack away the hundreds of books, articles and scrapbooks she'd collected and compiled on KAL 007 from the age of twelve. The obsession had consumed all of her adult life, but now it was all stacked in a storage locker several blocks away. Finally, it was time to move on.

Akiko wiped her *kami* with a cloth, placed the photo back on the shelf and gave a final bow. She stood back and regarded the altar. It wasn't impressive, but it was always clean and well cared for.

The microwave pinged, reminding her that it was her turn to eat. She took the instant noodles, gathered up the mail and settled onto the couch, picking through the pile as she ate. A hairdresser was offering free haircuts in exchange for promotional modeling shots. Akiko wondered whether the boy down the hall with the pink and white skunk hair had taken up the salon's offer. A computer shop was advertising ten percent off on second-hand portable hard drives. Pizza Hut was running a three-for-the-price-of-two teriyaki special. She could also have her drain deodorized for thirty percent off and get twenty phone numbers from a singles club for just ¥550. None of it appealed.

Komainu scratched in his box before crouching and urinating, neck craned forward, eyes narrowed to slits of concentration. The sound distracted Akiko. She watched him dig at the litter with his hind paws and then shake them as if he'd stepped into something distasteful.

She found the letter between a flyer for a dog-walking service and a solicitation to be a telemarketer. The envelope was white, her address penned with great precision in black ink. The handwriting was not familiar—old-fashioned, the Japanese characters almost calligraphic. Akiko could not remember the last time she'd received a personal letter.

And that's what this was—*personal*. She couldn't think of anyone who might actually post something to her. It hadn't happened in years. Perhaps it was from one of her students?

There was no return address on the flip side. She shrugged, opened it and pulled out a . . . *kuso!* Shit! A check with her name on it. For ¥10,657,460! Her heart leapt. Akiko could not believe her eyes. She read over her name and the amount several times. This had to be a joke, a mistake, or perhaps some stupid lottery-style promotion. She examined it again. No, the check was real; a cashier's check from the Bank of Japan, and it was made out to her. She looked inside the envelope and pulled out a note, a single sheet of paper, folded in thirds. As she opened it, an old newspaper clipping fell in her lap. Her breath caught in her throat. The article was so familiar she almost knew it by heart: 'The Tragic Survivors'. And she knew the photo—the original was in a frame on the nightstand beside her bed. It showed her mother and father and herself as a small child. She was asleep in her mother's arms; her father's arm around her mother's shoulders. It was the last photo taken of the three of them together before . . . Akiko had a sour taste in her mouth. Why would anyone be sending her this? Perhaps it was someone's idea of a cruel joke after all. She held up the note. It was handwritten in Japanese.

December 03, 2011

Dear Akiko

You are not the little one in the photograph any more. But I know she still lives, perhaps not so deep within you.

My name is Yuudai Suzuki. We have met. Perhaps you remember. We spoke a number of times, often in the elevator. It is unlikely that we will ever meet again because, by the time you read this, I will be with my ancestors and my good friend Curtis Foxx.

We talked on a couple of occasions about KAL 007.

I never told you that many years ago I worked for the Chosa Besshitsu, specifically the Annex Chamber, Second Section, Investigative Division. I was a radar operator and I manned the Wakkanai radar facility tasked to track and identify Soviet aircraft over Sakhalin Island.

In the early-morning hours of September 1st, 1983, I witnessed the terrible events that changed your life and the lives of so many hundreds of others. I saw the Korean Air Lines 747 Flight 007 transit prohibited Soviet airspace pursued by hostile fighters. I heard and observed the interception on my radar screen. It was widely reported that after the aircraft was struck by missile fire, it plummeted into the sea.

While I am sure KAL 007 sustained damage from the missiles, what I observed was a stricken aircraft, maintaining an altitude of 5000 feet, fly beyond the coastline of Sakhalin Island. It was on a heading for the Soviet air base of Dolinsk-Sokol before disappearing from my radar screen, too low to be tracked any further by my radar. I most definitely did not see the aircraft 'plummet into the sea' as was widely reported.

I can't tell you why it has been so important for the authorities to lie. However, I do know that my silence and the silence of others have been part of making it legitimate. Now that Curtis and I are dead, perhaps the world can know what really happened.

Little Akiko, I have no children to survive me, but our talks confirmed to me that my legacy would be in good hands if left to you.

What you need to know is that I believe your mother, and many other passengers on KAL 007, could still be alive. My friend Curtis had a son and he will help you find them. His business address is 3147 South Kennedy Blvd, Key West, FL, USA.

The money enclosed here, all I have left, is yours. It is not much, but hopefully it will be enough. Spend it wisely and in pursuit of the truth.

Yours sincerely
Yuudai Suzuki

Her mother, *alive?* Akiko reread the letter, her fingers trembling. Yuudai Suzuki. Yes, she remembered him well. He was a large man who lived alone, further down the hall. He was about the same age as Hatsuto, or perhaps a little younger—it was difficult to tell. She had met him often while waiting for the elevator. On one of these occasions, she'd been carrying an armful of reference books on aviation disasters. And thereafter they had talked about this accident or that, and on a couple of occasions about KAL 007, but only in the most general terms. She hadn't bumped into him for more than a year, but hadn't given it a second thought. If she had, she'd have simply concluded that he'd moved out. Why hadn't he just told her what he knew from the beginning? Had he been spying on her?

Akiko looked up at the *kami* and found her vision blurred, tears streaming down her cheeks. Nami, alive?

January 12, 2012

Shibuya, Tokyo, Japan. Once the initial shock had worn off, doubts set in about Yuudai Suzuki's bizarre letter. How had he known about her mother being a passenger on 007? She had never mentioned Nami. The more Akiko thought about it, the more she came to the conclusion that Yuudai Suzuki was just some kind of cruel troublemaker. But that had changed when the Bank of Japan processed the check and the funds appeared in her account. She had looked at the statement online wide-eyed for a full minute. Her next action was to google for a private detective in her local area. The money was real, but what about *him*?

There was a private detective with an office three blocks away from her school who, according to his website, specialized in missing persons. His name was Thomas Watanabe. Akiko had made an appointment immediately, seeing him during her lunch break. He was ex-Japan Defense Force and ex-Tokyo police, and had spent the last ten years of his career in missing persons, the experience and contacts from which he'd brought across into private practice.

She'd briefed him a week ago. And earlier this morning, Watanabe had called to inform her that he had a result, and apologized for taking so long.

After pressing the buzzer on his door, Akiko sat impatiently in the waiting room Watanabe shared with a wedding dress maker and a two-man tourist agency. Watanabe appeared after five minutes, a smile on his round face and his hand outstretched as he walked toward her. He was in his early fifties and a drinker, Akiko decided, from his capillary-crazed cheeks and the strong smell of sake that preceded him like aftershave. He was short and stocky, his shoulders tending toward round. His belly was thick, his loose gray suit pants secured by a thin, tight belt. His leather shoes needed polishing. He also had an old-fashioned Adolf Hitler mustache, which looked wholly at home on his lip.

'Akiko, Akiko, yes . . .' he said in a voice full of gravel, adding fish to the array of smells. 'Glad you could come over so quickly. Please . . .' His hand gently came to rest on her shoulder.

She got up and he motioned her into his small windowless and airless room, which was stuffed with a compact desk and chair, a laptop computer and printer, two filing cabinets and, hanging on a wall, a couple of citations as well as pictures of fellow officers from the Tokyo police force. He came in behind her wheeling a chair, taking the last square meter of space, and positioned it in front of his desk and said, 'Sit, sit . . .'

He then pulled a file from the cabinet and placed it on the desk in front of her. 'I have good news.'

'You traced him?' Akiko asked.

'Yes. The fact that your benefactor stayed in your apartment building made it relatively easy. There was a forwarding address, bank account details. And there were willing contacts in the military. Speaking of which, there are some added expenses incurred in loosening tongues. Nothing unreasonable.'

He placed an account on the table. Akiko's eye went to the bottom line.

'¥180,000? That's a lot of money.'

'Are we in agreement?'

Akiko hesitated, unused as she was to having any spare cash.

'If you are not completely satisfied, pay nothing,' he reassured her.

Akiko knew she had no choice. 'Okay.'

Watanabe opened the folder and a color photo of Yuudai Suzuki looked up at her. He appeared much younger than he was when she'd met him, but it was definitely the same man. And now he was dead.

'It's him,' she said, a tingle running up her spine and into her ears so that she shivered. *I believe your mother, and many other passengers on KAL 007, could still be alive.*

The private detective sifted through the folder and handed her a lease agreement on a Honda signed in December 1982 by Yuudai Suzuki. The dealership was located in the city of Wakkanai. Suzuki had given his residential address as an apartment in Wakkanai.

'This contract puts him in the right place at approximately the right time,' said Watanabe. 'And here is a photocopied page of his military record.' He produced a sheet with a Japan Defense Force logo at the top. The language was full of abbreviations and acronyms and difficult to decipher.

'What does it mean?' Akiko asked.

'This confirms Suzuki's transfer to the Chosa Besshitsu, and notes his area of expertise as radar and signals. He retired a sergeant first class. What do you know about the Chobetsu?'

'Enough. It gathers and analyzes radio and signals transmissions. Today, it spies on North Korea. In the Cold War, its chief target was the Soviet Union. It was, and still is, affiliated with the American National Security Agency.'

'Yes, all true. You know, you are a surprising young woman,' Watanabe said.

Akiko noted a sheen on Watanabe's forehead as he licked his upper lip, which deposited a fleck of saliva on his mustache. There was something other than business on his mind.

'I have been thinking,' he said. 'Perhaps we could come to some kind of accommodation on my bill.'

'Perhaps,' she said, wanting his cooperation for a little while longer.

Akiko had taken all her reference books and scrapbooks out of storage and her small apartment now resembled a ransacked library. There was very little in the public domain about KAL 007 that she didn't know about. There was, according to her research, a Chosa Besshitsu radar station in Wakkanai, on the very tip of Hokkaido, not fifty miles from the point where the Russians claimed the plane had crashed into the Sea of Japan.

'Did you manage to access the roster for Suzuki's shifts for the second half of 1983?' Akiko asked.

'No. So sorry. That information is still top secret. Perhaps it can be obtained through the right channels. I tried, but could not get confirmation.' Watanabe shook his head.

He sifted through the folder and handed Akiko another couple of forms, his forefinger stroking the top of her hand. It could have been an accident. Akiko doubted it.

'His discharge papers,' he said.

She scanned them. 'He left the military in 1986.'

'Yes. He found employment in the computer industry, working for Toshiba. When he lived in your building, he also kept a home in Sapporo.'

'Why did he move to my building?' she wondered aloud.

'One can only speculate. Perhaps he felt a special bond with you. Perhaps he came to spy on you. Perhaps you're not telling me the whole story.'

Watanabe held her eyes with his for a long moment, a cold smile lifting a corner of his mouth.

The private detective was right. She had told him nothing about KAL 007, nor had she shown him Suzuki's letter. Akiko wanted information. She wasn't giving it away.

Watanabe gave a small capitulating shrug. 'He was diagnosed with pancreatic cancer nine months ago and it claimed him at the age of sixty-one.'

'Any relatives?' she asked.

'No. Yuudai Suzuki was an only child, as were both his parents. Mother, father, grandparents, all deceased. He did not marry.'

Akiko nodded. The man she remembered had been comfortable in his loneliness, or had seemed to be.

'The folder is yours,' said Watanabe, closing it and pushing it toward her.

Akiko was far from satisfied. Yuudai Suzuki had been with the Chobetsu, as claimed in his letter. He had also more than likely worked at the facility at Wakkanai in 1983. But what of the meat of his declaration? Had he been on duty on the morning of September 1, 1983? Had he seen her mother's plane fly on after the missile strike, rather than crash into the sea? If what he said was true, then why had the Soviet Union contrived such a lie? And how could Moscow have pulled this off without the complicity of Japan? Or America? And if the plane had landed safely, what had happened to all the passengers; to her mother, Nami?

Akiko was suddenly aware that Watanabe was standing behind her. His hands were on her shoulders and they were working forward, down toward her breasts. She shrugged them off angrily and leaned forward to gather up her bag.

'That won't be necessary,' she snapped, feeling around among wallet, lipgloss, tissues and other items for her checkbook. 'I will pay you now, and in *full*.'

There was really only one other place she could go for answers. On the way back to her school, Akiko ducked into an internet cafe and booked a seat on a plane.

January 13, 2012

Orlando, Florida. The Otter required an engine overhaul, and excep-
tionally cold weather up north had pushed an unseasonal number of
tourists south to the Keys. The combination of these two factors had
made it impossible for Ben to fly up to Orlando sooner. But the delay
had given him time to think. And mostly what he thought was that this
whole business was just an attempt by Curtis Foxx to purchase himself
a clear conscience before he died.

The money bequeathed to Ben, the best part of a hundred grand,
had landed in his bank account as Bourdain had said it would, and he
was going to use it to pay off a big chunk of the Otter. Whatever that
bullshit about embracing the truth meant, Ben had no idea, but he was
more than happy to embrace being virtually debt free.

He stood across the road from the bank and took it in. With its
expanse of concrete, glass and steel, the branch exuded wealth and per-
manence. It was difficult associating a building like this with his father,
but then he'd felt the same about the offices of Kayson Bourdain. Ben
trotted across the street, dodging traffic, and went through the revolving door. He approached the enquiry section of a long granite counter
where a thin white male, his tie as thick as a noose around his neck,
looked particularly bored. 'Can I help you, sir?' he asked.

'Safe deposit boxes, please,' Ben replied.

'To rent or open?'

'Open.'

'Just head on down the stairs, sir.'

Ben took the two flights to the basement, the air temperature falling with each flight. In the basement, another granite counter overlooked by several surveillance cameras greeted him, this one occupied by a fat white teenage woman with blackheads trailing across her high forehead. A nameplate on her substantial chest informed him that her name was Petulia, if he cared to use it.

A black security guard with tight salt-and-pepper curls and bags like blisters beneath tired eyes stood in the corner with his hands behind his back. He rocked back and forth on the balls of his feet, staring at nothing.

Ben gave Petulia a smile and put the key on the counter.

'Can I see some ID, please, sir?' she asked.

'Driver's license, social security card?'

'Yes, thank you.'

Ben handed over both.

The woman shuffled through them a couple of times while she glanced at Ben, perhaps having difficulty getting past the 'Sex Addict' T-shirt he was wearing. She went to a computer terminal to check his details and returned with a more accommodating attitude.

'Okay,' she said. 'Sign here, sir.' She handed him a stylus and he scribbled on the screen. The formalities handled, she heaved herself off the stool. 'Follow me, please.'

Ben followed Petulia down a hallway scanned by more cameras, the cheeks of her large bottom bouncing like kettledrums slung over a horse's rump. A highly polished heavy steel and brass door featuring several large spoked wheels was open halfway on massive hinges. Inside, lit with bright halogen overhead lamps, boxes were set into numbered shelves from floor to ceiling.

'Box number 007,' Petulia repeated to herself.

It was located in the first row inside the vault, seventh box from the floor, secured in place by two locks. Petulia produced a key on a thick chain, inserted it into the lock, and waited for Ben to do the same.

'On the count of three, turn counterclockwise,' she informed him, stifling a yawn. 'One, two, three.'

The keys turned and the box sprang from its shelf half an inch, enough for Ben to grip it between thumb and forefinger and pull it all the way out. It was a couple of feet deep, twelve inches wide and six inches high—long and thin.

'The second viewing room on your left is vacant,' Petulia told him, pointing down the hall. 'Just let me know when y'all's finished.'

Ben tucked the box under one arm, said thanks, and left her inside the vault. He found the empty room, went in and shut the door. There was a table and chair, but no cameras. The walls were painted green and hung with prints of the city of Orlando 100 years before Disney and technicolor had come to town—wide dusty streets, more horses than cars, and everything in black and white.

Ben gave the box a gentle shake. Nothing rattled. He lifted the lid and found a legal-sized envelope taped to the bottom. He pulled away the tape and tore open the envelope. Inside was a smoky brown plastic spool of tape about the size of a beer mat, no label or markings of any kind on it.

'Tequila Sunrise' by the Eagles was playing on the car radio when Ben drove through the parking lot at Key West International. The sun was a velvet yellow button in a cool afternoon sky. The Eagles song gave way to the station ID, and then a familiar ad came on. The announcer sounded like he was bursting out of his skin with excitement: *You've got Key West surrounded by water, we've got seaplanes that land on water. What's all that telling you? Yeah. You need to come on over to Key West Seaplanes. We know where the deserted beaches are hidden, where the big fish are biting. Wanna see something special? Take a flight out to the Dry Tortugas* . . . The guy went on in that vein for a dozen more hyped-up seconds and then the ad concluded with the sound effect of a seaplane roaring overhead, a couple of testimonials, a musical sting and a phone number. Ben was sick to death of it. Cecilia had it piped into reception and playing on the phone when the caller was on hold. But the ad gave him an idea. Instead of turning left out of the airport, he took the exit heading east.

The girl at reception looked at the spool of tape in Ben's hand and weighed the request. She knew that the guy standing in front of her worked for Key West Seaplanes, a regular advertiser on the station. He was also cute.

'Okay, Ben. Take a seat and I'll see if anyone can help you. Can I get you something to drink, a Coke or something?'

Ben said no thanks and sat on the couch. He heard her try a couple of extensions until she located the technician and gave him a brief explanation of the situation. A minute later, a pale skinny guy with dyed black hair, black eye make-up and tight black jeans strolled into reception.

The girl gestured politely. 'This is Ben from Key West Seaplanes,' she said.

'Hi. I'm Omar,' he announced. 'So what you got there, Ben?'

Ben held up the tape. 'Thought you might be able to play this for me.'

'What's on it?'

'That's why I'm here. Haven't got a clue.'

'Let's see what we can do.'

Ben followed Omar through a door that warned 'Staff Only Beyond This Point'.

'So you're from Key West Seaplanes,' Omar said as they walked.

'Yeah.'

'I did your ad.'

'Really.'

'Yep. Wrote it, produced it. That sucker's on my resumé.'

'It's a great little ad,' Ben agreed, slipping into diplomacy. 'So, do you use reel-to-reel tape decks here much?'

'Occasionally. We've still got sound effects left over from the old days that we haven't digitized. Tape is better than disk, you know— better quality, more information. You lose something in the transfer.

I thought it would be best just to keep the tape, but management didn't agree.'

Omar pushed through another door into a room no bigger than a closet and filled with electrical equipment—black panels, cords and blinking lights. A tape deck with a sleek black facing and one large brushed-aluminum spool mounted on it sat on a shelf among a nest of twisted black and blue cabling. The technician swapped around a few leads, unplugging some, plugging in others, then stabbed the deck's power button and a small red LED standby light glowed.

'Okay, you got that reel?'

Ben handed it over.

Omar ripped out a length of tape, threw the spool onto a spline, wound the tape around various rollers and secured the end in the large aluminum spool.

'The sound will come though this,' he said, tapping a speaker propped beside the deck.

He turned the control lever to play. The spools turned, the rollers flexed, but the speaker was silent even though the levels needles on the front of the deck were dancing into the red.

'Hmm,' Omar said to himself. He replugged one of the leads and the small room was suddenly filled with 120 decibels of hissing and screeching. Ben winced and Omar's hand darted for a knob on one of the boxes.

'Oh, sorry about that,' he said as the noise dropped rapidly away.

'What's that?' Ben asked.

'The sound? Beats me.'

Omar fast-forwarded the tape, stopped it and again switched the lever to 'play', but the hiss and static continued. He sampled the tape in several other places, but more of the same resulted.

'You've got something on here, but whatever it is, it's ruined. Where'd you get it from?'

'Long story,' Ben said.

'Well, analog stuff doesn't last forever and this is definitely an antique.' He rewound the tape, removed the spool and handed it back with a shrug. 'Sorry, dude.'

So much for tape being the best way to store sound, Ben thought. He thanked the guy and left, shaking his head at the waste of a day. When he reached his car, he tossed the spool into the glovebox and slammed the door shut. 'Hey, fella,' he said to himself, 'I know what you need.'

Captain Tony's was a saloon on Greene Street. Outside, a giant jewfish was mounted above the front door, a model of the monster fish supposedly caught by Captain Tony himself. Tourists flipped coins into its mouth for good luck. Ben wasn't sure why. The fish had sure run out of luck to end up stuffed and hanging over the door. Inside, the place looked like the bedroom of an adolescent who'd raided a Victoria's Secret warehouse. Bras, more than a thousand of them, were pinned all over the walls and ceiling. In the middle of the joint grew a tree that had been used by vigilantes in the eighteenth century from which to hang a bunch of pirates. There was also a gravestone in the floor for someone's daughter who had died back in 1822. But the clincher for Ben, making Captain Tony's his favorite watering hole, was that some of the best-looking lager maidens in the whole of the Conch Republic pulled the beers here.

'Lock up your daughters,' Marsha called out from behind the counter when she saw him walk in. 'Ben Harbor's about to land.'

'Why don't you grab the microphone and announce it proper, sugar?' Ben said, mimicking her southern accent as he occupied a stool.

'Haven't seen y'all for a while,' she said, pouring him a Sunset beer without having to be asked. 'What's up?'

'Family stuff,' Ben explained. 'What's new with you?'

She gave him a shrug and placed the beer in front of him, the glass frosted, a lick of foam sliding down the side. 'My damn ride got boosted the other day right out of the Wal-Mart parking lot. And I caught my boo red-handed with that blonde skank who worked for his old man.'

'Ouch. You okay?'

'Yeah. My car was a pile of junk anyway,' she said, with a smirk. She leaned toward him across the bar, her breasts pressed against the wood. Her skin glowed with health. The bad luck and detritus of life that stuck to other people just seemed to slide right off her. She was wearing pink lipstick and her blue eyes sparkled. Even after twelve months, the picture of their one night of lovemaking, along with her personal preferences, were still vivid in Ben's mind.

Marsha cleared her throat. 'Think I'd better go serve someone else.'

'Yeah, you'd better.' He grinned.

'Give me a holler when you want to go another round,' she said ambiguously. Ben watched her move down the bar, swinging a runner's ass.

He glanced around. The band was setting up. The afternoon crowd had left and the night-time crowd was drifting in. Several old guys and their wives were having a quiet drink by the front window. A couple of tourists—a roided-up guy and his hyper-attractive girlfriend—were playing pool against a couple of older pro fishermen, one of whom Ben had taken on a charter flight to meet up with a cruiser that was fishing the Gulf Stream's deep blue waters out beyond the reef.

On the flatscreen over the bar, a debate between the front-running Democrats in the upcoming presidential elections had supplanted sports. Ben couldn't hear the sound but he didn't need to. They were both no doubt two-faced and untrustworthy, like all politicians, and probably neither deserved the Oval Office.

'Yo, Marsha!' Ben called out. 'Can we change the program here?'

She gave him a nod, found the remote and aimed it at the screen. NASCAR highlights took over.

Ben thought about calling a few friends to meet him for a drink, but decided against it. He had some thinking to do. He pulled out the picture of Curtis Foxx standing in front of what was probably the reconnaissance plane he'd flown and gazed hard at the man who looked so familiar, hoping to find a clue. The guy was young, he was smiling, he was a pilot and he was married to Nikki.

'So what happened to you, Curtis?' Ben asked out loud.

A hand suddenly slapped hard onto the bar beside his elbow.

'I believe you've been coined,' said a woman's voice.

Ben turned. It was the woman who'd been playing pool. The game was over and the two fishermen were standing around leaning on their cue sticks. The woman was tall and olive-skinned with full lips. Her longish hair had a wave in it and her dark eyes glittered with the effects of maybe a glass too many. She wore tight faded jeans and a blue Abercrombie & Fitch sweatshirt that smelled vaguely of the sea and coconut tanning lotion.

'You have no idea what I'm talking about, do you?' she gathered from the blank look on his face.

'No, I don't. What did you say? I've been "coined"?'

'You're not Air Force?'

'No.'

'Sorry, my mistake. I've got albums full of pictures just like that—with my dad and his friends standing in front of planes. I thought you might have been an Air Force brat, like me.'

'No.'

'Well, there's an Air Force tradition,' the woman said, 'that if you put a coin on the bar and the other person can't match it with a coin of their own, then that person has to buy the drinks for everyone who can.'

'And what if I did have one?' Ben asked, intrigued, looking at the thick medallion-sized coin beside his glass.

'Then I'd have to buy *you* a drink.'

'Interesting,' he said.

'So, sorry if I startled you.' She flicked her hair behind a tan shoulder. 'I just lost the game and had to buy those two boys over there a drink. You were staring so hard at that photo, I couldn't help but interrupt. This is a coin from my dad's squadron. He flew gunships—still does.' She picked it up and handed it to him.

It was heavy, made of brass. On one side were the words *4th Special Operations Squadron* above a hooded, ghost-like character, lightning bolts shooting down from its hands. On the flip side was a four-engined airplane banking in a steep turn, gunfire spitting from its side. There was a caption: *The AC-130—the real reason to fear the night.*

'Ben,' he said.

'Lana,' she replied and smiled, giving him a firm handshake. 'You know, I'm told I'm usually the reserved, stuck-up type who gives men she doesn't know the brush-off. But I'm wearing my vacation face at the moment.'

'This place has that effect on people. So, what are you drinking?' he asked.

'Forget it. I'm not sure what the rules say about coining someone who doesn't have a clue about the rules.'

One of the fishermen ambled up to her. 'Excuse me, miss, are you still . . . er . . .' He motioned toward the pool table.

'Oh, okay, just one second,' she told him, and turned to Ben, 'Look, my brother had to split to meet his girlfriend and—'

'That was your brother?' Ben asked.

'Yeah. And he's probably the world's worst pool player. I'd really like to beat these guys. Do you play?'

He considered the offer, then said, 'That table has a lean to the right and a dead cushion at this end.'

'I'll take that as a yes,' she beamed. 'Local knowledge.' She gave a hoot. 'I feel like my luck's about to turn.' She counted out some quarters with which to feed the pool table.

Ben turned toward the bar and caught Marsha's attention.

'What can I get you guys?' she said, coming over. 'Same again?'

'I'm good,' Ben replied, 'but I think—'

'Can I please have two Sunsets—make that three,' said Lana pointing at Ben's glass, butting in. 'And a white wine.'

Marsha raised a knowing eyebrow at Ben, then disappeared to fill the order.

'So what do you do when you're not on vacation?' he asked.

'I go—or rather, I went—to UCLA. I just finished.'

'I've met people from LA. Should I run away now?' Ben said.

Marsha assembled the drinks on the counter. Ben reached for his wallet, but Lana beat him to it and handed Marsha a note.

'Keep the change,' she said.

'Thanks,' Marsha replied, giving Ben a quick flash of approval.

'I'm not from LA,' she said. 'Being an Air Force brat means I'm from all over. Even spent a couple of years in Qatar.'

'What did you study?'

'Political science.'

The fisherman Ben had taken out to the Gulf Stream approached them. 'It's Ben, isn't it?' he asked.

'Yes, sir. And Jim, right?' Ben replied.

The guy nodded. 'So, you teamin' up with this pool shark here?' he said, gesturing at Lana. 'I reckon she's setting us up for the kill.' He turned to her. 'It's your break, honey, by the way.'

Lana took the triangle from his outstretched hand and passed it to Ben. 'You know these two fellas?' she asked as Ben hopped off his stool and went over to corral the balls.

'Just the one called Jim. I took him out to the reef a couple days ago.'

'Oh—you own a boat or something?'

'A seaplane.'

'A pilot? Why didn't you say so? I knew there was a reason I was attracted to you.'

They won the first game, but things fell apart after that.

'Hey,' Lana said after Ben lost them their third straight game, sinking the black ball too early on both occasions, 'I hope you fly better than you play pool.'

Across the bar a group of older men launched into a sing-along.

'C'mon, let's go eat,' Ben shouted. 'It's getting rowdy in here. I know a place.'

'I'm sure you do,' said Lana over the noise.

Twenty minutes later they were eating jumbo shrimp at Alonzo & Berlin's Lobster House over at the Key West Bight, Lana telling Ben about life growing up with an Air Force dad, the boats at the nearby marina slapping gently at their berths.

After that, it was a short walk to a couple of late-night margaritas at Ben's other favorite bar, The Green Parrot, which was smaller, a little quieter, but every bit as authentic as Captain Tony's.

As they walked arm in arm back toward the main street, Lana stopped and said, 'If you're heading straight ahead, this is where I get off. My hotel's up that way.' She motioned off to the left.

86

'Actually, there's one more place you should see on the real Key West tour.'

'Let me guess—that would be a real Key West bedroom? Now why do I get the feeling there's a beaten path to that attraction?'

'All right, I do have an ulterior motive, but it's not the one you're thinking.'

She folded her arms, skeptical.

'There's something I'd like to show you. An Air Force brat might know what the ribbons mean on the blouse of a uniform, wouldn't she?'

'Blouse? Since when are they teaching military dress vocabulary to seaplane pilots?'

'Since my father—the guy in the photo—died and left me his service dress.'

'Really? Wow, that's pretty cool.'

A few minutes later, Ben stopped at a small wood cottage painted green. 'My castle,' he said as he opened the door.

Lana walked in and her eyes swept the tatty open-plan living room/dining room.

'All my good furniture is in storage,' he told her.

'Is it?'

'Nope. Drink? I've got red wine, white wine, a Sunset, or rum.'

'White, thanks.'

'Make yourself comfortable,' Ben said as he walked toward the galley kitchen.

'This place yours?' she asked.

'No, I rent. Everything I've got is tied up in the Otter.'

A large framed air-to-air photo of a seaplane dominated one pale blue and white striped-wallpapered wall.

'The one in the photo?'

'Yeah.'

Lana took a stroll around the room, taking it in. There were gaps here and there in the old wooden floorboards, mismatched rugs scattered around. A circular wooden table with maps and papers scattered across it occupied the middle of the room. An old cupboard with a base for a remote phone was the only other furniture, aside from a television and a couch.

She sat on the couch, the color worn off the black leather cushions in patches.

'Here you go,' said Ben, handing her the wine.

'Thanks,' she said, looking up at him.

He put a glass of red on the table and retrieved the uniform from the back of the front door, lifting the plastic cover over the coat hanger.

'So you weren't lying about this to get me here after all.'

He gave her a grin.

'Hey,' she exclaimed when she focused on the blouse's ribbons. 'Your old man must have been some warrior.' Ben laid the uniform across her lap. 'This one's the Airman's Medal.' She touched it gently with a fingertip. 'You don't see too many of these. He must have done something unbelievably and conspicuously heroic to earn it. And this,' she continued, 'is the Air Medal, awarded for exceptional airmanship under pressure. Let me see . . . the Meritorious Service Medal, the Air Force Commendation Medal, and this is the Air Force Outstanding Unit Award. He also has the Combat Readiness Medal, the National Defense Service Medal, and the Air Force Longevity Ribbon. This last one is the Small Arms Marksmanship Ribbon. My dad's got some of these too, but your father has oak leaves on several of his, which means he got them more than once. No question, I'm impressed.'

Lana turned toward him, her arm sweeping away the sheet, breathing slow and steady with sleep. Her breasts were deeply tan—almost black in the moonlight streaming through the window—except for small pale triangle shapes around her nipples that showed the brevity of her bikini top. Lower down and hidden beneath the sheet was a small cornflower-blue butterfly tattooed just above and to the left of her pubic hair, as if it was about to alight there. Lana was definitely a girl worth getting to know.

They had talked for some time about Curtis. She'd seemed genuinely interested in him. He'd told her about the money left to him—without saying how much. And he'd showed her the 007 safe deposit key on his keyring, but wouldn't elaborate on what he'd found inside the box—teasing her. They fought for the keyring on the couch. She'd climbed up his outstretched arm to get at it. And that's when Ben kissed her. The rest was a blur of breasts and butterflies and Lana's athleticism.

Ben locked feet with her and drifted back off to sleep.

He woke again just after dawn, with a slight headache and an empty feeling he couldn't explain. He rolled over and saw that Lana wasn't there. He called her name, but there was no response. He got up, showered, and tried not to let it bother him. He didn't even have her damn phone number. Then he picked up his keyring and saw that the safe deposit box key was gone.

September 1, 1983

Somewhere over the Bering Sea. Major Curtis Foxx gave his instruments a cursory scan. His mind was elsewhere and the whole crew knew it. 'Hey, Tex,' he asked over his shoulder, 'where are we exactly?'

'Fifty-seven seventeen thirty-three north, and one sixty-five seventeen thirty-three east,' replied the navigator. 'In short, we're eighty-six miles from the nearest Soviet anti-aircraft battery on the Kamchatka Peninsula, give or take.'

Curtis nodded. So, seventy-six miles beyond airspace recognized as Soviet, but close enough to be making Ivan jumpy, mostly because they were also closing in on the coast of the USSR at seven miles per minute.

He looked through the window at the sky above—a palette of frozen blacks and grays. Beneath the wings of Cobra Ball Arctic 16, a blanket of ice-gray altostratus topped out at 17,000 feet. Occasional black holes of liquid cold opened up in it here and there, revealing the empty expanse of the frigid Bering Sea below. Overhead, wisps of cirrus clouds bore the faint luminescence of dim silver and, above it all, the solid black-ice dome of space pricked with needle-points of chilled starlight.

Curtis cradled his mug of coffee between both hands, feeling the warmth of it radiate through the Nomex gloves into his palms. He checked the outside air temperature: minus fifty-two degrees Celsius.

Brisk, for sure, but not especially so, and mostly just a factor of the altitude. When winter weather patterns forced the Siberian storms south and east off the plains, the sea-level temperatures in this part of the world often dropped to around the same numbers. How many nights had these super-refrigerated tempests grounded their converted Boeing 707 on Shemya Island, out on the whip end of the Aleutian Islands chain? Too many. As far as Curtis was concerned, hell wasn't a place of fire and brimstone. It was the numbing, relentless ferocity of black sub-zero cold.

'You're looking nervous, Curtis,' observed the navigator, Captain Dallas 'Tex' Mitchell, leaning on the back of Curtis's seat.

'Y'know, there's no need to be,' Captain Eli Grogan piped up from the co-pilot's seat. 'I've had two monsters myself. Really, Nikki will be fine.'

'Oh, yeah? Two? Show us your stretch marks,' said Tex.

A grin flashed across Curtis's face. This was the core of a good crew; two more were at the back of the flight deck, getting some shuteye. They were close-knit, which was essential on these long cold deployments. And they were damn good at their jobs. 'What's the time?' he asked yet again.

'According to my watch,' said Tex with a sigh, 'Nikki's been in labor fourteen hours, twelve minutes and thirty-two seconds—that's five minutes and ten seconds more than the last time you asked.'

'And that's normal, right?'

'What?' asked Eli. 'Your nerves or the labor?'

'If it's the labor, it ain't *abnormal*,' Tex reassured him. 'Like I keep telling you, man, everything's gonna be fine, just fine.'

'So what are you going to call it?' Eli asked. 'Not something weird like Aardvark, I hope.'

'We've got a few names up our sleeve. Nothing strange on the shortlist.'

'So, returning to the business at hand,' Eli said, scanning the banks of temperature and pressure gauges for their four Pratt & Whitney turbofans. 'Have the boys down the back of this bus deigned to tell us where we're going tonight?'

'Not exactly,' Tex replied. 'But my guess is it's going to be the typical profile, even though we're a little further south than usual. No doubt the buzzards will just set us up to loiter in the general vicinity of the most likely patch of sky, once they get word from Fort Meade.'

The 'buzzards' were more officially known as Ravens—NSA spooks—and twenty-five of them were on board tonight. Curtis Foxx and his USAF crew flew the plane and got it to where the Ravens wanted it to be. When they arrived there, the Ravens would scan the area with their top secret and highly sophisticated suite of measurements and signals intelligence apparatus, designed to detect and evaluate the performance of Soviet missiles, like the SS-20, and their multiple re-entry vehicles as they burned through the upper atmosphere. Telemetry collection and evaluation was a mission that the USAF had flown countless times over the years, and would no doubt continue to perform countless years into the future. Indeed, the mission was deemed so important that there was a Cobra Ball in the sky around the clock, always on station in these skies in the event that intelligence manna—an SS-20 MRV—would literally fall from heaven.

Keeping the Soviets honest—letting them know that they couldn't hide—was a significant plank in the strategy to secure those Hammer and Sickle missiles on their mobile launchers. And soon Curtis would have a very special and more deeply personal reason to help maintain the peace between the world's superpowers. He glanced at his wristwatch and said, 'So, how long has it been now?'

Tex announced over the intercom, 'We've got some new vectors from the buzzards.'

'Let's have 'em,' Curtis replied, instantly back in the groove.

'A revised flight level of three one zero, heading zero six five, speed zero point six six Mach.'

While Eli annotated the log, Curtis gave a readback on the information then thumbed the mike key: 'Anchorage Centre, Arctic 16 request higher . . .' A minute later the Boeing was trimmed for the climb, and on the revised heading.

'A new patch of sky,' observed Eli.

'Just like the old patch of sky,' Tex replied.

Curtis visualized the course change. The Ravens were directing them away from the Soviet coastline, which always settled the butterflies somewhat. In this part of the world, Russian defenses—radars and SAMs and anti-aircraft batteries—were the air defense equivalent of a porcupine with a nasty temper. It was always good to be flying *away* from those quills rather than into the thick of them.

☭

Des had some serious clout. Or maybe a few words from Clark's mouth had done the trick. Garret wasn't sure how the impossible had been achieved, but channels had been cleared, assets reallocated, programs reassigned. Someone upstairs had seen to it that he had the resources and the bandwidth to put the Bering Sea and the Soviet Far East under the microscope—all from the armchair comfort of Situation Room A, NSA HQ, Fort Meade, Maryland.

Eric Hamilton was sitting beside him, wearing a headset plugged into the console. As yet there was nothing to hear, only the usual back-scatter interference. But any moment now that would change as the assets came online.

'There's something we need to consider that hasn't been discussed,' said Hamilton.

'And that would be . . . ?' Garret asked, distracted, checking through the console's systems.

'There'll be an investigation afterward. Once it starts, it had better be with the right body or we'll have no chance at all of guiding it.'

'Who don't we want?'

'The National Transportation Safety Board.'

'Why not?'

'They'll leave no stone unturned *and* they have the power of subpoena.'

'Why would they get involved? It's not going to come down on US soil.'

'Gray area. 007 originated from US territory—the NTSB could make a case.'

'Then who *would* we want on the job?'

'Something ineffective that the public would nonetheless have confidence in. A body like the International Civil Aviation Organization, for example.'

'The ICAO? They're UN.'

'And toothless,' said Hamilton.

'Okay. I'll manage it,' said Garret.

The minute clicked over on the digital clock between the banks of monitors. The time was 15:58 GMT, coming up to midnight over the Bering Sea, and noon in DC—lunchtime.

'We are now inside the envelope,' Hamilton announced.

Garret knew his way around the console as well as any operator. He tapped a number of commands into the keyboard. Somewhere unseen a Cray Supercomputer reviewed its memory banks and data boards and obeyed his commands. The light in the room softened the way it did at the cinema. The monitors on the wall blinked on, fed with signals harvested by the giant dishes behind the Fort Meade facility. One monitor presented outlines of the Soviet Kamchatka Peninsula, the Sea of Okhotsk and the Bering Sea. The screen below it captured a wider view taking in Alaska, the Bering Sea, the Aleutian Islands, and the radar sweep provided by the Regional Operations Control Centre at Elmendorf Air Force Base, Anchorage. Lines on this screen showed the actual course of KAL 007 through Elmendorf AFB's radars, a dotted line indicating where things got a little speculative beyond Elmendorf's range, and the projected track of an RC-135 over the Bering Sea. The two lines were now intersecting, as planned. Four screens to the right collectively showed the world from the Arctic Circle to the islands of Japan. Also highlighted was the US facility at Shemya Island and the Cobra Dane phased-array radar, the US air base at Misawa, Japan, as well as the Japanese Defense Force radar facility at Wakkanai. In addition, Garret could see a radar ship—the USS *Observation Island*—cruising in international waters off the Kamchatka Peninsula. Overlaying all of this was the projected snake-like track of a US 'ferret' spy satellite, which would cover the operation in its critical phases over the Kamchatka Peninsula and Sakhalin Island.

'You think we've got enough assets on this, Roy?' asked Hamilton, his facetiousness failing to ease the tension.

'We'll soon find out,' said Garret, lighting a Chesterfield. He'd learned through experience that, in all reality, you could never have enough feeds. Things often went wrong through malfunction and random accidents and there was rarely enough redundancy built in.

'Where's the target?' Hamilton asked.

'The Cobra Dane radar on Shemya will pick it up when it comes online any time now,' said Garret as he took a bite out of his lunch—a ham and cheese on rye.

☭

Arctic 16 had completed yet another altitude change, this time climbing to flight level three three zero—33,000 feet—and accelerated to its maximum speed at this altitude of 434 knots indicated. The aircraft's speed wasn't something the buzzards usually stipulated, which intrigued Curtis. Heading: two zero five. They were on the very edge of the Russian radar envelope. He leaned forward against the harness and absently tapped a dial. All temps and pressures were in the green and there was plenty of gas in the tanks. Amen, he thought, glancing at the bleak world beyond Arctic 16's nose. This was a long sortie, though by no means the longest—some stretched beyond eighteen hours. And there was always the chance that if the weather was foul at Shemya, the crosswinds beyond the RC-135's maximum, they'd have to divert all the way to Eielson, more than 1300 miles away, which had happened enough times in the past.

Still no word about Nikki. Another watch check: 16:03 Zulu, which meant she'd been in labor now fifteen hours and . . . fifty-two minutes. Sitting back in his seat and trying to relax, Curtis took a deep breath, expelled it, and willed that Nikki would be okay.

'Boss, we've got something here from the buzzards. It's a first,' Tex informed him.

'Yeah? What?' Curtis replied, back on the job.

'Somewhere ahead in our one-o'clock, a thousand feet out, is another aircraft.'

'What kind of aircraft?'

'A heavy—a jumbo jet.'

'A what?'

'Yeah, you heard right, a 747.'

'What the fuck's one of those doing this far north?'

'Now there's a question,' said Tex.

Curtis verified their heading again—force of habit: two-zero-five degrees.

'I've got a visual,' Eli announced. He pointed up and to the right, through the windshield. 'It's dark. Look at where the stars are obscured.'

'No strobe, no nav lights, no tail light,' Curtis said, thinking aloud.

'Is she lost?' Eli said, asking the obvious.

'Inform the buzzards we've got a visual,' Curtis told Tex.

Tex, linked directly through to the buzzards, told them, and then turned to Curtis. 'Boss, they want us to maintain heading and adjust speed to close with it. They want us to join up with her.'

'It has to be civilian,' said Eli.

'Eli, you want to handle the maneuvering?' Curtis asked.

'On it,' he replied, adding, 'Doing this kind of flying with a civilian plane—it's illegal as hell.'

Curtis ignored the comment. Minor course and speed alterations drifted the RC-135 gently into position just fifty feet behind, below and to the left of the 747—close, but well out of its slipstream.

'What now, Tex?' Curtis asked.

'Maintain the formation, apparently.'

No one spoke for a moment as they looked at the huge aircraft filling the top right-hand quadrant of their windshield.

'Eli,' Tex said eventually, 'you've got the best eyes here. Whose is she?'

'Do I look like Superman? I can't tell in this light,' he said, alternately squinting and then frowning. 'It'd help if the moon wasn't hidden by cloud . . .'

'Or if the thing was running lights like it's supposed to,' Curtis commented.

'Do we make contact with it?' Eli asked. 'Maybe they're lost and need assistance. And this ain't a particularly forgiving part of the world to be blundering around in, as we know.'

'Tex, put it to the buzzards,' said Curtis.

'It's at least 200 miles north of Romeo 20,' Eli observed, putting voice to the thoughts running through Curtis's brain. 'A modern passenger aircraft getting so lost . . . Is that possible?'

'Boss, the buzzards say under no circumstances are we to compromise standard operational radio silence.'

Curtis said nothing in reply.

'Assuming that jumbo stays on this vector, she'll cross the Kamchatka Peninsula in twenty-eight minutes,' Eli said. 'I don't think Ivan is gonna appreciate that.'

'Tell that to the buzzards,' Curtis told Tex.

Moments later, Tex replied, 'I think they know, Curtis. I just got back more of that "maintaining radio silence" stuff.'

'Anything coming up on Russian combat frequencies?'

'Nope. But they'll know we're here. Bet on it. We're retracing an earlier orbit. We hit these same coordinates on the same heading an hour ago.'

'How many passengers do those things carry?' Eli asked, the glow from the instruments giving his skin a sickly green color.

Curtis didn't know for sure, but he was thinking in the hundreds.

'You realize we're making things a hell of a lot worse,' Tex informed them. 'In this position, we're ghosting. Not only that, because we formed up just outside Soviet radar range and we've been flying a regular pattern, the Russians will believe that this commercial 747 is us—a United States Air Force reconnaissance aircraft.'

'Is someone trying to start World War Three here?' asked Eli, voicing the question on all their minds.

Curtis had broken into a sweat. 'Tex, assuming they maintain their current course, where will they cross Kamchatka?'

'It's not so much where they'll cross. By my calculations, they'll virtually overfly Petropavlovsk,' Tex informed him.

Petropavlovsk—the Soviets' main submarine base in the Russian Far East. *Oh, Jesus . . .* 'We need to get a warning off on Criticom, and fast,' Curtis said.

Criticom, the critical intelligence communications system carried by the RC-135, gave them the ability to communicate with Washington over an ultra-secure network. A Critic dispatched from this system was the highest-priority message. It was sent via uplink to a satellite in geo-synchronous orbit above the equator and beamed straight to the NSA's Fort Meade complex. If the system worked as it was supposed to, the Commander-in-Chief would have the Critic outlining the plight of this civilian 747 on his desk within seven minutes. And within minutes of that, Arctic 16 could receive orders to communicate with the civilian craft and save it from certain annihilation. And perhaps avert a global cataclysm.

'The buzzards are fine with that, boss,' Tex told him. 'They're sending someone forward to take a letter.'

Curtis checked his watch, and this time thoughts of Nikki had nothing to do with it. Four minutes had passed since they had come into contact with the jumbo. In that time, they had closed on the Soviet coast by roughly twenty-eight miles and were now well inside what the USAF and the USSR alike considered to be the Russian buffer zone.

☭

Roy Garret was out of cigarettes, which added to the tension. Were they counting down on a thermonuclear war? Cobra Dane had picked up both the 747 and the RC. The tracks of KAL 007 and the RC-135 had merged for five minutes now. Radio intercepts indicated that the Soviets were beginning to stir on the Kamchatka Peninsula. The intrusion had been noted. The clock was ticking.

A sudden buzzing sound startled him.

'What's that?' asked Hamilton.

'The door.'

Garret slipped off the headset and went to answer it. The surveil-lance camera told him an army specialist was waiting outside. Garret punched in the code and the door opened. The specialist had an enve-lope for him, stamped in red across the top 'Top Secret. Eyes Only'. Garret returned to the console, took his seat, tapped the envelope on the bench.

'You going to open that?' asked Hamilton.

Garret sent him a flash of annoyance. He was trying to prepare himself. It could be anything—including a mission abort. He wound the string off the button and then broke the seal. Inside was a slip of computer printout. The code in the top right-hand corner indicated it was a decryption. This was a particular kind of message, one with the highest protocols—a Critic. His heart pumped an extra beat. He read the message.

'Get Bilson on the phone,' he told Hamilton. 'Use the secured line.'

'What's the problem?'

'The commander of Arctic 16.'

'What about him?'

Garret handed Hamilton the terse bulletin. 'This is exactly why I was against using an RC-135. The guys flying the plane aren't NSA.'

'I'm sure Des will have it covered,' Hamilton said, handing it back.

'Maybe.'

A few moments later, a familiar voice on the line said, 'I wasn't expecting a call. Not yet. Everything okay?'

'Arctic 16 fired off a Critic.'

'Oh.'

Garret waited for Clark's chief aide to elaborate, but all he got was silence.

'I can't stop a Critic, Des,' Garret said, an edge in his voice. 'I have to send it on, and it'll hit the President's desk within a matter of minutes.'

'In the White House, right?'

'That's the protocol.'

'Relax, Roy. The President's at Rancho del Cielo, Santa Barbara. And that's a long way from his desk.'

☭

'Any word from the buzzards?' Curtis asked, time ticking away, the silhouette of the 747's tail area floating over their windshield.

'Nope,' Tex replied, crouching between the pilot and co-pilot's seat, mesmerized by the sheer bulk of the jumbo jet just sitting in midair above them like it was levitating. 'But the Critic only went off three minutes ago. We need to give Washington at least another five minutes to respond.'

That would mean a total of eight minutes at seven miles per minute: fifty-six miles. Those civilians are getting way too close to the fire for comfort, Curtis thought.

'You know, I think that's a bird on the fin,' Eli proposed all of a sudden. 'Which airline has a bird as its logo?'

'Malaysian Airlines have one, don't they?' Tex asked.

'I don't think it's Malaysian,' replied Eli. 'Wrong hemisphere.'

'The buzzards have given us a new altitude and course,' Tex interrupted. 'We're dropping down to flight level one two zero, maximum rate of descent, whereupon we head zero eight five.'

Curtis was stunned. The look on his face was transparent.

Tex shrugged. 'That's what we've got.'

Curtis stared at the giant plane for what seemed like an age.

'Boss?' Tex prompted. 'Time to go.'

Curtis swallowed hard. 'Eli, you have the controls. Tell the buzzards to buckle up.'

The captain took over. The maneuver—diving steeply beneath the 747—made it appear as if the airliner was being sucked into the murk above. In a few short seconds, it had disappeared.

'Hey, Curtis,' said Tex, suddenly jolting him. 'I just heard.'

'Heard what?' The major's heart leapt. Washington had responded to the Critic after all and it wasn't too late to—

'It's a boy! Mother and baby doing fine.'

'What did she name him?' Eli enquired.

'She named him Ben. Benjamin Foxx. Damn sight better than Aardvark. Congratulations!'

September 1, 1983

Shemya Island, Bering Sea. 'Goddamn it, Joe,' said Curtis, stopping mid-stride in the belly of the plane, on his way back to the flight deck. 'What the hell is going on here tonight?'

Joe Marich, an NSA Raven, the signals monitor on Arctic 16, removed his headset and stood up. 'Hey, calm down, Curtis. Going on where?' He went to put a hand on Curtis's shoulder, but it was pushed aside.

'Did you send off that Critic?' Curtis asked.

'Of course we sent it.'

'And you got nothing back?'

'Not a word.'

'I don't believe you.'

'Believe whatever you want. I've got no reason to lie.'

'Bullshit,' Curtis spat.

'Just do your job, Major, and keep your goddamn nose out of ours, okay?'

The next thing Curtis knew, he was being pulled off Marich, arms around his shoulder and chest, restraining him.

'Jesus, what . . . what the fuck's got into you?' Marich stammered, sprawled against his station, blood oozing from his nostrils.

'You bastards signaled that 747. You lined it up for us,' Curtis shouted.

'Shit . . . it was a 747?' he heard someone behind him say, stunned.

Curtis suddenly realized that the buzzards may not have known what was going on, either.

'You need to take a break, Major,' said Marich. 'I'm going to forget about this, but it damn well better not happen again. Go get yourself some fucking R&R for Christ's sake.'

'Have you any idea what's going to happen to those civilians?' Curtis demanded.

'I don't know what you're talking about.'

Curtis felt the arms around him relaxing. He wiped his face with his sleeve, straightened his flight suit, and headed for the cockpit. The buzzards all turned to stare at him as he passed.

Curtis was returning to duty after an hour of fitful dozing, tossing and turning in the crew rest facility down the back of the plane, unable to shake the image of the black and gray 747 filling their windshield and the accompanying feeling that he was responsible for turning it into some kind of airborne *Mary Celeste*—a ship of the damned.

'You okay?' asked Tex as Curtis stepped past him.

'What landing weather have we got?' Curtis said, ignoring him.

'Wind at thirty gusting to three-five knots, from two-two-zero degrees. Scattered cloud at nine thousand, and broken at five thousand. Drizzle patches. Visibility, seven miles,' Tex said. 'The usual friendly homecoming.'

'Runway two-eight, and twenty-seven to thirty-two knots of crosswind,' said Curtis, thinking aloud. He took the wheel and put his feet on the rudder pedals, his eyes automatically scanning the instrument panel for errant dials. Ordinarily, these kind of crosswind numbers were quite a handful, unless your regular job was to land a 707 with no thrust-reversers, chute or tail hook on a speck of rock mostly lashed by far worse than what lay ahead of them. But the landing would still require concentration, and Curtis welcomed anything that would take his mind off the last couple of hours.

'Oh, by the way, boss,' said Tex through his headset. 'In case you were wondering, we haven't heard anything.'

Curtis didn't need to ask what Tex was referring to—a radio report that the Soviets had shot down a plane full of civilians.

He nodded. 'Places, everyone,' he said.

Twelve minutes later, Arctic 16 made a perfect landing, turned and then backtracked the runway blasted by a rain squall and headed for the hangar. Between sweeps of the windshield wipers, another RC-135 could be seen parked on the ramp.

'What have we got here?' Eli enquired.

'A training RC,' Tex told him. 'That's our ride to Eielson, those of us who are going back.'

Arctic 16 taxied to the ramp and lined up on the markings guided by a guy in a rain poncho waving glowing red wands. When the wands crossed, Eli engaged the parking brake and commenced the shutdown procedure.

Later, they jogged to the hangar door fifty yards away during a break in the downpour. Inside, the training crew was standing around with welcoming smiles. Somewhere a radio played 'Horse With No Name'.

'Nice landing,' commented a second lieutenant from the training crew.

'For a duck,' added another voice, followed by a little laughter, none of it shared by the crew of Arctic 16.

'Hey, Curtis,' said Kyle Hensley, a maintainer, coming up to him. The man suddenly stopped. 'Jesus, Major, you don't look so good. You feelin' okay?'

'Turn on CBS in a couple of hours,' Tex suggested as he walked past.

Curtis grabbed the bucket hanging from Hensley's hands and threw up into it.

September 1, 1983

Sea of Okhotsk, northeast of Sakhalin Island. The weather radar screen between Captain Chun's and First Officer Sohn's knees was switched to ground-mapping mode. Just ahead, at twelve o'clock, was the outline of Sakhalin Island; at ten o'clock, the northern tip of Hokkaido; at three o'clock, the coastline of the Russian mainland; at nine o'clock the southernmost islands of the Soviet Kuril chain. Chun allowed himself a nod of grim satisfaction—they were exactly where they were supposed to be. His eyes met Sohn's and a shared fear passed between them, along with a mad sense of elation and achievement. This was the mission of a lifetime, the likes of which they had never dreamed would be attempted, at least not by the Korean Air Force. But here they were, and flying it for a *civilian* organization.

If they could stretch their luck a bit further, complete success was minutes away. Through a combination of planning and sheer audacity, they had managed to achieve the impossible: flown within a handful of miles of the Soviet sub base at Petropavlovsk on the Kamchatka Peninsula, transited the Sea of Okhotsk, threaded the needle of the Soviet air-defense system, and beaten the enemy threatening their country's freedom. Ahead, only a handful of minutes away, lay the safety of international airspace.

Russian ground controllers were still making frantic attempts to contact them on 121.5 MHz, the international emergency radio frequency. But Chun and his crew had completely ignored them and would continue to do so. And if, somewhere to the south, KAL 015 was providing Tokyo Centre with fictitious reports of KAL 007's arrival at mandatory waypoints as planned, with a little careful maneuvering before they entered the controlled airspace around Seoul-Kimpo, they might even be able to claim that they had flown nowhere near the Soviet Air Defense Identification Zone. Chung, Sohn and Kim had discussed this among themselves, without involving the Americans. Wouldn't this be the best solution for them all? The Americans would get their intelligence assessments and they'd get to keep their reputations.

'Captain, the Soviets have said there will be no more warnings,' came Flight Engineer Kim's voice urgently in his headset. 'They are now threatening to shoot us down. We cannot hedge them with silence any longer.'

'If we communicate with them, then we will have to divert,' Sohn said.

'We have rolled the dice and lost,' Kim replied. 'Face it.'

'If we give ourselves up now, we will cause our country and our allies great embarrassment,' Chun pointed out.

'We are so close to international airspace,' Sohn added.

'We are playing Russian roulette with the people who invented it,' Kim said.

'The finish line is just ahead!' snapped First Officer Sohn.

Chun had wondered about his flight engineer's commitment. Kim had lacked a sense of mission from the beginning. He was not a fighter pilot; did not have the stomach for this work like himself or Sohn. Or the balls. But there was truth in what the flight engineer was saying. They *were* right on the knife edge of disaster; the Russians were out of patience. They had to communicate with the Soviets, but stall them at the same time. It was then that a possible solution occurred to him.

'Turn on the transponder,' he told Kim.

Sohn looked at Chun, bewildered.

'We need a few more minutes,' Chun explained. 'Perhaps we'll get them if we add a little confusion.'

'So who are we?' Sohn asked.

'That will be up to the Russians to guess. Kim, squawk something meaningless—squawk code 1300.'

Sitting in a small, dark, air-conditioned box with three other operators, Yuudai Suzuki stared transfixed at the screen in front of him. He had been following the progress of the aircraft the Russian Deputat and Trikotazh ground controllers were calling 'the target' since it had flown within the 210-mile range of the powerful military radar at Wakkanai, on this northernmost tip of the Japanese island of Hokkaido.

It was not Yuudai's job to interrogate the air traffic, but merely to sit and watch and ensure that the Wakkanai facility was operating at its peak so that any recorded data of Soviet air movements could be examined and analyzed by others trained to do so within the Chosa Besshitsu.

The mystery aircraft had just turned on its transponder, which was now helpfully broadcasting the plane's altitude and other details. But it was squawking the code 1300, which meant nothing in the tightly controlled and monitored world of civil aviation. Code 1300 did not ID the aircraft.

He'd been listening to Deputat and Trikotazh radioing message after message, asking, pleading and—finally—demanding that the plane properly identify itself. In response, all they'd received was silence. And now, code 1300. It was . . . odd.

Whatever was out there, it was a big aircraft with a huge radar cross-section; the active Wakkanai radar was getting a solid paint. And then Yuudai saw two, four, six other blips on his screen. These were easy to identify; their transponders were giving out Russian idents: fighter planes from the Sakhalin bases at Dolinsk-Sokol and Smyrnykh, climbing into his radar's range.

Yuudai was intrigued, then worried. This was looking like it could end in disaster. He broadened the radar's view, thereby bringing in the radio communications feed from Tokyo Centre, whose air traffic controllers handled the non-military traffic in the area. The screen now showed much of Hokkaido, and highlighted the civilian traffic as small triangles each properly accompanied by carrier, code, altitude and heading details coming and going along Romeo 20 and other lanes. It was after three in the morning, so there wasn't much. Yuudai accessed the Base Air Defense Ground Environment system into which all flight plans for commercial airliners had been automatically loaded. One aircraft was missing: a Korean Air Lines 747, Flight 007, flying New York to Seoul via Anchorage. KAL 015, a scheduled flight behind 007, was where it should be out on Romeo 20, but 007 wasn't. Strange . . .

And then the reality of what he was witnessing dawned on him. Could it be possible? Could this mystery 1300 squawk over Sakhalin—around 300 miles further to the north than it should have been—be KAL 007?

Yuudai suddenly realized the mystery blip couldn't be anything else. It was so far off course—how had 007's flight crew gotten it so wrong? Unless the plane was there because . . . it *wanted* to be there . . . Or someone *else* wanted it to be there.

Despite the air-conditioning, Yuudai's face became hot and his back clammy as the panic swept through him. Korean Air Lines 007 was a regular passenger flight. The blip up there over Soviet territory calling itself 1300 was an aircraft carrying potentially *hundreds* of passengers, all of whom would more than likely be asleep in their seats right now, oblivious to the murderous tide rising up from the island beneath them.

A presence behind Yuudai distracted him. He looked over his shoulder. An American officer had entered the operations room and was ordering all the operators other than Yuudai to leave.

'What the fuck is code 1300?' Garret asked, a frown of concentration causing deep lines in his forehead.

Hamilton stared at the radar return on the monitor. He took the headset off and gave one of his ears a rub. 'I have absolutely no idea.'

Garret ground his teeth. It was always the small details that could cause an operation to unravel—the unknowable, the unpredictable—

and this operation was full of both. Over the past six months he'd been given an intense indoctrination into the world of international aviation: air traffic control practices, avionics, communications, aircraft systems and so forth. He reviewed what he knew: aircraft flying international routes were given transponder codes so that they could be easily identified. There were also codes that communicated specific occurrences. For an emergency, code 7700. For radio failure, code 7600. All light aircraft were given a single code, like 1200, which identified them as being low and slow movers. Firefighting and emergency aircraft were given special codes. But code 1300 was a mystery.

'Well, I'll be damned,' Hamilton exclaimed, his face breaking into a smile. 'That Chun is a wily bastard.'

'What?'

'I think they're trying to confuse the issue.'

'Well, it's working, and you're not helping any,' said Garret.

'They're doing what they can to stay alive. The Soviets want to know who the intruder is—the ground controllers and interception aircraft are demanding they acknowledge the interception and identify themselves—so rather than coming clean as Korean Air Lines Flight 007, Chun is telling them they're something else, something completely unknown. A transponder code of 1300 will make the Russians scratch their heads, and maybe give the Koreans the time they need to cross over into international airspace.'

'Well, that's just great,' said Garret. 'Couldn't we have just disabled their fucking transponder beforehand?'

It had been a worthy attempt, but the ruse with the transponder didn't appear to be giving them the extra minutes they needed. The Russian-accented voice through their headsets was angry. In halting English, it told them to prepare for interception by aircraft from the Soviet Union.

'Do as they say,' Kim demanded.

Chun and Sohn ignored the flight engineer. Both having combat experience, they knew what would be happening in the sky behind them. Ground controllers would be vectoring SU-15 Flagons and MiG-23 Floggers onto their tail. Those aircraft, capable of well over 1400 mph, would easily run down a 747 cruising at 550 mph. Despite what the Russian ground controllers were telling them, in accordance with accepted international practice a fighter would pull out in front of them, waggle its wings, and then break to the left or right. They'd be expected to follow. If they didn't obey the command, gun or cannon would be fired across their path. Missiles would be the intercepting pilot's next and final option.

The radio fell silent on frequency 121.5 MHz. True to their word, the Russians had given up trying to talk them down. According to the weather radar, the southwestern coastline of Sakhalin was off their nose, the safety of international airspace now just two minutes of flying time away—barely nineteen miles. It would be touch and go.

Chun and Sohn did not need to discuss tactics with each other. A 747 might not be able to outrun a Soviet fighter, but it could go *slower*. The way to make this evasion maneuver appear innocent to any unfriendlies who weren't on the ball—to make it seem as if the 747 was behaving like a normal airliner—was to climb. And to slow the plane further, Chun chopped the throttles.

'Hey, Tokyo Radio. Korean Air 007,' said Sohn, contacting Tokyo Centre, working hard to keep the stress out of his voice.

'*Korean Air zero zero seven. Tokyo,*' came the reply.

'Request immediate climb to three five zero.'

Both Chun and Sohn reached down, pulled up their oxygen masks and put them on. Behind them, at the flight engineer's station, Kim Eui-dong was shaking his head, doing the same. There was a chance that the Soviet pilot might interpret their climb as less than innocent. If he viewed it as an evasive maneuver . . .

The moment of greatest danger had arrived.

Down in economy, seated in 52A, Nami Sato drew the blanket tighter around her shoulders. The air in the cabin was frigid, made worse by the cold seeping through the window beside her head. She slipped back into the dream she was having about Akiko. The child, older than Akiko in real life, was dressed in school clothes: a tartan skirt, navy jacket and tartan cap. Her daughter seemed sick. Her face appeared to be changing color. It started out white like a geisha's, then turned the pale blue of Arctic ice. Behind and around the child was a white glow, a mist with tentacles that curled around her like an octopus.

In the dream, Nami was calling Akiko's name and she could hear her own voice. But her daughter didn't hear, or couldn't hear, or chose not to hear as children do—Nami wasn't sure which. The child's lack of response made Nami feel angry at first, and then insecure and afraid. Akiko smiled, but it was a ghastly, frightening smile. Blood then gushed from the little girl's mouth as if from a faucet, under pressure. The torrent ran down her blue face and spattered on the white floor, where it was bleached white, like death.

Nami came awake in a cold sweat as the plane slowed dramatically. She told herself it was just a dream and meant nothing. She looked over the tops of the seats in front of her, at the sea of headrests beyond. Here and there an overhead light was on, where someone was reading. Tobacco smoke drifted forward from the rear of the plane where a small, concentrated assembly of people were kept awake by their habit. But mostly the plane was dark and quiet with sleep. Nami looked at her watch. Adjusted for Tokyo time, it was almost 3:25 in the morning. The cabin staff wouldn't be serving breakfast for at least another hour. She felt her ears compress and then pop as the plane suddenly began to climb, forcing her down in her seat.

Nami didn't want to sleep in case she slipped back into the nightmare, and she was too tired to read. So she turned to look out the window and saw, far beyond the wingtip, a stream of orange fireflies bursting from the vicinity of a white, blinking strobe light.

The shape of the Sakhalin coastline creeping past the bottom edge of the weather radar captured every molecule of Chun's and Sohn's attention. Mere seconds now separated them from breaking into the safety of international airspace, which commenced twelve miles beyond the coast.

Sohn had caught the cannon fire sparking from the nose of a Soviet fighter off to the right moments after they had begun the climb. The sight had caused him to soil his underwear even though, quite by accident, they'd managed to time the climb impeccably. There was a chance the fighter pilot might think the 747's climb—innocent or not—had prevented its flight crew from seeing his warning shots. He might give them the benefit of the doubt. He might decide to make a second attempt at it. If so, by the time he got himself into position to fire at them, they would have escaped over the line to freedom.

'Captain, Captain,' Kim called out behind them. 'We have made it!'

Sohn beamed with relief and clenched his fists above his head. Success! The Americans had been right. It *was* possible to drive a spear through the side of the Soviet bear without suffering retribution from its claws, and they had been the ones to prove it. He reached across and warmly shook Chun's hand, noticing as he squeezed it that the captain's palm was clammy with sweat.

September 1, 1983

Wakkanai Radar Facility, Hokkaido, Japan. Yuudai Suzuki bit his bottom lip and tasted copper. He leaned forward over the screen. The return from the Russian fighter had merged briefly a couple of times with the return squawking 1300—Korean Air Lines Flight 007. The Soviet plane, an SU-15 Flagon, had been flying close beside and then behind the Korean plane, all the while trying to get it to acknowledge on 121.5 MHz that it had been intercepted, but without success. The exchanges Yuudai was now hearing between fighter pilot and the ground controller called Deputat were chilling. If there had been any doubt in his mind about how this would conclude, it had evaporated. And he was absolutely powerless to prevent it.

Yuudai watched as the moment he had been dreading began to play out. The Russian fighter was dropping way back from 'the target'. This wasn't the SU-15 letting the Korean plane go, but rather the Soviet pilot allowing for the minimum distance air-to-air missiles required to arm. Separation was also necessary so that, when the missiles detonated, metal shrapnel and other airborne fragments wouldn't destroy the Russian fighter's engines.

The speakers in Yuudai's headset crackled. *'I'm dropping back. Now I will try a rocket,'* the pilot announced.

'Lock on,' Deputat told him.

'I am closing on the target. Am in lock-on. Distance to target, eight.'

Yuudai checked the screen. Yes, eight kilometers. There was a little more communication. And then came the words he most feared: *'Tsel unichtozena.'* The target is destroyed.

Yuudai shivered. He had just witnessed the deaths of possibly hundreds of people. He slumped in his chair, overwhelmed by utter helplessness.

And then an unexpected voice came through his headset.

'Tokyo Radio. Korean Air zero zero seven. Position at NOKKA one eight two seven. Flight level three five zero. Estimate arrival at . . .'

What? Yuudai was confused. He rechecked the radar screen. Korean Air Lines Flight 007 was announcing its arrival at waypoint NOKKA? NOKKA was *southeast* of Hokkaido, hundreds of miles south of where he knew 007 to be. How was that possible? There was nothing on his screen abeam waypoint NOKKA. KAL 015's squawk was in the vicinity, eight minutes away further up the lane, but not its sister ship. *Very* strange. So where had the transmission he'd just heard come from? There was only one possible answer. Yuudai realized that it could only have emanated from one source: KAL 015.

A thump that jolted the plane sideways was the first indication. The second was the decompression alarm. And then the cockpit became a sea of flashing warning lights and the air filled with clanging sirens. Chun, Sohn and Kim had no time to discuss what had happened, what had caused this. They knew.

Gauges told them engine three was on fire and useless, while engine one was losing power. Hydraulic pressure had taken a hit, but had stabilized.

Flight Engineer Kim slapped the EMER MASK DROP button on his panel that dropped the masks in the passenger cabin and began pumping oxygen into them. The sudden change in pressure caused Kim's left eardrum to rupture and blood began to fill his headset cup.

Condensation fogged up the windshields.

Chun disengaged the autopilot and pushed the control wheel

forward, sending the massive aircraft into a steep dive. There were two priorities: extinguish the engine fires and descend to a breathable atmosphere. Working together, Chun and Sohn put years of simulated emergency training to practical use, with no time to acknowledge that the likely reward for their efforts would be their deaths.

Nami had given up trying to get comfortable. The moment of sleep had passed and yet the unsettling effects of the nightmare about Akiko were still with her. She knew she was up and awake for the remainder of the flight. She leaned forward against her seatbelt to pull the magazine from the pouch on the back of the seat in front of her.

A sudden white-hot flash outside the window registered in her peripheral vision. An instant later the side of the plane just ahead of her window disintegrated, sucked away. In its place came a monstrous and ear-splitting scream. A white fog engulfed the cabin and swirling debris raced for the enormous hole that had opened up where the rows of seats in front of Nami had been just seconds before.

Dimly, Nami realized that the two people sitting in those rows had also disappeared. They were gone as if they'd never existed. A long groan of tortured metal, deep and painful, came up through the floor, which then began to buck violently beneath her feet. A hot orange ribbon of flame crosshatched with sparks streamed from the rear of the engine outside, just beyond the hole, the source of the howling noise. Fire engulfed the top of the wing momentarily, before being swept away by the terrible freezing shriek that filled Nami's ears.

Something flew past her shoulder. It was a young girl. She smashed into the twisted metal ripped away from the side of the plane, where she suddenly stopped. Flying objects battered her face and then tore away into the night, sucked through the hole into the blackness. The child gazed at Nami with dead eyes, fingers of gnarled aluminum rib arcing up and out of her shaking corpse. And there she stayed, impaled, buffeted by the hurricane rushing by her, rich red blood gushing and then slowly dribbling from her blue lips.

Nami was aware of the oxygen masks dropping down, the vomit

exploding from her mouth and the horrible weightless feeling in the pit of her stomach as the crippled airliner pushed over into a dive. She looked down into her lap where her own blood was pooling.

She lifted her dripping red hand and stroked the dead girl's hair by her knees. It was then that she heard the scream. Looking around, she saw the man with the hat sitting diagonally across the aisle. He was staring at her, his mouth open in shock, the scream hoarse and animal-like in his throat. Nami reached up for an oxygen mask and put the cup over her face. Then she stretched forward and put a mask over the girl's blue face. As she did, she caught a glimpse of her own reflection in the porthole window. Her scalp had been peeled back from the top of her head and pints of blood were running down her shoulders and arms.

'The ruse with the transponder—code 1300. It hasn't paid off,' observed Hamilton.

Garret was unable to move his eyes from the monitors. 'Except that they're right on the edge of international airspace, almost away.'

A shiver of conflict tightened the muscles at the base of his skull. Part of him willed the plane to safety, wrestling with his determination to see the mission through to its successful conclusion. The 1300 blip on the screen represented the lives of 269 people. He murmured the words, '"Take now your son, your only son, whom you love . . . and go to the land of Moriah, and offer him there as a burnt offering."'

'What's that from?' asked Hamilton.

'Genesis 22. God talking to Abraham. Don't know your Bible?'

'To tell you the truth, no. Though I do know one thing that Abraham said. I can't tell you where it comes from, what part of the Bible—maybe Genesis—but it was something my mother used to drum into us kids.'

Garret looked at him.

'Blessed are the peacemakers,' he said, 'for they shall inherit the earth.'

Garret gave him a wry smile. 'Peacemakers' was Clark's suggested name for the new MX nukes with their multiple re-entry vehicles. 'And I'm sure they will,' he said. 'I don't suppose you have a cigarette?'

'Nope. Give 'em up, Roy. They'll kill you.'

'Good advice. Maybe I'll take you up on it.'

'See how the fighter's dropping back?' said Hamilton, his attention shifting to the screen. He pointed at the outline of the southern end of Sakhalin Island. 'It's happening. Just the way I said it would, and not a moment too soon. 007 has just crossed into international airspace.'

A new minute ticked over on the digital display set to Greenwich Mean Time—18:26.

Garret worked the computer keyboard and the image onscreen covering the pursuit of the 747 suddenly expanded and took over the entire wall.

A burst of staccato Russian crackled from the speakers.

'You speak some Russian, don't you?' asked Hamilton. 'Care to translate?'

Another barrage of Russian. The tone implied commands followed by responses.

'Zakhvati tsel.'

'Take aim at the target,' said Garret.

'Tsel zakhvatchena.'

'Aim taken.'

'Ogon.'

'Fire.'

'Ya vypolnil pusk.'

'I have executed the launch.'

'Tsel unichtozena.'

'The target is destroyed.'

The tone of the exchange was businesslike, devoid of excitement.

'Well, that's that,' said Garret, his eyes fixed on the small glowing radar return squawking 1300. The seconds drifted by. Long seconds. The numbers attached to the blip showing 007's altitude began to fall, and fast. And then the numbers slowed and stopped.

Another radio transmission came through.

'Tokyo Radio. Korean Air zero zero seven. Position at NOKKA one eight two seven. Flight level three three zero. Estimate arrival at . . .'

'What the hell?' Garret exclaimed.

'Jesus. That's 015.' Hamilton frowned at the monitor. 'They don't realize what's happened to 007. They're too far away—they didn't hear what we just heard.'

'How do we explain *that?*' asked Garret.

Another transmission crackled through their headsets. This one was distant, etched with interference and stress. It was also in heavily accented English: *'Tokyo Radio, Korean Air zero zero seven.'*

'Korean Air zero zero seven, Tokyo.'

'Zero zero seven . . . ***fifteen thousand** . . . holding with rapid decompressions. Descending to one zero thousand . . .'

'Doesn't sound at all to me like the target has been destroyed,' said Garret.

'No, sir, it doesn't.'

BOOK TWO

January 13, 2012

NBC Studios, 30 Rockefeller Plaza, New York City. New Mexico governor Roy Garret glanced at camera one and reminded himself to look natural in case the producer zoomed in for a quick reaction cut. The live televised debate—long awaited by the voters—had seesawed across the issues and now it was in its final moments. Garret thought that he'd come out on top, but it was going to be tight.

His opponent, Louisiana senator Lou Chevalier, was the moderate Democratic nominee in the race for the White House. Chevalier's credentials were impeccable. At fifty-one, he was comparatively young, and he was black, from a poor working-class family living in Tallulah, Louisiana. His father was a preacher and his mother had been a housecleaner. Both were still alive, in their nineties. Senator Chevalier had been a Gulf War I hero, earning the Distinguished Service Cross, and the evidence of his bravery was a patch over the destroyed socket of his right eye. After the war, he'd completed a law degree at Stanford and opened a low-cost legal aid service, which had grown in size and stature, attracting corporate sponsorship from Microsoft and others, and spreading to twelve state capitals—so the man was wealthy to boot. He was also an eloquent performer in front of the cameras and doing very well in the polls. It was an understatement to say that Garret hated his guts.

'We've heard the governor of New Mexico tell us about our priorities and how we've got them all mixed up,' Chevalier said, moving into the final stretch of his two-minute rebuttal. 'Governor Garret tells us that being a teacher isn't as important as being a soldier, but our children are our future. He tells us that providing universal healthcare will never work, but there are well over 47 million Americans who can't afford to get sick. He tells us that helping the poor only entrenches poverty; that equal pay for women will only encourage them back into the workforce and lead to the break-up of families; that rape victims who bear children have in fact received a blessing from God; that forced deportation at the point of a gun is the only way to deal with illegal immigration; that we need to lower taxes and cut spending on virtually everything except the military.

'Governor Garret tells us that, after having four years of a moderate in the White House, we've gotten our priorities all wrong. He can barely hide his glee that the current President is retiring from office for reasons of poor health. But that shouldn't surprise us, because the man on my left, well, he's a Cold War soldier, a reluctant migrant from the land of conservative fear-driven mistrust. And what do we really know about him? In the 1980s, he was in the clandestine world of the NSA. And then, suddenly, out of nowhere, he becomes the assistant deputy director of the CIA! A few years after that, he made director! What did he do to deserve all that? Well, my friends, we'll never know because the governor of New Mexico's employment records are top secret, a matter of *national security*.'

The half of the audience supporting Chevalier roared with applause, while the other half hooted and hollered, angered by their man's mistreatment at the hands of this do-gooder.

'Another thing we know,' Chevalier went on, his voice rising in pitch and ardor, 'is that before becoming governor of New Mexico, and while *I* was defending people unable to defend themselves, Roy Garret was sitting in the boardrooms of a number of high-powered companies from the Chase Manhattan Bank to Bechtel, a company awarded over $2.4 billion in no-contest contracts to rebuild Iraq's infrastructure, despite its well-known reputation for reconstruction failures. We know that as the director of the CIA for ten years, he used the agency as an instrument of his own brand of legalized terror: wire taps, the mysterious deaths of Venezuelan and Syrian presidents, the silent war in southern Thailand, the support of bloodthirsty rebel troops in the jungles of the Democratic Republic of the Congo, and the reseeding of civil war in Kosovo.'

'And that's time, Senator,' moderator Tim Russert called out over the clamoring of the audience, who were practically rioting in their seats at the accusations that had—until now—just been whispers. Russert tried to calm things down with placatory hand gestures.

'Okay, okay. Settle down, everyone,' he said. 'Hoo, boy, we're passionate tonight.' He turned to Chevalier. 'Now, I know you were supposed to have the last word, Senator, but we'll have to give your opponent one minute to respond—and that's your fault for leaving the best till last.'

His comment extracted a laugh from the audience, which had the effect of blowing off a little steam. Russert glanced at the producer for a signal and then addressed Garret. 'Governor, you have one minute.'

The audience waited for his response the way a man who'd poked a rattlesnake with a stick would wait nervously for the retaliation.

Ordinarily, Roy Garret loved the camera. But today it wasn't doing him any favors. He tried to keep the smile on his face, though he had a feeling that the longer he kept it in place, the more the muscles in his cheeks were reorganizing his features into a grimace. And he'd started to sweat, a droplet greasy with make-up running down his temple. Chevalier had managed to twist his policy ideas just enough to make them seem extreme. That was politics, the name of the game. But what really crawled under Roy Garret's skin was having his service questioned.

'Is there a problem, Governor?' Senator Chevalier prompted. 'Cat got your tongue?'

The light on top of camera one was glowing. It was coming in for that close-up and the split seconds were mounting into an uncomfortable protracted silence.

'No, the cat hasn't got my tongue, Senator,' Garret said, relieved to hear the sound of his own voice. 'Though I'm afraid the cow may have jumped over the moon here tonight.'

Surprised laughter rippled through the audience.

A movement in the corner of Garret's eye momentarily distracted him. It was Hank, his long-time aide, standing in the wings along with his campaign manager, Felix Ackerman. Both men were giving him an encouraging thumbs up.

'What I mean by that, Senator,' Garret continued, 'is that it seems to me you have a nursery-rhyme grasp of the CIA. As you correctly point out, secrecy acts won't allow me to talk about my tenure at the Agency. Nevertheless, let me try and address your accusations in general terms. The fact is, I took my orders from the government of the day and while I was director, sir, the CIA was never my plaything. What you are, Senator, is a carnival trickster who wants to con the American people with BS. And let's talk about your tactics. Frankly, they're cheap. You're spreading innuendo hoping that the voters will see it as truth, which says to me you don't put a lot of stock in the intelligence of the American people. But they're a lot smarter than you think, Senator.'

Garret took a breath and pushed on. 'Now, back to your accusation. In 1981, Senator, President Reagan outlawed assassination as a tool of foreign policy. If you're not aware of that fact, you should be. And it has *never* been my habit to contravene presidential orders, no matter what the politics of the man issuing them.'

'Yes, Governor,' Chevalier interjected, 'but you must—'

Garret raised his voice. '*You* must allow me to speak, Senator. Your statement went way beyond implication and into slander. You posture like a gentleman, but your words are as common as your intent. All you want to do is besmirch my record and character for political gain. You want to know what is on the public record? Under my directorship, the CIA served the administration of the day admirably and honorably. End of story.'

The yellow light came on. Garret's one minute had expired.

He raised his voice to an indignant tone. 'Senator, my record is on the public register. And unlike yours, mine has been a *lifetime* of service to the United States of America.'

Russert interrupted him. 'That's time, Governor . . .'

124

After signing half a dozen campaign posters for eager supporters, Governor Garret, Hank Buck and Felix Ackerman walked briskly through the network's secure back entrance to the underground parking lot, flanked by a screen of secret service security.

'I'm serious, Governor,' encouraged Felix Ackerman, the 250-pound man referred to by some Washington insiders as a sweaty one-man avalanche, 'the switchboard lit up with support for you. I'm ecstatic with the result.'

'My campaign manager's happy? That's a first,' Garret said. 'I must be in trouble.' Despite reassurances to the contrary and his earlier confidence, he knew the debate had gone against him.

'Look, you showed America that you're a strong leader, agile on your feet, passionate *and* patriotic. Your performance tonight was pure gold. Chevalier might have had his nose in front, but you pulled down his pants on camera. You even managed to include a subtle dig about that bayou cottonmouth's trivial part-time service—a few short years in the army.'

'I wouldn't call the DSC trivial, Felix,' said Hank.

'If he's such a great warrior, then why doesn't a single soldier he served with have anything to say about him—good *or* bad? I tell you, Roy, coming into the final stretch, the timing of this debate couldn't have been better. You'll win the Democratic nomination for sure. The party's looking for strength. Bringing things into the open like that did you a favor. Believe it.'

Garret wasn't so confident.

'Listen, I have to stay back here and talk to the print media journalists,' Ackerman said. 'I'll catch up to you later this evening when the latest poll results are released.'

'Okay,' Garret said as he climbed in the back of the Lincoln with Hank, the secret service detail deploying to its vehicles. The driver shut the door and it gave a heavy, bulletproof clang. Garret settled into the aromatic leather seat.

'Hank, I want that hick nigger's head on a plate.'

'And you'll have it, Roy. But Felix is right—Chevalier did you a favor.'

'On a plate, Hank. I want you to peel back his life, look into his past, lift up the damn seat on his john. Find some dirt on this cocksucker we can use. Somewhere along the way he screwed the wrong woman, inhaled, didn't pay a bill, tripped up an old lady. I want to know why he got that fucking medal. I will not have my service to my country called into question. Not ever. You hear me?'

'I hear you, boss,' said Hank, and, furthermore, he approved. Garret had come a long way from those early days at the NSA. A decade as CIA director had been the making of him, honed his edge. And now he was shooting for the highest office in the land, which meant Hank's own stocks were on the rise.

'Before I forget,' Hank said. 'Some stuff has come up.'

'What kind of stuff?' Garret asked, fixing himself a scotch from the bar.

'Good stuff. Those two KAL players we've been keeping an eye on, Foxx and Suzuki, finally kicked the bucket. They both died of natural causes, by the way.'

'It's about time.'

'So I think we can afford to relax a little, maybe let our Russian friend go.'

'What about the tape?'

'If it exists, I'm pretty sure it would have surfaced by now, but just in case it has been passed along we're checking on family members.'

'How many are there?'

'I should have said, family *member*. We're lucky—it's just one, an American citizen.'

'That's fortunate,' said Garret. 'Who've you got on it?'

'Our connections are still good at the NSA. We've given a couple of their best people a watching brief—low level. What about General Korolenko? I'm pretty confident we won't need the Russian any more.'

'I'll leave that decision up to you, pilgrim.'

Hank allowed himself a private smile. Pilgrim—he hadn't been called that in quite a while.

January 14, 2012

Key West, Florida. The courier exchanged a signature for the cardboard box. Ben kicked the door closed and took the package inside. He sliced the tape with a box cutter and lifted out the stainless-steel urn encased in bubble wrap. Curtis's body had been picked up from the hospital by the funeral parlor, and his cremated remains FedExed to Ben. Nice and simple, and, as Curtis had requested, God had been excluded from the loop.

'Where am I going to put you?' Ben said. 'The mantelpiece is in my other mansion.'

He placed the urn on the floor, against the skirting board, near Curtis's uniform. There he was, Curtis Foxx—his father—all nine pounds of him. Having him in the house in any form felt way beyond strange.

'Hey, Curtis,' he said. 'Nice of you to drop by after all these years. When you've got a minute, there are a few questions I'd like to ask you.'

Ben shook his head and went back to what he'd been doing before the courier arrived, which was turning the place over searching for the safe deposit box key, still finding it hard to believe that Lana had woken early, stolen it and run off. That just didn't make a hell of a lot of sense. More than likely, the voice in his head assured him, the key had somehow fallen off the ring and become stuck behind a cushion when they were messing around. And even if she did steal it, the voice continued, what did it matter? There was nothing in the box anyway.

'But that's not the point,' Ben said out loud, surveying the room, wondering where else it could be.

Twenty minutes of searching later, the key hadn't turned up and the whole business was disturbing him in ways he hadn't thought possible. Something odd was happening, and it was somehow connected to Curtis Foxx. His cell rang. The ringtone told him it was a call from work.

'Hello,' he said, distracted by the morning's events.

'You know, Ben, you should really consider a job at the United Nations,' Cecilia said.

'Why?'

'You met any Japanese women lately?'

'No . . .'

'Really? 'Cause there's one here in reception who wants to see you.'

'Akiko Sato,' she said with the slightest of bows.

'Ben Harbor,' he responded, giving her a warm, tourist-operator smile. 'Pleased to meet you.'

Akiko looked him up and down.

'Is there something wrong, ma'am?' he asked, smile faltering.

Akiko hadn't been sure what to expect, but it wasn't someone who wore torn jeans with his underwear showing and a T-shirt with the voluptuous silhouette of a seated naked woman and the words 'Trucker dude' on it.

'I have a pilot's uniform if it would make you feel more comfortable. Some people prefer—'

'I'm not here to fly.'

'Oh, then how can I help you?'

'Are you the son of Curtis Foxx?' she asked.

'I beg your pardon?'

'Your father wanted us to meet.'

'What?'

A group of people wandered into reception, laughing, taking up a lot of the room.

Ben told them someone would be with them in a moment, and called out, 'Cecil!'

He then led Akiko to a smaller room full of airplane memorabilia— photos of old warplanes, propellers and a chromed dismantled airplane engine on a stand.

'Please, take a seat,' he said, motioning at a couch while he leaned against the engine bench with folded arms. 'Now, do you want to run all that by me again . . . And I'm sorry, what did you say your name was?'

'Akiko.'

'Okay, *Akiko*,' he said, appearing to speak her name aloud in order to make it stick in his brain. 'What's all this about? You knew Curtis Foxx?'

'No, I never met him. He was friends with a man called Yuudai Suzuki. Have you heard this name before?'

'Suzuki? Of course. They make motorcycles and—'

'No, not *that* Suzuki.'

The man Akiko had crossed half the world to see obviously had no idea why she was here at all, which increased her frustration and concern. She held an envelope toward him.

'Look, lady,' he said, avoiding it and instead taking a step toward the door, 'I'm not sure what you want or how I can help, but I've got a job to do so if you wouldn't mind . . .'

'Please,' she said. 'Read this.'

Ben looked at her.

'Please.'

He reluctantly took the unsealed envelope from her, opened it and removed a sheet of fine, almost translucent paper. It appeared to be a letter, and it was written in Japanese. An English translation had been written below the signature. He read it, and as he read, he rested his forehead on his hand, looking stunned.

'Your father, Curtis, and Yuudai were friends,' Akiko said. 'The tragedy of Korean Air Lines 007 bound them together.'

'007,' he said, his lips barely moving.

The way he said it, the number meant something to him, that much was clear. The one and only positive sign, Akiko thought.

'It says here that this Yuudai guy left you some money,' Ben said, looking up. 'How much?'

'Over ¥10,600,000.'

'What's that in American dollars?'

Akiko pulled out her cell phone and performed the calculation on it. 'A little more than $96,000.'

Ben almost seemed in a daze. 'When Curtis died, he left me $96,000 plus change,' he told her. He scanned the letter again and this time read the last line aloud. '"Spend it wisely and in pursuit of the truth." Curtis wrote almost the same thing to me in his will. He said, "I am proud of you and will be prouder still if you embrace the truth."'

Akiko nodded. 'Now Yuudai and Curtis have bound us together.'

'Really? To do what?'

'They both say, to find the truth.'

'And where's the truth to be found, if you don't mind me asking?'

'In Russia.'

☭

'Look, I have no idea who Yuudai Suzuki is, or was. I've never even heard of him, let alone met the guy,' Ben said, getting them both a drink of water from the cooler in the corner. 'And it's pretty much the same with Curtis. He was my father, but he left my mother and me when I was still in diapers. I hadn't heard anything about him or from him till a lawyer read me his will a little more than a week ago.'

Akiko seemed disappointed, almost angry. She'd obviously come expecting answers, not ignorance.

'Until I read your letter, I hadn't heard of KAL 007, either.'

'So none of this means anything to you at all?'

'No. Yes. I don't know. Maybe.'

'I don't understand.'

Ben was reluctant to tell her what he did know. He had a feeling it came with strings and that he'd get dragged into something messy.

'Please,' said Akiko.

Ben sighed. 'Look, I have no idea what it means, but when Curtis died, he left me a key to a safe deposit box. The number of the box was 007.'

'Oh!' Akiko was startled. 'Can I see it?' she asked.

'There's a problem. I lost the key.'

'You . . . lo-lost it?' she stammered with disbelief. 'How?'

'It doesn't matter,' Ben said, picking at a seam in his jeans, trying to hide his embarrassment. 'The box contained a reel of audio tape, which I have.'

'What's on it?' she asked, the expectation returning.

'Nothing—just static. The tape was old. The technician who played it for me said there might have been something recorded on it at one time, but the tape is ruined.'

Ben felt Akiko's disappointment. It had mass, like a breeze against his skin. She'd come a long way, and for what? She reached into her bag and pulled out a thick scrapbook. She opened it to the first page and took out a newspaper clipping, which she held toward him with two hands. Ben took it from her in the same manner. At first, it confused him. The article was in Japanese. The newsprint was old and yellowed, the color of tobacco. But he could see it was a picture of a happy Japanese couple, a child in the woman's arms.

'The man is my father, Hatsuto,' Akiko said. 'He died not so long ago. This was my mother, Nami. She was a passenger on KAL 007. It was taken on the night of departure.'

'The little girl here is you?'

'Yes.'

Ben saw small quivering dents appear in Akiko's chin, her top lip clamped between her teeth. Her slender body was absolutely still, held rigid as she fought the emotions threatening to break through to the surface.

He handed back the clipping.

'Do you have a picture of your father?' she asked.

'Yeah, sure,' he said. He found his satchel and the photo and passed it to her. 'That's Curtis on the end. The rest of the guys are, or were, his crew.'

Ben sensed Akiko stiffen. 'Is something the matter?' he asked her.

'The plane. It's an RC-135.'

'Well, yeah, I think it is.'

'There was an RC-135 implicated in the crash.'

Ben took the photo and re-examined it.

'It was never proved,' she said. 'There were many questions.'

'When was all this supposed to have happened?'

'September 1, 1983.'

Ben digested this news. 'That's the night I was born,' he said in a state of mild shock. The mission, the one that had changed Curtis's life, changed his mother's life, his life; all their lives. KAL 007; the 007 key. The timing. Was it possible?

'Your father was a pilot. You told me that he left when you were a small child. Why did he leave you and your mother?' Akiko asked, as if she could read his thoughts.

Because he was a violent drunk.

'I don't know. It's a little family mystery. He's staying at my place at the moment—I'll ask him.'

'What?'

'Sorry, black humor. His ashes arrived this morning. He was cremated.'

There was a knock on the door. It was Cecilia.

'Excuse me,' she said to Akiko as she popped her head in. 'Ben, sorry, but your nine o'clock is here. They want to head out to the Dry Tortugas.'

Ben gave Cecilia a nod and said that he'd be there in a minute.

'Where are you staying, Akiko? Can we organize anything for you? Do you need a cab?'

'I have a rental, and I'm staying at the Crowne Plaza.'

'Okay, well, I have to go to work and then I have to go and see someone. I'll be back later this evening. Could we maybe get together then?'

'Yes, okay,' she said, standing.

Ben sensed her hesitation.

'Are you okay?' he asked.

'You don't know what to think about any of this, do you?'

'Honestly? No, I don't.'

'I don't blame you. There were many things about the KAL 007 disaster that have never been explained. A Soviet fighter launched two missiles at it. When it crashed off Sakhalin Island in the Sea of Japan, it triggered the biggest air and sea search in history. There were many Japanese, American and Soviet ships. And do you know what they found?'

'No, what?' Ben asked.

'Nothing. They found nothing at all.'

January 14, 2012

NSA HQ, Fort Meade, Maryland. NSA investigator Lana Englese ran her fingers across the numbers etched on the key. She leaned back in her chair, aware of the headache tapping away at both her temples—nothing serious, just a couple woodpeckers making themselves at home on either side of her head. She had taken paracetamol tablets, downing them with a full glass of water. But one pill had become lodged in the pipe above her stomach and was giving her a burning sensation. Great, she thought, just what I need.

The cause of the discomfort had been a late night followed by an early start, kicked off with a helicopter ride from Key West International to Miami International Airport in order to make a connecting flight to DC. And now she was facing a blank laser screen that covered the entire wall in a special room called a virtual investigation booth, sandwiched between her partner, Investigator Miller Sherwood, who thought this low-priority case was a complete waste of time, and the operator, who was taking his time getting his shit together. On top of all that, she was breathing manufactured air in a room with no natural light and walls that unnaturally sucked all sound from the atmosphere—typical in a VI booth. It was going to be one of those days.

Suddenly, Lana caught his scent again. She must have washed her hands half a dozen times, but the guy was still on them. Or maybe his smell was on her clothes. Or maybe, she told herself, it's just you feeling fucking guilty. Lana had broken her own number one rule: you don't sleep with your work.

'Okay, what have we got here?' said the operator.

His name was Saul Kradich. Lana had never teamed up with him before, but he had a reputation for being thorough. He was wearing a ratty, faded Indians ball cap. He was a young guy for such an old cap, Lana thought. It had to be much loved. Maybe he slept in it, though he looked the type who never slept at all—or did anything other than sit on a chair in front of screens; the extra folds of pale skin under his chin reminding her of unbaked pastry.

'Let me get this straight,' Kradich turned to ask her. 'Your surveillance target was outbound from Key West International yesterday and you want his destination, right?'

'Among other things,' Lana said, distracted.

'You okay, Englese?' asked Sherwood. Sherwood could lift his own body weight in steel plates on the machines in the gym, and his biceps stuffed his shirtsleeves the way meat filled sausage skins. He was either calm and rational, or a red-faced hand grenade with a missing pin, nothing in between. 'You look a little off color.'

'I'm fine,' she replied, discreetly belching a little paracetamol gas behind her fingertips.

'That asshole didn't slip anything into your drink, did he?'

'No. Self-inflicted. Margaritas.'

'Then I'll be taking back that sympathy.'

'You got photos of this guy for me?' Kradich asked, now impatient to get on with it.

'Check your mailbox,' Sherwood told him. 'I sent them through half an hour ago. I've also given you his name and address.'

'You're making this too easy.'

A window opened on the screen set on the wall, followed by another window and then an email and a photo file attachment. A dozen pictures of Ben Harbor on his own appeared, along with several of him together with Lana. In all the photos, Ben and Lana were both either laughing or smiling.

'Someone loves their work,' Kradich commented.

Heat washed into Lana's face.

'I've been to that bar,' Kradich went on. 'It's in Key West. Captain Tony's, right? Bra heaven.' Mistaking the look of discomfort on Lana's face for offense caused him to add, 'If you like that kind of thing.'

He closed down all the windows. 'Okay, now I add his name and address to the function,' he said, muttering to himself, 'and then we . . .' He held his index finger over the control screen symbolically, then let it drop. ' . . . wait.' A little cartoon eye winked in a corner of the giant screen, indicating that the command was being processed. 'But we don't wait too long.'

The laser screen filled with window after window, each overlaying the last—Ben Harbor's entire life from the day he was born, every school report and parking ticket, right up to the last time he used his credit card, made a phone call, and passed a surveillance camera.

'Wow, this guy has a real big filling in his left upper M2,' observed Kradich, tapping his screen.

The system harvested identification photos from various official documents and deposited them in a window that also contained the pictures taken by Investigator Sherwood.

'So now we've got Harbor's mug shots from his passport, aviation license, Florida driver's license and credit card. The aviation license photo is a month old—that's good, gives the software a control image to work against. You want this guy's bank and phone records?'

Lana nodded. 'Uh-huh.'

Kradich's fingers rolled across the glass control screen in front of him. 'What else can I get you?'

'His father died recently. He left a will. I want to check whether it's been through probate.'

Kradich picked up a pencil and clamped it between his teeth.

Lana consciously ran her thumb over the key again, feeling the ridges of the numbers.

'Yep, the will has been probated. The IRS also has a copy,' said Kradich. 'You want a copy, too?'

'Yes, please,' Lana replied. 'While you're at it, you might as well give us some background on Ben Harbor's father. His service record, discharge and so forth.'

'Let's see here,' Kradich said, chewing the pencil, his fingers a blur over the control screen. More information frames tiled across the screen. 'Curtis Eugene Foxx … birth certificate … service records … medically retired. According to this, it seems he came down with a bout of acute paranoia. He believed people were following his every move.'

'Were we?' Lana asked.

'What? Following his every move?' Kradich asked.

'Yes.'

The laser screen on the wall filled with new windows, some of which stayed while others disappeared.

'Only around the clock, apparently,' he said.

'Can you tell us why?'

Kradich put his head down and began digging. A 'classified' graphic came up along with fields that required access codes.

'Nope,' he said after a handful of attempts. 'Not unless you can fill in these boxes. Sorry.'

During their briefing, their section head, Sam Whittle, had told them that Ben Harbor, the son of Curtis Foxx, a recently deceased former RC-135 pilot and a 'person of interest' to the NSA, might be hoarding information pertaining to the shootdown of Korean Air Lines Flight 007 on September 1, 1983, which could affect national security. The purpose of the investigation was to determine whether this was, in fact, the case. Until that could be ascertained one way or the other, this was a low-priority enquiry. Nevertheless, Lana was intrigued. The KAL 007 incident had happened almost twenty-nine years ago, before she was born. How could *any* information that Ben Harbor might have on the incident affect national security in the year 2012? And then there was the guy himself. He was a harmless hedonist, nothing more.

'Curtis Foxx flew RC-135s out of Shemya Island,' she said. 'What was he doing on the night of September 1, 1983?'

Kradich entered various commands and kept getting denied access.

'You've never tried to dig into MISREPs before, have you?' he asked.

'MISREPs?'

'Mission Reports.'

'No.'

'Looks like missions flown by RC-135s from Shemya on that date have been sequestered and coded SAR—special access required. You can only get into SAR-coded files if you're authorized for that compartment.'

'So you're saying that the MISREPs have been buried. Should I be suspicious about that?'

'As in maybe they contain some deep, dark secret?'

'Yes.'

'Not necessarily. That mission happened back in the Cold War days. The MISREPs could well have been sequestered not because of what they contained, but rather *how* the information was obtained. The methods of intelligence-gathering back then were often more closely guarded than the intelligence itself. You wanted the other guy to think you held four aces in your hand, even if you had nothing—*especially* if you had nothing.'

'So how do I get access to Foxx's MISREP for September 1, 1983?'

Kradich swung around to face her. 'Access for a compartment isn't granted by clearance. If you're not in a billet that requires that information to do your job, or because your need-to-know isn't high enough, you won't get access.'

'And being an NSA investigator on a case looking into events around the mission flown by a particular pilot from a particular base on a particular day doesn't qualify as need-to-know?'

'Don't ask me, lady, I just work here.'

'Call me Lana.'

'Sure—Lana.'

'Who decides need-to-know on this?'

'Well, Lana, you could try the people on the billet.'

'Who are they?'

'I don't know. Their names are also compartmented and protected by codeword.'

'We're getting nowhere on this,' Lana said, frustrated.

'Sorry. You'll have to find another way in, I'm afraid.'

'What about Curtis Foxx's crew members from September 1983?' said Sherwood. 'Are any of them still around?'

'Okay,' said Kradich. 'Give me a minute . . .'

File photos of five men came up. 'All smoked except for this guy, Dallas Mitchell. He lives in Homestead.'

Oh great, thought Lana. Back to Florida we go.

'We're about ready to roll here,' said Kradich.

They watched the software finish constructing a wire frame of Ben Harbor's head and shoulders, based on the photos. Saul tapped a few keys and flesh and coloring began to overlay the wires as the bust revolved in three axes.

When the image was complete, Kradich asked, 'Look familiar?'

'Yeah,' said Lana. 'In a creepy kind of way.'

'Now, we just feed this re-creation into the face-recognition program and the software will start scanning all the surveillance-camera footage in the airport's hard drive, looking for a match. They've got a few hundred cameras there so it'll take a minute. Let's just hope he's not wearing a hat. Ceiling-mounted cameras hate hats.'

'Is that why you wear one?' Investigator Sherwood asked him.

'No, I wear this because I'm a fan.'

'Right,' said Sherwood. 'A fan of the *Indians*?'

'Yes, as a matter of fact. You know, you could go get a coffee or something while I do this,' Kradich suggested, offended.

'No, it's okay. Happy to wait,' Sherwood said.

Kradich shrugged and said, 'Okay, Happy, suit yourself.'

Lana smiled. Sherwood grunted.

Kradich's fingers issued a few commands and then he sat back in his chair, one foot up on the edge of his bench. His Nikes were as old as his baseball cap.

Up on the main screen, small thumbnail stills from video clips began filling a separate window. Within a minute the cursor flashed in the bottom right-hand corner of the frame, the search complete. Kradich gave the software permission to edit the clips together in sequence.

'You ready?' he asked.

'Hit us,' said Sherwood, who'd been passing the time cleaning his fingernails with a plastic fast-food fork left behind by someone from a previous session.

Kradich tapped away and the footage began playing at double the normal speed, like a film from the silent movie era. He said, 'Okay, your target flew US Airways Flight 4062 to Orlando. After he arrived there, he took a cab. I've got the license number of the cab. You want to tail it? Orlando is crawling with surveillance cameras.'

'Thanks,' said Lana. 'We want to know where he went and who he saw. And then we want to know when he returned home, and what he was doing until he arrived at Captain Tony's Saloon, Greene Street, Key West.'

'Scary—you're starting to sound like my ex,' Kradich said. 'And after that?'

'I know where he was after that,' Lana said, once more feeling the heat rise into her face.

January 14, 2012

Homestead, Florida. A cowboy wearing a ten-gallon hat, spurs on his boots and a couple of fake revolvers belted low on his hips, walked from the shadows of the Radio Shack's front entrance carrying a sale sign under his arm. Apparently, cell phones and audio systems were on special today.

Sitting in his car, Ben watched the man go to the highway, set up the sign and position it for the passing traffic, then walk back. With a name like 'Tex' this had to be Mitchell, though from a distance he didn't look anything like the man in the photo. But then, Ben considered, the man in the photo with Curtis wasn't dressed for a rodeo.

He gave the guy a minute's head start before following him into the store, and found him near the cash register, twirling two nickel-plated six-shooters around his fingers for the entertainment of a customer's small child. Closer up, the man did look familiar. Same height, a few more pounds and lines, the same amused mouth and eyes.

'How can I help you, sir?' he asked when Ben approached.

'Dallas Mitchell?'

The man hesitated, seemed uncertain. 'Er, yes . . . ?'

'Do you mind if I have a word with you? In private.'

The man hesitated, unsure what to make of the request.

'It's about Curtis Foxx,' said Ben.

The added information seemed to do the trick.

'Curtis? Sure. Let's, er, go into my office.'

Tex gave the little girl a lollipop from under his hat. She snatched it and then ran off. Ben followed Tex past displays of auto navigation systems, video cameras and computers to a small room with high, narrow windows that opened onto the highway. Drifting through them was a high-speed traffic hum that sounded like overworked air-conditioning. Mitchell ditched the hat and unclipped the spurs.

'You know, I've never ridden a horse,' he confessed. 'The damn things give me a rash. Closest I've ever been to a horse was eating it one time in France.'

'Not from the Lone Star state?'

'Boston, born and bred, partner.'

'Then why the fancy dress?'

'There are eight Radio Shacks between here and Miami-Dade. Folks keep coming back to this one. Maybe it's to see the fool who looks like Gene Autry and keeps candy on his head. Now, what's this about Curtis?'

'Curtis Foxx was my father.'

'You're Curtis's boy?'

Ben nodded.

'Now that you mention it, I can see the resemblance. So, you're Ben Foxx . . .'

'Ben *Harbor*,' Ben corrected. 'My parents were divorced.'

'Right.' Tex cleared his throat. 'You know, I was flying with Curtis the night you were born. If I remember rightly, he was pretty excited about it.'

'September 1, 1983,' Ben said.

At the mention of that date, something rippled across the man's face, as if the power to every muscle had been cut for the briefest moment.

'So, what brings you here? Just in the neighborhood?'

'I live in Key West,' Ben replied.

'Nice part of the world.'

'Curtis died recently,' Ben said, small talk not his favorite activity with anyone other than paying customers.

Tex sat heavily, the news appearing to hit him in the solar plexus. 'Oh . . . that's . . . I'm very sorry to hear that. Curtis was an original. We were all pretty close back in the day.'

'I came across this photo.' Ben took the group shot from his pocket and showed it to him.

Tex shook his head. 'Seems like yesterday. This was taken at Eielson.'

'Who are the guys in the middle?'

'Jim Svenson and Mark Harlow—both pilots. They were killed along with Eli Grogan, the man standing beside Curtis here, in a C-130 crash. Happened in '89.' Mitchell handed back the photo with another shake of his head. 'Military aviation is a high-risk pursuit.'

'So I've heard. Curtis left me his service dress uniform,' said Ben. 'I was wondering what he won the Airman's Medal for.'

Tex leaned back and pondered the ceiling. 'Your old man was a born hero. He was at the Austin municipal airport updating his landing currency. The way I heard it, on the way home Curtis saw smoke coming from an apartment building just beyond the airfield fence, so he raced over there, climbed the fire escape and entered the burning building. Brought out a child and an infant. Then he turned around and went back in, carried out the mother and resuscitated her. They were saying that the fire was so big the air traffic had to be diverted.'

The picture Ben conjured up was of Curtis, covered in black soot, running through fire, shielding a baby in his arms. His father a hero? That was a man he never knew.

'Curtis also won the Air Medal,' Tex continued. 'I was there for that. He landed an RC-135 in severe weather with nothing but fumes in the tanks and almost no communications or navigation equipment to speak of. We're talking about a *big* aircraft here. The RC was basically a Boeing 707. And at the time we'd suffered a complete and total electrical failure. Yep, your old man was the best aircraft commander—the best pilot—I ever flew with.'

'So what happened to him?'

'Pardon me?'

'What happened to him?' Ben repeated. The question hadn't sounded quite so blunt when he'd practiced it on the drive up, but that was how it came out.

'I'm not with you,' said Tex.

'From what you've said, Curtis was quite a guy. And yet one day he just dropped out and took up alcohol. What sort of man who's prepared to jump into a burning building and risk his life to save complete strangers walks away from his career and his family and becomes a bum?'

What kind of a man leaves his one-year-old son and never comes back?

'I . . . I don't know,' Tex said.

'You were his buddy, his navigator.' Ben paused for rehearsed effect. 'It had something to do with Korean Air Lines Flight 007, didn't it?'

Tex went pale, the color sucked out of his skin. 'I have *no* idea what you're talking about.'

'I think you do,' Ben insisted. 'There was a mission and it went wrong, and it happened on September 1, 1983—the night KAL 007 was shot down, the night I was born. You admitted it—you were there!'

'Look, I don't know what you want me to say,' said Tex, looking uncomfortable. 'There was no mission that differed from any other. We went out, we took pictures of Soviet missile re-entry vehicles, and then we came back. That was our job. And I don't even think I'm allowed to tell you that much.'

'I'm not leaving till you give me some answers.'

'Your father was like a brother to me, Ben.'

'So, that makes me like your nephew?'

'Look, what happened back then happened. No one can change it. We've all moved on and that's something you're also going to have to do.'

Ben remained seated. 'I start asking the hard questions and down come the shutters. You *do* know something. I know you do.'

Mitchell picked up a phone handset and held it to his ear. 'Security? Yes, could you come to my office . . .'

'In case you change your mind,' said Ben, placing a Key West Seaplanes business card on the table as he got up.

He opened the door and walked out. A big soft guy with acne and a wispy goatee, wearing a branded Radio Shack knitted shirt, approached him. 'Sir . . .' he said as Ben brushed past.

Ben saw Tex in his rear-view mirror as he drove off, standing at the entrance, feet apart, hands resting on the nickel-plated six-shooters in their holsters, staring after him.

'You're late,' said Cecilia, impatiently tapping on the booking schedule with a pen.

'Yeah, sorry. I got held up,' said Ben.

'Akiko's here.'

'She is? Where?'

'I set her up in the spare office.'

'Thanks, Cecil.'

'Don't mention it,' she said, peeking out between the slats of a window blind. It was dark outside. 'Can I go home now?'

'Why ask me? You're the boss.'

'Yeah? Sometimes I wonder.' Cecilia stood up. 'Akiko seems like a nice lady.'

'She does.'

'What's going on? You want to fill me in?'

Ben leaned on the reception counter. 'Do you remember an incident back in 1983 when the Soviets shot down a 747?'

'Yeah, I do. It was somewhere off Japan, I think. If memory serves me correctly, it was full of civilians. The Soviets put a couple of missiles into it, and there was some talk about it being a spy plane, on a mission for the CIA.'

'Really? Well, you know more about it than me.'

'So?'

'Akiko's mother was on that plane.'

'Oh, Lord . . .'

'She believes the business had some connection with Curtis.'

'Is that why she's here?'

'Yeah.'

Cecilia whistled softly. 'Well, if you need any help from me, just ask.'

'Thanks, Cec,' said Ben as he turned and walked down the hall. 'As you're offering, you could order us some take-out before you go. Maybe some Japanese,' he added with a grin.

He found Akiko playing solitaire on a desktop computer. 'Hi,' he said, closing the door behind him.

'Hello,' she replied, her face brightening.

'Sorry. Took longer than I thought.' Ben pulled up a chair and sat beside her. 'Been here long?'

'No. I walked around, went for a swim. The water was so clean. And then I had lunch at a bar, a funny place with bras all over the walls. Have you been there?'

'Once or twice,' he said as he took the photo of Curtis and his crew out of his top pocket. 'I'm late because I went to see this guy here.' He pointed to Tex. 'He has a shop a few miles up the road. He was flying with Curtis in an RC-135 on the night of September 1, 1983.'

Akiko examined the face in the photo with interest.

'I was hoping he'd tell me what happened.'

'And did he?' she asked.

'No. He kicked me out. It might have helped if I knew more about what happened that night. '

'You should have asked me. I've read everything there is.'

'You've studied it?'

'I wanted to know as much as I could. I lost my mother in that crash.'

'Your English is perfect,' said Ben.

'I hope so. I teach it in a school in Tokyo. Russian, too.'

'Russian. Is that a coincidence?'

'No, I thought learning the language would help me understand the people, why they acted as they did.'

'And has it?'

'No. I went to Sakhalin Island, and for the same reason. I was four when I lost my mother. I remember the day. I don't remember the day before, but I have been aware of every moment since. Perhaps September 1, 1983 was the day I grew up. My father and I, we looked after each other. He was devastated.'

'Did he remarry?'

'Yes, when I was ten, but he divorced two years later. I don't think he was ready. In his case, six years of mourning was not enough.'

Ben didn't comment. 'What about you? Not married?'

She held up her ringless left hand. 'I've had boyfriends, but it never seems to work out longer than six months. I get bored with them. Or they get bored with me. You're not married?'

'No,' he said.

'Why not?'

'Life's a party.' He shrugged. 'Why spoil it?'

She gave him a smile.

There was a moment of silence and Ben's eyes slid off her face.

'What's the matter?' she asked.

'What am I getting into here?'

'Nothing.'

'Just like the search for the plane found. I'm sorry . . .' The meeting with Tex was still fresh in his mind. 'Look, Akiko, bottom line: I don't think I can help you.'

'Why not?'

'I don't know anything about this. I don't know any of the people involved. It's not my problem.'

'It's not your problem?' Akiko asked, anger now in her voice and face. 'We have a lot in common. I think you also lost your father because of what happened on September 1, 1983.'

Ben hadn't looked at it like that. If the mission no one would talk about really was somehow involved with KAL 007, then Akiko could well be right. But did that really change anything? Curtis had left a long time ago. They'd never had any kind of relationship, except for a dull resentment he'd felt for a father who'd taken off and never made any attempt to contact him. Until he'd passed away. And that, as far as Ben was concerned, was just too damn late.

'What exactly do you want from me?' he asked. 'What were you expecting when you came here?'

'I was hoping you would know what happened.'

'Why?'

'The letter—because Yuudai said you could help, and he knew your father.'

'I wish people would stop calling Curtis Foxx my *father*, for Christ's sake.' Ben got up, walked to a bench on the far side of the room and sat on the corner of it. 'The crash happened a long time ago. All we have is that tape and there's nothing on it. Maybe there never *was* anything on it. There's one guy alive who can tell us what happened that night and he won't talk. What am I supposed to do? What more do you want from me?'

Akiko stood up and gathered her shoulder bag. 'This was a waste of time, obviously. Your father misjudged you.'

'So, what? You're just going to go back to Japan now?'

'What do you care? It's not your problem, remember?'

Ben took a deep breath. 'Maybe it would help if I knew what all this was about.'

'Look it up on the internet,' Akiko said as she opened the door.

Ben didn't want her to leave like this, so full of anger. And perhaps because she had come such a long way to see him, he told himself, he owed it to her to at least hear the story. He hopped off the bench and put his hand on the door, pressing it closed.

'C'mon . . . what happened to that plane? Tell me. Maybe, once I know, something will click.'

'Why should I bother? You don't care. You don't want to spoil the party.'

'They really found nothing of KAL 007? No wreckage at all?'

Akiko hesitated. She fought a strong desire to run from the room, catch a plane back to Tokyo and go back to teaching. But if you walk out that door, she told herself, it will be over. All hope of knowing what really happened will end. Perhaps if this man knew the facts, something good *might* come of it. Yuudai Suzuki had believed that Ben would help find the truth. And so had Ben's father. There was a reason for his involvement, even if he couldn't see it. Even if she couldn't see it.

She walked back to the couch, opened her bag and pulled out her scrapbook. It was the size of a phone book and twice as thick. She sat, let it drop onto the cushion and then leaned over to flick through the pages. Ben took a seat beside her.

'None of the ships or planes conducting the search found anything—or at least *admitted* to finding anything,' she said, flicking through until she found what she was looking for—a newspaper article showing a Russian MiG fighter buzzing a ship flying the Japanese flag. 'There were 269 people on board, but only a couple of bodies washed up on Hokkaido beaches, and they were unidentifiable. A little wreckage also washed up—a few bits and pieces.'

'Doesn't seem likely for a plane the size of a 747.'

'There were many things about the crash that didn't seem likely.'

'Did the Russians really shoot it down?'

'You *don't* know anything about this, do you?'

'Why should I? It happened the day I was born.'

'Yes, you told me,' she said.

'Do you think that's somehow significant?'

She shrugged and flicked through more pages until she found a map, which had been folded and unfolded so many times over the years that the paper had worn out at the creases. 'No. An interesting coincidence, perhaps.'

The map showed the world from Alaska to Japan, and took in a large chunk of the Bering Sea and the northern Pacific Ocean. The track KAL 007 had taken over the Soviet Union was marked on it, as was its designated route much further south, and other points of interest. There was a lot of divergence between the two tracks, up to 300 miles at one point.

'Korean Air Lines Flight 007 was a regular passenger service flying between Anchorage and Seoul,' Akiko said, tracing the route with her finger. 'For some reason that no one has ever explained satisfactorily, it flew hundreds of miles off course and headed to the north over Soviet Kamchatka.'

'747s don't fly hundreds of miles off course—not even the ones back then.'

'It flew over a secret Soviet submarine base and continued back into international airspace until it reached Soviet Sakhalin Island. This time, the Russians were waiting for it. They claimed the airliner maneuvered to avoid its ground anti-aircraft defenses, and then again when its interceptors caught it. They said they thought it was a spy plane.'

On the map, the plane's demise was marked by a red, yellow and white flash.

'Why did they think that?'

'Because it wouldn't answer radio calls. It was also flying with its lights off and behaving strangely—not like a civilian plane. The Russians fired two missiles and shot it down. At first the Japanese authorities thought the airliner had crashed into the water east of Hokkaido. There was a lot of confusion. No one knew for sure where it actually came down. There was even a report that it landed safely on Sakhalin Island.'

'Like it says in your letter.'

'Yes, but the Russians denied it. And they were actively searching the waters off a place called Moneron Island, so that's where everyone sent their ships. But the Russians wouldn't let the Japanese or American ships search its waters. They even dropped pingers on the sea floor to distract the other boats. Both sides were more interested in locating the black boxes than they were in finding any possible survivors.'

'Why?'

'Because it was the Cold War. Each side wanted to prove that the other was at fault. The Americans blamed the Russians for killing innocent civilians. The Russians blamed the Americans for using civilians as the cover for a CIA mission. The Russians eventually returned seventy-six items to the relatives of the passengers—things they said had washed up on Sakhalin. When Soviet divers were interviewed years later, they said they investigated the wreckage a couple of weeks after the crash and found no luggage, no bodies or even pieces of bodies—and not a single life jacket.'

'That's spooky,' said Ben.

He took over from Akiko and became absorbed in going back and forth through the clippings, some of which were in Japanese while others were in English.

'The Soviet divers said that they believed the plane had been dragged to the site and blown up.'

'What about the black boxes. Were they found?'

Akiko gave a wry smile. 'There was a rumor that the CIA had them, and that they'd been classified in the interests of national security and would never be released. But then Boris Yeltsin turned up with the black box tapes at a press conference in 1993 and handed them over.'

'And did the tapes clear up the mystery?'

'No. They were analyzed and many experts thought they'd been tampered with. Some of the information found on the flight data recorder seemed to have come from another flight entirely.'

'Your letter is starting to make more and more sense.'

'Yes.'

'What about the RC-135? How was that involved?'

'Do you know what ghosting is?'

'No.'

'It's a maneuver where two planes fly so close together that their radar returns merge. That night there was an RC-135, a plane called a Cobra Ball, flying reconnaissance over the Bering Sea.' Akiko turned to another map that, according to the caption, had originally been printed in the *New York Times*. The map showed the track of the RC flying a figure-eight pattern intersecting with 007's course. 'The Russians said it rendezvoused with KAL 007 on the edge of the buffer zone between Russia and America. The two planes flew so close together that Soviet ground radar operators thought they were looking at just one plane. Then the blip separated into two—one flew away while the other kept coming. The Soviets thought the aircraft headed for their territory was the RC.'

Ben snorted quietly. 'It's hard to believe something like this happened.'

'It happened.'

A buzzer rang. Ben went out to investigate and came back with take-out.

'I hope you like sushi,' he said, unpacking it.

'I prefer Italian.'

'Next time. So, this RC-135 . . .' he went on.

'There is so much you don't know. Please, before you make up your mind about helping me or not, do me one small favor.'

'What?'

She closed the book with a thud, lifted it up and dropped it in Ben's lap.

'Read.'

January 15, 2012

Saint Petersburg, Russia, USSR. The weather was mild, thought Valentin Korolenko. He guessed at the temperature. No lower than minus ten degrees Celsius. And it was mid-winter! Definitely, the world was warming. The retired major general of the Federal Security Service and KGB nevertheless tied the fur flaps of his *ushanka* under his chin—not easy to do with thick, gloved fingers, despite all the years of practice— and lifted up the collar of his padded coat. A young couple sauntered past, lovers arm in arm. The man was dressed in nothing but jeans and a sweater. No gloves and no *ushanka*. You never used to feel the cold either, he told himself. One's blood became lazy with age.

Czar, a golden retriever and his sole companion these days, snuffled at the base of a tree. The dog lifted a leg on it before cantering on a few paces, tongue hanging over his lower jaw like a wet pink blanket.

Korolenko started walking again, pulling on the leash, angling Czar back toward the Chesma Church, a beautiful old strawberry-sorbet-colored building with white vertical stripes, as familiar as an old friend. The grounds were small, but it was still his favorite place, even though tourists often swarmed here like flies over fresh wounds.

'Czar! Come,' he commanded, giving the long leash a firm tug to discourage the dog from mounting a male German shepherd, the tip of Czar's organ the color of an unlit match.

A bus pulled up and disgorged a load of tourists who milled about the church's forecourt, their guide speaking loudly in English as she threw her voice over their heads. 'Ah, the flies,' Korolenko called out in Russian, giving them all a wave, chuckling to himself as half a dozen waved back.

How the motherland has changed, he observed, and not all for the better. There was so little respect these days, though the Kremlin, still drenched in oil money, had reasserted itself. At last.

Czar bolted after a pigeon pecking at crumbs in the grass, practically wrenching off Korolenko's arm and aggravating the mild arthritis in his hands. He returned the favor with interest, pulling back hard on the leash. 'Czar! Stop!'

The animal coughed and swallowed a couple of times and looked up at him with warm brown eyes, an apparent smile on his panting jaws. Korolenko forgot his anger. He removed a glove, patted the dog's head and took a treat from his pocket. 'There, Czar. Good boy.' The dog snatched it, leaving slobber on his hand, which he wiped on a handkerchief.

It was time to go home. Enough exercise for the day. He took the path off to the right, as he always did when he came here, the force of habit mixed with expectation. It had been almost a year since he'd last seen the tin propped against the base of the tree—the agreed sign established more than twenty years ago; a connection to powerful friends, friends with money. Korolenko remembered the day in the Parisian park clearly.

It had started when US$50,000, plus a return ticket to the French capital, arrived at his door. On that day, with the Soviet empire collapsing around his ears, his double life had begun. The offer had caught him when he was vulnerable, at his weakest. The state hadn't paid him for six months because the state, effectively, had ceased to exist. It was a lifeline when he'd desperately needed one.

The meeting in Paris with no less than the assistant director of the CIA and his aide had gone well, and he was presented with another pregnant envelope containing US$50,000. There were conditions that came with the payments, of course. As a high-placed officer in the KGB

Fifth Directorate, he had to move across to the new organization being formed—the FSB. If he succeeded, his role was to see that all foreign nationals held on Russian soil were never released. The reward for this service would be a steady stream of money, making him rich in a land of paupers.

Korolenko had held up his part of the bargain and, as the years passed, the payments had continued. The contact had always been sporadic, but for the past twelve months it had all but ceased. Soon, too, the payments would also stop, he could feel it in his . . .

Korolenko swallowed. The tin! The signal. It was propped exactly as it should be—upside down. He counted the trees. Yes, it was the correct tree, third from the fence. He turned on his heels and hurried toward the milling tourists. After tying Czar's leash around the base of a young tree, he pushed his way through the crowd and arrived at the pink-and-white-striped church's entrance just as the attendant, a fat old babushka with a patchy gray mustache, was telling the tourists that the Chesma was closing for the day.

'No, no . . . I must say a prayer,' Korolenko insisted. 'Please . . .'

The fact that he was wearing an old Soviet-era coat and was obviously Russian overcame the old woman's reluctance. She jerked a thumb over her shoulder, then rudely closed the door in the faces of the crowd.

Although an atheist, Valentin Korolenko crossed himself, in the event that he was being watched, and hurried around the pillar to the piano pushed into a corner. Behind it was a coat rack with a number of hooks. On the third hook from the left hung a woman's old black winter jacket. He removed a glove and felt for the front right-hand pocket, then thrust his hand inside and dug around for the prayer book he knew would be there. He pulled it out and moved across to the altar. Getting down on one knee, he crossed himself again and then stood, head bent, in front of the painted Christ. Using his body as a screen from the old woman closing down the souvenir stall by the front door, he opened the prayer book to page thirty. There, wedged in the spine of the book, was a cigarette paper.

He put on his reading glasses and angled the book at the overhead light. The old thrill flooded through him, tingling in his scrotum and across his shoulders. It took a moment for his eyes to adjust. There was nothing written on it. His heart thudded with concern, his worst fear realized. He pinched the thin rice paper between thumb and forefinger and turned it over, just to make certain. There was nothing written on the reverse, either.

'*Govno!*' he swore under his breath. Shit!

The cigarette paper was utterly and completely blank. The signal that the relationship, a regular and significant source of income, had come to an end. The excitement he'd felt evaporated, leaving a bitter taste in his mouth. There would be no more new Mercedes.

January 16, 2012

Key West, Florida. Cecilia was laughing at something or someone—
the wall blocked Ben's view. He stuck his head around the corner. Tex
Mitchell was leaning against the counter, entertaining her. The Village
People cowboy outfit was gone and the guy was almost unrecognizable.
What the hell was he doing here?

'Hey, Ben,' Cecilia called out when she heard the door open. 'Come
and meet your first flight of the day—we've got us a real Cold War warrior in the house.'

Ben walked in.

'You look tired,' Cecilia observed. 'How'd it go with Akiko?'

'Not the way you're thinking. I was up all night reading through
stuff. She'll be over soon,' he said, checking his watch. 'Can you look
after her?'

'Call me mother hen.'

'Thanks, Cecil.'

Ben went straight into the paperwork for the flight. 'Got a headset?'
he mumbled without looking at Tex, who signed off on the booking
form and then pulled out a well-used headset from the Nike gym bag
at his feet.

'Why do I get the feeling you two know each other?' Cecilia
asked.

'We've met.' Ben turned and walked out, Tex following. 'You're the last person I expected to see today.'

'I wanted to talk to you.'

'What's the difference between yesterday and today?'

'Wait till we're airborne. So you're a pilot. Curtis would have approved.'

'Who the hell cares?'

Fifteen minutes later they'd climbed out of the bay and the Otter was trimmed for straight and level flight 1000 feet over a calm fall sea. Sitting in the co-pilot's seat, Tex reached behind him and pulled a gadget with a gauge and a needle on it from his bag. He waved it around the cockpit and passed it across the instrument panel. 'Okay,' he announced. 'You're clean.'

'You want to tell me what's going on?' Ben asked.

'You don't have any idea what you're involved in, do you?' Tex asked, examining Ben's face. 'No, you don't . . . After you left yesterday I had a visit from a couple of NSA investigators. They're snooping around, asking questions about Curtis and reminding me about the secrecy agreement I signed. I'm here to warn you. The NSA isn't the kind of agency you want digging around in your life. The last time I had those fuckers in my face was September 2, 1983.'

'The day after the Soviets blew KAL 007 out of the sky. Thanks for the heads up.' Ben banked to take them out to the edge of the shelf where the turquoise water turned black.

'What do you know about that flight?' Tex asked.

'I know that when a plane like a 747 weighing half a million pounds hits the water you get a slick of body parts and wreckage a couple miles long. I know that after 007 went down enough wreckage to suggest a Cessna might have crashed in the vicinity washed up on the beaches. I know that the wife of the Korean pilot took out extra life insurance on her husband before he left home because he told her that his next flight was going to be a particularly dangerous one and that he might not make it back. I know that a plane with the tail identification number HL7442—the number of the plane shot down by the Russians—arrived at Andrews Air Force Base in company with an RC-135 a couple weeks before the crash, and taxied to building 1752 operated by E-Systems, a US defense contractor that specializes in electronic warfare. Shall I go on?'

Ben glanced down and saw several dark shadows in the shallow luminescent water. Tigers or hammerheads from the look of their size, a mauled loggerhead foundering between them.

'When did you become such an expert on this?'

'Someone loaned me a book on the subject.'

'I suppose next you're going to tell me one of the more bizarre conspiracy theories—that the US Air Force shot 007 down to cover an air battle that took place over Sakhalin Island?'

'I was going to mention it,' said Ben. 'I was also going to bring up the fact that an RC-135 rendezvoused with KAL 007 on the edge of the Soviet buffer zone and flew so close to the airliner that the radar returns of both planes merged, confusing the Russian air defense network.'

'That's a theory, not a fact.'

'You want to explain a maneuver called "ghosting" to me?'

'As you know what it's called, I think you also know what it is.'

'The Soviets shot down the 747 because they thought it was the RC—your RC. You and Curtis Foxx fingered the Korean airliner for the Russians, didn't you?'

Ben took the Otter into a steep turn, carving a tight 90-degree arc over the line that separated the shelf from the deep ocean. Tex was looking out the window at the Gulf below.

'That photo of Curtis, you and the others,' said Ben. 'Curtis left it to me. You're the last man standing. I think he wanted me to contact you about 007.'

'And I've already told you that I won't comment on the specifics of any mission I may or may not have been involved in.'

'Spoken like a true politician.'

'Spoken like a guy who doesn't want to end up in prison for the rest of his life. That's the score when you sign a secrecy agreement.'

'No debris and no bodies, Tex. That adds up to no crash. What do you know about the report that came from the CIA a few hours after the plane went missing, the one that said it had landed safely on Sakhalin?'

'I know that no one seriously believed it.'

No one except for maybe a Japanese radar operator only fifty miles away at Wakkanai, thought Ben.

'The report was never verified,' continued Tex. 'And since when has the CIA ever made public reports?'

'If 007 crashed in the water, what happened to the wreckage along with the remains of the people aboard it?'

'The fighter that shot it down had to return to base, low on fuel, so there were no eyeballs on the airliner when it hit the water. But it crashed *somewhere*, obviously. Maybe the plane came down further up the Tartar Strait and the currents took the wreckage away from the search and rescue operations. There was a report that the 747 flew on for another twelve minutes after the missile strike.'

'I know. Was KAL 007 on a spy mission, flown deliberately over the USSR to light up its radars?'

'That's what you think?'

'It's the theory doing the rounds that makes the most sense to me.'

'I don't think it makes any sense whatsoever. With the assets we had pointed at the Soviet Far East back then, we knew *everything* worth knowing about their defenses. And what we knew was that the Russians had more holes in their turf than the greens at a gopher convention. The fact that 007 overflew so much Soviet territory before they caught up with it is proof of that. If 007 *was* on a spy mission, I have no idea what mission it might have been on. And as for the supposed E-Systems/Andrews AFB stopoff you mentioned, that doesn't make any sense either. What if that 747 fell into Soviet hands and they found intelligence-gathering equipment on it? Can you imagine the stink?'

The same thought had occurred to Ben.

'This is as much as I'm going to tell you,' Tex continued. 'KAL 007 arrived at waypoint NEEVA a full *nine minutes* later than its original estimate given at NABIE, the previous waypoint. Nine minutes is a long time for a commercial airliner not to show up.'

Ben turned to look at Tex. 'And?'

'You're a pilot. Figure it out.'

'Gee, thanks for the insight.' Ben banked the Otter again and put it on a heading back to Key West. 'So those guys who paid you a visit— the NSA agents. What did they look like?'

'Who said they were guys?'

The realization hit Ben like a slap. 'Was one of them an attractive brunette with a tan?'

'You got a visit too, huh?'

'Jesus . . .'

So Lana was NSA, some kind of secret agent. And she'd slept with him. Was it just to find out what he knew? Did secret agents really do that shit? And now she had the key. Did she know about the tape, too? This was not Ben's world and he felt completely out of his depth. He glanced at Tex. There was a reason Curtis had wanted him to contact his old navigator. He hoped to hell that trust had something to do with it.

'Tex, there's someone I think you should meet.'

'Is Akiko here yet?' Ben asked Cecilia, Tex close behind him.

'In the TV room,' Cecilia replied, waving to a couple of customers heading off with one of the other pilots.

'Tex, come and meet the woman I was telling you about.'

Akiko was reading the *Tokyo Shimbun* online, sitting on the couch with a laptop on her knees. She glanced up and was about to say something to Ben when Tex put his finger against his lips, silencing her. He took a pad and pen out of his bag and scribbled a note, which he tore off and handed to Ben. The note asked that all electrical equipment in the room be turned off at the wall socket. The words 'wireless internet' were underlined. Tex then pointed to the lights and the laser printer, and walked around the room tapping his pencil on the LCD TV, the DVD player, the wall fan, the air-conditioning unit, an electric clock, the desk lamps and Akiko's laptop. He wanted all of it off. He wanted Ben's and Akiko's cell phones turned off and left on the table. The note also asked for a wet mop.

'You want to do some cleaning?' Ben asked.

Tex shook his head and put a finger against his lips.

Ben did as Tex asked—turned everything off—then stepped out of the room to get a mop. When he returned, Tex was standing on a chair and waving his gadget around a bank of fluorescent lights in the ceiling. When he saw the mop, he stepped down off the chair and checked that the head was wet enough, then went over to the window, propped it firmly against the glass and drew the blind. He then passed his instruments over their cell phones before taking them apart and examining the circuitry. Satisfied, he put them all back together.

'We're clear,' he said.

There was a large question mark on Akiko's face.

'Akiko, this is Tex Mitchell,' said Ben. 'He's the guy from the photo I went to see yesterday, the navigator who flew with Curtis in the RC-135.'

'Oh,' she said, breaking into a smile. 'I'm honored to meet you.'

'Hello, Akiko,' said Tex, shaking her hand. 'Ben has told me a little about you. You've come all the way from Japan, I hear.'

'Yes.'

'He also told me you lost your mother on KAL 007. I was very sorry to hear that.'

'There are many things I'd like to ask you,' she said.

'That makes two of us,' said Ben. 'Why don't you start with what the mop's all about?'

'Okay, well, what I just did was conduct a diode search, using a sniffer to find radio frequency emanations that shouldn't be coming from things like this paperweight, for instance.' He waved the instrument over the small model of a seaplane. The needle didn't move. 'But there are easier places to hide bugs—like in any electrical gear. A wireless computer network is a prime surveillance target. It can be used as a transmitter or as a switching mechanism for listening devices— to turn them on when they're needed, and off to avoid detection. Cell phones are another easy place to secrete a bug. And just because the cell's turned off doesn't mean the bug stops working.'

'Do you think we're being bugged?' Akiko asked.

'Tex thinks the NSA might have rekindled an interest in 007 since Curtis died,' said Ben.

'The NSA is the National Security Agency,' Tex added. 'It's the agency that—'

'I know what the NSA is,' said Akiko. 'Did you find anything just now?'

'No. That's why we're talking.'

'And the mop?' Ben prompted.

'Right. Well, when you talk, the sound waves strike the windowpane, which vibrates and acts as a big diaphragm. There's a device that can bounce a laser beam off the glass and pick up those minute oscillations and then convert them back into sound. The wet mop dampens the glass and stops it vibrating.'

'What makes you so sure the NSA has an interest in us?' Akiko asked as Ben turned on the lights and the internet router.

'Akiko, I told you about the key and how I lost it?' Ben said.

She nodded.

'I didn't lose it. The key was taken—stolen by an NSA agent.'

'Whoa,' said Tex. 'Hold it right there, partner. What key? You didn't mention anything about a key.'

'Curtis left me a key to a safe deposit box. The number on the key—the box number—was 007.'

'You're shitting me,' said Tex.

'The NSA investigator who came to my house yesterday stole the key when I wasn't looking.'

'Fuck,' Tex said, sitting down. 'So let me get this straight. Curtis left you something in a safe deposit box, the number of which was 007?'

'Yes.'

'And the investigator stole the key?'

'Yes.'

'*Fuck*!' he repeated, this time with emphasis. 'What was in the box? Did you open it?'

'Yeah. I cleaned it out, so having the key won't do the NSA any good.' Ben opened a cupboard and revealed a small safe. He punched in the four-digit code and the door sprang ajar.

Tex's eyes went wide when he saw what Ben removed.

'Don't get too excited. I've played it and there's nothing on it,' said Ben.

'Nothing at all?'

'Unless you consider a sound like whales copulating something.'

'Let's have a look,' Tex said.

Ben handed him the tape.

'I don't think Curtis would have gone to the trouble of leaving you this in a safe deposit box if it was useless.'

'I took it to a sound technician. He said he thought the tape was too old, or damaged in some way.'

'But there's *some* sound on it, right?'

'Static.'

'It could be encrypted.'

'Could be, I guess . . . I wouldn't know.'

'Ben, the NSA came to see me after they paid you a visit. That means there's a good chance we're both going to come under surveillance. Most likely it'll start with a knock on the door from the electric company or the phone company, someone with a van and a clipboard. They'll say they need to check this or that. Or maybe they'll cause a fault in your air-conditioning. You'll call to get it fixed, and you'll get a bug up your ass.'

'Akiko, do you have the letter?' Ben asked.

'Yes.'

'Tex should see it.'

'What letter? How many more rabbits are you gonna pull out of your hat?' Tex asked.

Akiko hesitated, then took the letter from her bag. Tex took the thin folded paper and opened it up. As Ben watched him read, he saw the man's face go pale.

'Jesus Almighty,' he whispered. 'Is this genuine?'

'I met him,' Akiko said. 'He lived in my apartment building and we talked on a few occasions. I was shocked when I received the letter. I didn't know what to think, what to believe, so I hired a private detective. He confirmed that Yuudai Suzuki was stationed at Wakkanai during 1983 and worked for the Chosa Besshitsu.'

'Sounds like a breed of dog,' Ben commented.

'The Chosa Besshitsu is the Japanese NSA,' said Tex. 'I think perhaps Yuudai Suzuki was checking you out. What did you talk about, anything in particular?'

'Airplane accidents,' said Ben. 'It's a hobby of hers.' He went to the desk and scooped the heavy scrapbook left by Akiko for him to study under an arm. 'Have a look.'

He put the book on the couch beside Tex, who opened it at random to a color photo of the ill-fated Korean Air Lines 747. He turned through several pages revealing maps, articles and interviews.

'I have several more of these at home,' Akiko said.

'You talked to Suzuki about all this specifically?' Tex asked.

'A little. I can't remember the details.'

'With the letter came a check for almost $100,000,' Ben said.

Tex whistled. 'The money kinda puts this all beyond hoax territory, don't it?'

'Curtis left me almost the exact same amount,' said Ben. 'What do you think that means?'

'Curtis and Yuudai were in this together. Perhaps it means that now you and Akiko are, too.' Tex sat back. 'So let's think this through. What Yuudai says he saw is at complete odds with the official version of events. Coming from someone like Yuudai, a Chosa Besshitsu radar operator working the screens at Wakkanai on the night KAL 007 went down? That's what I call a bombshell.' Tex tapped the spool of tape with his thumb. 'The Regional Operations Control Centre at Elmendorf Air Force Base destroyed its tapes of that night.'

'Who?' said Ben. 'What?'

'The Regional Operations Control Centre at Elmendorf Air Force Base, Alaska,' said Akiko. 'There were many radars on the Alaskan coast that looked out over the Bering Sea and these were remoted to the Elmendorf facility. There was an NSA communications intelligence unit based there, and it was also home to the 6981st Electronic Security Squadron.'

Tex's mouth was slightly ajar.

'You'll get used to it, Tex,' said Ben. 'She has an encyclopedic knowledge of the subject.' He turned to Akiko. 'Go on . . .'

'The aircraft movements the radars picked up were recorded on tape at Elmendorf, the tapes examined and then recycled every thirty hours. But for some reason, on the night KAL 007 flew through its sector, the tapes were recycled—destroyed—within hours.'

'Had they not been destroyed,' said Tex, 'those tapes might have shown the aircraft flying a perfect great circle line before changing course, hooking a right and heading toward the USSR.'

'Is that actually what happened?' Ben asked.

'I don't know,' Tex replied. 'And if I did, I couldn't say.'

'You were *there*. You'd *know*.'

'Ben, as I've told you already, I can't and won't go there. And besides, we were just Air Force. We flew the plane, nothing more. The guys down the back did all the snooping. They never told us what they did or didn't see and we never asked—against the rules.'

'Is that what you think we might have here?' Akiko asked, gesturing at the spool in Tex's hand. 'A copy of the Elmendorf tape?'

'No. Your Mr Suzuki wouldn't have had access to that material. A lot of stuff was never turned over to the investigation, aside from those Elmendorf tapes. As I'm sure you know, there were tapes of the communications between the Japanese ground controllers and the 007 flight crew. Never released.'

Akiko nodded.

'There were also the communications between the Russian military controllers and their fighter pilots and the airliner—also never released.'

'Why not?' Ben asked.

'Because the Soviets didn't want something that was on their tapes revealed,' said Akiko. 'They claimed they tried to contact the plane before they shot it down. Perhaps they lied about that.'

'If you want my opinion,' said Tex, 'more than likely those tapes just showed how truly incompetent the Soviet defenses were—and that wouldn't have suited anyone's purposes, theirs *or* ours. No point arming yourself to the teeth against an enemy with no fangs of their own. And we never released anything of real recorded value either, citing reasons of national security.'

Tex went back to tapping the tape with his thumb. 'Maybe that's what we've got here—those Russian ground controllers frantically trying to contact 007 and the Koreans ignoring them. The Russians claimed they called up the plane on 121.5 and asked them to divert to a military field. They also claimed the flight crew never responded. Our side denied that ever happened. If the Russians were telling the truth, then it heavily suggests the Koreans were engaged in a little selective radio silence, playing dumb to the Russians while they acted like responsible aviation corporates to Tokyo Radio. You don't play those games unless you've got something to hide.'

'Yes, I see,' Akiko said.

'The post-crash investigation conducted by the International Civil Aviation Organization came to the conclusion that KAL 007 had blundered off course because it had no hard evidence beyond the circumstantial—no smoking gun—that proved otherwise. The ICAO, being a UN body, had no power of subpoena, no way to go hunting for evidence. And no one, the Russians or us, was prepared to release anything damning. It was the Cold War.' Tex stared at the spool as if trying to absorb its secrets by force of will. 'Do you mind if I read the letter again?' he asked.

Akiko handed it to him.

'What are you thinking?' Ben asked when he saw Tex nodding slowly to himself.

'I'm changing my mind about what this could be. Maybe this *is* the smoking gun. Everything we collected on our flights was recorded for later analysis. And it would have been the same at the Chosa Besshitsu facility at Wakkanai. Perhaps this isn't audio tape, but radar tape. I'm starting to think that, just maybe, what's on here is what Yuudai Suzuki actually *saw* on the morning of September 1, 1983—a plane heading for an emergency landing at the Soviet Dolinsk-Sokol base on Sakhalin Island.'

'Just like in the CIA report,' said Ben.

'Yeah,' Tex agreed. 'You know, I can see why Curtis kept this in a vault. There are people who'd kill for it.'

'Like the US government?' Akiko asked.

'Possibly.'

'Oh, c'mon,' Ben snorted.

'Where are you staying, Akiko?' Tex asked.

'At a hotel—the Crowne Plaza.'

'It's in Key West?'

'Yes.'

'Good. Don't go anywhere near Ben's home. It would also be best if you didn't come back here. In the meantime, I'll figure out a way the three of us can communicate with each other reasonably securely.'

'Um,' said Ben, 'aren't you overreacting a little?'

'No,' said Tex. 'I don't believe I am.'

September 1, 1983

Sea of Japan, southwest of Sakhalin Island. The 747 dived at close to its maximum speed. Vibration caused the lights across the instrument panel to shimmy like incendiary fires. Chun's knuckles were the color of bleached bone as he gripped the control wheel, his feet braced hard against the rudder pedals for additional leverage. Beside him, First Officer Sohn's face was etched with the strain induced by the physical effort required to help the captain maintain command of the mauled airliner.

Outside, the airflow was howling. A harmonic vibration rumbled up through the airframe and into the controls, informing Chun and Sohn that the plane had suffered severe damage to its control surfaces, though how bad that damage was, and which surfaces had sustained it, they wouldn't know until the plane leveled out from the dive. On the positive side, at least they were able to maintain a wings-level attitude in the dive with minimal tendency for the aircraft to roll inverted. But the vibration itself—that was worrying.

'Eighteen thousand!' yelled Sohn, his voice cracking.

'Now!' Chun called out a moment later over the shriek of high-speed air ripping past the windshields.

Both men pulled back on their yokes, employing every ounce of their strength. Slowly the nose came up and the G-forces built, squashing them down in their seats. Chun's eyes flicked to the gauges. Their speed was reducing rapidly. Engines two and four were operating within the normal parameters, the hydraulic pressure low but stable.

The G-forces peaked and then rapidly faded as they attained level flight. Chun added throttle to keep their attitude steady, but as the aircraft accelerated it began to shake violently. He reduced throttle and the ferocious vibration abated somewhat. He eased the throttles forward until the shaking started again, then backed them off a touch, the limit established.

'That's the best we can manage?' Sohn asked.

Chun nodded.

'225 knots and we cannot maintain level flight,' Sohn observed.

The captain was aware of the problem. The altimeter was registering 15,000 feet of altitude, but there was a descent rate of around 400 feet per minute. An airspeed of 225 knots was higher than the minimum speed normally required to maintain level flight, but they were still descending. There was a reason and Chun believed it had something to do with the wings, which was why he hadn't descended to the emergency height of 10,000 feet that training mandated for a cabin decompression. They might end up needing every foot of altitude they could get.

The aircraft shook under them like a car with a buckled front wheel. Chun, Sohn and Kim all knew they'd been struck by at least one missile, and probably two. Explosions and shrapnel had destroyed the number one engine on the left wing, number three engine on the right wing close to the fuselage, and caused a depressurization event. But what else?

The light on the internal phone system had been blinking almost continuously since the missile hits, accompanied by a beeping tone. Chun slid off his headset and answered it. 'Captain Chun,' he said, keeping the tone of his voice as even as he could.

'Captain! Captain!' The stewardess was shrieking at him down the line.

'Calm yourself,' he snapped. 'You are a professional.'

The rebuke had the desired effect, the woman regaining a measure of composure. 'Captain, what . . . what has happened?' she blubbered.

'Is there damage to the cabin area?'

'Yes. There is a hole. We have dead and injured.'

In his mind's eye, Chun could imagine the situation near the missile strike. The shrapnel would have been a whirlwind of steel knives, killing, slashing, maiming.

'Administer first aid as per procedures. Are there any doctors among the passengers?' he asked.

'Yes. They are doing what they can.'

'We think it was a bomb—terrorists.'

'Terrorists?!'

'I will make an announcement shortly,' he said, 'once we have assessed the damage. I will send someone back to inspect. Now, go and see to your passengers.'

'Yes, Captain!'

Chun hung up the handset.

'We have to maneuver to see what is possible,' said Sohn. 'I think they have crippled us.'

Chun agreed. 'Okay. I have the controls,' he informed the first officer.

'We were in international airspace!' Kim shouted.

'Yes. We will sue them,' Chun said over his shoulder. 'I will try a turn to the left.' He moved the wheel. The vibration through the controls increased and the aircraft made a small turn of no more than ten degrees. 'A problem there,' Chun said, speaking as much to himself as Sohn. 'Now, a turn to the right.' The aircraft banked thirty degrees to the right, but again with markedly increased vibration.

'Kim,' said Captain Chun, 'go back and have a look at the wings. Reassure the cabin crew and the passengers.'

'Reassure them yourself. If it weren't for the both of you and your fighter-pilot egos, this would not have happened. We wouldn't even be here.'

'I'll go,' said Sohn.

The captain could handle the controls by himself now that they weren't in a dive or a turn. The descent rate hadn't increased. Chun gave him a nod. 'Be quick,' he said.

The first officer released his seat restraints, removed his headset and oxygen mask, and pushed himself up and out of his seat. He stepped past the flight engineer, glaring at the man.

Chun checked the weather radar. Sakhalin Island was behind them. He began running through their options in his head. As he saw it, they had just two: ditch in the sea, or backtrack to Soviet territory and try for a landing. Neither was palatable.

Sohn moved through the upper deck of the business-class section, which now resembled a trash heap of oxygen masks and strewn personal effects. The passengers were mostly holding onto each other, or retching into the yellow cups still over their mouths. He saw one man snoring loudly, oblivious to the situation, unable to be woken, his mask hanging against his cheek and his shirt and pants stained wet with alcohol and cola. Here and there passengers looked up at the first officer with a primeval fear. Sohn did his best to soothe them. 'It's okay . . . it will be okay,' he said, patting shoulders, even though he knew in his heart it probably wouldn't be.

A flight attendant, her mascara smeared, sat in a chair rocking a young teenage girl whose body was racked by sobs.

Trash, blankets, clothing, food, headsets, books, luggage and vomit filled the aisles. Sohn tripped and slid on it all as he made his way to the staircase. He gripped the rails as the aircraft shook like a sick man having a seizure, and took the steps carefully one at a time down to the main floor. Here the flight attendants were doing the best they could, administering first aid, speaking with the passengers, trying to answer questions they didn't have answers to. Sohn was amazed at how calm some people appeared to be. The effect of naked shock, he decided, or the quiet reverence of individuals making peace with their gods, preparing to die.

'Down the back, down the back. Aircraft right,' yelled a flight attendant, rushing up to him, her eyes wide, a nasty gash on her forehead, the trail of blood smearing half her face.

Sohn kept moving, bending down occasionally as he approached the area where the wing joined the fuselage, looking out through the portholes, scouting for damage. The noise levels increased markedly here, an unmuffled scream of jet noise mixed with the violent winds. Newsprint and tissue paper danced in the air beyond the economy lavatory and galley sections, tugged at by invisible vortices.

That's when he saw the hole in the starboard side of the plane, as the flight attendant had said. His mouth opened in shock. It was a yard and a half in diameter. A bundle of clothes appeared to be caught on the perimeter of the hole. Then he realized that the bundle was half a body—a young girl—her legs chewed off by the jagged metal of the torn fuselage and the airflow. Whole rows of seats adjacent to the hole—three in total—were gone.

Sohn crossed to the opposite aisle, to the port side, and saw that the rear of the plane had been evacuated. He looked over his shoulder, back toward the galley. It had become a makeshift triage area, the flight attendants having augmented their emergency first aid training with the help of any additional chance medical experience among the passengers. There was a lot of blood. A woman was having her head bandaged by a man in a bloody shirt. Nothing Sohn could do here. He crossed back to other side of the aircraft and continued moving aft past the hole. Engine number three was visible through it. He crouched to get an angle on the wing.

'Shebal!' he said aloud when he saw the jagged tear in the upper wing surface. Motherfucker! A whole section between engines three and four was gone. He crossed again to the other side of the cabin, leaned forward on a seat back and looked out through a porthole at the left wing, and the bottom of his stomach fell away. It was difficult to see in the starlight, but the entire wing section beyond engine number one appeared to be missing. Sohn tried not to let the fear show in his face. It was astonishing that they were flying at all. He noted that the fuselage skin was punctured in numerous places with shrapnel holes and many seats were bloodstained. A number of bodies were laid out across the center seats, blood-soaked blankets covering their faces. He counted six in all. A human leg was also wrapped in a blanket, the shoe exposed. Sohn tripped on something embedded in the carpet. He bent down and discovered a long blade of dull metal—missile fragmentation material.

'What's happened?' a man shouted at him over the roar filling the cabin.

Sohn stood up. It was an American. He recognized him as the US congressman the purser had introduced him and the captain to in Anchorage when the aircraft was still on the ground. The congressman's sleeves were rolled up and bloodstained, and there were wide crimson blood spatters across the front of his white shirt. He was the man who had been bandaging the woman's head.

'Are you alright, sir?' Sohn asked.

'Yes.'

Sohn nodded and began to move. The man gripped his arm with strong fingers.

'What in God's name happened?' the congressman demanded.

'A bomb,' Sohn said, shaking his arm free. A flight attendant was running down the aisle toward them.

'First Officer Sohn,' the woman said, her face gaunt. 'First Officer Sohn, Captain Chun wants you on the flight deck immediately.'

☭

Nami's scalp throbbed dully as the bandage was carefully wound around her head and then secured by surgical tape.

'You've lost a fair bit of blood,' the man told her. 'You might feel weak when you stand up. I had to stitch your scalp back on.'

The man was older than she was, but he had a pleasant face. The white, bloodstained sleeves of his business shirt were rolled up beyond his elbows. She recognized him. 'You're the congressman.'

He nodded. 'Congressman Lawrence McDonald, at your service, ma'am.'

'One of the other passengers told me your name.'

'What's yours?' he asked.

'Nami.'

'Pleased to meet you, Nami.'

'Thank you for this,' she said, tipping her head slightly.

'I used to be a flight surgeon in the navy, though my training was in urology, not head wounds. Pity you don't have a prostate.' He gave her a smile. 'Your head wound could have been worse,' he said as he stuffed a handful of bloody gauze in a plastic bag. 'You're very lucky.'

'Yes,' she agreed and looked across at where she'd been sitting. Lucky they hadn't seated her a row further forward; lucky her seatbelt had been done up tightly; lucky that whatever had scalped her hadn't struck a few inches lower and taken the top of her head clean off.

'I wasn't even supposed to be on this flight,' he said as he gave his handiwork with the bandages a final check.

'No?'

'I was booked on a flight two days ago, but I missed it—decided to stay on in New York a couple of extra days instead.'

'I think you were meant to be on board, to help.'

'Well, you're okay now, Nami.' He put his hand up and beckoned one of the cabin crew, who hurried over. 'Go with the flight attendant. They're seating everyone from this section further forward.'

'Thank you,' she said, standing, helped by his hand under her elbow, feeling faint for a moment.

One of the flight crew appeared on the other side of the galley to inspect the damage to the aircraft.

'I'll come and check on you later,' said McDonald. 'Take these when the local anesthetic wears off in around an hour's time.' He dropped two pills snipped off the end of a blister pack into her palm. 'And if the pain persists, see your family doctor.' He smiled at her again.

Nami appreciated the gentle humor.

The congressman moved off to talk to the pilot.

Around her, passengers were dead and dying, sliced up by flying metal. It was like a battle zone. She made way for two men carrying a body between them down toward the makeshift morgue. Nami glanced at the pills the congressman had given her. An hour's time? She hoped she'd still be alive then.

'We must make a decision,' Chun said as Sohn squeezed past him, took his seat and glanced at the altimeter: 14,200 feet and descending at the same previous rate of just under 400 feet per minute.

'What is the situation back there?' Chun asked with a gesture over his shoulder.

'Bad. There's structural damage to the fuselage and we have lost wing panels between engines three and four. We may have flaps or we may not—it was hard to see. The biggest problem is the left wing outboard of engine one—it's gone.'

'Put out a mayday call,' Kim demanded. 'Do it now.'

'Shut up, Kim,' Sohn spat.

'Well, that explains our lack of turning ability,' said Chun, fighting the shaking wheel. 'How are the passengers?'

'Frightened. There are many dead and wounded.'

'Their deaths are *your* responsibility,' Kim called out.

'And yours, too, Kim,' Sohn told him. 'You agreed to this just as we did.'

'You must make a mayday call,' Kim again pleaded.

'Why? We don't need to. We can still fly,' said Sohn.

'There will be no mayday call,' commanded Chun. 'We can't acknowledge that we know where we are. What about 015? They have given position calls in our name. We will incriminate them.'

'Forget about their reputations. Our lives, the lives of our passengers, are what's important now.'

'We have spent the last half an hour ignoring Soviet calls on the emergency frequency,' Sohn reminded him. 'How do we explain that now we are suddenly able to transmit on 121.5?'

'The ruse is over,' said Kim. 'We have failed.'

'Enough!' the captain shouted. 'We have little time. Do we ditch or try to make landfall?'

'If we ditch, you *must* send a mayday call,' said Kim.

Chun and Sohn ignored him.

'What do you think?' Chun asked his first officer.

Sohn shook his head. 'If we ditch, with little control at night? Our chances of survival would be nil.'

Chun nodded. 'That's my thinking also.'

'What is this rock below us?' Sohn asked, checking the weather radar.

'Moneron Island. It's Russian. As you say, it's a rock. Nothing on it.

We can't make a runway in Japan. Sakhalin Island is our only alternative,' said Chun. 'The Soviet base at Dolinsk-Sokol.'

Sohn frowned.

Chun knew what was on his first officer's mind. 'When we land, we can plead ignorance, disorientation, like the captain and crew of KAL 902.'

'What about him?' Sohn asked, gesturing over his shoulder.

'If we make it, I'll say what's necessary,' Kim insisted. 'I don't want to go to prison.'

'We must make a turn,' Chun said. 'I'll need help. Keep a hand on the throttles.' He gripped the wheel firmly with two hands.

Sohn placed one hand on the wheel and one hand on the throttle levers.

'Keep the turn slow,' Chun said. 'No more than twenty degrees of bank.'

Sohn nodded and Chun fed in the pressure, turning the wheel. Suddenly, the aircraft banked sharply to more than forty degrees and their altimeter needle began to wind backward. The wheel shook and trembled.

'Bring it back!' Chun yelled, fighting the plane's tendency to want to roll over. 'Bring it back!'

'I'm trying!' Sohn told him, taking his hand off the throttle lever and putting his shoulder into turning the control wheel in the opposite direction to their turn.

'Throttle!' Chun bellowed.

He saw that Sohn's hand was no longer on the levers. He snatched across and jammed them forward. There was a roar of thrust and a forward surge. Chun hoped that more air over the control surfaces would give them extra authority. It worked and the plane began to pull out of its spiral, though the vibration caused by the additional speed was now almost bone-jarring. Chun reduced the throttle and the plane gradually resumed a wings-level attitude. He throttled forward to the previous setting and allowed his eyes to flick to the compass. They had lost almost 4500 feet of altitude and completed two and a half orbits of the island. But at least they were now pointed in the right direction.

The light on the intercom phone came on. Sohn picked up the receiver and cradled it under his cheek. Droplets of sweat dribbled into the holes in the plastic over the mouthpiece. Chun could hear a woman's hysterical voice coming through over the noise in the cockpit. Sohn reassured her that everything was going to be okay, and replaced the phone. Chun found himself wondering whether ignorance of their current plight would be preferable.

They were at 10,000 feet with a sink rate now of less than 300 feet per minute in the thicker air. Airspeed was also now slower at 220 knots. Chun did the math in his head. Assuming the numbers didn't change for the worse—and there was absolutely no guarantee that they wouldn't—they had a little over thirty-three minutes in the air until they hit the water. In that time they could cover 123 nautical miles. Dolinsk-Sokol was 82 nautical miles from their current position. So they were within range, though there was very little room for error, especially if they had to ride the throttles to maintain speed.

'It's going to be close,' Sohn said, arriving at the answers at the same time as Chun. 'Do we have charts for Sakhalin? Are there mountains between us and Dolinsk-Sokol? When we cross the coastline we'll have about 5600 feet of air under our wings.'

'If we still have wings,' said Kim behind him. 'And no, we have no charts for Sakhalin.'

'Sohn, take the controls,' Chun commanded. 'It's time to inform the passengers.'

'I have the controls,' the first officer confirmed.

Chun lifted the handset off its cradle, turned the switch to 'Announcement' and increased the volume. 'This is Captain Chun Byung-in speaking. A bomb has been detonated in the cabin just behind the wings. You can be assured that we have the aircraft under control. Please don your life jacket and follow the instructions of the cabin crew, who will now prepare for an emergency landing. We are confident of having you all on the ground safely in thirty-one minutes.'

The radio suddenly crackled to life: *K*** *** **ro zero se**. Tokyo R****

Air traffic control in Tokyo was trying to raise them. The message was faint, garbled. KAL 007 was very low and far beyond range.

Chun replaced the handset and constructed the reply in his head before sending it. 'Tokyo Radio. Korean Air zero zero seven.' He waited for a response. There was none.

'Tokyo Radio. Korean Air zero zero seven,' he repeated.

Silence.

Sending a radio message was futile. He glanced at Sohn. KAL 007 was now completely on its own.

'Tokyo Radio. Korean Air zero zero seven.'

'Korean Air zero zero seven, Tokyo.'

'Zero zero seven . . . ***fifteen thousand** . . . holding with rapid decompressions. Descending to one zero thousand . . .'

If there had been any doubt in Yuudai's mind about 1300 being KAL 007, the radio message edged with fear clarified it. He put out of his mind the earlier bizarre radio call from 015 claiming to be 007 cruising along on Romeo 20.

The Chosa Besshitsu radar operator watched as 007 accelerated vertically downward from 35,000 feet, the altitude numbers attached to the blip tumbling away. He saw it all on the screen, the blood thumping in his temples, keenly aware that he was witnessing hundreds of men, women and children hurtling to their deaths.

But then he realized that perhaps he was seeing something else. If the plane was falling out of the sky, the descent rate would be much higher. He scrutinized the numbers with renewed interest. And hope.

And then, miraculously, the numbers slowed and steadied at 15,100 feet. The airliner had pulled up at a breathable altitude. The 747 had not suffered a catastrophic failure of its systems or airframe as a result of the missile attack. He examined 007's heading. It was now on 220 degrees. The Russian fighter pilot had launched his missiles and one or more had struck home, but the big jumbo had survived the hits—at least for now. On his screen, he could see that the fighters had bugged out, low on fuel, the pilots certain their quarry had been obliterated.

The aircraft was continuing on its heading, now in international airspace, but far from land. How badly had the missiles damaged it?

Obviously, there was something seriously wrong with the plane—it was flying very slowly, crawling along. What were the pilots' intentions? They hadn't broadcast a mayday call.

The radar return on his screen began to turn to the north around tiny Moneron Island. It was a descending turn, a rapid one. The target continued through 360 degrees. '*Bikkuri shita!*' he murmured. Damnit! 007 was circling the island. Were they intending to ditch into the sea? If so, where was that mayday call? The airwaves were silent.

The aircraft proceeded to turn around the island, losing a lot of height. Yuudai shook his head. Ditching was not a good option. What were the pilots thinking?

'Keep turning,' he whispered, willing them to take the only real course of action open to them. The blip circled the tiny, wind-blasted island, losing more height and very rapidly. Was he witnessing the plane's final moments? And then it suddenly straightened its course and maintained altitude. A new heading of thirty-two degrees. Yes! The pilots were backtracking toward Sakhalin, into Soviet airspace.

The speaker crackled to life, the Russian Deputat controller vectoring two new fighters to search for the plane. Yuudai saw their radar returns appear on his screen as they climbed within range of the powerful Wakkanai facility, but the Korean plane had departed the area.

'*Korean Air zero zero seven. Tokyo Radio.*'

The only response was static.

'*Korean Air zero zero seven. Tokyo Radio. That's unreadable. Radio check on one three two decimal eight.*'

Tokyo Radio was trying to raise Korean Air Lines 007. There seemed to be some response, but it was unintelligible. Perhaps it wasn't 007 that had tried to respond, thought Yuudai. Tokyo Radio tried again several times but without success. And still the blip on Yuudai's radar screen flew on.

The 747 had lost around 6000 feet of altitude as it spiraled over Moneron, but now it had leveled off and the island was miles behind it. Extrapolating the heading, Yuudai could see its probable destination: the military base at Dolinsk-Sokol on Sakhalin Island.

'There is a runway there,' he said, his lips barely forming the words.

KAL 007 was managing around 220 knots, very slow by a 747's standards. It was barely making four miles per minute. On the aircraft's current heading it would be over the coast of Sakhalin in just under eight minutes.

For every agonizing second of those minutes, Yuudai watched the airliner limp toward Sakhalin. The Russian fighters were continuing to search for it, but in the wrong place. The airwaves were completely silent now, the 747's VHF and HF radio out of range, too low to be picked up by anything other than perhaps Russian ground controllers. The airliner had lost more height, bleeding it off slowly. It was at 6100 feet, maintaining the descent rate of 300 feet. Ahead were low ranges with hills topping out at 1700 feet. The crippled 747 would scrape over them with a couple of thousand feet to spare.

Yuudai willed the aircraft forward. The blip flickered, now well over Sakhalin Island. And then it disappeared. It was on his screen and then it wasn't. Yuudai was sure it hadn't exploded. The 747 had merely slipped under the curved rim of the horizon, beneath his radar coverage.

'Airman Suzuki. Airman!'

All at once, Yuudai became aware that someone was speaking to him. He turned and saw an American lieutenant colonel. A patch on the man's uniform told Yuudai the colonel's unit was the 6920th Electronic Security Squadron.

'They're going to make it,' Yuudai said. 'They've got a chance.'

'We don't know that,' the American told him.

'Yes, we do. Didn't you see?'

'I didn't see anything,' the colonel insisted.

'But—'

'I didn't see anything. And neither did you, Leading Airman. This is an international incident. We are dealing with the Soviets. You will be told what you saw.'

'Sir.'

'Secure the radar data tape of the incident and deliver it to my office immediately so that it can be provided for the investigation.'

'What investigation is that?'

'The investigation that will undoubtedly follow.'

'Yes, sir.'

When the officer had gone and his shift was over, Yuudai secured the tape.

☭

'What does that mean?' Garret wondered. 'Has it crashed?'

They'd watched the transponder code representing KAL 007 lose height over Moneron Island, a controlled descent to 15,100 feet, and then lose more height in a spiral over the speck in the Sea of Japan. It had then set a course back toward Sakhalin, while the Russians were flying around seemingly blind—chickens without heads. It was comical. Almost.

'I can't tell you with any degree of certainty,' said Hamilton, his neck cramped from looking up at the monitors, all his fingernails peeled off and dropped onto the thick sound-absorbing carpet at his feet.

'Terrific,' Garret replied.

'It could have blown up in midair, suddenly dived, or it could simply have flown below the horizon of the facility providing the feed.'

'That's Wakkanai,' said Garret, checking.

'Yes, sir.'

'Fuck,' said Garret. 'All the technology in the known universe at our disposal and we have no sure way of knowing what just happened to an object bigger than a football field and weighing 250 tons, give or take. What do we do?'

'We wait, sir. The Russian reaction will fill in the blanks.'

'They've already notified their navy to start searching the water for wreckage,' said Garret. 'Why do that?'

'They're either flying totally blind, or they've already begun a program of disinformation.'

'What do you think?' Garret asked.

'Sir, my years of operational experience tell me the Reds wouldn't know if a pogo stick had been shoved up their ass sideways.'

January 20, 2012

Key West, Florida. Ben thanked the FedEx guy and took the package inside. He cut off the top of the bag with a kitchen knife and a cell phone encased in bubble wrap dropped into his hand, along with a charger. Akiko would be receiving hers at the same time.

According to Tex, the rules were simple. When contacting each other, there would be no SMS texting or video calling, no direct references made to KAL 007, no names to be used—of each other, Curtis Foxx or Yuudai Suzuki. They weren't to store numbers in the phones' memories, and they were to wipe the phones' logs after every number dialed or received. All calls were to be under thirty seconds' duration and should be used only to establish and/or confirm meeting places and times. The cell phones used pre-paid SIM cards, the handsets were new, and everything had been paid for with cash by one of Tex's employees.

'Owning a Radio Shack has to be good for something,' Tex had said.

The phones could not be used out in the open, as they'd then be susceptible to directional listening devices and conventional surveillance techniques. It was amazing what could be done with a video camera and a lip reader, Tex told them. The NSA had vast resources and if they were seriously employed, it would be impossible to keep the phones secure. Nevertheless, if the three of them played by the rules, Tex believed they'd be safe to use for possibly up to two weeks, but only because, like a lot of mega organizations, the NSA had issues with inertia.

Tex said he would notify both Ben and Akiko when their private network was operational—their cell phones would ring twice. They were to then find a suitably private location in which to receive the call that would follow exactly half an hour later. Tex would be phoning to let them know where and when they were to meet next.

Ben unwrapped the cell and turned it on. The icon indicated that it was fully charged. He placed it back on the bubble wrap and returned to his breakfast: a boiled egg and a couple of slices of toast. He'd gone back to work, and Akiko was staying at the Crowne Plaza, taking in the sights like any tourist would. They hadn't had any contact with each other or Tex since the meeting four days ago. But that didn't mean Ben had stopped chewing things over. What did Akiko want from him? It wasn't a roll in the hay, though the thought had occurred to him—she was attractive. This went way beyond anything he'd experienced before. It was like being been pulled into something he couldn't get out of, and Curtis and Yuudai Suzuki were the ones doing the pulling.

The doorbell rang. Ben checked the time. He was due at work. Who could that be? Akiko? The bell rang a second time as he opened the door.

'Good morning. I'm Investigator Englese and this is Investigator Sherwood. We're with the National Security Agency. Mind if we come in?'

Ben blinked with surprise. It was Lana. Sherwood was the bodybuilder guy she'd told him was her brother. The lady had balls showing up, he had to give her that. He caught the initials on their shields before they were taken away: NSA against an eagle clutching something in its talons. It was a key. How appropriate. Lana was wearing a navy pantsuit and a cream-colored shirt. Her hair was brushed back off her face and behind her ears. She looked considerably different from the last time he'd seen her.

'I have to go to work,' he said.

'This won't take long.' Lana was smiling. The muscle man behind her was smiling, too.

'Just say what you've got to say and then say goodbye,' Ben told her.

Lana's smile faltered. Her bodyguard's disappeared.

'You're in a lot of trouble, Ben,' she said.

'So are you. I didn't use a condom.'

Lana glanced down, then looked up, rearmed. She knew damn well he had.

'Can I have my key back now?' Ben asked.

'That's what I want to talk to you about. Now can we go inside, please?'

'Seeing as you asked so nicely,' Ben said.

Turning, he walked inside with Lana and her partner following. He saw the new cell phone sitting on the cupboard and cursed himself for forgetting about it. Keeping his body between it and the two investigators, he moved to the cupboard and clumsily swept the opened FedEx bag and bubble wrap into the trash along with the phone and charger.

'Last Thursday you took US Airways Flight 4062 to Orlando,' Lana said, reading from a PDA. 'You took a cab to the Bank of America on Sand Lake Road. At the bank, Petulia helped you use this key to open box number 007.' The key made a tinkling sound when she placed it on the table. 'You then left the bank and returned to Key West on US Airways Flight 3073. You arrived at 4 p.m., picked up your car from the short-term parking lot and then drove to MEOW radio station. Why did you do that?'

'Why don't you tell me?' Ben said, his pulse racing, his mouth dry. He had to think fast. Had they been following him all this time? If not, how had they managed to piece together all his movements? Did they know about Akiko? 'You seem to know everything else I did,' he continued, doing his best to keep the anxiety out of his voice.

'I'm giving you a chance here, Ben,' said Lana, her eyes dead and flat. 'You risk being in a lot of trouble. You're withholding sensitive material.'

'I'm going to call my lawyer.'

'You're not under arrest, Ben. We're not cops. We just need a few answers.'

'I have no idea what material you're talking about.'

185

'Why did you go to the radio station?'

'MEOW do our advertising. I went there to congratulate the guy who wrote the ad—pat him on the back. The man's a genius.'

'You saw a man by the name of Omar Mavis. You had something you wanted him to play. A reel of tape. We want it.'

The hair on the back of Ben's neck prickled. They *knew*.

'And why's that?' he asked. 'Why's it so important?'

He examined her face, looking for the woman he'd made love to. She didn't appear to be in.

'I'm not at liberty to say,' Lana replied.

'It takes two to have a conversation. If you won't talk, then why should I?'

'This is not a conversation, Ben. This is the National Security Agency asking a law-abiding citizen to cooperate with a matter of national security.'

'Bullshit.'

'We want the tape,' Sherwood said, stepping forward.

'As you talked to Omar,' Ben said, facing Lana, 'you'd know the tape was junk. He'd have told you we played it and got nothing. I had it in my car when I met you at Captain Tony's. It was in my bag when we came back here and you fucked the daylights out of me.'

Lana's eyes sparkled dangerously.

'Watch your mouth,' warned Sherwood.

Lana raised her hand in a gesture that said, 'It's okay, I can handle this.'

'I threw the tape in the trash after you left,' Ben said.

'I don't believe you. Just hand it over.'

'It's gone to landfill, Lana. So you can go back to wiretaps or whatever it is you do in between pretending to be a Bond girl.'

The muffled sound of an old fifties wall phone rang twice.

Lana paused and turned toward the source. 'It seems your trash is ringing, Ben. Now why's that?' she asked, glancing at her Seiko to mark the call time.

September 1, 1983

Over Sakhalin Island, USSR. Nami found herself seated beside the man with the cowboy hat, up behind the galley in what she believed was the forward-most economy section. With the passengers from the rear of the plane evacuated and relocated forward, the section Nami was seated in was crowded. But the wind and engine noise weren't so bad here, and the air wasn't alive with flying papers.

The plane hit an air pocket and bounced. A collective gasp peppered with screams rippled through the passengers. The engine noise rose to a shriek and then dropped back. The ride was rough. Everyone could feel the tenuous grip the pilots had on the enormous bucking, seesawing, rolling beast. What would happen when they tried to land it? Nami wondered with a shudder.

Some passengers had horrific injuries. One woman had lost the muscle on her upper arm, peeled off like a banana skin back to the bone. She had fainted. Twenty minutes later she was still unconscious. It was probably a blessing, Nami decided. A man had lost several fingers off one hand, and she'd overheard two of the flight attendants saying that another man had lost an eye and the tip of his nose. There were other injuries, too. She wasn't sure what they were, but the congressman and another doctor were attending to many people.

Nami's head had started to throb and itch, so she'd taken the pills the congressman had given her. She glanced around, feeling as if she was floating an inch or two off her seat. She noticed that the couple across the aisle were writing farewell notes to loved ones. The woman was distressed, sobbing, clutching a photo, looking at it and then sobbing some more. Nami wanted to comfort her but she knew that the woman was beyond a few words of reassurance. She wished that she had a photo of Akiko and Hatsuto to look at. In the back of her dazed mind she recognized that the photo taken at the airport would be the last one her husband and daughter would have of her.

☭

'Korean airliner. You will follow or risking serious consequences,' the Russian voice warned in halting English.

'Korean Air 007. Wilco,' Chun answered.

'Look,' said Sohn, pointing out the window beside Chun's head at the SU-15 cruising past in the faint moonlight. They watched it maneuver into position 300 feet ahead of them. The fighter then waggled its wings up and down, establishing its authority. The Soviets would make no more mistakes. Chun radioed compliance.

The altimeter was registering a little over 4000 feet of altitude. At least the arrival of the Soviet fighter had ended their fears of having a midair with a mountain. The Russian pilot would hardly position his plane out in front and lead them into a rock face.

KAL 007's speed had dropped to 215 knots and the aircraft's nose was riding very high. If their speed dropped much further they would stall unless the flaps were lowered. Their sink rate had increased and was again nudging 400 feet per minute.

'We're seven minutes out,' said Kim.

'We need to see if we can deploy those flaps while we still have some air under them,' Chun told Sohn. 'Take a flashlight and make a final inspection. Don't be long.'

The first officer unbuckled his restraint and pushed himself out of his seat.

Chun was feeling every one of his forty-eight years, cramped with stress, unable to move. His hands were slick on the control wheel and sweat trickled down from his damp hair into his eyes and stung them. Neither he nor Sohn had any simulator experience modeled on the problems they were facing with getting the 747 safely on the ground. While he waited for his first officer to return, Chun rolled his neck and shoulders, timing the movement between the peaks of the harmonic vibration that shuddered through the controls every ten seconds or so, then reached for the handset and made a short announcement to the passengers and cabin crew.

'This is the captain speaking. In a few minutes we will land. Please assume the brace position.'

☭

A wave of fear rolled through the cabin when the captain made the announcement. Flight attendants followed it up, moving from seat to seat, hurriedly instructing the passengers on the proper body position where necessary. Several babies were crying, picking up on the changed pitch of the engines as well as the heightened tension in the air. Some of the wounded passengers were moaning.

In a private prayer, Nami said goodbye to her husband and daughter, and promised to guide them and watch over them when she crossed over and became an ancestor.

☭

Sohn hurried through the door to the flight deck, puffing, and strapped in. Chun noted how badly the man stank.

'There is a piece missing out of the flap outboard of engine three,' Sohn informed him.

'Then we can't risk deploying them. Get ready,' Chun commanded. 'You have the throttles,' he told the first officer.

Sohn readied himself.

The fighter made a gentle turn to the left, which Chun tried to mirror, the big 747 coming around slowly until they'd settled on the SU-15's revised course. Ahead, laid out on the dark ground, he saw the unmistakable lights of a runway threshold burning brightly in the clear, cold pre-dawn air. He saw the nozzle of the fighter's engine glow with a lit afterburner, and in an instant the SU-15 was gone, vanished into the night.

The 747 began to shake violently and Chun fought to hang onto the control wheel. And then, just as quickly as it began, the vibration stopped.

'The undercarriage,' he said. 'Let's get it down.'

Sohn pulled the lever. The aircraft rocked as the landing gear deployed. Their speed was reducing, but they were still coming in hot. At their current rate, they would flare over the runway threshold at 190 knots, cut the throttles and touch down on the runway at a fast 160 knots.

The vibration returned, rattling the control wheel, but Chun was expecting it this time. His fear of it was gone.

The runway ahead was brightly lit. Down the far end, red, yellow and blue emergency beacons gathered in a concentrated knot. The red and yellow revolving lights of firefighting equipment dotted the open ground on either side of the runway. There would be a reception committee, thought Chun, but it would hardly be welcoming.

'Throttle,' he commanded as they cleared the perimeter fence.

Sohn pulled the throttles back to idle and a calm enveloped the aircraft. Without flaps, the nose was riding so high that they flew blind for several moments.

☭

Everything became still and quiet. Then the plane's tires lightly touched down on the runway, like someone dipping a toe in the water before diving in. The silence was ended abruptly by the thump of the undercarriage rumbling over runway cracks, the scream of reversing engines, the wail of brakes being brutally applied. The deceleration forces squeezed Nami hard against her lap restraint. They were landing very fast.

A tortured groan from the brakes penetrated the howl of the reversing engines and the tires thumping over the joints in the runway. But then the plane slowed, the danger evaporated, and Nami lifted her bandaged head, amazed to be among the living. Other passengers looked around, like bewildered survivors of a violent earthquake. Emergency service vehicles flashed by the portholes, momentarily filling the cabin with their multicolored lights. Nami felt pure joy welling up inside her. She was alive. She had lived. She would see Hatsuto and Akiko again, get to hold them, kiss them.

Here and there, applause broke out, thanking the skills of the captain and crew as well as the gods for sparing them a fiery death. Others hugged each other and sobbed with relief. They had all been flown to the gates of hell, and given a reprieve.

The massive plane slowed remarkably quickly, took a sharp turn off the runway, then came to a bucking stop, the brakes giving a final tortured squeal. The flight attendants raced for the emergency exits, threw back the levers, pushed the hatches open and activated the emergency slides.

Cabin staff began herding the passengers toward the exits, forbidding them to carry hand luggage. Surprisingly, there was no panic. Nami felt a hand under her armpit, lifting her up. It was the American with the hat.

'Here, let me help you, ma'am,' he said.

He and Nami joined the queue and shuffled toward the door.

The flight attendant asked her if she would be okay going down the slide. Still dazed, Nami said that she would. The attendant reminded her to fold her arms across her chest, helped her to the door, and then Nami found herself sliding toward the ground. A soldier in uniform with a rifle slung over his shoulder helped her to her feet and pointed at a group of passengers assembling beyond the wingtip.

As she walked, Nami looked back over her shoulder at the plane. The engine nearest the cabin was charred and smoking. A fire truck began spraying the ruined engine with foam while another approached the aircraft's nose. It pulled up below the forwardmost door and extended its ladder toward the opening. Three men with machine guns scaled it, the man leading holding a pistol, and disappeared inside. A few moments later, Nami saw the pilot and his crew pushed down the slide at gunpoint. They were met at the bottom by more armed soldiers who roughly escorted them to a van, put their hands on their heads and pushed them inside. With an urgent tire squeal, the van drove off into the cold night.

The sight of the flight crew being manhandled like criminals made Nami stop. A soldier beside her gave her a gentle push with the side of his rifle to get her walking again.

'What the hell's going on here?' said the American with the hat beside her.

Banks of harsh lights came on, flooding the plane with a brutal glare. More truckloads of soldiers arrived, disembarked, and formed up between the plane and its passengers.

Nami and the American continued moving toward the assembled passengers, who, Nami realized, were surrounded by soldiers and snarling dogs.

The congressman who had treated her was shouting at one of the soldiers who had pushed an old man so hard that he had tripped and fallen. The soldier suddenly pulled out his pistol and aimed it at the congressman's forehead with an outstretched arm. There was a collective gasp and a hush came over the crowd.

A man of about forty years of age, wearing a uniform with braid and ribbons and a high-peaked cap, walked up beside the soldier, placed his gloved hand over the pistol's barrel and lowered it. Words were exchanged between the two men in a language that Nami couldn't understand. The soldier holstered the weapon, saluted, then took a step back.

'Jesus,' the American whispered, his face ashen. 'Where the hell are we? I just noticed—there's a a goddamn hammer and sickle on that guy's cap!'

The officer climbed onto the hood of a nearby truck, and another officer accompanying him jumped up on the running board.

'If I could have your attention,' the officer on the roof said in passable English, his words translated into Korean by the man on the running board. 'Until further notice, you are all under arrest as enemies of the Union of Soviet Socialist Republics. The charge is spying. Until we can decide what to do with you, you will be kept under guard and tight security. You will remain silent. I warn you now—talking among yourselves will be severely punished. You can expect to be interviewed personally one by one. If anyone has anything to confess before being interviewed, it would be wise to come forward now and talk to me. I am Colonel Valentin Korolenko. I am an officer in the Komitet Gosudarst-vennoi Bezopasnosti. You may know of this as the KGB.'

September 1, 1983

NSA HQ, Fort Meade, Maryland. The digital clock indicated 19:31 GMT. Garret had run out of Chesterfields again, having chain-smoked the last six. A little over an hour had passed since the Soviet pilot had announced, 'The target is destroyed.' Garret checked his watch: 3:31 p.m. It would be 12:31 p.m. in Santa Barbara where Clark, Meese and Bilson were staying. All three men were occupying rooms at the Pacific Biltmore Hotel, the President staying twenty miles down the road at his ranch. Garret picked up the phone, nervous as hell, and placed the call.

'Bilson,' said the voice.

Garret put it on speaker and hung up the handset. 'It's Garret.'

'We expected to hear from you sooner.'

'The situation's complicated, Des. We have two possible scenarios.'

'What?'

'We don't yet know for certain exactly what happened out there, sir,' said Hamilton, stepping in. 'The Soviets waited till the last moment, till 007 was in international airspace, fired two missiles into it, then let it alone to die. By the time they came back to finish the job, they couldn't find it. We tracked the plane till we lost the contact. The options are that it either exploded in midair or it landed.'

'Landed?'

'On Sakhalin Island. Our best guess is the Soviet base at Dolinsk-Sokol,' said Garret. 'There's an 8000-foot runway there.'

'You're fucking kidding me?'

'The Russians immediately launched a search and rescue effort off the coast,' said Garret. 'We believe they thought they splashed it.'

'Jesus . . .'

'A jumbo's harder to kill than we thought,' observed Hamilton.

'Remind me to call Boeing and fucking congratulate them,' replied Bilson. 'Jesus Christ . . .'

The blinking green cursor on the computer screen by Garret's elbow suddenly raced along, laying down half a dozen sentences.

'Des, just a moment. A prelim's just come in from South Korea.' He read the curt decryption and passed on the gist of it. 'It's an unconfirmed report out of Seoul. Sources are quoting the CIA. 007 is down on Sakhalin. The passengers and crew are safe.'

'Our CIA?'

'That's what it says.'

'Jesus, I'd better go brief the Judge,' said Bilson. 'The shit is seriously going to hit the fan.'

'Des, before you go, what happened to the Critic?'

'Forget about the Critic, Roy. We followed the protocol. President Reagan will find it when he goes through his papers once he's home from vacation.'

'It was sent to the White House?'

'That's the protocol. We checked the fine print. Some low-ranked bureaucrat will get rapped over the knuckles for not using his initiative.'

'Okay.'

'Don't sweat the small stuff, Garret. Criticoms were introduced as a back channel to stop an inadvertent nuclear war. You got mushroom clouds blooming over Maryland?'

'No, sir.'

'I rest my case. Send me a summary.'

'You'll get it in five.'

'Anything comes up, let me know, pronto.'

'The damn Contras are going to sit around drinking tequila, or whatever it is they drink down there, until they see some zeros in their bank accounts,' said Meese. The President's chief counselor sipped his late lunch and watched the ice cubes reorganize themselves in the bottom of his glass. 'We can't very well expect them to throw coconuts at the commies.'

'No, I guess not.' Clark was contemplative. No money, no weapons, no war. A simple equation; one Congress understood all too well. There was a knock on the door. 'Come!' he said, raising his voice. The door opened. It was Des. 'Well?' Clark asked.

'The Soviets are more pathetic than we thought,' said Bilson.

'Why?' asked Meese.

'According to the CIA, it landed on Sakhalin Island, at the Soviet Dolinsk-Sokol base. Passengers *and* crew safe.'

'Aw, shit,' said Meese.

Clark felt a surge of anger. 'What happened?'

'It was intercepted. The Soviets fired two missiles, which did enough damage to force the plane down. Chun must have chosen to backtrack to Sakhalin rather than ditch.'

'Jesus,' Meese said.

Clark admonished him with a glare. 'What are the Soviets saying?' he asked.

'Nothing yet, except that they're conducting search and rescue in the Sea of Japan.'

'That's odd,' said Meese. 'If they've got the plane, why would they do that?'

'Garret thinks they thought they shot it down, and then 007 just turned up over Sakhalin, slipped under their radar.'

'So what have we got?' said Clark.

'A damn cluster fuck,' Meese commented. 'What about the Japs? Have they released anything?'

Bilson referred to the notes sent through by Garret and Hamilton. 'The Japan Defense Agency is saying nothing, and neither is Korean Air Lines.'

'Let's keep it that way,' said Clark. 'We want them following our lead on this.'

'As far as anyone knows,' continued Bilson, 'KAL 007 is delayed. In practice, what the JDA has done is start conducting a search and rescue operation east of Hokkaido.'

'East of Hokkaido?' asked Meese. 'Why the hell there?'

'Because 007 gave its position report at waypoint NOKKA, which is east of Hokkaido, moments *after* it was hit by missiles.'

'How is that possible?' asked the counselor.

'KAL 015 was transmitting 007's position reports. 015 didn't know 007 had been struck by a missile because they were beyond 007's radio range.'

'Shit.' Meese slumped into an armchair. 'We're fucked.'

'We need to get a grip on all this,' said Clark. 'It's bad, but not catastrophic. The facts are that the Russians shot the plane down, a 747 full of innocent people. They're searching the Sea of Japan. We'll search alongside them and so will the Japanese.'

'What about the Russians?' asked Bilson.

'What about them?' Clark replied.

'They're going to turn up with the plane and the passengers.'

'We don't know that. They won't say anything till they know what cards they hold. It all depends on what Moscow thinks and the Russian Far East is nine time zones away. There'll be confusion. All the Soviets will be certain of is that they shot down a plane that overflew some of their most secret facilities. What we need to do is control the flow of information from our side. The CIA report will leak—has leaked—but we need to make sure it stays unconfirmed. That will keep a lid on things for a while—the press won't want to go public till they can confirm it as fact. And let's make sure we have no satellites passing overhead. Whatever's going on down on the ground on Sakhalin . . . The point is, we want deniability.'

Bilson and Meese both agreed.

'In the meantime, we need to mobilize our troops,' Clark continued.

'The army?' asked Meese.

'No. Get Bill Casey on the line, as well as Shultz and Eagleburger.'

Bilson jotted down 'CIA', 'Secretary of State Shultz' and 'Lawrence S, Undersecretary, Political Affairs'.

'We'll also need a point man from State. Who's on the team?' Clark asked.

'How about Richard Burt?' Meese suggested.

'Yeah, Dick's a good man. He's perfect. The State Department, rather than Defense, is going to have to take the lead on this.'

'What are we going to tell them?' Meese asked.

'What's in our best interests for them to know: that the Evil Empire is even more bloodthirsty than any of us supposed—they've just shot down a civilian airliner full of women and children that innocently strayed off course into their airspace.'

'What about the President?' asked Bilson.

'What about him?' Clark replied.

'Shouldn't we inform him?'

'Why? Officially, *we* don't know anything yet. When we know for certain how monstrous those Soviets really are, that's when President Reagan will be briefed. Besides, right at the moment he's taking an afternoon nap.'

☭

Once the passengers had disembarked, the plane was pulled off the runway onto the grass. Soldiers climbed all over it with netting, gray blankets and painted plastic.

Nami shivered violently, the cold seeping into the bandages and the gash in her scalp. The pain was becoming excruciating, causing tears to well into her eyes. The soldiers were forcing the passengers and cabin crew to sit on the freezing tarmac while they removed the six deceased and loaded them onto a truck. People like herself, with wounds or injuries, were not getting treatment.

The hand luggage was next off the plane, and lined up in rows opposite the passengers. One passenger at a time was made to get up and identify what was theirs. Two of the KAL cabin crew had been drafted into assisting the Soviets with this task, going through the passenger manifest and pointing at the passengers, starting with the people traveling first class.

'The bastards want our passports,' whispered Lawrence McDonald sitting beside Nami, his teeth chattering in the cold morning air. 'They want to see who's fallen into their laps.'

Nami was suddenly frightened for McDonald. He was right. What would the Russians do with him when they learned he was a United States congressman?

A soldier detached himself from two others, walked up to McDonald and drove the butt of his rifle into the side of the man's face. He slumped against her.

'No talk,' the soldier shouted.

From the corner of her eye, Nami saw both the flight attendants pointing in her direction. 'No,' she said quietly, shaking her head, but the soldiers approached her anyway. They lifted the congressman to his feet and he swayed unsteadily. A soldier urged him forward with a push. The congressman staggered, then regained his footing and moved toward the bags while the flight attendants cowered beside the Russians.

☭

The telephone conference call had concluded and only the secretary of state, George Shultz, remained on the line. When briefed, everyone could see the opportunity that the Soviets had just handed them. It was a gift, as Ed Meese had succinctly put it.

'It's just you and me now, George,' said Clark, glancing at Meese sitting across the table. 'Tell me what's on your mind.'

'So what's *really* going on here, Judge?' asked the secretary of state.

'What we've got, George, is what we all agreed—the biggest single public relations opportunity to have come along in years. And if we manage it correctly, we can punish the Soviet Union like never before.'

'That's not what I mean. You know as well as I do that 747s don't fly hundreds of miles off course, let alone just happen to pass within spitting distance of the Soviet's most secret submarine base.'

'I'm not sure I know what you're implying, George. Would you care to speak openly of your concern?'

'Judge, let me just say that this had better turn out as planned.'

'Planned? I'm sorry?'

'I'm not stupid, Judge. Give me some credit. Just promise me we're not going to have another Powers/U2 event on our hands. Something like that could set us back years.'

Clark remembered the incident from 1960 like it was yesterday, and Shultz was right—there were similarities. Gary Powers, flying a U2 spy plane over the USSR, had been shot down. Washington denied all knowledge of the flight, at least until Moscow produced wreckage from the plane as well as Powers himself and paraded him in front of television cameras.

'There's a big difference between the Powers incident and flight 007.'

'And what's that?'

'There weren't any babies on board that U2, George.'

Garret had been locked in Situation Room A since KAL 007 had disappeared. Information from sources all over the US, Japan and South Korea was flooding in by the moment, much of it contradictory. The Russians were denying they'd shot the plane down, which was the most interesting development. The Japanese had called off the search in the seas east of Hokkaido, centered on the NOKKA waypoint, and were sending ships to search the waters around Moneron Island, an uninhabited rock in the Tartar Strait. If Garret hadn't known better, from everything going on he'd have believed Moneron was where 007 actually *had* come down.

'Roy, we've just received a call from someone in the State Department. They've had an enquiry from a guy called Tommy Toles,' said Hamilton.

'Who's he?'

'Toles says he's the press secretary for a congressman by the name of Lawrence Patton McDonald.'

'Oh, yeah, I know McDonald.'

'Seems the congressman missed an earlier flight and ended up on 007.'

'No way,' Garret snorted. 'I don't remember seeing his name on the manifest.'

'That's because it wasn't *on* the manifest,' said Hamilton. 'The passenger list we had was updated seventy-two hours prior to the flight's departure. McDonald's arrangements were rescheduled *forty-eight* hours prior. Looks like the congressman has just been drafted into the front lines of the Cold War.'

☭

Colonel Valentin Korolenko opened the door to the office being used to question the passengers, many of whom had been overcome by the stress of their situation, and the stench of vomit rushed out and assaulted his nostrils. The officer behind the desk, a younger KGB man with the rank of lieutenant, stood and snapped to attention.

'Is that his passport, Lieutenant Illich?' Korolenko asked, gesturing at the document the lieutenant was flipping through.

'Yes, Comrade Colonel.' The lieutenant presented the blue cover to his superior officer. Clearly visible in silver was the seal of the United States of America: a bald eagle, bolts of lightning in one talon and an olive branch in the other. Above it were the words 'Diplomatic Passport'.

'I'll handle this interview.'

'Of course, sir,' said the lieutenant.

He picked up his cap and moved smartly to the door as the colonel took the chair behind the desk.

'Bring him in,' said Korolenko.

'Immediately, Comrade Colonel,' said Lieutenant Illich. He turned and strode out the door.

Korolenko opened the passport, reviewed the owner's details, and then flicked through it, noting entry and exit stamps for a number of countries including the United Kingdom, West Germany, Venezuela, Iran, Italy and France. He felt vaguely offended by the freedom that allowed someone to move about so easily. It was an uncomfortable emotion, tinged with envy, and he shut it down as he closed the passport.

There was a slight commotion in the hallway outside the office. Two stocky, broad-faced enlisted men from air force security brought in the prisoner and sat him forcibly in the chair facing Korolenko. They then took a step backward.

'I demand to see a representative of the government of the United States of America,' the prisoner said.

Korolenko ignored the plea and took a moment to examine the man seated opposite him. His face was round, a well-fed face, an old scar from his left nostril to the top of his lip. A good-looking man, Korolenko thought, made for television.

He opened the passport. Lawrence Patton McDonald, born in the state of Georgia, April 1, 1935. That would make him forty-eight years of age. Korolenko glanced up. Despite his disheveled appearance, the man looked more like a young forty year old. He estimated the man to be around 1.8 meters tall, although with his slouched and seated posture it was difficult to be sure. Weight: a little over 105 kilograms. There was much dried blood on his white shirt. A dark red welt spread across the right side of his face and black blood had crusted on his ear. Korolenko doubted the blood on his shirt was a result of the blow to his face—there was too much of it. The look in the man's dark eyes was intelligent and defiant; whatever he'd received the blow as punishment for, it hadn't intimidated him one bit.

'Lawrence Patton McDonald,' said Korolenko, reading aloud from the passport. 'Patton, the US general. Any relation?'

'I demand to see a representative of the government of the United States of America.'

'Please just answer my questions.'

'You have no right to hold us. One of your men assaulted me. What you're doing here is wrong. We have done nothing wrong.'

'Are you related to Patton, the famous general?'

The question appeared to faze the American, or perhaps it was Korolenko's persistence or his reluctance to respond to the American's demands.

'A cousin,' McDonald said finally.

'You are a cousin of General Patton's? Well, I am impressed.' Korolenko picked up the passport again and flicked the pages past his thumb. 'You are traveling with a diplomatic passport. Why is that?'

'Where have we landed?' McDonald asked.

'I will ask you once again. Why are you traveling with a diplomatic passport?'

There was a knock on the door.

'What?' Korolenko called out, irritated by the interruption.

'Comrade Colonel, we have his luggage here.'

'Bring it in,' said Korolenko.

The door opened and the air force security man brought in three suitcases—one large, one smaller and one hand-luggage sized. It was a matching set. Black. The padlocks securing the zippers had been cut. One of the men passed Korolenko a thin black leather satchel.

'This is your luggage?' the colonel asked.

'Again, I demand that you contact a representative of the government of the United States of America.'

Korolenko noted the man's sudden anxiety. It had something to do with the satchel. He stifled a yawn, opened it and sifted through the documents, most of which appeared to be travel related. He pulled out an itinerary and the hint of a smile animated his lips, dry and cracked by the cold. This McDonald had every reason to be anxious.

'So, *Congressman* Lawrence McDonald, I asked if this is your luggage?'

McDonald refused to answer.

'Well, is it?'

'Yes,' he said finally.

'You are a US congressman?'

'I demand—'

The colonel cut him off, raising his hand. 'Yes, yes, of course. You are injured? I will get a doctor to see to your wounds.'

'I'm okay, but there are people out there who are not. And I must *strongly* protest your treatment of all the passengers. Keeping them out there in the cold all this time is—'

'Do not tell me how to act in my own country, especially toward spies, Congressman.'

'Spies? We're not spies!'

'I trust your stay with us will not prove overly stressful,' Korolenko said, tempering his natural inclination to get up, walk around the desk and smack the arrogance out of the American.

'Will you contact the US government?'

'There's no need. I'm sure your government, particularly your CIA, already knows of your whereabouts.'

'And where's that?'

'In a great deal of trouble, Congressman.'

The colonel directed a slight movement of his head at one of the security men. Both immediately stepped forward and lifted the American to his feet. In Russian, he told them, 'Keep him segregated from the rest. I do not want him damaged further. And if he won't stop making demands, tape his mouth.'

The security men hustled the American from the room, lifting him between them. Korolenko skimmed through the passport again and then eyed the man's luggage, wondering what other interesting items it might contain. Before taking the interrogation further, it would pay dividends to know more about the congressman.

January 24, 2012

NSA HQ, Fort Meade, Maryland. Investigator Lana Englese had too much on her plate, simple as that. There were other cases she and Sherwood were working on: backing up the FBI's investigations into a Colombian cocaine lord who appeared to be getting some helpful assistance from a mole within the Drug Enforcement Agency down in Texas; an ongoing investigation into the unlawful financial activities of Kim Jong-il, the crazy-ass leader of North Korea, and his regime; and a program to upgrade and improve the security of the US Navy Pacific Fleet's signals intelligence. And that was just the big stuff. The rats and mice—paperwork mostly—also took a big chunk of time. So it had been four days since she and Sherwood had interviewed Ben and there hadn't been time to follow up on it.

Lana settled herself into the co-pilot's chair beside Saul Kradich, the operator she'd been allocated. She liked Kradich, though Sherwood couldn't stand to be in the same room with the guy—one of those stupid alpha male things, probably. She noted that Kradich was still wearing the ratty Indians ball cap from the other day and experienced an uncomfortable flash of him showering in it.

'Where's Sherwood Forest today?' Kradich asked.

'Investigator Sherwood's busy with other cases.'

'That's a shame,' said Kradich with zero sincerity as Lana handed him the code for his time, the case code and her swipe card. 'So, what are we doing?'

'Tracing a call made to a cell phone.'

He entered her codes into the system and swiped the card. 'What's the number of the cell that received the call?'

'I don't know.'

'Oh. I don't suppose you've got the cell's serial number?'

'No.'

'A make or model number?'

Lana shook her head.

'Hmm, then not so easy. Is there *anything* you can give me?'

'The cell received the call from the number at exactly 8:12:15 a.m. on Friday, January 20. The receiving handset was stationary at 49 Elizabeth Street, Key West.'

'Did you log the time with that wristwatch?'

'Yes.' Lana showed it to him, a Seiko.

'How often do you adjust the time? Does it gain or lose?'

'I never change it,' she said.

He checked its accuracy against the cesium clock and found the timepiece was running two minutes and twenty-one seconds fast.

'So then, going with the assumption that it keeps *consistent* time, your actual inbound call time was at approximately 8:09:54,' he said, jotting down the numbers on the back of a folder. 'Any idea who the carrier of the receiving handset was?'

'Nope, sorry,' said Lana.

'Was the call answered?'

Lana wasn't sure about that, either. When the cell rang, Ben had reached into the trash, picked it out and turned his back on her. The ringing stopped almost instantly, which meant he could have ended the call. But he could also have sent it to a mailbox. In fact, thinking about it, there were a few options. He could even have accepted the call but not spoken to the caller.

'I can't be sure,' she said. 'Is it important?'

'No, not essential, but knowing the call duration would help narrow the search field. Hmm . . .' Kradich rubbed his chin and then started

206

working the control screen, a thin panel of gray-colored glass roughly the dimensions of a sheet of paper. Within a few moments, a map of Key West came up on the wall-mounted laser panels, covered with interlocking circles. 'Those circles represent the footprints of the base transceiver stations for cell phone communications on Key West.' Kradich tapped in a command and the street map of Key West overlaid the circles. 'Looks like 49 Elizabeth Street is serviced by two BTSes. Now, what we need is access to the mobile switching center for each BTS.' His fingers went to work again on the control screen, coaxing, cajoling. 'Okay,' he said, speaking as much to himself as to Lana. 'Fortunately, both BTSes use the one MSC. Yes, here we go. It's a Nextel MSC. I don't think they'll mind if we just lift up the lid and take a peek inside.'

'What are you looking for exactly?'

'Calls transmitted to cell phones serviced by those two base transceiver stations. We'll look at calls transmitted to cell phones in our footprint ten seconds either side of our target time of 8:09:54.'

He pulled up a menu of reference codes from the NSA's vast databank and entered one of them into a box. This activated a Nextel-branded index, which popped up with lists of acronyms that meant absolutely nothing to Lana.

'So, I've established the criteria and activated the search engine and we should get . . . Yeah, here we go.' Fifteen nine-digit numbers appeared in one box, matched with fifteen nine-digit numbers in an adjacent box. 'If we were doing this for a block in Manhattan, the phone numbers would be in the thousands. These are the numbers that went through the mobile switching center during our search period. The numbers in the left-hand box are the inbound calls, by the way. On the right are the phone numbers of the receiving handsets. You recognize any of them?'

'No. How do we eliminate them to get the one we want?' asked Lana.

'I'm not sure, but we could go out to dinner tonight and discuss it?'

Lana gave Kradich a smile. 'I never date Agency people. It's a rule.'

She'd broken a long-standing rule with Harbor and now she'd become almost obsessed with this KAL thing. See what happens, she told herself.

'You're a nice guy, Saul. And you play that control screen like Beethoven, but let's just keep it professional. Maybe we could go for coffee sometime.'

'Okay, not quite a rejection. I'll settle for that. So, let's do a search on these phone numbers and see which are on contract to a carrier and which are pre-paid. Is it likely your target is using a cell in the hope of keeping the calls low profile?'

'It's probable, but I'm not certain.'

'Hmm . . . then maybe we shouldn't use that filter. We risk eliminating the number we want.' Kradich picked up his pencil and tapped a beat on the front edge of the bench to help organize his thoughts. 'So, fifteen little Indians hanging on the wall. I don't suppose you have any idea of the general area the inbound call might have originated from?'

'No, that's why we're tracing it,' she said, working hard to keep the 'duh' out of her voice.

'By general area, I mean North America, Antarctica . . . ?'

Lana shook her head. 'No. But there's a good chance it was a new cell.' Someone had sent Ben the phone and he'd tried to hide it, dumping it in the trash as they walked in. She had glimpsed bubble wrap, cardboard packaging, plastic and a FedEx envelope stuffed in there too.

'A *new* cell?' Kradich brightened, the suggestion prompting a fresh line of thought. 'Hell, why didn't you say?' He hunched over the keyboard. 'We eliminate all phone numbers first registered on the system more than a week ago . . . And Bingo was his name,' he exclaimed when all the numbers except one in each box disappeared. 'In case you've forgotten, the number on the left belongs to the phone on Elizabeth Street.' His fingers continued working. A new window appeared on the laser screen. 'You have to thank the rules that govern the buying of new cell phones. Before they came along, you didn't need to provide ID. In some states now it's easier to buy a gun than a cell.' A name and an address appeared in a separate box. Saul read it out. 'The cell that called the one in Key West was recently bought by Tony Park of 3 Zambezi Drive, Pinecrest, Florida. Do you know him?'

Lana frowned. 'No. There's no connection for me with that name.'

Kradich picked up his pencil and sat way back in his chair, assuming the position of an astronaut on a launch pad. He tapped out a beat on his thigh with the pencil, his body language saying, 'Where to from here?'

Lana had never heard of Tony Park, but there had to be some connection with Ben. 'How many cell phones does this Park guy own?'

Saul Kradich shrugged, reached forward and removed the control panel from its dock. He then reassumed the takeoff position, this time with the panel in his lap. 'Four,' he said after a short while. 'He has one on contract to Verizon, which he's had for fourteen months . . . Well, look at this. The other three are pre-paid Virgin Mobile, which he bought last week on Thursday, January 19. And look here at one of the allocated phone numbers—it's another of our little Indians, the number of the cell phone at 49 Elizabeth.'

Lana felt a surge of excitement. She was on to something. 'Where were the phones purchased?'

It took Kradich only a handful of seconds to come up with the answer. 'Radio Shack, Homestead.'

Lana smiled. A connection to Tex Mitchell. 'Let me take a guess that Mr Park is employed at the Homestead Radio Shack.'

Kradich tapped away, searching the tax files of all the store's employees. And there he was—Tony Park. 'You're good at this, aren't you?' he said.

'Good at guessing,' she said.

Tex had probably given the money to Park to buy the phones and use his driver's license or social security card to minimize the chances of detection. She may have been right or wrong about that, but it hardly mattered. The important thing to note was that Ben and Tex were communicating, and trying to keep their communications secret from the NSA.

'Has either handset dialed the remaining cell?' A third cell indicated the probability of a mystery third person.

In a moment, Kradich had the answer. 'Your third cell received a call at around the same time as the Elizabeth Street cell on Key West—at 8:12:32 a.m. on the 20th. And lookee here . . . the call went through an adjacent base transceiver station on Key West. Seems your cell owners are neighbors.'

'Oh, I almost forgot. Here are your new phones,' Tex said, pulling a plastic bag out of the Silverado's center console as he drove.

'You really think it's necessary to ditch the other ones?' Ben asked, taking the Samsung labeled with his name on a Post-it, and passing Akiko's to her in the back seat.

'You said the first thing the NSA investigator did was look at her watch when I called you.' Tex checked the rear-view mirror. 'She did that for a reason. If the NSA knows the time I called you, I have no doubt the agency could find my cell's phone number. From there you can bet our network would be compromised. Calling me at work and using a payphone to fill me in on your latest NSA visit tells me you have good instincts, Ben.'

'Well, maybe my instincts know something I don't. I can't help thinking we're being overly dramatic.'

'This is not paranoia, this is playing it safe. Those replacement handsets look tired because they're second-hand units. The SIMs are pre-paid from different carriers, bought for us by different people I know. The same rules apply about not sending texts and so forth. We have to assume we're now under the NSA's microscope given the interviews we've both had, and especially your *hands-on* experience with whatshername.'

'Lana,' said Ben.

Tex glanced across at him with a raised eyebrow. 'Yeah, Lana.'

Ben looked out the window at the suburban street. The Port Charlotte neighborhood felt small town—not rich, not poor. 'How're you doing back there, Kiko?' he asked.

'Good. I'm sightseeing,' she said. 'None of this is in the brochures.'

'We're here,' said Tex, pulling over past a driveway blocked by a substantial steel gate. A heavy steel-mesh fence and a thick screen of pines secured the rest of the perimeter.

They got out of the Chevrolet and walked to an entrance gate. Tex pressed a button on the security system.

'Yes?' said a female voice.

'It's Tex.'

There was a buzz and Tex pushed the gate open.

At the head of the pathway stood a large, rambling single-story weatherboard home painted gray with a white trim. A flock of pink flamingos stood on wire legs in the middle of a manicured lawn.

'Remember what I told you about Lucas. Try not to stare. And don't let his appearance fool you. Lucas Watts is one of the smartest people I've ever known.'

'Why are all the windows blacked out?' Ben asked as they approached the house.

'Lucas has privacy issues.'

'Really?' said Ben. 'Never would have guessed.'

The steps up to the front entrance had been replaced by a ramp. Tex pressed the button beneath a small television screen on the wall then waved at the surveillance camera when a green light glowed.

A few moments later the door opened, held by an extremely attractive tall woman dressed in navy slacks and a light blue shirt. Her straw-blonde hair was worn in a thick plait that ended just above her waist. Ben guessed she would have been in her early thirties.

'Hey, Vanessa,' said Tex, giving her a quick hug. 'How are you?'

'I'm fine, Tex. You?'

'All good, all good. And the man?'

'He's big, he's bad. Come on in. We were talking about you just the other day. I'll tell him you're here.'

'She's a *nurse*,' Tex whispered and, by way of explanation, added a wink.

Inside, the house was gloomy. Vanessa switched on a light as she disappeared around a corner. The floor was pale green and white checked linoleum. The hallway was wide and the doorway also appeared to be far wider than usual. The air smelled of powerful artificial fresheners and something vaguely animal. The sound of electric motors whirred, getting louder, and the largest human being Ben had ever seen came through a doorway down the hall in a motorized wheelchair. The heavy vehicle turned through ninety degrees like a tank, the wheels on one side stopping, then motored forward. Tex had told them not to stare but it was impossible to look anywhere else. Ben estimated the man's weight at around 700 pounds, and he filled the wheelchair the way a pudding filled a bowl.

'Hey, Lucas, my man. Wuss happening?' said Tex.

'Oh, you know, not much—just sitting around thinking up ways to bring the world to its knees.'

And chomping through enough food to sustain the state of Florida for a month, thought Ben.

Vanessa made an appearance behind Lucas, her shoes squeaking on the floor. 'Just holler if you need something,' she said as she walked into another room and closed the door behind her.

Ben could think of a few things, but chose to keep them to himself.

'So, Tex, who do we have here?' Lucas asked.

'This is Akiko.'

'Pleased to meet you, sir,' said Akiko, bowing.

'Akiko, delighted,' Lucas said, giving her a small nod. 'This is me bowing to the floor, by the way.'

Akiko smiled and said, 'Thank you for helping us.'

'Well, that remains to be seen, doesn't it? But any friends of Tex's . . .' Lucas manipulated a joystick and motors whirred, angling the wheelchair at Ben.

'And this is Ben,' said Tex.

'Ben,' Lucas repeated, holding out his hand.

Ben took it and was surprised at how small the hand was, like a boy's, except that it was attached to a thick column of white wobbling flesh, the fingers damp with sweat.

'Well, they passed the test. Very little staring. Tex, you obviously warned them.'

'Being somewhat larger than life, Lucas, you tend to overwhelm people.'

The wheelchair spun around and began moving down the hall. 'Can I get Vanessa to fix you folks anything to drink or eat?'

Both Ben and Akiko shook their heads.

'We're okay,' Tex said.

'Well then, follow me.'

Ben noticed that, walking in Lucas's wake, the animal smell was stronger. He put it out of his mind.

'So Ben was asking why all your windows are blacked out,' said Tex.

'Have you told my guests what I used to do? What I do now?'

'Not really.'

Lucas turned his vehicle to the left and they followed him into a large room painted black. It was filled with electrical equipment, computers and monitors, countless LEDs twinkling in the darkness like colored, faraway stars. Lucas docked his wheelchair into the thick of it and the electronics around him seemed to come to life. Screens lit up, music played, various message boards buzzed with activity.

'I was a Raven in the NSA. Tex and I flew together for a while in the mid-eighties out of a place called Shemya Island. Heard of it?'

'In the Aleutians,' Ben said.

'Ben's father flew RC-135s,' said Tex.

'Ah, well, I think that makes you part of the family.'

'Lucas went on to become one of the NSA's best codemakers—if not *the* best,' Tex added.

'Well, alright, if you insist. But after the Cold War came to an end, I couldn't see the point any more, so I left. I drifted around for a bit, playing at being a genius, developing algorithms for predicting the stock market. I finally got it right, just in time to make a killing during the recession of '93.'

'I always wondered why you never sold that algorithm,' said Tex. 'You'd have made an even bigger fortune.'

'Because as soon as a large number of people start using it, the algorithm no longer works. And anyway, how much money does one need? In my case, too much was a curse. I didn't have to work any more. In fact, I didn't even have to leave the house—which has had its obvious downside, as you can see. These days I run a high-end webzine for electronic nerds, which keeps me interested.'

'The NSA has taken Lucas to court several times for breaching national security, but has never managed to make the charges stick.'

'I sail close to the line, but never over it. It's a circuitous route to your question, Ben, but that's why all my windows are darkened. It's a material that absorbs energy within certain radio frequency and microwave ranges. There are also various sniffers secreted in the walls, ceilings and floors that let me know when Uncle Sugar is tiptoeing around. I do the best I can with my phone lines, but I can't guarantee the integrity of anything external. Fortunately, I've been left alone the last couple of years, so either the NSA has decided I'm no longer a risk, or it's trying to lull me into the ol' false sense of security.'

'Could be you're just too smart for them,' said Tex.

'Tex, one thing I will *never* do is underestimate my former employers, though they do have weaknesses: the bureaucracy and their political masters. Mine's KFC. No one's perfect.'

Something beeped and Lucas switched it off.

'Now,' the big man said, 'down to business. Why are we here?' His chair pivoted on the spot so that he faced Ben, Akiko and Tex.

Ben glanced at Tex, who gave him a nod, so he reached into his satchel, pulled out the spool and handed it to Lucas.

'A tape. I'm intrigued. You want to tell me about it?'

Ben and Akiko spent the next twenty minutes briefing the former Raven and NSA code whiz on what they knew, leaving out nothing, starting with the letter Akiko received from Yuudai and the mystery of the 007 safe deposit key left to Ben by Curtis. Lucas listened with a frown, occasionally shaking his head and asking a question or two. In the middle of the story, he reached below the bench top, opened a fridge, and pulled out a two-liter bottle of Pepsi. He drank it all in half a dozen gulps.

When they'd finished, Lucas concluded, 'So, in a nutshell, you want me to decode it.'

'If possible,' said Ben.

Lucas whistled quietly. 'You don't think something like this would be best left unresolved?'

'No,' said Akiko adamantly.

'The reason I ask is because once we let this knowledge loose, there'll be no stuffing it back in the cage. If it's what you think it is, it'll probably change your lives forever.'

'We're ready,' said Ben, glancing across at Akiko.

Akiko checked with him and nodded. 'Ready.'

'Well, I'd best get on with it then,' Lucas said, suddenly animated, the intimacy of the mood broken. Motors whirred and he pivoted around to face the banks of black boxes and monitors. 'You might like to sit. This could take a while.'

Akiko and Ben sat on a black sofa against the back wall.

'Just as a matter of interest, how are you going to read it?' asked Tex.

'First I have to know what language it was written in. On the basis of what you've told me, I agree with you that this is most likely radar tape. Therefore, a good starting point would be to find out what kind of radar system the Chosa Besshitsu operated at Wakkanai back in '83. I'm guessing a forerunner to the Raytheon AN/SPS-49 long-range air surveillance radar. We'll see . . .'

Half an hour later, Lucas took a break. 'You know, I initially thought decoding something like this would be like asking a Ferrari engine builder to tune a weedwhacker, but this is tough. 1983 saw out the last days of analog, which was a bit before my time. It turns out that the mathematical architecture of the encryption algorithms back then was spectacular, like skyscrapers built from sticks. Pull the wrong ones and the whole structure comes tumbling down and you have to start all over again. I'll get there, but it'll take some time. You might like to come back later, but you're also welcome to hang around.'

'We'll stay,' said Akiko, before Ben or Tex could answer.

Tex agreed. 'I don't think driving back and forth is a good idea.'

'Me, either, given what you think is on this tape and that the NSA may be wise to it,' said Lucas. 'Make yourselves at home. I've got plenty of food.'

☭

Lana waited for the session to finish before going in, squeezing past a couple of analysts on their way out.

'Hey, Saul,' she said.

'Hey yourself,' replied Kradich, stifling a yawn as he cleaned up his desktop after the session.

'I know it's been a long day but just quickly, have we got any bites on those lines?'

'I'll take a look. Don't let your section head in on it, but I set up a surveillance nodule over all three cells.'

'Silence or death,' she said with a smile.

This was a low-priority enquiry. Her boss and chief-pain-in-the-ass Sam Whittle wouldn't appreciate having NSA resources tied up in it. She leaned forward with her elbows on the bench while Kradich fed codes into his control screen.

'Nope, nothing,' he said eventually. 'None of the cells have logged on to the network, which means they haven't even been turned on.'

Lana hid her disappointment.

'But there is some good news.'

'Yeah?'

'I'm free for that coffee.'

☭

'Okay, gather round,' said Lucas. 'I think I've just about cracked it. The tape runs for twenty-eight minutes and six seconds. There's no sound.'

'Have you seen what's on it?' Ben asked.

'Only the first few seconds. You both ready for this?'

Ben and Akiko glanced at each other and then nodded.

'It'll come up on that monitor,' Lucas said, gesturing at a large flat-screen sitting on a bank of black electronic boxes. He tapped at the keyboard. An image suddenly jumped onto the monitor. Ben instantly recognized the green outline of the claw-like shape of the southern part of Sakhalin Island, and the northernmost tip of Hokkaido where the Wakkanai radar facility was located. There were seven blips visible over Sakhalin, each representing an aircraft. Six squawks had transponder settings with Cyrillic letters against them—Soviet fighters. Out on its own in front of the fighters was a blip tagged with the code 1300. The numbers attached to this radar return indicated that it was at 33,000 feet on a course of 240 degrees with an airspeed of 488 knots.

'Well, I'll be damned . . .' said Tex into the silence.

There were numerous boxes of information around the screen, most of which meant nothing to Ben, except for the date: 1983/09/01; and time: 18:10:54 GMT.

Lucas tapped a key and things began to move. The seconds reeled

216

off and the blips progressed across the screen in small jumps, heading generally southwest.

'1300?' asked Lucas.

'That's the transponder setting 007 used when it got to Sakhalin,' said Ben. 'No one knew why. It didn't mean anything. One of many anomalies.'

Akiko gave him a fleeting smile, acknowledging that he'd come a long way from their first meeting.

The returns representing the fighters closed on 1300. Ben put his arm around Akiko's shoulders. As one of the fighters pulled almost level with the 747, the airliner slowed dramatically and began to climb. The fighter overshot the 747 and was forced to loop back around behind its quarry. And, as every agonizing second passed, 1300 edged closer to the safety of international airspace beyond the outline of Sakhalin Island. The cat and mouse game was mesmerizing.

After closing with the airliner a second time, the fighter began to drop back as KAL 007 crossed over into international airspace. And then the altitude of 1300 suddenly began to fall. Ben noticed that Akiko wrapped her arms around herself, and he realized that he was breathing hard. What must it have been like for the passengers on that plane, the missile strikes followed by the plunge?

Then the plane's dive slowed. It pulled up at 15,100 feet. Ben had read several accounts of the end of KAL 007. What he was seeing on the screen more or less jelled with them. The generally accepted hypotheses held that the plane had spiraled into the sea north of Moneron Island. As he watched, the plane indeed began a spiral, quickly losing 5000 feet of height. But then the blip straightened its course and leveled out, flying a heading that meandered between thirty-eight and forty-two degrees. It was being flown manually, limping back toward Sakhalin Island.

'Sweet Jesus wept,' said Tex softly.

Meanwhile, several Soviet fighters crisscrossed the sky, changing altitude and course, searching for the aircraft their pilots no doubt thought had plummeted into the sea. Several interceptors, probably low on fuel, returned to base.

A few minutes later, 1300 was losing height according to the information transmitted by its transponder and captured on the tape. All of the original fighters in the chase had by now gone home. New fighters were flying into the Wakkanai radar's horizon, trying to find the 747, but they were looking in the wrong place. KAL 007 was heading north and east.

The time was 18:37:40 and still 1300 flew on. It was over the coast of Sakhalin Island now, on a heading that, extrapolated, would take it to the Soviet Dolinsk-Sokol base, just as Yuudai Suzuki had said in his letter to Akiko.

Then, at 18:38:12, 1300 disappeared from the screen. It was low, just above 5000 feet. More than likely it had merely dropped below the Wakkanai radar's range.

At 18:39:00, the screen went black, the end of the tape.

'Well, fuck me,' said Tex, exhaling.

Ben looked at Akiko; her eyes were red-rimmed. Yuudai Suzuki had been right.

September 1, 1983

Santa Barbara, California. The phones were silent, a brief lull in the storm.

'You want me to get in some dinner?' Des asked.

'I could use something,' said Meese. 'I think it's going to be a long night.'

'A club sandwich will do me fine,' Clark replied. 'And you might ask if we can get a couple more phone lines in here, if that's possible.'

'Make that two club sandwiches, Des. And fries,' said Meese. 'And whatever you want, of course.'

The phone rang. The National Security Advisor pounced on it. After a moment, he said into the handset, 'Hang on, Roy. I'm going to put you on speaker.' Clark pressed a button and announced, 'It's Roy Garret.'

'Sir, I just faxed to you 007's final passenger manifest,' Garret said as Des handed Clark several curled pages of facsimile paper hot off the machine.

'Just got it,' said Clark, flattening it on the table.

Another phone rang. 'It's Bill Casey,' Meese said, after picking it up.

'Roy, we've got the director of the CIA on the other phone,' said Clark. 'Bill, Roy Garret from the NSA is on the line.'

'Hello, Roy,' said Casey.

'Good evening, sir,' Garret responded.

Clark signaled to Des. 'Hold all other calls. So what have you got for us, Roy?'

'Sir, it seems US Congressman Lawrence McDonald was a passenger aboard 007.'

'Aw, hell,' Meese swore.

'Larry McDonald . . . ?' Clark shook his head, and ran down the faxed manifest with his finger until he got to the Georgia congressman's underlined name. 'Why was he on that flight? Why didn't we know?'

'According to his press secretary, a guy called Tommy Toles,' said Garret, 'the congressman was on his way to Seoul at the invitation of the President of the ROK. He was attending a conference there, as well as celebrating the thirtieth anniversary of the US–Korea mutual defense treaty. Seems the congressman was supposed to be on an earlier flight, but he missed it.'

'How did Toles know there was a problem with the plane?' asked Meese.

'He heard a newsflash on the TV that 007 was missing. No details,' said Garret. 'He called the Federal Aviation Administration in DC and spoke to the duty officer there, a guy by the name of Orville Brockman. Toles recorded the call. I've got a transcript.'

'Read it to us, Roy,' said Clark.

'Yes, sir . . . "We have just received information from our FAA representative, Mr Dennis Wilhelm in Tokyo, as follows: He has been advised by the Japanese Civil Aviation Bureau headquarters, Air Traffic Division, Mr Takano—T-a-k-a-n-o—who is his counterpart in Japanese aviation, as follows: Japanese Self-Defense Force confirms that the Hokkaido radar followed Air Korea to a landing in Soviet territory on the island of Sakhalinska—S-a-k-h-a-l-i-n-s-k-a—and it is confirmed by the manifest that Congressman McDonald is on board."'

Garret's voice hung in the air.

Meese massaged his forehead.

'Leaving Larry McDonald aside for a moment, couldn't that be considered confirmation of the CIA report?' Des pointed out.

Meese ran his fingers through his hair. 'We can't let that happen.'

'It sounds to me like someone told someone who told someone who told someone,' reassured Casey. 'That's not a confirmation, it's Chinese whispers. And by the way, we don't know where the initial so-called CIA report claiming that the plane was safe on Sakhalin came from. We think it might have been cooked up by a TV station in Seoul.'

'Though it's not far from the truth, evidently,' Meese replied.

'Anything else, Roy?' asked Clark.

'Sir, it's now clear that the Soviets believed they had an RC-135 on their hands. They didn't know 007 was a civilian airliner.'

'That strains credibility,' said Meese. 'They got right up and personal with it?'

'Yes, sir,' said Garret.

'Close enough to see what it was?'

'We believe so, yes.'

'And they still got it wrong?'

'Apparently.'

Meese snorted and shook his head. 'Then they're even more hopeless than we thought.'

'Roy, there was no misunderstanding about what kind of plane it was,' Des insisted. 'That's the party line and we're sticking to it.'

'I copy that, Des.'

'Roy, we need you to do something for us,' said Meese.

'Yes, sir.'

'Get in touch with Richard Burt in DC. He's expecting your call. Dick's the assistant secretary of state for European and Canadian affairs. He's put together a task force to control the flow of information. The task force will be meeting daily until further notice, monitoring consular reaction to the shootdown worldwide, as well as the press reports. CIA, Defense and State have seats at the table, and we'd like you to be our inside man.'

'Yes, sir,' said Garret.

'Dick knows you're NSA, but that's about where it ends, if you know what I mean.'

'I think so, sir.'

'You'll report back to us after each task-force meeting, keeping us abreast of developments.'

'Will do, sir.'

'Roy, we'll speak again soon.' Clark cut the connection with Garret. 'So, what's happening on your end, Bill?' he asked the CIA director.

'We knew about Toles and his congressman. That's why I phoned,' Casey replied. 'Toles has been calling everyone in the known universe about it, which Garret just bore out.'

'Larry's a good Christian. I've met his wife, Kathryn. They have two nice kids,' said Clark, shaking his head.

'Judge, McDonald was also a member of the House Armed Services Committee. There's not much he doesn't know about our defense strategies, budgets and programs—the President's strategic defense initiative, the MX and so forth. And that means if he *is* still alive, the KGB knows what he knows, or *will* know it.'

'Wonderful,' Meese said to the ceiling.

'Calm down, Ed,' said the CIA director. 'If you think about it, this is a stroke of luck.'

'I'd love to know how.'

'We were going to get a once-in-a-lifetime opportunity to bury the Soviet menace without having to fire a shot. That was the plan. It hasn't worked out quite the way we intended, but we can still pull it off. If you think about what will happen if the Soviets turn around and release those passengers, and especially the crew, we have no choice.'

'Just to be clear, you're saying that we give them Congressman McDonald,' said Meese.

'Yes, exactly. If they want him, they'll have to keep everyone. Our challenge now is to make them want him *badly*.'

Clark frowned, unconvinced.

'What do y'all know about Larry McDonald?'

'Well, I know he accused you of being a commie lover on television a couple of months back,' said Meese with a humorless chuckle.

'Yeah, Ed, McDonald's quite a character,' said Casey. 'He also believes there's a worldwide conspiracy funded by the Rockefellers to create a global government along communist lines. I'm supposed to be part of it, and so are George Shultz and Vice-President Bush. McDonald has been operating his own private surveillance network within various government departments and embassies, looking for communist sympathizers and other "globalist" undesirables.'

'What?' said Clark, incredulous.

'Which bit don't you believe, Judge? The globalist paranoia or the fact that he was spying on his own government?'

'Well, all of it, clearly. I had no idea. He has his own espionage ring?'

'He does indeed. Senator Joseph McCarthy was a left-winger compared to Larry McDonald.'

'Larry's ultra-conservative,' said Clark, shaking his head. 'As chairman of the John Birch Society, you have to be. But this?'

'You don't know the half of it, Judge,' said Casey. 'You know that Larry McDonald is General Patton's cousin?'

'Yes, of course. Who doesn't?'

'Well, it seems Larry inherited the general's records. What might surprise you to learn is that toward the end of the war, Patton and a German spymaster named Reinhard Gehlen were working toward a plan to re-arm the German army and mount a joint German/US invasion of the Soviet Union. Gehlen's men—those who are still alive—now work and recruit agents for Larry McDonald's personal secret service.'

'That is totally outrageous!' said Meese, aghast.

'If McDonald's still alive, and we have to assume that he is, you know what he'll be thinking?'

'What?' asked Meese.

'That the downing of 007 was a plot to put him into communist hands—further confirming to him that Washington and the Soviet Union are cooperating in a global conspiracy.'

'This is mad,' said Clark.

'Judge, two weeks ago, Larry McDonald told his staff he was intending to run for the Presidency of the United States in 1988 as a conservative Democrat.'

Clark was shaking his head.

'He believes Vice-President Bush will run,' the CIA director continued. 'He further believes that if Bush wins, he'll create some kind of international catastrophe that will allow him to proclaim a "New

World Order". McDonald wants to head that off at the pass, if he can.

'The point is, gentlemen, even without dressing it up, Larry McDonald is a real prize for the Soviets. Not only can he give them an insight into our military's strategy, tactics and hardware, but thanks to the Patton/Gehlen connection he'll be able to provide them with a list of *every* communist sympathizer and enemy within our government, the bureaucracy and big business, along with a whole network of former German spies and their contacts.'

'Shit,' Meese murmured.

'So what do we do?' Clark asked.

'It's simple, really. We salt the mine. We make absolutely certain the Soviets know *exactly* what they've got in Lawrence Patton McDonald; make the man worth his weight in gold. We need to leave them in no doubt as to his value to the KGB and its war on the west. In the meantime, we have the tactical issue of this JDF report Garret just told you about. We need to smother it. Now.'

'I'll do that,' said Clark.

'What will you tell them?' Casey asked.

'I'll speak to the director of the FAA personally. I'll say that the FAA is to make no comment whatsoever to anyone about 007. We're fighting a war with the Soviets and, as such, the downing of KAL 007 is a national security incident.'

'What about the President? Does he know yet?' asked Casey.

'We briefed him half an hour ago,' said Meese. 'All he knows is that the plane is missing. We told him that the reports are sketchy and unconfirmed.'

'When will you give him a fuller picture?'

'Before he retires to bed this evening. We'll let him know that we believe it's in the water.'

'What about the public?'

'George Shultz is preparing a full announcement. He's taking it to the networks tomorrow morning. And we're going to give it to the Soviets—both barrels—in the United Nations General Assembly tomorrow as well.'

'Who's our man on point?'

'If the President agrees, Charles Lichenstein,' said Clark.

'Yeah, Chuck's good on his feet. Well, that about wraps up my end for the moment.'

'What about McDonald?' asked Meese. 'Salting the mine.'

'Leave that to me. The CIA has contacts.'

'I'm sure you do, Bill,' said Meese.

'We play this right,' said Casey, 'and we'll have the Soviets on the ropes. Things are going badly for them in Afghanistan. They're starting to get bogged down. This KAL thing is going to totally blindside Moscow.'

'That's the idea,' said Meese.

'Like I said, we can still pull this off. I'll call you later,' the CIA director said and then the line went dead.

There was a knock on the door. Des got up and opened it. A secret service agent wheeled in a trolley carrying two dishes covered with domed, polished-silver lids.

'Not joining us, Des?' asked Meese.

'No, thank you, if you don't mind. Just lately I seem to have lost my appetite.'

January 24, 2012

Port Charlotte, Florida. They'd run through the Yuudai tape four times, but the sheer impact of it—what it meant—was still almost too big to grasp.

'They lied,' Ben fumed. 'The bastards fucking lied.'

Lucas reached for another two liters of Pepsi. 'Have you any idea how completely the downing of that plane changed the world?'

'It changed my world,' said Akiko, the years of grief drop-forged into hot anger, her fists white and clenched in her lap.

'When KAL 007 came down, it almost brought the Soviet Union down with it,' said Lucas. 'So where does that leave us? Or, rather, you?' His eyes flicked between Akiko and Ben.

'We go to the media,' Ben said bitterly. 'And we do it now.'

Curtis was the kind of man who pulled children from fires and then dived back into the flames. He was also the kind of man who felt bound by a secret so terrible, the keeping of it destroyed him and his family. And the whole time he knew it was a lie. For the briefest instant, Ben experienced an emotion he'd never felt. He was proud of his father. He also felt loathing for the kind of men who chewed people like Curtis up and used them as fodder for their own purposes. At that moment, Ben wanted revenge. And he wanted to set the record straight.

'The media? No, I don't think that's such a good idea,' said Tex.

'I agree. Dumb,' nodded Lucas.

'I don't give a damn what anyone thinks,' Ben told them.

'Look, we don't know who's read-in on this,' the big man said. 'Some of them could still be alive and kicking. The shootdown of KAL 007 would have involved a wide range of intelligence assets—the mission flown by Curtis Foxx and the crew of Arctic 16, for example, was just a small part of it.' He raised an eyebrow at Tex.

'And your silence helped sell this bullshit,' Ben said, stabbing his finger at his father's navigator.

'Curtis and I were *not* part of *this*,' Tex insisted.

'My point,' Lucas continued, calming things down, 'is that without a shadow of a doubt anything that connects American assets to the demise of 007 will be sequestered in a compartment with a SAR code protecting its integrity. Do you understand what I mean by that?'

Ben shook his head, frustrated.

'You produce that tape and the people who are read-in on this material, the people who know the facts, will do their damnedest to discredit it. You can bet someone will come out and claim the tape is a hoax, compare it to the Hitler diaries. They'll do a complete hatchet job on the tape as well as everything and everyone connected with it. Can we prove it's genuine? No. Could a tape like this be fabricated? Yes. Discredit this evidence and it would cement in place forever the real hoax—that Korean Air Lines flight 007 hit the water and all souls aboard were lost.'

'I agree,' said Tex. 'The people read-in on this are going to be powerful enough to get the NSA hunting around on the whiff of a suspicion. But I guarantee you that the investigators who paid us a visit, Lana whatshername and her friend, have no real idea what they're looking for. They're far too junior. There's no way they'd be read-in.'

'So, what?' asked Ben. 'Akiko and I just forget about this and get on with our lives?'

'Hell, no,' said Lucas, waving an arm. 'I'm just saying that I don't think you should post it on YouTube, or whatever. Yuudai and Curtis would have realized that all this tape does is convince you of one thing.'

'Which is?' asked Ben.

'That my mother could still be alive,' said Akiko.

'I didn't know her. Why should I care?' Ben said.

The others turned to face him.

'Hey, I'm not being an asshole, I'm just saying— why me? Why am *I* involved?'

'That's easy,' Tex said. 'You're Akiko's link to me, and hence to Lucas. You're also all Curtis had.'

Ben looked down at his feet and took a long deep breath.

'So, now you know, you find just one passenger who was on that plane,' said Lucas, 'and *all* the lies come tumbling down.'

'Whoa . . . slow down, big guy. So Akiko and I are going to cruise into Russia and find someone who's been missing for, like, thirty years?' Ben asked, ridiculing the idea.

'Well, you ain't gonna find her in Key West,' Tex replied.

'We will need visas for Russia,' said Akiko.

'Hey, c'mon. This is going too fucking far,' Ben protested.

'You've got a point. Russia is a big place,' said Lucas. 'Where do you start looking? I've got a buddy, a former Defense Intelligence spook. He might have a few ideas. He worked out of the West German embassy in the late seventies and mid eighties, one of the top experts on the Soviets back then. He lives over in Gainesville. I'll set it up.'

'Okay, okay . . . Just *stop* for a moment?' Ben demanded.

Akiko put her hand on his forearm.

'Like I warned you, kiddo,' said Lucas, 'you can't stuff it back in the cage.'

September 2, 1983

Rancho Del Cielo, Santa Barbara, California. President Reagan, freshly showered, his cheeks shaved and ruddy, his hair combed and smelling of tonic, finished a prayer of thanks to the Lord and picked up a slice of lightly buttered toast. 'Judge, you don't look like you've had much in the way of sleep. You neither, Ed. Why don't you two join me in a cup of coffee while we talk? Orange juice, if you'd rather.'

'Why thank you, Mr President,' said William Clark, sitting on the President's right.

'Thank you, Mr President,' Ed Meese echoed, also taking a seat.

They both gave orders for coffee to the attendant who'd suddenly appeared. He filled their cups and then melted away toward the kitchen.

The men sat at the old country table in the sun-drenched room. They could see a couple of chestnut horses being walked across the paddock beyond by a stablehand. President Reagan was dressed in loose faded jeans and a plaid flannel shirt, set for a relaxing day's work around the ranch.

'Well, looks like another morning in paradise, doesn't it?'

'Certainly does, Mr President,' said Clark.

'So what's been happening in the wider world overnight? You two look like you've eaten something that hasn't agreed with you. Any more news on that missing plane? Has it turned up?'

Clark and Meese exchanged a glance.

'As a matter of fact, it has,' said Clark, keeping the tone of his voice low and slow. 'I'm afraid we are the bearers of news of a terrible tragedy, Mr President.'

President Reagan looked up, the smile faltering on his lips. 'What's happened?'

'Sir, it looks like the Russians shot it down,' Meese told him.

'What?'

'Yes, sir. In fact, there's absolutely no doubt about it.'

'How . . . ? Why . . . ?'

'We think it got lost somehow, strayed into Soviet airspace, and they simply shot it down. We have a transcript here of the Russian fighter pilot speaking with his ground controller who gave him the order to fire his missiles.'

National Security Advisor Clark slid a sheet of paper toward the President, who put on his glasses, picked it up and held it out until the writing came into focus. His lips moving, he skipped over the Russian and read the English translation. Horror was mixed with disbelief on his face, the paper quivering in his fingertips.

'That's incredible . . . incredible.'

'Mr President, there were 269 passengers and crew aboard the plane, sixty-one of whom were Americans. I'm afraid Congressman Lawrence McDonald was also confirmed on the passenger manifest.'

'Oh, my . . . Larry McDonald?' Reagan hung his head. 'Where was it shot down?'

'We're not 100 percent certain on that point, Mr President. Somewhere in the Sea of Japan, off Sakhalin Island. The US Navy, as well as the Japan Defense Force, is conducting search and rescue. The Russians are also searching the same area. So far no wreckage has been found and no bodies recovered.'

'What are the Soviets saying about this?' the President asked, white circles of rage starting to surface on his cheeks.

'Typically, they're admitting nothing and denying everything,' said Meese.

'Why was the plane off course?'

'The civil aviation corridor comes quite close to the Soviet Kamchatka Peninsula. As far as we know, it looks like a simple navigation error on the part of the Korean pilots. In fact, we're sure the flight crew had absolutely no idea they were in any danger.'

'The Soviets didn't warn them?'

'No, sir,' said Clark, taking over. 'It looks to our intelligence sources as if the Soviets tracked the plane for a full two and a half hours before shooting it down. Their fighters got right up close to it, close enough to see it was a civilian passenger plane. They fired no warning shots, as they were required to do by international aviation law. Then, just as the airliner crossed over into international airspace, the Soviet fighter fired two missiles at it and the 747 plummeted into the water.'

Reagan took a deep lungful of air and expelled it. 'An awful, awful business. Couldn't *we* have warned it?'

'Unfortunately, no, sir. The plane was flying beyond the range of civil aviation radar. We've got a lot of military intelligence-gathering assets in that part of the world—as you know—but none of them track *civilian* air movements. We did have an RC-135 spy plane in the vicinity of KAL 007 at one stage, but it was tracking Soviet intermediate-range ballistic missiles at the time. And, in fact, it was in its hangar more than an hour before the Soviets shot down the airliner. Frankly, Mr President, we only knew there was trouble *after* the Soviets took action. We have here full written assessments prepared by the NSA and the CIA for you to read at your leisure, sir.' Clark placed a thick folder on the table.

President Reagan eyed the formidable stack of paper. 'That won't be necessary, Judge. Just tell me the facts.'

'Yes, sir.'

'George Shultz is in Washington,' said Meese. 'He wants to make a statement on this incident to the media. Jump on it before the rumors start.'

'Of course, Ed. You tell him to go right ahead.'

'Yes, sir.'

'Has Kathryn McDonald been informed?'

'Yes, she has,' said Clark. 'With your permission, Mr President, we'd like to lay the facts of the case before the United Nations Security Council later today. At least make some kind of a statement. The Soviets can't be allowed to get away with this despicable act.'

'You do what's necessary, Judge. Apply the blowtorch. Let's bring Jeanne Kirkpatrick in on this. As the UN ambassador, she'll need to prepare a response.'

'Sir, we thought of giving the job to Charles Lichenstein—he's the American delegate. He's a great performer and can write one heck of a speech. Let him fire the first shot across Moscow's bow. Then, when we have a better grasp of the situation and all the facts are available, we can bring Jeanne into the fray.'

'Okay, I agree. Go with Charles first.'

'We also think it would be worthwhile if *you* made a statement, Mr President,' said Meese. 'Perhaps later this afternoon. Larry Speakes is nearby, staying over at the Sheraton. Since he's the official White House spokesman, we could have him call a press conference and deliver your views on this senseless attack.'

'Good advice, Ed. That's why you're my counselor. Let's do that.'

'We've taken the liberty of drafting some initial thoughts for you to go through with Larry,' said Clark, taking a couple sheets of paper from a briefcase and handing them to the President.

'Mr President, I know you're on vacation, but this is going to heat up,' said Meese. 'We've spoken to State. They're talking about the possibility of you cutting your vacation short—to deal with this disaster directly from the Oval Office.'

The President jealously guarded his downtime. He frowned and clasped his hands in front of him on the table. 'Let me talk that over with Nancy.'

'And, depending on the Soviet reaction, we're all thinking it would make a powerful impression if you were to go on television. The American people, indeed the free peoples of the world, will need your guidance and reassurance.'

'Yes, I think you're probably right,' the President agreed.

Clark finished his cup of coffee. With a flick of his eyes to Meese, he said, 'This is a terrible tragedy, Mr President, but perhaps some good can come of it. God willing, we'll be able to turn the tide of world opinion against the Soviet menace and show them for what they really are—a cold-blooded and calculating peril, hellbent on world domination.'

☭

Richard Burt, the assistant secretary of state for European and Canadian affairs, leaned over a desk strewn with newspaper clippings from well over two dozen countries. The Soviet attack on the civilian airliner was the world's biggest news story. Burt picked through the clippings along with several other members of the task force. With rare exceptions, the headlines were uniform: outrage. A few with late deadlines showed maps of Sakhalin Island and KAL 007's flight path across it ending in a jagged starburst over the Sea of Japan.

'We've got the bastards!' Burt exclaimed. He turned to Garret. 'Roy, your role here is simple. We'll be relying on the resources of the NSA to keep an ear to the ground. I want a daily briefing. What we're particularly interested in hearing about is any divergence from the core issues, namely that the Russians brutally shot down a civilian airliner and killed several hundred innocent civilians. I note, for example, that there are a few articles and editorials questioning *why* the plane was off course and *why* the US military failed to warn the flight crew. We'll have to head off that kind of enquiry, come down hard on it if we have to. It's about keeping the media on message.'

'Yes, sir,' said Garret, nodding along with the others.

Burt addressed the room. 'I want the local press put under a microscope. Any deviation from the official line should be brought to my personal attention immediately. If individual journalists won't play ball with the administration, we'll make it difficult for them to get interviews—squeeze them right back. State has direct channels with all the major networks and media groups and we'll use them if we have to. I don't need to remind you that we are at war with the Soviets and they have just murdered sixty-one of our countrymen, including a congressman. They need to be shown that we're absolutely unanimous about such behavior being unacceptable.'

He turned to Garret once more. 'Roy, I was wondering if you could possibly help us out with some of the more intractable consulates? It would be helpful to know who's not playing ball as soon as possible—get the drop on them.'

'Can do,' said Garret. 'By the way, sir, has anyone contacted the National Transportation Safety Board?'

'No, why?'

'As of right now, the NTSB will be demanding all materials on this incident from every source it can think of in preparation for the investigation, which it probably thinks it's going to handle. We'll need to exert some influence there. The NTSB won't give a damn about the national security issues at stake. The NTSB also has the power of subpoena and we don't want this ending up in the courts.'

'I hear you,' said Burt, a hand on his chin, the other on his hip. 'What should we tell them?'

'There'll have to be an inquest. Until we settle on the right body, tell them State is going to conduct the investigation.'

'We don't do air disasters.'

'I know, sir, but State could certainly manage it into the hands of the appropriate body.'

'Such as?'

'Such as the United Nations.'

'The ICAO?'

'The International Civil Aviation Organization would be ideal—they're even-handed, international, unbiased . . .'

'And no power of subpoena?'

'None whatsoever, sir. But, armed with the right information,' Garret reassured him, 'the ICAO would do a great job.'

'For us.'

'Yes, sir.'

'Good. Then we'll deal with that straightaway. Perhaps Lawrence Eagleburger can give the NTSB the news.'

'I'll give you the numbers to call, sir,' said Garret.

'You see?' Burt exclaimed, facing the table. '*That's* the kind of forethought we need on this. And while I think of it, if we get *any* calls asking for the latest information, the correct answer until further notice is that there is *no* new information. The press is going to move at *our* pace, not theirs. Like I said at the outset, it's up to us to manage the official US response.'

A young woman in a tight knitted wool suit, her hair cut short in a bob, rushed through the door holding a sheet of paper. 'This is just in from TASS, Mr Assistant Secretary,' she announced. Burt snatched it from her. Everyone went quiet. It was the second TASS bulletin to be released, and it would reflect Moscow's official line.

'Gromyko. He's at it again,' Burt muttered once he'd skimmed it.

Andrei Gromyko, thought Garret—the Soviet foreign minister. He'd authored the first TASS bulletin to comment on 007.

Burt read from the paper. '"In violation of international regulations, the plane flew without navigation lights and did not react to radio signals of the Soviet dispatcher services, and made no attempt to establish such communications contact. Anti air-defense aircraft were ordered aloft; they repeatedly tried to establish contact with the plane using generally accepted signals and to take it to the nearest airfield in the territory of the Soviet Union. The intruder plane, however, ignored all this . . ." . . . et cetera . . .'

Garret had heard it all before. So far, TASS had merely rehashed its first press release.

'"Over Sakhalin Island,"' Burt continued, '"a Soviet aircraft fired warning shots and tracer shells along the flying route of the plane. Soon after this, the intruder plane left the limits of Soviet airspace and continued its flight toward the Sea of Japan . . . The US services followed the flight throughout its duration in the most attentive manner . . . a *preplanned* act . . ."' Burt gave a wry, lopsided smile. 'Okay, this is new. TASS says: "It was obviously thought possible"—by the CIA, I assume this means—"to attain special intelligence aims without hindrance *using civilian planes as cover.*" They then go on to call the US response to this atrocity a "hullabaloo". Can you believe that? A hullabaloo. It's almost laughable.'

Burt lowered the paper. 'Those bastards are going to lie and cheat and deny, deny, deny. At least we now know along what bullshit lines they're going to fight this. But most importantly, we know the truth, people, we know the truth.'

Des Bilson sat in the gallery, looking down on the scene below.

The room that usually held the fifteen-member United Nations Security Council could not handle the number of representatives that wanted to have their say, so the extraordinary session dealing with the events off Sakhalin Island had been moved to the Economic and Social Council Hall. And now a capacity crowd awaited the initial United Nations reaction to the Soviet atrocity.

Bilson craved the horizontal comfort of his bed. Even in the air-conditioning, his skin felt oddly sensitive and was clammy with sweat, the only obvious outward symptom that his own body had turned on him. A team of doctors of various persuasions was convinced that he had some kind of virus that was stopping his body's ability to defend itself against disease. There were similar cases being reported around the country. Everyone was afraid. The doctors had given him a timeline that would come to an abrupt end in the not too distant future. While the doctors weren't prepared to confirm why this virus had chosen to attack him, there'd been insinuations. Perhaps, after all these years, his secret was going to be aired.

Bilson listened intermittently, distracted by his own health issues, as the first speaker, the South Korean ambassador, Kim Kyung-won, angrily called for a full and detailed account of the downing of the airliner from the Soviet deputy delegate, Richard Ovinnikov. As expected, the Russian sat motionless, reacting to the demand with the alacrity of a granite block.

Next to speak was Canada's delegate, Gerard Pelletier, who bluntly charged the Soviets with murder. Bilson noted that Ovinnikov, trying a different approach to what was going to be a difficult session, was now absorbed in the ritual of packing his pipe.

Australia's delegate followed Pelletier, then Pakistan's and Zaire's, and a host of other nations. The language was unanimously anti-Soviet, and not a single delegate rose to speak in Moscow's defense. Bilson took out a notebook and, with shaky handwriting, jotted down for his report to Clark some of the more potent words used to condemn the communists: 'massacre', 'incomprehensible event', 'premeditated violence', 'an animal act', 'callous'.

He watched Ovinnikov lean back and regard the ceiling, the embers in the tobacco bowl between his thick thumb and forefinger glowing red as he puffed. Whether Ovinnikov reacted to the condemnation or not, it was all heading in the right direction, thought Bilson. The plan was working.

Charles Lichenstein, the deputy delegate of the United States, stood. The crowd held its breath. The heavyweight bout everyone had come to see was about to start. The undercard had finished and the main event had commenced.

The US delegate led with a flurry of body punches from the beginning. Gone was the usual equivocation of the diplomat. Lichenstein was going for the knockout.

'Let us call this crime what it clearly is,' he railed, tapping into the indignation and revulsion of the preceding delegates' mood. 'Wanton, calculated, deliberate *murder*. This is a ruthless totalitarian state responsible for killing more people and enslaving more nations than any state, any regime, in the history of mankind.'

It was an award-winning performance, Bilson thought as he tried to write down Lichenstein's words. He was increasingly unable to keep up with the transcription and his heart was fluttering like a startled bird's. Was the world accelerating, or was he dropping behind? It was a question he didn't find an answer to before he fainted, slipping out of the chair and slumping to the carpet.

January 27, 2012

Fort Meade, Maryland. Investigator Lana Englese had hit a brick wall. It had been several days now and still the cell phone network set up by Tex Mitchell had not been activated. She had to assume, therefore, that they'd established a new one. And second time around, Tex Mitchell would be even more circumspect. She was still most interested in discovering the identity of the holder of the third cell phone. How did that person fit into the triangle between Ben Harbor, his father Curtis Foxx, and Mitchell, Foxx's navigator?

The folder on her desktop held a copy of Foxx's record, which she now knew reasonably well. He was a great pilot who went bad as a result of events that happened on September 1, 1983, the evening the Russians put a couple of missiles into KAL 007. The conspiracy websites were full of theories about 'what really happened', and most included the antics of a USAF RC-135 in the airliner's demise. There was little doubt in her mind that Foxx had been the RC pilot, which meant Mitchell was likely to have been the navigator on that mission. She was unsure whether Mitchell would have said anything to Harbor about what happened that night—especially after Foxx had gone to his grave without revealing it. She felt a surge of admiration for these men, and especially for Curtis Foxx. Looking at the guy's record, he'd been one hell of a warrior.

Lana tapped in the access code and opened the folder. Saul Kradich had deposited the items she'd requested—Foxx's bank records, his IRS returns, his will. She opened the will and –

'Are you *still* chasing ghosts on that 007 caper, Lana?' Sherwood asked over her shoulder.

'What? No . . . I –'

'C'mon, we've spent far too much time on this conspiracy crap. Why don't you look into 9/11 instead? I've got news for you—there's nothing out there. Move on.'

'I don't agree,' Lana argued. 'And this investigation has no lesser priority than anything else we're on.'

'You and I both know this is a long way from an investigation,' he said, then clapped his hands together and rubbed them to change the mood. 'That shit happened more than a quarter century ago. Forget about it. This afternoon we're in on the bust down in Texas. It's battle stations, baby.'

'You know, I really think you joined the wrong service, Sherwood. And if you call me baby again you'll get a knee where it hurts.'

'Alright, sorry about that. But look, it's time to go.'

'No, it's not,' she said, irritated. 'The plane leaves in forty-five minutes. I'll see you downstairs in fifteen.'

'Okay,' said Sherwood, squeezing past her workstation, disappointed at her apparent lack of enthusiasm. 'Don't keep us waiting.'

Lana puffed out her cheeks as she exhaled. The guy really should have joined the US Marshals, or something. Maybe the Chippendales. She clicked on the icon of Curtis Foxx's will. It opened, and she read it.

Chena Lake. She'd been there. It was a nice place to spend an afternoon so why not eternity? Foxx had been based at Eielson, near Fairbanks. Nothing unusual about that. There was no mention of a key, a tape, or of 007 in the will, which, at the very least, would have been a handy confirmation of suspicions. Curtis Foxx had been wary all the way to the grave, but, to be fair to the guy, with good reason. Overall, it was a strange will—informal, almost chatty in places. The bit about embracing the truth—that could mean anything and nothing. What significance had the father wanted the son to take from it? The two had

239

been estranged almost all of Ben's life. A little late to start preaching values.

She wondered how much money Curtis had left to Ben. She clicked on Curtis's bank account; he had only one—a basic checking account. She reviewed the last six months up to when the account was closed because all the money had been withdrawn. She followed the numbers and the statement to the IRS. The amount of $96,000 and change had been paid to Benjamin Harbor. Ninety-six grand. That was a lot of money for someone who was essentially a vagrant. Where had it come from? Lana found the entry almost immediately. In the month before he died, Curtis Foxx had received an amount of $88,221.34.

'Who gave you that?' she asked aloud.

She followed the account numbers and came to a short-term dead end. The cash had come via a company that handled international money transfers. Someone overseas had sent Curtis the funds. The question was, who? Ten minutes with Saul Kradich and she knew she'd have the answer.

Her cell rang. The number on the screen told her it was Sherwood.

'Jesus,' she said, quitting her computer access and then grabbing her coat and bag. She was late.

September 4, 1983

Dolinsk-Sokol, Sakhalin Island, USSR. Colonel Korolenko's footsteps crunched on the gravel as, deep in thought, he walked toward the prisoner's cell. There had been several telephone discussions with superior officers about the prisoners in general and about Congressman McDonald in particular. Indeed, Korolenko had been ordered to fly to Khabarovsk the following day to meet with Colonel General Penkeyev, the number two man in the Soviet Far East Military District. The bloated old war hero wanted to be taken through Korolenko's thinking personally before making a recommendation to Moscow. Which way would the cards fall? The KGB colonel was still unsure. In his private opinion, the leadership had been erratic since Premier Brezhnev's death. Right now, the Americans were applying intense pressure through the United Nations over the KAL 007 incident and there was a trial of international public opinion going on. Maps, diagrams, translated voice tapes were the exhibits. Soviet forces had captured the spy plane three days ago and still there was no admission from Moscow that they had fired on it, so perhaps there was hope.

Of course, the admission about the shootdown would come eventually—there was pride in defending the motherland against all comers. It was the other questions he was unsure of: Would Moscow inform the world that many of the passengers were alive and safe? Would they all be sent home?

The information he now had in his hands might increase the certainty in favor of incarceration and secrecy. McDonald's complete annotated diary had been found in his luggage, along with notes taken while attending various US defense committees and meetings. Possibly of even greater value was a package about the congressman that had come through the Soviet embassy in Tehran. It seemed this McDonald was quite a catch after all.

Korolenko gave the KGB prison guard a nod and together they walked to the end of the cell block. A quick visual on the prisoner through the grille by the guard and then the key rattled in the lock. The door opened.

Congressman McDonald was sitting on the bare concrete bench in his rumpled gray suit, a bucket of feces pushed into a far corner. The American had no tie, no belt, no socks and no shoelaces. Korolenko had spared him a body search. He didn't think the congressman would be the type to hide things in body cavities. At least, not yet.

Korolenko heard the door close with a metallic clang behind him.

McDonald looked at him and said nothing.

'Not going to ask me about contacting the US consulate today?'

McDonald didn't answer.

'Ah, a new tactic. Silence. It will do you no good. We know more about you now, Congressman. It seems you are a true enemy of the USSR. How ironic that you will ultimately prove of such great value to us.'

McDonald's frozen silence continued.

Korolenko took a different tack. 'You will be removed from this place soon. Another airplane flight, I'm afraid. You will be taken to a place that many people have regretted visiting over the years. There will be no escape. Your days will be filled with misery. Your nights will be worse. Unless you talk. Talk is rewarded. Silence is punished. You will come to accept this simple relationship, as everyone does. For your sake, I hope you come to realize it quickly.'

McDonald made no response.

'Does the name Reinhard Gehlen tell you anything, Congressman?'

Silence, though Korolenko saw the muscles in the American's jaw tighten.

'Yes, it should. It should tell you that now we know which questions to ask. I pity you.'

Pure bravado, thought Korolenko. Equally likely was that the congressman would be on a plane home within a day, his pockets full of Moscow's weak-kneed apologies.

☭

Nami had spent the last four days in a railway freight car with thirty other passengers. They had been forbidden to speak—a rule enforced with a rifle butt. There was barely enough room to sleep lying down and the four buckets provided were soon full and stinking. But now, a guard was pulling her from the boxcar. The first blast of cold fresh air she had breathed in days was sweeter than any dessert.

The man had his hand under her armpit, lifting her so that she walked on her toes. He marched her toward a door, opened it, shoved her forward, and then led her to a chair. He pushed down on her shoulder and she sat heavily.

Seated behind the desk in front of her was a hard woman with dyed blonde hair, a thick black line down her center part, and heavy black eyebrows. She glanced up at Nami, checked the passport between her fat, blunt fingers, and then put it down. 'This luggage is yours?' she asked in passable English.

Nami followed the woman's gaze. 'Yes,' she said after a moment. There was a red T-shirt tied around the handle to help identify the nondescript black suitcase on a carousel. The T-shirt was an old one that Akiko had grown out of. The sudden memory jolt—seeing Akiko in that T-shirt—moistened her eyes.

'Where is this place?' she asked.

The woman ignored the question as if she hadn't heard Nami speak— as if she didn't exist—and referred instead to some paperwork before her. The male guard opened the suitcase on the floor and sifted carelessly through the neatly folded clothes. Next, he opened her carry-on bag. Nami knew that all he'd find were cosmetics and a book—nothing of real value or interest.

The guard spoke abruptly in Russian to the woman behind the desk.

243

There was a brief exchange between them, and then Nami felt the man's hand under her armpit again, lifting her.

'Wait!' she cried out.

The woman behind the desk didn't look up as Nami was pushed out the door.

September 5, 1983

Khabarovsk, Siberia, USSR. It was late in the evening by the time Colonel Korolenko arrived in the Siberian city of Khabarovsk. Colonel General Alexander Penkeyev, the man he had been summoned to see, had abandoned the cold concrete climes of the Far East Military District HQ for the cozier atmosphere of his home on the outskirts of town, a rambling cottage made of wood in the peasant style perched high on a hillock and positioned to look southwest over the Amur River, toward China.

The general was taking his time with Korolenko's report, flicking back and forth through the pages, occasionally grunting, and then pausing to pour himself another vodka or relight his Cuban.

Korolenko sat stiffly in an armchair off to one side, facing the blackened empty hearth. His eyes swept the room. The decor was surprisingly feminine—painted dinner plates hanging on the wallpapered walls, paintings of young women and men dancing, and two vases of flowers on the mantelpiece. The only masculine touch was a collection of photos shot in Afghanistan that showed the general and a bunch of young Red Army soldiers on top of a Soviet T64 tank.

General Penkeyev was a big, stocky man—a combination of muscle and over-feeding—whose former physical power still lingered in his thick forearms. His scalp was bald and patterned with scars collected over a lifetime on the front lines, and reminded Korolenko of a marble head pitted and chipped by hammer blows. His cheeks were round and full, like a trumpet player's, and ruddy from a long friendship with the bottle.

Korolenko knew the man's background. Who didn't? In the Great Patriotic War, Penkeyev had been the ranking sergeant within a dwindling company of men being smashed during what would be the Nazis' final assault on Stalingrad. At sunrise one frozen morning, Penkeyev woke to find his position being strafed by a platoon of Waffen-SS armed with seven MG-42 heavy machine guns. The officer leading his unit and four of the seven men still able to walk refused Penkeyev's demand to charge the enemy emplacement. So he shot each of them in the head with his revolver and forced the three men remaining to assault the position with him. But the moment Penkeyev's back was turned, the soldiers immediately deserted, leaving the sergeant to charge the enemy stronghold by himself. The story went that Penkeyev grabbed a German helmet and put it on, marched into the emplacement and took the Ukraine conscripts by surprise, shooting all but one of them dead. Out of ammunition, he apparently smashed the remaining man's head in with the butt of his revolver. Soon after the action, the sergeant, who'd lost half a hand in the engagement, was given a battlefield commission to lieutenant and later granted the title of Hero of the Soviet Union.

General Penkeyev was a Soviet in the old mold—hard-nosed, opinionated, conservative and authoritative. He was also a survivor who had drunk with Stalin and Beria on many occasions and lived to tell about it.

'Vodka, Comrade Colonel?'

Korolenko was not a drinker, but to refuse would have been the height of rudeness and professional suicide.

'Yes, thank you, Comrade General.'

'This is quite a haul. Four scientists, two engineers, an electrical engineer, two computer experts, five ex-military men from a variety of countries, two journalists. And, of course, our congressman,' said the general as he poured the vodka through a haze of cigar smoke.

Our congressman. A good sign, thought Korolenko.

'I have spoken with some people, made some discreet enquiries. Lawrence McDonald's connection with Gehlen is most interesting. A friend of mine came up against Gehlen when the man was chief of the Third Reich's Foreign Armies East, back in the war. Gehlen was a fascist pig of the highest order. The Americans loved him. Perfect CIA material. He ran to them and they snapped him up immediately. Gehlen helped organize the B Faction in the Ukraine and Romania's Iron Guard, to name but two of his counterrevolutionary organizations. The GRU thinks there are perhaps thousands of Gehlen's agents, little spiders, still operating within the Soviet bloc, spreading anti-revolutionary poison. You think this McDonald might provide leads that would help us track these people down?'

'Yes, Comrade General, undoubtedly. I also believe he could provide far more than mere leads. He has names and places. If you would permit me to speak freely . . .'

The general rolled his mangled hand a few times in a gesture of continue, continue, topped up Korolenko's vodka and puffed heavily on the thick cigar stub.

'As I have documented, sir, Lawrence McDonald himself actually recruited spies with the help of Gehlen to gather intelligence from institutions *within* the United States.'

'He has his own personal spy network?'

'Yes, sir.'

Penkeyev grunted. 'Sounds like one of us.'

'Comrade General, he penetrated the FBI, the CIA, and other agencies. The intelligence windfall could be of incalculable benefit.'

'Hmm . . .' Penkeyev nodded his scarred head. 'What do you think McDonald might know about this Star Wars nonsense of their President's? Drink up, Colonel. I don't trust men who don't drink.'

Korolenko threw back the half glass remaining, his second. General Penkeyev immediately refilled it to the brim.

'We think he might know a considerable amount, Comrade General. I suspect he is as much a fascist as that Nazi Gehlen, and his cousin, General Patton—'

'Patton—*pha*! A great general,' Penkeyev interrupted. 'He was born on the wrong side of the fence.'

The general motioned for Korolenko to drink up, which he did, even though his head felt heavy on his neck and he was having difficulty selecting the correct words, let alone speaking them. He noticed an empty bottle in the trash bin beside the general's writing desk and wondered how much Penkeyev had drunk before he arrived.

The old man filled their glasses again and sat back with a wheeze, his collar loosened, a couple of jacket buttons unfastened, gray chest hair sprouting from the black shadow beneath his loosened collar, wet cigar stub in his mouth. The vodka bottle swayed in the hand resting on the arm of the armchair. He was gazing at the empty hearth as if entranced.

'This is going badly for us,' Penkeyev said, in a tone that suggested he was having a conversation with himself. 'If we give the passengers back now, five days after the air force failed to do its job, the world will ask why we kept them so long. They will also think we are finally caving in to capitalist pressure. Will either outcome be helpful, enhance Soviet prestige?' He shook his head, answering his own question. 'The west believes the plane and all its passengers are on the bottom of the Sea of Japan,' he continued. 'Perhaps the best course we can steer is to let the world continue to believe it.'

He turned his head to face Korolenko. 'Do you realize, Colonel, that the air force followed this CIA decoy for a full *two and a half hours* as it entered our airspace, flew over our submarine base, passed back into international airspace, and then altered course, dodging and weaving over Sakhalin?'

'No, Comrade General, I was not fully aware of this.'

And it was true. No one on the air force side, either in flight ops or ground defense, was saying anything. Heads were expected to roll in the wake of the incident, and no one wanted to help sharpen the blade lest it land on their own neck.

The old man coughed richly, then wiped his mouth on the back of his sleeve. 'The stupid Jewish Cossacks should have either let the plane go or stopped it at the front gate,' he said. 'Then we would be seen as either tough or understanding—something positive, at least. As it stands, we're viewed as incompetent, dithering *and* cold-blooded. The

Americans must be rubbing their hands with joy. Our air force couldn't shoot semen onto a virgin's chest.'

Korolenko saw that Penkeyev was staring at his glass, so he lifted it quickly to his lips and drank, finishing the vodka.

'Where are you staying, Comrade Colonel?'

'There is an Intourist hotel on the river—'

'Nonsense. We have plenty of room here, as well as vodka. You like a drink, I can see. I will get my wife to bring another bottle. Tell me more about this McDonald. This is the best news I've had in days.'

Roy Garret took his third scotch and sat on the arm of a chair, his gut a nest of coiling snakes. He drank half the tumbler and read the decoded notice sent through by the 6920th Electronic Security Squadron, Wakkanai. A radar tape of the last minutes of KAL 007's doomed flight had gone missing. There was no explanation. The tape had apparently been secured, logged, tagged, and then it had simply disappeared. An internal investigation at the Wakkanai facility was under way to find out what had happened to it. The notice from the Security Squadron concluded with a statement that the tape could also have been accidentally destroyed. The point that it could therefore also *not* be destroyed was the issue.

Garret glanced at the television. On the screen was a graphic of the White House at night, its arches accentuated by floodlights. The camera's view widened and panned to the right until President Reagan appeared centered on the TV screen, behind his desk in the Oval Office. He was flanked by the Stars and Stripes and the flag of the President of the United States. On the sideboard behind him were various happy family photos of Nancy, their kids and grandkids. The President's mood appeared subdued but determined.

Garret's mood was turning maudlin. There could well be a ticking time bomb circulating.

'*My fellow Americans,*' Reagan began, '*I am coming before you tonight about the Korean Airlines massacre, the attack by the Soviet Union against 269 innocent men, women and children aboard an unarmed Korean passenger plane. This crime against humanity must never be forgotten, here or throughout the world.'*

Garret's attention drifted in and out as he wrestled with the stress brought on by this latest development. He had apprised Hank of the situation, and Hank would bring it up with Des Bilson.

'Let me state as plainly as I can: There was absolutely no justification, either legal or moral, for what the Soviets did. One newspaper in India said, "If every passenger plane . . . is fair game for home air forces . . . it will be the end to civil aviation as we know it."'

Garret got up, wandered into the kitchen for more ice. He grabbed the bottle of Dewar's and brought it back to the sitting room, pouring a tall drink and downing it along the way. The President was doing what the President was good at—talking like a concerned parent. Pouring another, Garret sat in front of the television again and saw two Presidents, his eyelids the weight of lead shot.

' . . . But despite the savagery of their crime, the universal reaction against it, and the evidence of their complicity, the Soviets still refuse to tell the truth. They have persistently refused to admit that their pilot fired on the Korean aircraft. Indeed, they've not even told their own people that a plane was shot down . . .'

Garret turned in the chair to get more comfortable. He smiled drunkenly as a passage of the President's speech penetrated the alcohol.

'Let us have faith in Abraham Lincoln's words, "that right makes might, and in that faith let us to the end dare to do our duty as we understand it". If we do, if we stand together and move forward with courage, then history will record that some good did come from this monstrous wrong that we will carry with us and remember for the rest of our lives.

Thank you. God bless you, and good night.'

'Good night,' Garret mumbled, his eyes closed, the empty bottle of Dewar's on the floor by his feet.

January 28, 2012

Gainesville, Florida. Ben sat at the bar and allowed himself to be distracted by the big screen. The Bulls were hammering away at the Timberwolves, a replay of one of the previous season's games that had won the Bulls a place in the playoffs. The volume was up and the Bulls commentator, Tom Dore, was laying into the Timberwolves for fielding a team that, he said, 'gave second-rate a bad name'. Ben smirked, sipped the Dr Pepper and switched his attention to another sweep of the booths. He was meeting a man here, a friend of chubster Lucas Watts, a former spook whose name was Jerome Grundy. Lucas had described Grundy as being in his mid-sixties, bald, short, with small eyes fixed in a permanent squint. Looking around, Ben could see no one by that description among the mostly student types scattered here and there in quiet conversation.

Ben wondered at the direction his life had suddenly taken. Akiko, Tex, Lucas . . . ever since Curtis's death, his world had been flipped on its head. Instead of sand and sun, it was now all spies and secrets.

The door opened, letting in traffic noise and a woman in her early twenties. She was wrapped tight in a trench coat, the collar up. Maybe this Grundy character was also a master of disguise, he told himself.

'You want another, Ben?'

Hearing his name startled him. Ben looked up. The barman: early sixties, bald, short and squinty-eyed. 'Did you serve me the first time?' he asked.

'I did.' The man held his hand over the bar. 'Jerome.' They shook. 'People see what they want to see, and, unless it's wearing a skirt, the barkeep is a nobody.'

The girl in the trench coat was no longer wearing it. She was now in a tight vee-neck T-shirt and low-slung jeans and she'd joined Jerome behind the bar.

'Another Dr Pepper here, Jacqui,' Jerome told her, pointing at Ben's glass.

'One Doctor for the surfer dude,' she said.

'My daughter, Jacqui,' said Jerome, introducing them. 'Jacqui, Ben.'

'Hey, Ben.' She flashed him a pearly-white smile and then freshened his drink.

'Jac works the bar on Saturday nights with a girlfriend or two. You'd be surprised what a difference it makes to the bottom line.'

'No, I wouldn't,' said Ben.

Another woman was strapping on a low-slung apron, joining Jerome's daughter. She was a strawberry blonde, emerald eyes, very tall, and she wore the same spectacular tight, low-cut uniform Jacqui had on.

'Speaking of whom, that's Tiffany.'

Ben returned Tiffany's wave.

'If I'd known retirement was going to be this tough,' Jerome said, toasting her, 'I'd have done it sooner.'

'Wouldn't everyone?' Ben caught himself staring at Tiffany.

'Let's talk,' said Jerome. 'Grab that table over there in the corner before someone else does.'

The place was filling fast and the music volume was creeping up. Within an hour, it'd be standing room only. Ben took his drink and made for the corner table. A minute later, Jerome joined him.

'So, you're a friend of Lucas's,' said Jerome. 'Known him long?'

'Nope. A few hours, max.'

'Well, you must have made an impression. Where's the Japanese woman? I was told to expect her, too.'

'Akiko had to do a few things.'

In fact, Tex suggested that it would be safer for them not to be seen together, not unless it was absolutely necessary, given what they now knew they had in their possession. So Akiko had taken a bus to DC to organize visas for Russia, and Ben had gone back to work.

'Count yourself lucky that we're still talking,' said Jerome. 'In the old days, that kind of deviation would have been enough to terminate the rendezvous.'

Ben shrugged. What was it with all these adults playing spy games? 'Next time I'll remember to bring my cloak *and* dagger. So what has Lucas told you about all this?'

Jerome took a crumpled letter from his pocket and handed it to Ben. The letter mentioned Akiko and him by name, gave the date that they'd be coming by, but not a lot else. Mostly, it was about the weather.

'Lucas has never sent me a letter,' said Jerome. 'And I mean *never*. He's Mr Internet. So the fact that he wrote this at all tells me quite a lot. You want to keep something secret, don't create a digital file. Put it in an envelope with a stamp on it. The NSA isn't employing nearly as many grandmas to steam open letters as it used to. So, whatever it is you do know, it's obviously very big and very secret, and, as my expertise was the USSR, it has something to do with a world that doesn't exist any more.'

Ben finished his soda with a slurp. 'You've got the big picture,' he said.

'What do you know about me?' Jerome asked.

'Lucas told us that you worked out of the US embassy in West Berlin in the seventies and eighties. He said that you were former Defense Intelligence Agency and that, as you say, you knew a thing or two about the Soviet Union.'

Jerome nodded. 'Now that we have the formalities out of the way, what can I do for you?'

Ben found himself scoping the bar.

Jerome reassured him. 'You're safe here, kid, believe me.'

'That's a relief,' Ben said. He found what he'd been looking around for—Tiffany. And she was reaching for a bottle on the top shelf.

'So let's talk,' said Jerome.

'Do you remember much about the downing of Korean Air Lines Flight 007 off Sakhalin Island?' Ben asked.

'I do—that was a biggie. It made things very tense, a great year for the end of the world. Yuri Andropov was the Soviet Premier. He was a sick man—kidney trouble—and none too bright, neither. He believed NATO and the US were planning a nuclear first strike on the Soviet Union. So he had the KGB and the GRU out scouring the world for telltale signs to confirm this hunch. Meanwhile, Reagan was calling the Soviets the "Evil Empire" and talking about missile defense shields, which didn't help. And then the Korean 747 came along, flew 200 miles off course and almost directly over the USSR's secret sub base at Petropavlovsk. It jinks left and right over military installations on Sakhalin Island, and then heads straight for Vladivostok, home of the Soviet Pacific fleet. So they shot it down, thinking it was a spy plane. Quite a few of us were worried that the Russians, being so jumpy, might believe we'd use the incident as an excuse for that first strike, which would, *ipso facto*, increase the risk of a pre-emptive first strike on us by them. World peace was pretty finely balanced back then.' Jerome took a mouthful of ice and crunched it. 'From memory, all the passengers on the plane were killed.'

'Two bodies were recovered, both unidentifiable.'

'If the bodies were unidentifiable, who's to say that they came from the airliner?'

'Good point,' said Ben.

'There were a whole bunch of unanswered questions, right? Didn't we lose a senator on that plane?'

'A congressman.'

'Yeah . . . That business was one of the final bastard acts of the Cold War. A tense time was had by all. What's your connection with it?'

'My father flew RC-135s—a Cobra Ball. His plane was somehow involved in the incident.'

'He tell you that?'

'Not in as many words. He died and left me a tape, a radar tape.'

Jerome seemed dubious, but also curious.

Ben continued. 'Lucas decoded it. It shows that the Korean airliner didn't crash into the sea as reported, but made it to Sakhalin Island. It was headed for one of the Soviet air force bases there.'

'Jesus. I see why Lucas didn't want to write any of this down. Where did the tape come from?'

'Lucas thinks the joint Japan/US radar base at Wakkanai.'

'What do you think?' asked Jerome.

'I think I'd like to go back to Key West and sit on the beach.'

'Then why don't you?'

'Akiko, the Japanese woman who was supposed to be here with me, her mother was a passenger on that 747.'

'Right . . . And if the plane landed, there's a chance there were survivors who became prisoners.'

'That's the theory.'

'Shit.' Jerome exhaled, sat back to catch his breath, and then leaned forward. 'So what do you want from me?'

'Akiko and I are going to Russia, apparently.'

'To look for her mother?'

'That's the plan. You have any thoughts on where she might have ended up?'

Jerome looked at Ben's empty glass. 'You want a refill, kid? Something harder? I sure as shit could use something.'

'Can't. The FAA says eight hours bottle to throttle.'

'You a pilot like your old man?'

'Uh-huh.'

'What do you fly?'

'Seaplanes, mostly. Choppers occasionally.'

'What kind of helo?'

'JetRanger.'

'Been in a few Hueys in my day. I believe Tiffany wants to learn to fly. You should give her a few pointers.'

Ben glanced over at the bar. Tiffany was sharing a joke with a customer while she worked. She caught him looking at her and gave him a small wave. 'Yeah, pointers,' he said.

'Have a drink, Ben. You and I aren't going anywhere for a while.'

Ben thought about it. He'd flown up in the chopper—a guy had walked in wanting a ride to Orlando and all the other aircraft were booked solid. Gainesville was just a short hop north from Orlando, and he'd needed a few hours in the JetRanger to stay current anyway. Two birds, one stone. Now it was almost dark and it had been a while since he'd flown anything with a rotary wing at night. And there was an added reason behind the bar not to rush this meeting.

'Okay,' he said. 'You've twisted my arm.'

'What'll you have?'

'A Sunset, thanks.'

'Hey, Tiff,' Jerome called out over the music. 'A couple of Sunsets and a jigger of rye.'

Tiffany indicated that she had the order.

'So, where to start looking?' said Jerome, posing the question to himself. 'They landed on Sakhalin, in the Soviet Far East. There's not much out there and so they don't have to rush.'

'Who's "they"?'

'The Soviets on Sakhalin Island. They're going to keep everyone together till they know what they're going to do.'

'From what I've read, the Russians took forever to admit they shot it down,' said Ben. 'They finally came clean on September 6, five days after the attack.'

'That fits. They would have looked at it from every angle before making up their mind about which way to jump. Making the decision to keep everyone locked up is one thing that does make sense—the Soviets were scroungers, especially when it came to information. They fessed up on the sixth, you say?'

Ben nodded.

'Then pretty soon after the sixth you can assume the passengers the Soviets considered VIPs would have been flown to Moscow and taken to either the Lubyanka or Lefortovo prison. My money would be on Lubyanka. Lefortovo's less conspicuous, but the Lubyanka's set up for secret deliveries.'

'What about all the other passengers? Akiko's mother, for instance.'

'Was she a rocket scientist or a nuclear physicist?'

'Nope, just a mom.'

'Was she healthy?'

'I don't know.'

'If she was, then she'd have been transported to any one of countless labor camps and put to work.'

'Are we talking . . . like a gulag?'

'More or less. The Soviets stopped calling them that after Stalin's time—but a rose by any other name, right? There are still labor camps today in the Soviet Far East. They're full of North Koreans.'

'What?'

'They were slaves in the seventies and eighties,' said Jerome. 'The Democratic Republic of North Korea owed Moscow money, so its President, Kim Il-sung, paid some of it back with a labor force. The North Koreans are still there, but they're paid these days. Not much, but a fortune by the standards of the Korean People's Paradise. They mostly work in forestry and mining, I believe. My point is that if Moscow wanted to hide Asian foreign nationals, like Akiko's mother, those labor camps would be as good a place as any to look. Siberia is a big empty wasteland. For all we know, there might also be camps holding European foreign nationals. And if there are, you can bet the Russians aren't *ever* going to let them go—way too embarrassing.'

'Where are these labor camps?' asked Ben. 'The North Korean ones. A street address would be helpful.'

Jerome chuckled. 'Somewhere in the Ulan-Ude/Lake Baikal region, which is over the top of Mongolia. There are also supposed to be some north of the city of Khabarovsk. Best I can do.'

'Any suggestions for narrowing that down?'

'The only way I can think of would be to get into the records at the Lubyanka. The Soviets were pretty good with their record-keeping.'

'How do we do that?'

'Beats me. The Lubyanka was the home of the KGB, an agency that amalgamated state security, the secret police and intelligence under the one big, ugly roof.'

'I know about the KGB,' said Ben.

'I'd be real surprised if you didn't—mean dispositions and crummy black limousines. When the Iron Curtain came down in '91, the KGB dumped its old uniforms in the trash, put on some new cheap vinyl jackets and called itself the FSB. The Lubyanka is still its HQ, along with a new building built just next door, right in the heart of downtown Moscow. When the communists fell, the new government said it would give some of the Lubyanka's files a public airing, but it ended up being all talk. Never happened. The FSB, like the KGB before it, isn't exactly amenable to freedom of information enquiries.'

'So, no ideas on how we might get a look around?'

Grundy massaged his chin. 'At the very least, you'll need some serious connections. Do you know President Medvedev or Prime Minister Putin?'

'No.'

'Then I don't like your chances. There's a KGB museum in the Lubyanka. Have a snoop around there. It's practically the only point of friendly contact the old Soviet world has with the general public.'

'What's in it?'

'Just what you'd expect. A trip down memory lane of favorite methods of torture, assassination and espionage.'

'What if we strike out there?'

'Then you're screwed. I don't know . . . Run an ad. If you *do* manage to get a look at the records on some kind of pretext, I'd watch out for prisoners processed as a group between the seventh to the fifteenth of September, 1983. If you find a cluster of admissions, that'll be suggestive. If you're real lucky, you might even get the names of a few of those camps.'

Jerome sat back in his chair. He was frowning, conflicted about something.

'You know, assuming your tape is real—and I'm sure it is—it says that the whole episode was a massive conspiracy aimed at bringing down the Soviet Union. In retrospect, you'd have to say it worked. Two hundred and sixty-nine lives traded for world peace? The imminent threat of global thermonuclear war lifted? You weren't alive then. Trust me, I'm thinking it was a fair trade . . .'

'I know one person in particular who'd disagree with you.'

'I'm sure I could find more who wouldn't. The people who cooked up the whole operation and double-triple-quadruple-guessed the Soviet reactions were strategic geniuses.'

'Here you go, guys.'

It was Tiffany, interrupting with a drinks tray. Ben grinned up at her, glad for the momentary diversion, and got a smile straight back.

'I have to go,' Ben whispered in Tiffany's ear.

She made a sound like, 'Do you have to?' and then promptly went back to sleep, turning toward him and hugging her pillow.

He kissed her lightly on her tangled strawberry hair, tied his remaining shoelace, and slipped quietly away.

It was still dark outside, though the sky was lightening off to the east. Sunrise around 7 a.m., he guessed. He hailed a cab and headed for the airport, doing the math. He'd stopped drinking at ten. It would take a while to log the flight plan and perform the pre-flight checks, so takeoff would be a little after 8 a.m. That made it over ten hours. He hadn't drunk too much, but he still felt pretty wiped out. As it turned out, Tiffany hadn't wanted to talk all that much about flying. She'd had other things in mind.

September 6, 1983

New York City, New York. Roy Garret found a clear spot by the wall and leaned against it. There was standing room only in the United Nations Security Council chamber, every square inch of remaining carpet occupied by aides, assistants, lobbyists, UN diplomatic personnel, and media. The atmosphere reminded him of the type of collective voyeurism usually reserved for public hangings and celebrity trials.

In the center of the auditorium, the permanent representatives had all taken their seats at the horseshoe-shaped table, and were adjusting their headsets through which they'd hear a translation of the day's proceedings.

The crowd stirred as several video screens were brought into the chamber and set up at strategic points around the room, positioned for the news cameras. Oleg Troyanovsky, the USSR's Security Council representative, glanced over his shoulder at the activity going on behind him with the look of someone being followed down a dark alley.

The session was scheduled to start and the US ambassador to the United Nations, Jeanne Kirkpatrick, sifted through the papers in front of her. She was continuing the debate begun by Charles Lichenstein on September 2, twenty-four hours after the Soviet attack on KAL 007. Now, Clark, Meese and Burt, satisfied that world opinion was on the US side, were comfortable about releasing more information and

Kirkpatrick had been preselected as the messenger. The presence of the video screens indicated that she had quite a show planned, and in fact the White House had issued an earlier statement saying that a 55-minute unedited tape of the Soviet fighter pilots' air-to-ground transmissions would be released.

Garret glanced around the room, noting quite a few faces he recognized in the crowd, eventually finding the one he was after. He eased his way through the press of bodies to the far side of the gathering. 'What did Des have to say?' he asked under his breath.

'Hey, I saw you over on the other side. I waved,' Hank said. 'Come to witness the evisceration, huh?'

'The missing radar tape. What was Des's reaction?'

'Forget Des.'

'Why?'

'Because Des is looking for God on some hill in Vermont.'

'What?'

'He's dying. He has a virus. Something-immuno-something-or-other. He contracted pneumonia. They've given him a month.'

Garret thought back to the last time he'd seen Clark's chief aide. The guy's tan had looked like badly applied make-up, and he realized he'd known the man was sick.

'They're calling it the gay virus,' said Hank.

Garret was surprised. 'Des was a faggot?'

'Hid it well. So we'll be working together a lot more from now on.'

'Gee whiz.'

'I thought you'd be happy.'

'The tape. Anything?'

'I looked into it. Things go missing all the time. It's a big organization. And there's the cultural barrier to contend with at Wakkanai. The tape's probably just fallen between the cracks.'

'Sounds like a whole lot of wishful thinking to me,' said Garret. 'You're saying that we just forget about it and hope for the best?'

'Unless you've got a better plan. They're looking at everyone, especially the radar operators who were on duty last Thursday, but, so far, nothing.'

The session opened and the crowd fell silent. US Ambassador Kirkpatrick was given the floor for the opening address. She stood, holding her glasses in one hand in the event that she'd need them. She let her eyes roam around the chamber before commencing, finally settling them on Ambassador Troyanovsky.

'Most of the world outside the Soviet Union,' she began, 'has heard by now of Korean Air Lines Flight 007, carrying 269 persons between New York and Seoul, which strayed off course into Soviet airspace, was tracked by Soviet radar, and was targeted by a Soviet SU-15 whose pilot, coolly and after careful consultation, fired two air-launched missiles that destroyed the plane and, apparently, its 269 passengers and crew.

'This calculated attack on a civilian airliner—unarmed, undefended, as civilian airliners always are—has shocked the world.

'Only the Soviet people have still not heard about the attack on KAL 007 and the death of the passengers, because the Soviet government has not acknowledged firing on the Korean airliner. Indeed, not until September 5 did Soviet officials acknowledge that KAL 007 had disappeared in its icy waters.'

Garret looked around the chamber. The crowd was enthralled at the spectacle of the superpowers duking it out on the world stage. Forget Broadway, he thought, this is the best show in town.

Ambassador Kirkpatrick made eye contact with one of the news teams as she said, 'Immediately following my presentation, the Russian-to-English transcript will be made available to all who may wish to study it. After this session of the Security Council, an audiocassette on which voices are still clearer will be provided to any interested mission.

'Nothing was cut from this tape. The recording was made on a voice-actuating recorder and, therefore, covers only those periods of time when conversation was heard.'

The chamber filled with a crackling sound, followed by garbled exchanges in Russian, the sound laden with static and electrical interference. It was difficult to decipher, but Garret already knew every word. Several gasps were heard among the audience as the tape played out to its violent conclusion. Throughout, the expression on

Troyanovsky's face shifted back and forth between concentration and disdain.

The audio presentation ended.

'That didn't sound like fifty-five minutes to me,' whispered Hank.

Garret checked his watch: only ten minutes had passed. 'They've edited out the dead air between the exchanges.'

'Didn't she say, "Nothing has been cut from this tape"?'

'I'd call dead air "nothing". What would you call it?'

'Those politicians sure have a way with words, don't they?'

'The transcript we have heard needs little explanation,' the ambassador continued, her voice cutting into the stunned silence. 'Quite simply, it establishes that the Soviets decided to shoot down this civilian airliner, shot it down, murdering the 269 persons aboard, and lied about it.

'The transcript of the pilot's cockpit conversations illuminates several key points. The interceptor that shot KAL 007 down had the airliner in sight for over twenty minutes before firing its missiles. Contrary to what the Soviets have repeatedly stated, the interceptor saw the airliner's navigation lights and reported that fact to the ground on three occasions.'

That's stretching it, thought Garret. He believed that when the Soviet pilot had mentioned lights, he'd been referring to his *own* lights and not, as the translation on the videotape had helpfully included in brackets, 'the target's'.

'Contrary to Soviet statements,' Kirkpatrick continued, 'the pilot makes no mention of firing any warning shots, only the firing of the missiles, which he said struck "the target".'

Garret switched his attention back to Troyanovsky to see how he was reacting to Kirkpatrick's assertions, because, on the very tape just played, with a little judicious filtering of the interference, the intercepting pilot would clearly be heard telling his ground controller that he had selected cannon and fired warning bursts ahead of 'the target'— just as the Russians had claimed. Troyanovsky, however, sat stiff and mute.

'Contrary to Soviet statements,' said the ambassador, 'there is no indication whatsoever that the interceptor pilot made any attempt either to communicate with the airliner or to signal for it to land in accordance with accepted practice. Indeed, the Soviet interceptor planes may be technically incapable of communicating by radio with civilian aircraft, presumably out of fear of Soviet pilot defections.'

Another nice touch, thought Garret. In fact the Russian SU-15 *did* have such a radio, and the pilot *had* tried to communicate with 007 because Garret had heard it. Interesting. Obviously, the Russians must have decided that keeping their own communications practices secret was more important than giving anything away in their own defense.

'Wouldn't you hate to have this woman as your mother-in-law?' whispered Hank. 'She's a goddamn terrier. You married?'

Garret shook his head.

'Me neither. At the moment I'm between threesomes.'

'Shhh,' whispered someone beside Hank.

'We know the interceptor that shot down KAL 007 flew behind, alongside and in front of the airliner,' said Kirkpatrick, looking around the chamber, 'coming at least as close as two kilometers before dropping back behind the plane and firing its missiles. At a distance of two kilometers under the conditions prevailing at that time, it was easily possible to identify a 747 passenger airliner. Either the Soviet pilot knew the Korean plane was a commercial airliner, or he did not know his target was a civilian passenger airliner. If the latter, then he fired his deadly missiles without knowing or caring what they would hit. Though he could easily have pulled up to within some number of meters of the airliner to assure its identity, he did not bother to do so. In either case, there was a shocking disregard for human life and international norms.'

Ambassador Kirkpatrick paused, readied her notes and changed tone smoothly, like a Cadillac's transmission shifting gears.

'I'm going to head out and have a smoke,' Garret said under his breath.

'I thought you'd kicked the habit.'

'I'll mooch one.'

Hank reached into his pocket, pulled out a pack of Marlboros and his lighter and handed them over.

'Thanks,' said Garret. 'Come get me when she's done.'

He made his way to the exit and slid through it. The foyer was relatively quiet, though knots of people had gathered around monitors set up here and there. Garret found a seat near a window, out of the way, and took out the smokes and lighter. He flicked the zippo open and closed a few times and enjoyed the sound it made, like a bolt in a rifle. He wanted a cigarette badly, but decided not to have one. Instead, he watched a four-pronged contrail high over the city, a fleck of twinkling silver at its head, and tried not to think about the 269 passengers and crew.

Fifteen minutes later, snapping fingers echoing through the foyer brought him out of his trance. Garret glanced up and saw Hank beckoning him from a doorway. He got up and walked over.

'The old battleaxe is wrapping up,' said Hank.

Garret handed him back his cigarettes and lighter. They re-entered the chamber in time to see Ambassador Kirkpatrick gathering up her notes, her final words hanging in the air like the echoes of a bell tolled in a church.

The two men moved around the chamber to get a better view of the Soviets. Troyanovsky, the Russian ambassador, was gazing up at the ceiling, his index finger pushing the headset cup against his ear as the delayed translation finished up.

Voices murmured through the chamber. Anticipation was in the air. How would the Soviets react?

Rather than standing, Troyanovsky leaned forward in his seat, his shirt collar thickening his neck and making his face turn red and his eyes bulge like a toad's. He adjusted his notes and read a statement, rarely looking up from it into the lenses of the television cameras focused on him. His accent was as thick as the Kremlin's walls.

'I applaud the US ambassador's ability to take the facts and twist them,' the female translator's voice began, 'for you have just experienced nothing more. Do not allow yourselves to be fooled. This is purely a propaganda campaign and its aim is to purchase an increase in the size of the defense budget sought by the Reagan administration.

'We know that the flight path of the intruding aircraft was deliberate.

It was cleverly crafted to monitor our air defense reaction. The Soviet Union is not the guilty party. These people lost their lives not because of the Soviet Union but because of the Cold War.

'Today, we have all here been subjected to a provocative anti-Soviet spectacle; nothing more than an instrument of psychological warfare mounted by the US against the USSR. And it is well known that in the job of disinformation American propaganda has no equal.'

His brief denouncement concluded, the Russian sat back, adjusted his collar and shared a few quiet words with the assistant seated behind him.

'Is that it?' Hank asked.

'Looks like,' replied Garret.

'You think anyone believed him?'

'That it was all our fault? No.'

'Then I'd say we've done a damn good job.'

The phone rang. Colonel Korolenko's eyes sprang open. He'd been dozing at his desk. Sleep had been hard to come by these last few nights. He picked up the handset.

'Colonel Korolenko?' asked the voice down the line.

'Speaking.'

'I have Comrade General Penkeyev for you.'

'Yes, of course,' Korolenko said, suddenly feeling as if his face had been splashed with ice water.

'Valentin,' came a familiar voice. 'How are you? Recovered yet from our marathon session with the delights of the distilled potato?'

'Yes, Comrade General. It was most enjoyable. Your hospitality is boundless.'

'Thank you for your warm note of thanks, and for the caviar, of course.'

'Not at all, Comrade General.'

Korolenko had sent the general several tins of the black Beluga caviar he was said to favor. It was always wise to cultivate a potential patron when such an opportunity presented itself.

'I wanted to call and give you the news,' said the general. 'I've just received word from Moscow. On the news tonight, a TASS statement will put an end to speculation. It will confirm that in the early hours of September 1, a Soviet interceptor fired upon an intruder aircraft believed to have been a reconnaissance aircraft performing specialist tasks.'

'Good news, then, Comrade General.'

'I thought you'd think so, Valentin. If I were you, I would make arrangements to transport your important cargo as soon as possible.'

'Yes, sir,' said Korolenko, suddenly charged with energy. 'And thank you, Comrade General.'

'Not at all, Valentin. Perhaps you can wring some profit from this disaster for us.'

'I will certainly try, Comrade General.'

'Good,' said Penkeyev, and the connection broke off.

January 29, 2012

NSA HQ, Fort Meade, Maryland. Investigator Englese strode across the parking lot, still furious over the way the arrest of the corrupt DEA agent had gone down in El Paso. It had been a damn fiasco. The bent agent had somehow received word of the bust at the last moment. He'd left his home and was climbing into an Agency four-by-four when the DEA and FBI agents closed in on him. Oh, and let's not forget NSA Investigator Miller Sherwood, thought Lana, who'd somehow managed to strap on a set of FBI body armor and a DEA 9 mm Sig-Sauer P228 sidearm.

The agents had fanned out and surrounded the suspect in the parking lot. He knew he had nowhere to go, except perhaps to a federal correctional facility where he'd be welcomed by the Aryan Brotherhood, among others. So the suspect had had a brain fart and taken himself prisoner. It was almost comical, like something out of a Will Ferrell movie. He was surrounded, and so he'd stuck his own firearm under his chin and threatened to pull the trigger, unless he was given safe passage across the border and into one of the luxury Mercedes SUVs chauffeured by his Colombian associates. And that's when Sherwood had shot him in the head. Just like that. It was a great shot, no doubt about it, but that was hardly the point. There were hostage negotiators who could have been brought in, psychologists . . . But Sherwood was pumped up on testosterone and untrained for the situation he found himself in. There'd be an investigation, of course, to determine whether it was a righteous shoot. And there was also the outstanding matter of who'd tipped off the now dead DEA agent in the first place, spooking him into making a run for it.

Sherwood would have to remain in El Paso for a couple of days while the investigation was concluded, but there was no doubt that he'd be exonerated. The deceased wasn't liked or respected and had a reputation for abusive, and occasionally violent, behavior toward his subordinate agents. Indeed, an hour after the shooting, Sherwood and several of the witnesses from both agencies had been in the bar high-fiving each other over tequila shots. So Lana had flown back to Maryland on her own.

She went through the security gauntlet on the ground floor and made for the elevator, the doors of which were open and waiting. As they slid shut in front of her, she was startled by Saul Kradich's face appearing in the shrinking gap, followed by his hand.

'Mind if I hitch a ride?' he asked, hopping in when the doors opened.

'Morning, Saul,' she said.

'What are you doing in here? It's Sunday.'

'Catching up on paperwork. You?'

'I thought I'd clean the toilets.'

'What?'

'Haven't you heard? I live here.'

'Yeah, actually I *had* heard that.'

The elevator arrived at Lana's floor. Kradich held the doors apart with his finger on the button.

'If you've got time, come on up to number six,' he said. 'See if we've had some hits on your friend.'

'Yeah, okay,' Lana replied. Anything to take her mind off El Paso. 'What would be a good time?'

'Whenever. I'm not that busy.'

'Then I'll see you in ten. I'll just dump my stuff,' she said.

Kradich gave her a wave as the doors closed and called out, 'I'm joking about the toilets.'

A little over ten minutes later, Lana was settling into the spare seat in virtual investigation booth two, Kradich's domain.

'I heard about your partner,' Kradich said as he completed various security checks required whilst logging in.

'What did you hear?'

'That you called him a meathead in front of the FBI folks.'

'Yeah, I did.'

Lana handed him her smart card. She then keyed in her code on a touchpad that simultaneously verified the DNA captured from the sweat on her fingertips against the biometric profile reduced to a bar-code in her record.

'A damn fine shot, though,' he observed, handing her card back once he'd swiped it.

'You saw it?'

'There was a digital surveillance security system covering the park-ing lot. I got eight angles on the shot. Better coverage than an NFL game. Wanna have a look?'

'No, thanks. Caught it live.'

Kradich shrugged and went back to work on the control screen. The lights in the room dimmed. The laser panels covering the wall in front of them filled with rolling waves, porpoises diving through the crystal sets. Above, the clouds were yellow, orange and purple in the sunrise.

'Feeling soothed?' he asked her.

'Is it that obvious?'

'There are thermal sensors in your seat. According to your heat sig-nature, you're angry and frustrated.'

'Saul, I appreciate the concern.' She didn't. 'I really do.' She really didn't. 'But do you mind if we just get on with it?'

'Oh. Sure.'

The waves dissolved to black and windows full of data burst like bubbles to the surface.

'So, let's see what we've got,' he said. 'Hmm . . . still nothing on those cell phones, as you can see. But then we think they're a dead end, don't we?'

Lana nodded.

'However, Ben Harbor hasn't been able to do much of anything recently without the NSA riding shotgun on his every move.' A new window popped up. 'Well, let's see here. Yesterday he logged a flight-plan and flew a Key West Seaplanes Bell JetRanger II from Key West to Gainesville via Orlando.'

'I wonder what he was doing in Gainesville,' Lana said. 'Where did he stay?'

Kradich got busy. A moment later, he said, 'There's no entry. He either took a room somewhere and paid cash, or he bunked in with friends.'

'Any record of him flying to Gainesville in the past year?' she asked.

Kradich's fingers were a blur. 'No,' he said after a minute. 'No flight-plans logged with him as the pilot, no plane tickets bought with a credit card. He could have borrowed a friend's car and driven there. You want me to check bus and rail options? See if he picked up any speeding tickets?'

'No,' said Lara. Gainesville—it could be something, it could be nothing. 'Let's move on.'

'He has two email accounts—hotmail and gmail. The hotmail one doesn't get much use. Looking at his gmail account, he's received dozens of emails from his mother and father, as well as from the Federal Airlines Administration and Amazon.com. You want to see what books he reads?'

Lana shook her head.

New windows opened. 'He gets hammered with the usual junk,' Kradich continued, 'including jokes and porn from several buddies who live in the Keys; there are several from a crematorium as well as a hospital in Atlanta. There are also a couple of emails apiece from a Jane Sanderson, Christina Meadows, Abigail Mercurio, Donna Velasquez, Vanessa Sebring, Melissa Tang, Margot—'

'I think I get the idea,' said Lana, uncomfortable, and annoyed with herself for feeling anything on a level that wasn't professional.

'And just this morning, one from a Tiffany Lane.' Kradich went back to his keyboard. 'Hmm . . . As for his cell phone—the one he's not hiding—the records for the last couple of weeks show that he's called his parents in Norfolk several times, Key West Seaplanes innumerable times, a firm of lawyers in Miami a few times, several of his buddies who feature in his in-tray, that crematorium and the hospital in Atlanta twice each . . . He's canceled the standard search and rescue entered as part of the flight-plan to Gainesville, and—oh, this morning, two calls from Tiffany Lane. Just stop me if anything here strikes your interest,' said Kradich.

Lana couldn't resist the pressure. 'Tiffany Lane. What's her address?'

'According to the records lodged against the SIM card . . . 1126 North East 14th Street, *Gainesville*.'

Lana caught the significance. 'Assuming that's still her address, can you tell me what she does?'

A few moments later, Kradich had the answer. 'Tiffany Lane is in her final year at the University of Florida. She studies veterinary science. Her grades are average.'

'Okay,' said Lana. 'She on Facebook, MySpace or Twitter?'

'Nope. Here we go . . . She also works at a bar, part-time. A place called Grundy's.'

Lana didn't want to know any more details. She had gotten the picture loud and clear.

'Hey, we've got photos,' said Kradich, pushing on regardless.

Up on the screen, a life-size photo of Tiffany Lane appeared. It was part of a one-page article in *Maxim* magazine where the woman had been named 'Beerwench of the Month'. Lane was strikingly tall, her long legs accentuated by a baby doll dress with a very short hemline, had prominent breasts and eyes that were surely too green not to have been retouched. She held a pitcher of beer in her hand.

'Hubba-hubba,' said Kradich. 'I think I know what your guy was doing in Gainesville.'

Lana didn't have to wonder what those heat sensors in her chair were reading.

'Shall we see what she wrote him?' Saul asked.

'I don't think that's necessary,' said Lana. 'Has he returned the call?'

'No.' Kradich admired the picture. '*No one* has a figure like that, not for real.'

'Would you like me to leave you alone with it for a few minutes?' asked Lana, seething.

'Huh? Oh, sorry . . . Gainesville's a university town. There are hundreds of bars there. Why would Ben have gone to this one specifically?'

'You've got your answer up there, haven't you?' said Lana, tilting her head at the picture of Tiffany Lane.

'She only turns up in the guy's comms this morning. Nothing from her before he went to Gainesville.'

'So you think he could've gone to that specific bar for some other reason?'

'Yeah, maybe. Let's see who owns it.'

Lana looked at the time. She'd already committed herself to working on this case for the day and it was still early.

Kradich dug into the bar's IRS records and had the answer within a minute. 'Grundy's is owned by a Jerome Morton Grundy.'

Lana shook her head. 'Who's he?'

'I'm working on it.' Kradich leaned over the control glass. Data blocks came and went onscreen. 'He's a guy who pulls beers,' said Kradich eventually. 'At least, that's who he is these days. But once upon a time, Jerome Grundy worked for the US Defense Intelligence Agency. He was an expert on the USSR during the last big spike in the Cold War before the wall came down. His main gig was at the US embassy in West Berlin. He was a heavy-hitter back then—personally briefed President Reagan on two separate occasions.'

The pieces swam through Lana's mind. Jerome Grundy, a Cold War expert, up on all things Russian. KAL 007, Curtis Foxx, the mystery tape, Tex Mitchell, Ben Harbor . . .

'I want to have a look at a money transfer that appeared in Curtis Foxx's bank account. And you can kill the floor show.'

The full-length shot of Tiffany Lane, which was still occupying a third of the wall, shrank to a white dot and disappeared. In its place appeared a tiled selection of bank statements.

Lana checked her notes. 'The amount we're looking for is $88,221.34,' she said.

Kradich quickly located the statement that displayed the transfer.

He then went to work on his control glass, accessing databases supposed to be closed to all external probes. 'The money was sent through a company called Shinju Global Processing,' he said. 'They're like Wells Fargo—a Japanese version thereof.'

'Can you trace the transfer to its original account?'

Numbers rolled over in a box displayed on the screen, quickly stabilizing. A name came up.

'Yuudai Suzuki,' Lana murmured, reading it. 'The money came from him? It is a *him*?'

'Yep. Yuudai is a male name. I assume it means nothing to you?' asked Kradich.

'No.'

'That's a Bank of Japan account, opened in Tokyo. Says here the account was closed not long after the transfer was made.'

'We got an address for Yuudai Suzuki?' Lana asked

'Sure do—a place called Horonaibuto.'

'Go there,' said Lana.

A map of Japan appeared and the view closed in on the northern island of Hokkaido, the city of Sapporo captioned on its southwest end, and then the township of Horonaibuto around thirty miles northeast of the city. The view settled above what appeared to be a garden with small houses crammed into it.

'What's that?' asked Lana.

Kradich went in for a closer look. 'A cemetery,' he said. 'Unless he's the caretaker there, I guess that explains why the account was closed—Yuudai's dead.' Kradich hunched over his control glass. 'And I can confirm that. Yuudai Suzuki died on January 8 at Sanjukai Hospital, Sapporo. Pancreatic cancer. He was sixty-one. Before he died, he resided in Sapporo.'

'So Suzuki sent money to Curtis Foxx, who then passed it along to his son, Ben Harbor,' Lana said, thinking aloud. 'Yuudai and Curtis died at approximately the same time—within days of each other. Did they have some kind of death pact?'

'You want to have a look at this other large debit from Suzuki's account just before he died?' asked Kradich.

'Oh, yeah? Which one is that?'

'This one for over ¥10,600,000.'

'That sounds like a lot of money,' said Lana.

'Unless you're Donald Trump—around $96,000 US.'

Lana blinked.

'That's around the same amount Curtis Foxx left his son,' Kradich observed.

Lana nodded. The pattern was revealing itself.

'This one was debited from the account via a bank check.'

'Who cashed it?'

'I'm working on it.'

After a minute of silence, Kradich announced, 'Akiko Sato—a resident of Tokyo. A 31-year-old female. A teacher.'

Lana shook her head. The name meant nothing, but there *had* to be a connection between these four people: Akiko Sato, Yuudai Suzuki, Curtis Foxx and Ben Harbor. She just had to find it. Where to look . . . ?

'What do we know about Moneybags Suzuki?'

Kradich leaned way back in his familiar astronaut-on-the-launch-pad position with the control screen in his lap, settling in for the long haul. Up on the laser screen, the familiar eye symbol of the computer's cursor seemed to be winking at her. And then a head shot appeared—distinctly Asian, male, round, almost fat, wearing a blank expression. A passport-style photo. The man was in his late twenties, possibly early thirties. Chunks of information began to fill the screen, all of it in Japanese.

'Yuudai was in the military.'

Promising, thought Lana.

'You want to start there?' Kradich asked.

She nodded. 'Can you put a translation filter over the Japanese?'

The Japanese characters were suddenly replaced with English. Lana's eyes widened as she read. Yuudai Suzuki had been a radar operator in the Japan Defense Force. For most of his career, he was seconded to the Chobetsu. He was stationed at Misawa Air Base, June 1981 to October 1982; Wakkanai, October 1982 to November 1983; Kadena Air Base, November 1983 to September 1984; Misawa Air Base, September 1984 till his discharge from the military in May 1986.

'Where are these facilities located?' she asked.

The map of Japan widened so that the main islands were visible. Kadena was pinpointed on Okinawa in the far south, Misawa on the main island of Honshu, and Wakkanai on the far northern tip of the island of Hokkaido, almost within spitting distance of Sakhalin Island.

'Okay . . .' Lana whispered. 'Can you tell me if this guy was on duty on the night of August 31 to September 1, 1983?'

Kradich worked his control screen and the larger screen filled with data blocks.

'No. Someone's been lazy. Records that far back are yet to be digitized; 1985 is as early as they go.'

'Let's assume that he was,' said Lana, thinking out loud. 'What's the range of the Wakkanai facility?'

Kradich dug into the facility's specifications. 'To summarize,' he said after a minute, 'they had low and high level, primary and secondary coverage. Out to 210 miles.'

'So the Wakkanai radar would have tracked the Korean airliner long before it reached the Sakhalin coastline,' she said. Kradich waited while Lana ran through what she knew. 'So we have the pilot who possibly shadowed KAL 007 as it entered Soviet airspace, and the radar operator who possibly witnessed its destruction, and both are in contact with each other. Had Yuudai ever traveled to the US?'

Kradich searched the US State Department's records first. Lana got up and moved around the room, her fingers tingling with electricity. At last they were getting somewhere.

'He might have rotated through here while he was in the Chosa Besshitsu, but there's no mention of it in his records. I've got his passport number and checked it against immigration records, all of which are now held by Homeland Security, but the guy's passport number doesn't register a hit. So, as far as I can be sure, Yuudai Suzuki has never been to the US.'

'What about Foxx? He ever go to Japan?'

It didn't take Kradich long to come up with the answer. 'Look at this,' he said as a list of entry and exit dates came up onscreen.

'This is good,' Lana exclaimed when the information was displayed.

'August 29, 1984; August 28, 1985; August 26, 1986; August 30, 1990. '92, '95, '99, 2002, 2003 . . . Pretty regularly since '83.'

'Looks like he never stayed longer than ten days. You want exit dates?' Kradich asked.

'No—let's keep moving,' Lana replied.

Foxx had gone to Japan for a specific reason. She was as sure as she could be that he'd headed to Wakkanai. Perhaps he thought of the journey as a kind of pilgrimage. She remembered his mental state detailed in his medical discharge—maybe he went there to assuage feelings of guilt, to atone.

'His entry port was always Narita,' Kradich said. 'There are no records for through connections.'

'I want to see if we can put Suzuki and Foxx together. Is there a way we can do that? Where did they meet? Foxx went to Japan often, landing just before the anniversary of the 007 incident. Perhaps the two men met on one of those occasions—perhaps on all of them.'

'I'll limit the search to Japan, have the names Curtis Foxx and Yuudai Suzuki grouped together, and enter the periods a week either side of the dates Foxx is incountry.'

'Sounds good. Anything I can do?' Lana asked.

'Nothing you'd be prepared to,' replied Kradich, giving her a grin. 'Maybe get us both a cup of coffee?'

'Done.'

'Cream and sugar,' he told her.

'Back in a minute.'

Lana ducked out and closed the door behind her. The corridor was deserted. She went to a nearby kitchen. Someone had thoughtfully brewed a pot of coffee. She took out a pair of mugs, running on autopilot while she considered who this Akiko Sato might be, where she might fit in. The woman was still a mystery. She was Japanese, obviously, and connected in some way to Yuudai Suzuki. Why, otherwise, would he leave her a small fortune?

Lana swiped her way back into Kradich's domain, juggling the mugs of coffee. She was surprised to see that the screen on the wall was occupied by the picture of a large seagoing vessel.

'What's that?' she asked, taking her seat and putting Kradich's coffee on the bench beside him.

'That's the *Soya Maru Number 7*,' he replied.

'And it's significant because . . . ?'

'The search wasn't as difficult as we thought.' He touched the control glass and a list of names in both Japanese and English appeared. 'On September 2, 1984, the Japanese ferry *Soya Maru Number 7* embarked for the Sea of Japan between Moneron Island and Sakhalin Island with seventy-nine grieving relatives of the passengers of KAL 007 on board. Apparently they went to throw flowers and clothes into the water for the spirits of the dead passengers—a Buddhist/Shinto thing. Look who also made the journey.' Two names became highlighted on the list: Yuudai Suzuki and Curtis Foxx.

The skin on Lana's forearms turned to gooseflesh. 'So we know where they met.'

'A fair assumption. And turns out there were a couple of other interesting people on board that ship,' said Kradich as two other names became highlighted: Hatsuto Sato and Akiko Sato.

'Oh, wow,' said Lana, a smile of wonder on her lips.

'There was a Nami Sato, thirty-one years of age, on 007. My guess is that she was Hatsuto's wife. Akiko was their daughter. This is Akiko today.'

A passport photo of a woman in perhaps her late twenties appeared. Even in the typically unflattering passport shot, the Japanese woman was pretty, thought Lana.

'What can you give me on her?' she asked.

'I'm putting together a dossier on her now,' Kradich replied.

Up onscreen, hundreds of documents appeared and disappeared in the blink of an eye as massively powerful processors trawled through trillions of bits of information, sifting the relevant from the chaff. A box opened with a glowing red code. Kradich frowned and went to investigate. A second photo of Akiko Sato appeared on the screen.

'What's the significance of that?' Lana asked.

'On January 15, Akiko Sato passed through the port of LAX on a tourist visa. This is the immigration photo.'

Lana shook her head, in awe of the investigative power that could be commanded from the comfort of a leather-backed chair in one of these VI booths. 'Let me guess . . . Akiko had a through connection to Key West.'

'Uh-huh,' said Kradich after he'd fed an enquiry into the system. 'Flew Continental.'

A familiar map appeared onscreen—Key West covered by interlocking circles of cell phone base transceiver stations. Lana knew exactly where Kradich was going.

'Those circles cover a couple of pretty big hotels,' he said. 'I'm just interrogating their guest registers.'

A box opened with the following information: *Name: Akiko Sato; Nationality: Japanese; Passport: LM9897692. Check in: Jan 15. Check out: Jan 16; Jan 22; Jan 31.'*

'She's extended a few times,' said Kradich.

'What's the hotel?'

'The Crowne Plaza La Concha, 430 Duval Street, Key West. And guess what? That's right in the middle of our BTS circle,' said Kradich as a glowing green dot, indicating the hotel's address, appeared almost in the center of the transceiver station's footprint. 'Looks to me like you've got your third cell phone user.'

As he spoke, the information from the hotel amended itself. The check out now read Jan 29.

'What does that mean?' asked Lana.

'Akiko Sato has just shortened her stay.'

'Today's the twenty-ninth.'

'Then we've missed her. She just checked out.'

September 8, 1983

Dolinsk-Sokol Air Base, Sakhalin Island, USSR. The engineers were climbing all over the Boeing 747 beneath the camouflage netting, working out how best to dispose of it. The job would be a big one and it would have to be done soon. American spy satellites had not yet passed overhead, but surely it was only a matter of time. Korolenko had been informed by the engineers that explosives would do most of the cutting, which was why the firefighters were pumping foam and fire retardants into the Boeing's fuel tanks, other fire trucks standing by. A man was grinding out a portion of the fin bearing the plane's identification number: HL7442. When Soviet civilian divers inspected the wreckage on the sea floor, there would be no mistake. Korolenko had been informed that a site had been chosen in the Sea of Japan, far to the north of Moneron Island and well within Soviet nineteen-kilometer territorial waters. The coordinates of the site were secret.

The KGB colonel got back into the vehicle and gestured to the driver to move on. The black sedan turned through 180 degrees and accelerated back down the taxiway toward the Tupolev 154 with Aeroflot markings parked near the prison block. As he approached the familiar T-tail aircraft, Korolenko could see two men, both chained at the wrists and ankles, black hoods over their heads, being led from the rear of a truck to the stairs positioned behind the aircraft's wing. The prisoners shuffled, leaning against their armed escorts. In eight hours, they would have a new home.

The driver swung the GAZ limousine behind the truck and headed for the aircraft hangar where the segregated prisoners were housed. Armed guards jumped to attention when the colonel stepped out of the vehicle. He ignored them and walked to the shipping container that held KAL 007's most valuable cargo. Two armed sergeants standing by the only door came to attention. Korolenko motioned at them to open up. One man checked the slot in the door. Satisfied by what he saw, he unlocked the heavy padlock, released the chain and slipped the greased bolt. The door opened and Korolenko stepped inside.

'Good morning, Congressman,' he said to the disheveled man sitting on the side of a cot welded to the floor of the container.

Lawrence McDonald had been asleep when he'd heard the door opening and one of his eyes was gummed partially shut. 'What do you want?' he asked.

Korolenko noted the man's tone. He was angry.

'Today is the day.'

'The day for what?'

Korolenko folded his arms and regarded the prisoner. So this man was a representative of the American people, he thought. Not so formidable after all.

'A decision has been made that affects you.'

'What decision?'

'Yesterday Moscow announced to the world that it shot down an intruding aircraft, an aircraft believed to have been on a reconnaissance mission. Do you know what this means?'

'It means that your commie friends in Moscow were too cowardly and sniveling to admit from the start that they're bloodthirsty pirates.'

A half smile occupied Korolenko's mouth. There was still plenty of defiance left in the man. 'In fact, it means that the world believes KAL 007 is somewhere on the bottom of the Sea of Japan. It means that you are now our permanent guest, along with your fellow passengers.'

The Adam's apple in Lawrence McDonald's throat bobbed up and down. 'Washington will never fall for it. You can't make a 747 disappear.'

'Perhaps your omnipotent CIA is not as pervasive as you have been led to believe, Lawrence.'

'You won't get away with it.'

'I wondered whether you would say that. I have heard it said many times in your movies.' Korolenko snapped out an order over his shoulder and the two sergeants came in with leg and wrist chains. He then chuckled and said to the congressman, 'I believe the correct answer is that we *are* getting away with it.'

The guards strode past the colonel. One of them pulled his nightstick and tapped McDonald's arm. From recent experience, the congressman knew what was expected of him. He compliantly presented his hands to his captors, who fitted the chains. He then slid his feet forward away from the cot, the ankles slightly apart, so the manacles could be locked into place. The two guards lifted him to his feet.

'If Washington has turned its back on us, then it's because the administration can see a benefit in it. You're being manipulated, Colonel. How does it feel to be a pawn?'

Korolenko nodded at the guards and a black hood was produced and slipped over the American's head.

'This is not necessary,' came the congressman's muffled voice from beneath it.

'I'm afraid it is,' said Korolenko. 'Also it is necessary for you to stop talking. You will not speak until I say otherwise. This rule will be enforced.'

Colonel Korolenko pointed at the guard's nightstick and then at the congressman's leg. The guard nodded, drew the nightstick back and smacked it hard against the American's thigh. The unexpected shock of the impact made McDonald cry out as his leg buckled beneath him. The guards were ready and half dragged him out of his temporary cell.

Colonel Korolenko chose to ride with the captain of the detail in the back of a glossy black Fifth Chief Directorate ZIL. Ahead, five armored vehicles provided by the Fourth Transportation Directorate accompanied the two Ural trucks moving the prisoners. The convoy sped through busy Moscow intersections, the cross traffic held back by at least half a dozen military police officers on speeding motorcycles. It was the quickest trip Korolenko had ever made to the center of the sprawling city from Ramenskoye Airfield forty kilometers to the southwest. Korolenko had felt that a lower-key passage through Moscow might have been more suitable. Others within the Fifth Directorate had wanted no chances taken. Their desire was to have the prisoners safely under lock and key as soon as possible, and their collective voice won the decision. Who or what was possibly going to intercept the prisoners in the heart of the Soviet Union's capital? Korolenko had wondered. Nevertheless, he gave way to discretion. He had played his part. High-security prisoner transportation was their job, not his. It was time others took the lead.

Colonel Korolenko and the Fifth Directorate captain did not speak. It was Korolenko's prerogative to begin any conversation with the junior officer and he chose not to. It had been a long day. Nine time zones had been crossed in the last eight hours and he was tired.

The convoy took the Sadevaya–Sukharevskaya ulitsa route, approaching its destination from the north to avoid the worst of Moscow's inner-city snarl. As the convoy turned to the right, Korolenko glanced out the window and recalled the familiar streetscape of Myasnitskaya ulitsa, buildings lingering from earlier in the century rubbing shoulders with more masculine structures from Stalin's time. Muscovites hurried along the sidewalks in the late evening gloom, looking at their feet as they walked in their black overcoats and jackets. The mood of the city was said to be uncertain. Korolenko believed he could feel it. After the stability of Brezhnev and now the rumored failing health of Andropov, these were indeed uncertain times.

The colonel had driven down this very ulitsa countless times, first as a captain and then as a major, en route to work. Another right-hand turn and the convoy motored into Furkasovsky perelok, a dark cobbled cave of a street. The motorcycle police fanned out, blocking the street at both ends. The armored vehicles pulled to the side, allowing the prison trucks to take the lead. They stopped a little further on, and waited as a heavy gate set into the wall rolled up into its recess. The trucks and the

ZIL then began to inch slowly forward, into the rear receiving entrance of the Lubyanka—KGB headquarters and the most feared prison in all of the Soviet Union.

The gate came down behind Korolenko's ZIL and the courtyard filled with uniformed KGB officers, enlisted men and dogs.

'Nicely handled, Comrade Captain,' Korolenko told the man he'd been sitting beside as the car door was opened from the outside.

'*Spasiba, ser,*' replied the younger officer. Thank you, sir.

Colonel Korolenko received a salute from the enlisted man holding open his door.

'Valentin! *Zdrastvuytye, zdrastvuytye!*' A voice from behind called a greeting.

Korolenko turned and recognized an old friend. 'Colonel Ozerov! Hello to you, too. *Kag zhihzn?*' How's life?

The two men shook.

'*Nye zhaluyus,*' Ozerov said. Can't complain.

Both men had been young captains at the Lubyanka together, learning the ropes from the old hands, those who had survived the purges—tough men, hard.

'Is that gray hair I see?' Korolenko asked, examining the back of Ozerov's neck, the short-cropped growth beneath the band of his broad peaked cap.

'Yes. Unlike you, I haven't been vacationing all these years out in the mysterious Far East. You haven't changed at all.'

'*Pha,*' Korolenko scoffed. 'Then I see your memory is failing, too.'

Colonel Ozerov smiled. 'I have received word, Valentin. You have done some good work for the motherland by all accounts,' he said, getting down to business as they watched the hooded, shackled prisoners being led down a ramp, one of them being carried.

'Lucky to be in the right place at the right time,' said Korolenko. 'I heard you would be heading up the project at this end.'

'Yes. For once the rumors are true.'

'I have written up a full report for you.'

'Once we get them settled, share a glass or two of vodka with me and give me a verbal debrief to go with it.'

Drinking, especially on an empty stomach, was the last thing Korolenko wanted to do, but, as with General Penkeyev, he couldn't refuse, though this time it was for different reasons. With Ozerov, an old comrade, leading the interrogation there was a chance that Korolenko could maintain a connection with Congressman McDonald and witness the man's inevitable dissolution. *That* was something he wanted to see. And, indeed, General Penkeyev had slipped a temporary attachment for him through the system. Once his affairs were wound up in Sakhalin, Korolenko could return to the Lubyanka where he was to be attached to the Fifth Chief Directorate, the arm responsible for the interrogation of Soviet and foreign citizens.

'Which one is the congressman?' whispered Ozerov.

'I believe that's him now,' said Korolenko, nodding at a man being assisted from the back of the truck and led down the ramp.

'He doesn't look anything special. I hope he is worth it.'

'He's worth it,' said Korolenko.

'Has he talked?'

'No.'

'What about the rest of them?'

'They are sponges that will require only the gentlest of squeezes to give up their water. In my report you'll find many notes and observations.' He lifted the bulging briefcase by his side.

'Excellent. Well, Valentin, excuse me for a moment,' said Ozerov. He walked a few paces from Korolenko and stopped beside a large man in a drab green greatcoat. 'Form them up, Sergeant,' he said.

The sergeant immediately shouted an order. The sudden sound of a human voice appeared to bewilder the hooded prisoners; their shoulders turned toward the source. One of the dogs barked, its handler choking off the sound into a snarl and then a whimper. The security unit pushed the sixteen men and two women into a single line and then removed the hoods. Fear widened the prisoners' eyes. All seemed to prefer the blind security provided by the utter blackness of the hood, beneath which they could comfort themselves with the security of their own breathing and the warmth of their breath. One of the women and four of the men were weeping.

The situation they found themselves in was grim in the extreme: surrounded by drab green trucks, panting attack dogs and around thirty bull-necked guards, their eyes hidden beneath peaked caps. The high enclosing walls of the courtyard were pale yellow above rain-slicked cobbles and stonework blackened with almost a century of grime and tears.

'Welcome to Moscow, the capital city of the glorious Union of Soviet Socialist Republics,' said Colonel Ozerov with a smile, his English as lubricious as the Volga in mid-thaw. He strolled down the line. 'Welcome to the Lubyanka, though do not expect to get too comfortable. All of you will be moved to other establishments in due course. For those of you who know nothing of the Lubyanka, it holds a special place within the revolution of the Soviet peoples. It was for many years the tallest building in Russia because the Road of Bones in Siberia could be seen from its basement.' The colonel chuckled at the very old joke. 'Comrade Stalin had many enemies imprisoned here. For countless thousands, its walls were the last things they saw. I am telling you this to serve as a warning. Here, you will follow instructions or you will pay the consequences. Fortunately, you will only have to pay them once. Nod if you understand me.' All the prisoners nodded. 'Good,' he said.

Ozerov switched to Russian and said something to the sergeant, who immediately started shouting at his men. The former passengers of KAL 007 found themselves being pushed and shoved and herded up broad stairs toward the Lubyanka's thick double doors, open like the mouth of some massive and hungry carnivore.

'Where will you conduct the interrogation of 98987?' Korolenko asked as he and Colonel Ozerov descended the stairs. The vodka burned like a hurricane lamp inside his stomach, making him forget how fatigued and hungry he'd been feeling.

'There is a dacha near Zavidovo, just outside Moscow,' said Ozerov. 'It looks like a peasant villa, but it has an extensive cellar. Soundproofed, of course. They say Beria made use of it.'

'If it was good enough for the old master . . .' said Korolenko, impressed. Lavrenty Pavlovich Beria, chief of the now defunct NKVD, was Joseph Stalin's supreme architect of mass murder and disappearance. It was said he even did away with Stalin, the old Georgian, himself.

'We're planning to move him there within seventy-two hours. I'll install my mistress in the town, spend the week there on important state business—or so I'll inform my wife—and commute back to Moscow on the weekend. It's perfect.'

'As always, you have it all worked out, old friend.'

'Food and televisions might be scarce, but the warmth of a young Russian maiden is still a resource the Soviet Union has in abundance,' said Ozerov. 'Did you marry?'

'I came close to it once or twice, but no. I never married.'

That wasn't true. Korolenko hadn't come close to marrying anyone. In fact, he hadn't had a relationship in years, unable to form any worthwhile attachment to anyone or anything aside from work.

'Well, if you feel the urge come upon you, we have some willing inmates here at the moment. There is one Kazakh woman in particular. Breasts like snowy peaks. She is a screamer . . .' He shook his head, looked to the heavens and added a soft whistle.

A single bare light bulb burned in the overhead socket mounted on the angled concrete roof of the stairwell. It failed to keep at bay the shadows, which clung to the corners like living things cowed by unspeakable terror. The walls were painted a red that reminded Korolenko of clotted blood. The red stopped halfway up the wall; above it, the concrete was a dirt and grit-caked white. The air was bone dry and laced with ancient dust and the pungency of human excrement. Korolenko found the nostalgic familiarity of these sights and smells from his younger days oddly reassuring.

The stairwell ended in a heavy steel door with a sliding metal plate at eye level. Colonel Ozerov slid back the plate and received a visual ID check from the single bloodshot eye of a security guard on the other side. Bolts greased for silent operation were released and the door swung open soundlessly. Beyond it, the concrete corridor was lit much like the stairwell—bare light bulbs burning at regularly spaced intervals. The walls also shared the stairwell's bleak color scheme. The most significant difference was on the floor, where a thick brown carpet had been laid to reduce the conveyance of sound. The air was still and as utterly quiet as death itself, and the smell of human excrement was almost thick enough to slice. Both Ozerov and Korolenko kept absolutely silent. They signed the security guard's schedule and made a mental note of the cell number holding prisoner 98987.

Korolenko counted down the numbers on the cell doors as they passed. Up ahead, a guard peeped through the judas hole into a cell. Not liking what he saw, he drew his rubber truncheon, opened the door and rushed in. Korolenko heard a series of thumps and slaps, along with a grunt and a few cries. The cell was number 163, the one holding the prisoner they were here to see. The guard backed out just as they arrived, closing the thick concrete door silently.

'What's going on? How's the *zek*?' Ozerov asked under his breath.

Korolenko noted the use of the abbreviated slang for prisoner— *tyurzek*. Yes, McDonald was now truly in the system.

'He fell asleep,' the guard whispered, his anger mixed with nervousness at the unexpected presence of the two high-ranking officers. The prisoner's wakefulness was his responsibility and he had been derelict in his duty.

'Hmm . . .' Ozerov frowned with disapproval at the man. 'See that this crime is not repeated.'

'Yes, Comrade Colonel, *ser*,' the guard whispered, his back ramrod straight.

Ozerov shook his head in disgust and turned to look at the prisoner, putting his eye against the judas hole. Satisfied by what he saw, he beckoned Korolenko forward to have a look. The cell, two meters long by a meter wide, was so brightly lit with banks of high-watt globes behind grated recesses in the walls and ceiling that Korolenko's eye began to water after just a few seconds. Congressman Lawrence McDonald was standing in the center of the cell, the low ceiling forcing him to stoop. There were fresh welts on his face and his chest was heaving, trying to capture a breath.

The cell itself was bare. A bench too narrow to lie on jutted from the wall opposite the door. The only furniture was a plastic bucket—empty. McDonald, bare-footed, still wore his gray suit pants, though his shirt had been confiscated and replaced by a graying undershirt. His face was dirty, and fresh blood seeped from the wound on his cheek. His hair was unkempt and he wore a week's worth of beard. It was hot in the cell under all those lights and he was sweating. As Korolenko watched, the congressman shifted his weight from one foot to the other and his hooded eyelids drooped and then closed. He had just fallen asleep standing up.

The colonel backed away from the door and made a gesture to the guard, who stepped forward for a peek. When he saw what McDonald was doing, he swore under his breath, unlocked the cell and rushed in. Korolenko heard slapping sounds. The congressman made a muffled grunt. The guard backed out of the cell, keeping his eye on the prisoner, and again closed the door behind him.

Korolenko took another look at the congressman through the judas hole. The man's face was red and he looked angry, but he stood where he'd been told to stand and he was getting the very simple yet terrifying lesson: sleep was forbidden.

'After seventy-two hours without sleep,' Ozerov observed, 'he will beg us to kill him.'

January 30, 2012

Courtyard Miami Airport South, Miami, Florida. Akiko handed over the passport, opened at the page on which the visa had been affixed. She watched Ben take it and examine it, holding it close.

'People actually read this language?' he commented.

'Mind if I have a look?' asked Tex, sitting at the dining room table, a large map of the Russian Federation spread out in front of him.

Ben handed it over, saying, 'Looks like writing reversed in a mirror.'

'Wait till you hear it spoken. Did you have any trouble getting these visas?' Tex asked Akiko as he examined the document.

'No,' she said. 'Money dissolves Russian red tape—the more you pay the easier it gets. I paid a lot and they issued them within a day instead of the usual three weeks. What about the tickets?' she asked, surveying the hotel room. Backpacks and clothes were piled here and there, some of it still carrying labels and tags. Various items had also been purchased for her, a goose-down jacket and pants among them.

'Easy: US Airways to London's Heathrow, and then British Airways to Moscow. Paid with the Radio Shack corporate AmEx. Less chance of being flagged on NSA watch lists. The flights were booked—I had to buy business-class tickets to get you on. You leave Miami International tomorrow afternoon at one o'clock.'

'Tomorrow?' Akiko asked, eyebrow raised.

'The quicker the better,' said Tex. 'Even though we used a hard-to-trace payment method, air tickets have been issued in your names using your passport numbers. Who knows what kind of filters the NSA have running to keep tabs on Ben. And perhaps you. We're playing it safe, remember. If I'd had my way, you'd have been on that plane today.'

'We need to get all our documents photocopied—four copies of everything—so that Ben and I can keep duplicates of each other's papers, as well as our own,' said Akiko.

'Why the caution?' Ben asked.

'Russia isn't America, or Japan,' Akiko replied. 'When I was last there, I was stopped by a policeman. He asked to see my passport. I showed it to him. He confiscated it because he said it "contained irregularities". I was told later at the Japanese embassy in Moscow that the police often do this—authentic passports fetch a high price on the black market. Identity theft is big business in Russia. We have to be careful.'

Tex agreed.

'Where are we staying?' she asked.

'I've booked us a suite at the Moscow Park Hyatt,' said Ben. 'Nothing special, except for the room rate.'

'It was expensive, wasn't it?' Akiko said.

'Keeps the honest folks out.'

Akiko smiled. 'Moscow is the most expensive city in Europe. It is also the business hub for that part of the world. On the weekends, many of the hotels reduce their rate by half. How much was it?'

'A very reasonable US$1800 per night.'

'Maybe Yuudai and Curtis left you all that money because they knew this was going to be a pricy exercise,' Tex suggested.

'Or maybe the people at the Park Hyatt know a sucker when he rings them,' said Ben. 'What about credit cards? Can we use them? Does the NSA's reach extend to Russia?'

'I doubt it,' said Tex.

'But there are other problems. Every third night we stay in Russia we have to report to the tourist police,' Akiko informed them. 'It's the law and the hotels stick to it.'

'The place sounds friendlier by the minute.'

'How did you go with Lucas's Gainesville friend?' Akiko asked Ben, changing the subject. 'Did he have any advice?'

'Don't bother was his first suggestion.'

Akiko's face darkened.

'Hey, Stalin made 20 million people disappear in Siberia. And we're looking for *one* person.'

'So you got nothing worthwhile?' Tex asked, diplomatically stepping in.

Ben sighed, leaned over the map, took a pencil and circled a body of water three-quarters of the way across the eastern end of Russia. 'Apparently this is one area worth poking around in.'

'Lake Baikal,' said Akiko. 'Yes, I've heard of it.'

'It's a very exciting place if you like fresh water. The lake apparently contains one-fifth of the world's supply of it. It's also very popular with ticks—millions vacation there every summer. It's such a pleasant area, in fact, that quite a few gulags were located here. The inmates were used as slave labor in the local forestry industry. Your mother being Japanese and looking not too dissimilar to the local Mongol population—no offense, Akiko . . .'

'None taken.'

' . . . there's a chance she could have been sent to one of the camps here. Grundy also suggested sniffing around Ulan-Ude.' Ben circled the town just above the top of Mongolia, and another town hundreds of miles further to the east. 'And over here, north of Khabarovsk. Making things trickier, the positions of the gulags weren't indicated on any maps. I guess because they never expected tourists.'

Akiko was suddenly struck by the magnitude of their task, which Ben's sarcasm only accentuated. They'd be wandering around an area larger than the United States, asking questions of people who were notoriously distrustful of strangers. What were the chances of success? Nil, if she understood Ben correctly.

'I looked on the web. It's currently minus thirty degrees in Khabarovsk,' Akiko heard Tex say. 'Ben, you won't have experienced cold like that in Miami.'

'You've convinced me. Let's not go.'

'Pack thermal undies and you'll be fine,' Tex replied.

'Any ideas how we move around?' Ben enquired. 'I don't see any roads on this map.'

'The sub-zero temperatures will help,' said Akiko. 'At this time of year, the rivers are all frozen solid. They use them as roads. Lake Baikal is one gigantic ice rink. There are also trains.' She leaned over the map. 'See? The Trans-Siberian Railway connects Khabarovsk and Irkutsk— that's the main city at Lake Baikal.'

'Once you're incountry, I want to know where you're both headed,' said Tex. 'If something happens, I need to know where to look for you.'

'We'll send postcards,' said Ben.

'The postal service out there will be at least three weeks behind your movements.' Tex was thoughtful. 'SMS me. Keep it short. It's worth the risk. What are you going to do first?'

'Grundy thought it would be a good idea to check into the Luby-anka,' said Ben. 'Who knows, maybe someone scratched a clue into a cell wall.'

No one smiled.

'And if that fails,' he continued, 'there are always the prison records. We might find someone prepared to give us a look.'

'At the Lubyanka? Don't hold your breath,' said Tex.

'We might get lucky.' Ben shrugged. 'And if not, it'll be a short trip.'

Ben turned and walked to the window, frustrated. Miami International Airport was just across the expressway. They'd be back in a week with nothing to show for it. What they were planning was plain dumb and somehow his dead father had manipulated him into it. A Continental 747 landed on the runway parallel to the expressway, its engines scream-ing in reverse, a plume of water mist and vapor billowing around the wings.

He felt a presence behind him. He knew who it was before she spoke.

'Thank you,' Akiko said.

'Thank you for what?'

'For everything you've done; for everything you will do.'

Ben turned to face her. 'I'm not Curtis Foxx, Akiko. He ran into burning buildings to save people. You still don't get it . . . I'm way too selfish to do anything like that.'

January 31, 2012

NSA HQ, Fort Meade, Maryland. Lana swiped her way into the briefing room with her right hand, a thumb drive keeping the fingers of her left hand occupied. A buzzing sound followed by a green light on a panel at eye level told her the lock had disengaged and that she could enter. She pushed through the door and saw two men sitting at the pale, rose-colored wood table, waiting for her. One was Sam Whittle, her section head, a guy who must have had something compromising tucked away on the current NSA director because she had no idea how someone so inept could remain on the payroll, let alone climb through the ranks. The other man was a complete stranger.

'Ah, Englese,' said Whittle in his distinctively nasal voice. 'Where's your partner?'

'Down in Texas, sir.'

'Still? I wanted to tell him his transfer had come through.'

'Transfer, sir?' Lana asked, puzzled.

'He's going over to the dark side—FBI. I see you didn't know.'

'No, sir,' said Lana. She was surprised, but sanguine about it. The Bureau was the best place for Miller Sherwood, the bullshit fiasco in El Paso—the reason for his absence—proof of that.

The stranger with Whittle gave a polite cough.

'Okay, well, moving right along, this is Mr Buck from CIA.'

'Mr Buck,' said Lana.

'Ms Englese,' Buck replied.

Whittle sat back, slouched, his fingers interlocked across a beer belly, his unfashionable black-framed glasses pushed up on his head, holding back a mane of long gray hair that should have been chopped off long ago.

Lana passed her investigator's eye over the CIA man. He was in his early sixties; so, close to retirement. He wore a blue business suit, white shirt, red silk tie. The suit was quality: microfine wool fabric and tailored; the tie, silk. He was short, lean, somewhat rodent-looking with sharp features, dyed brown hair, some old scarring on his neck. He had the look of a man who'd seen combat in his time. He also looked too well paid, a fact confirmed by the plain black Mont Blanc refillable pencil that lay across a leather-jacketed notepad on the table in front of him.

· Lana took a seat opposite the two men. She glanced up at the screen on the end wall. The hard drive was running so she inserted her USB thumb drive into the laptop on the table between them.

'What have you got for us today?' asked Whittle, a smile on almost non-existent lips.

'Just to recap, a former RC-135 pilot by the name of Curtis Eugene Foxx, recently deceased, was a person of interest to the Agency. There were indications that Foxx may have had privileged information, perhaps even classified material, concerning the crash of a Korean airliner in 1983 that he passed to his son after his death. The son is one Benjamin Harbor of Key West, Florida, a charter pilot.'

Both men agreed with a nod.

'The source of these indications or the nature of the material wasn't included in my brief. And while the enquiry has had a low priority,' she continued, running her finger over the touch pad on the laptop and opening up the file, 'I can confirm upfront that I believe sensitive material not only exists, but is in circulation.'

Buck shifted in his seat, somehow more keenly focused.

'Take us through your thinking, Investigator,' said Whittle.

Both men listened intently as Lana outlined what her investigation had uncovered, mentioning Ben Harbor and the items bequeathed to him by his late father, Curtis Foxx, and concluding with the key to a safe deposit box.

Up onscreen, these objects appeared as captions within unconnected squares.

'A safe deposit box,' Buck repeated.

'It was numbered 007,' she said. 'I managed to acquire the key to this box, which was held at a branch of the Bank of America in Orlando. There was nothing in it. Whatever the contents might have been, Harbor had already removed them.'

'What do you think was in it?' Buck asked.

'A tape,' Lana said.

'A tape of what?'

'Using surveillance equipment, we tracked Harbor to a radio station on Key West where he tried to have the tape played. This proved unsuccessful. My partner and I subsequently approached Mr Harbor and asked for the tape. He declined to hand it over, claiming it was unreadable and had been thrown out.'

Lana paused to collect her thoughts, using the growing flow chart up on the screen to help her order them.

'Is that it?' asked Whittle.

'No, sir,' Lana replied. 'While my partner and I were interviewing Harbor at his place of residence, he received a call on a cell phone he was trying to hide. We managed to trace the call. An employee of the Homestead Florida Radio Shack purchased the phone, plus two others. The owner of this Radio Shack is Lieutenant Colonel Dallas "Tex" Mitchell, USAF, retired, the last surviving crew member known to have flown with Curtis Foxx.'

Lana noted that Buck seemed agitated as he scrawled some notes.

'Investigator Sherwood and I believed that Mitchell, being somewhat experienced with NSA methods, had established a closed communications network where he, Ben Harbor and a third party might communicate with each other with some degree of security.'

'Why did Mitchell think the NSA might be snooping around?'

'Because my partner and I interviewed him early on in the course of our investigation,' said Lana.

297

'How do you know Mitchell and Harbor had contacted each other prior to the establishment of the cell network between them?' Whittle asked.

Lana took a deep breath and launched into sanitized details of her first meeting with Ben. She then moved on to the money trail, which led to the former Chobetsu radar operator, Yuudai Suzuki, and to Akiko Sato, the daughter of one of the passengers onboard KAL 007.

As she expanded on these details she could see that Buck was tense, the aura of cool dissipating as he scratched notes onto his leather-bound pad.

An old yellowed newspaper clipping with a captioned photo written in Japanese appeared on the screen, inset in a box beside the flow chart that was now quite complex.

'Akiko Sato is a little girl in the arms of the woman, her mother, Nami Sato,' Lana explained. 'Today, Ms Sato is thirty-three years of age. She arrived in the United States on January 15. Up until two days ago, she was staying within a few hundred yards of Ben Harbor's residence on Key West, at the Crowne Plaza Hotel. Incidentally, we traced a call placed to the third cell bought by Dallas Mitchell's employee, to the vicinity of the Crowne Plaza. Three phones—one for Mitchell and one each for Ben Harbor and, we believe, Akiko Sato.'

'What's the latest on these two—their whereabouts?' asked Whittle, aware of Buck's agitation, which seemed to be growing by the minute.

'Sir, on January 28, Harbor flew to Gainesville to meet with a former Defense Intelligence Agency expert by the name of Jerome Grundy. We don't know yet what they discussed. Jerome Grundy was stationed at the US embassy, West Berlin, from '85 to '88—his expertise was the Soviet Union, its internal structure both political and social.'

'Where was the Japanese woman during all this?' Buck asked.

'We don't know.'

He grunted and pinched his nose between thumb and forefinger, so that when he released them there was a sucking sound. 'When do I get a written report?' he asked.

'I still have some interviews to conduct, sir—Grundy, for example.'

'Get it to me as soon as possible. I want this tape found and out of circulation,' said Buck, pocketing his notebook and Mont Blanc. 'I'm going to see if I can get the status on this case raised a few notches, Sam. I'm thinking Priority Orange. That should get you the resources you need to expedite things.' He stood and turned to Lana. 'Ms Englese, terrific work.' He then shook Whittle's hand. 'Sam, I'm looking forward to that report.'

'Yes, sir,' said Whittle.

Mr Buck walked out.

Whittle faced Lana and said, 'I'm going to get you a partner, Englese. Someone who can break down doors.'

Hank Buck hailed a cab and rode it some distance from NSA HQ into the anonymity of the 'burbs. He was looking for a public phone—still the safest way to make a secure call. In the age of the cell phone, they weren't easy to find. He eventually stopped at a laundromat, and found one inside. He dialed the number and got through right away.

'Governor? Hank.'

'Hank. Where are you?'

'I've just spent the morning being debriefed.'

'You sound . . . anxious.'

'That's because I am. And when I tell you what's up, you will be, too.'

Buck just didn't add up. Maybe it was the designer pencil. Those things cost thousands, didn't they? Lana swiped the sensor and tapped in the code to open her door. She sat down behind her laptop, performed the fingerprint and retinal scans to bring it online, and wondered who Whittle had in mind for her new partner. Her desktop came to life and she saw that there was a message to call Saul Kradich. She picked up the handset and dialed the number.

'Hey, Lana. What's up?' he said.

'Hi, Saul. I think you wanted me to call *you*.'

'Oh, yeah, that's right. I did . . . um . . .'

Silence.

'Well, just call me when you remember—'

'No, I remember why now. Sorry, I've just been in a real heavy session with a couple of jerks from the DoD. Look, I've kept up the surveillance on those people we've been tracking and something's popped up.'

'What?'

'Harbor's and Sato's passport numbers checked through US Customs and Immigration an hour ago.'

'Shit. Where?'

'Miami International Airport.'

'Damnit,' Lana said under her breath. She'd been a couple of moves behind from the start. 'They've gone to Russia, haven't they?'

'Hey, I'm impressed,' said Kradich. 'How'd you know that?'

'I threw a dart at a map of the world and that's where it landed.'

'Well, it's a big country, so I guess your chances were good. They've gone via Heathrow.' With the sound of voices in the background, Kradich added, 'They have a connection to Moscow, but you probably know that, too, right? Hey, gotta go. The DoD is back in the house.'

Lana swore quietly as the line went dead.

'Senator Chevalier earned the medal fair and square,' said Felix Ackerman. 'It's all in here.' He put a manila folder on the governor's desk.

'Give me the summary,' said Governor Garret.

'No one wanted to talk about how he won the decoration because Chevalier talked to them all personally and asked them not to.'

'Why'd he do that?'

'They said that he didn't want to use his service record as a means of gaining political advantage. The senator didn't believe it appropriately honored the three men in his unit who had died in the engagement.'

'Jesus Christ,' muttered Garret. The more he knew about this guy, the more he loathed him.

'But we do have something.'

'What?'

'Ten years ago, Chevalier's nephew went down for auto theft. His uncle didn't defend him.'

'Why not?'

'Because the kid was also a crackhead.'

'Thank God. At last . . . What's the angle?'

'Chevalier prides himself on being the defender of the poor and the disadvantaged. Maybe the kid was a complete fuck-up, but we can spin it that Chevalier distanced himself from the unsavory elements of his own family because he had his eye on politics down the track.'

'I like it, Felix. Let's work it up.'

'Oh, and there's more good news. You've regained some of the lost ground in the latest Gallup poll. We're heading in the right direction again.'

Hank walked in.

'Good work, Felix,' said Garret, dismissing him. 'Let's get on to that thing with Chevalier.'

'Yessir.'

'What's up?' Hank asked.

'Felix will fill you in later.'

The campaign manager was stuffing papers back into his briefcase. He stood up with a grunt and left, mopping the sweat from his forehead.

Garret got out from behind his desk and did a circuit of his office, a tumbler of scotch welded into the palm of his hand. 'Okay, give it to me.'

Hank delivered a précis.

'I told you that damn tape would rear its ugly head someday,' said Garret. 'And the timing stinks.'

He took a mouthful of scotch and tried to look at the brewing situation positively. 'Okay, so what have we got? Harbor and this Sato woman will go to Russia. What will they do when they get there? Get lost in Siberia? Hunt around for a trail gone cold well over two decades ago?' He took another gulp, the aged liquor caressing his palate. 'The tape we can handle if it surfaces. It's a hoax. These days things like that can be created fairly easily . . . After so long, perhaps we don't really have anything to worry about.'

'Well, *I'm* worried,' said Hank. 'This isn't random. And there's the connection with Suzuki and Foxx.'

Garret returned to his chair, leaned back and regarded his long-time associate. 'What concerns *me* most is that this is most uncharacteristic of you, Hank. You're usually so glib. What's your recommendation?'

'Reactivate our Russian friend.'

Garret took a deep breath and then emptied his glass. 'He'll want to renegotiate.'

'He's Russian, so of course he'll want to renegotiate. They're all crooks.'

'Then you'd better go over there and do it face to face. Ensure we get value for money.'

September 10, 1983

Vladivostok, Siberia, USSR. Colonel Korolenko had the KGB driver who had picked him up from the civilian airport take the scenic route to the railway yards, around the foreshore of Golden Horn Bay. Korolenko was fond of Vladivostok. It appealed to the KGB man within, the one who appreciated a city closed to all but essential Soviet Navy personnel. Even many of the Russians born here had been resettled elsewhere. The city's one purpose was to provide the motherland with a warm-water port from which naval operations could be conducted securely year round.

A large number of ships were moored in the bay: several icebreakers, half a dozen Soviet naval vessels, including an Udaloy-class destroyer. Most impressive of all, however, was the nuclear-powered battlecruiser *Kirov*, which, Korolenko had been informed by his driver, was on a shakedown cruise after a minor refit. It had stopped into Vladivostok as part of a flag-waving exercise, and the sidewalks were bustling with its seamen in their jaunty blue uniforms and white caps.

The driver turned the ZIL away from the bay and headed toward the city center. A short while later, the vehicle rumbled over railway tracks and pulled into a freight yard. From inside the car, at least, it seemed as if everything was running smoothly to schedule. The prisoners had been flown from Sakhalin overnight, packed into an Antonov An-124 transport plane, and then trucked to this siding. Around fifty armed KGB Fifth Directorate guards were handling the security arrangements of the transiting former KAL 007 passengers.

The high-value prisoners had been removed, and now it was time to divide the remaining bulk ethnically into groups for the next stage in their internment. The old and the infirm were also a problem. Korolenko's recommendation, which had been approved, was that they should be dispersed among the forced-settlement towns up in the Arctic Circle that were still heavily monitored by the KGB. Life up there was harsh and survival rates were low and they would quickly cease to be a problem.

For the rest of the day, before returning to Moscow, Korolenko was to oversee the dispatch of prisoners to the correct labor camps. This operation was his brainchild and he didn't want it going awry due to poor handling by subordinates.

The driver held the door open for him and saluted. Korolenko idly returned it as he climbed out. The air was warm, but there was a blustery, salt-laden wind. The biggest ethnic group aboard KAL 007 were Korean, which made sense, followed by citizens from Japan. There were also citizens from the Philippines, Taiwan and Hong Kong. Most of these would be sent to the labor camps populated by North Korean nationals north of Khabarovsk. The North Koreans had been forcibly deported from their own country to work in the timber industry. They kept to themselves, and their own masters were far stricter than the Soviet representatives in these camps. Once there, the 007 collateral assets were as good as buried.

The Europeans among the passengers would find a new home in the towns in the Kolyma region, populated when the gulag prisoners were released in the early sixties. These villages were some of the most remote townships in all of the Soviet Union. No road in, no road out. The vastness of the Siberian wilderness would swallow them whole.

The captain managing the current prisoner transfer approached and saluted. Korolenko returned it and asked, 'Any problems?'

'Comrade Colonel, *ser*. Five prisoners have died. One was crushed, one died from dehydration, and two from—we believe—heart attacks. One had a broken arm and died from blood poisoning.'

Korolenko thanked him. Deaths among these prisoners by natural causes were not problematic. 'Are all preparations still running to schedule?'

'Yes, Comrade Colonel. The trip will take thirty-seven hours as planned. The train will travel only at night, and pull into sidings so as not to inhibit regular passenger and freight trains.'

'I see you have had the railway cars stenciled "Automotive Parts".'

'Yes, *ser*, in case anyone is interested.'

'Good. Very good. I should have stayed in Moscow and let you handle it.'

The captain beamed. 'Thank you, Comrade Colonel.'

A ferocious animal snarl followed by a woman's scream distracted them.

The colonel looked up in time to see a man running toward him, his arms outstretched, pure hate in his eyes.

The dog handler released his animal, which broke away at a sprint and launched itself at the prisoner. The impact of the dog hitting the man from behind threw him face down onto the ground. The dog wheeled and mauled the prisoner, snapping teeth tearing at his neck.

'Don't let me keep you from your work, Captain,' said Korolenko.

The officer saluted, turned, and strode briskly away, shouting an order at the dog handler to bring his animal to heel.

Colonel Korolenko rubbed his hands. By this time tomorrow, he would be back in Moscow at Beria's old dacha, watching Congressman McDonald come apart at the seams. In fact, everything was going so well out here that he admonished himself for not staying in Moscow.

Standing out in the open by the railway cars, blinded by daylight, Nami was more tired than she believed possible. The feeling that at any moment she would break down and not be able to move was still with her. She had given up all hope of waking from this nightmare and finding it a ghastly figment of her imagination. Brutal imprisonment was now her life.

A Russian transport plane had brought them to a landing strip in the dead of night, from which they'd been trucked to this new destination. One of her fellow KAL 007 passengers had whispered on the flight that they'd landed in the Soviet Union nine days ago. This had surprised Nami. The time frame was difficult to grasp. It seemed to her that she'd boarded KAL 007 back in Anchorage many sleepless years ago.

Back wherever it was that they'd landed, their jailers had kept them in shipping containers. These were crowded, but it had been possible to find enough space in which to lie down. It was explained that there weren't suitable facilities on the base for keeping so many people under guard. Water had been reasonably plentiful and the food adequate. But some indeterminable time between then and now, the attitude of the Soviets had changed markedly for the worse. The guards had removed the Europeans, leaving just the Asians, and many more Asians had been allocated to their steel box. With the overcrowded conditions inside the shipping container came an end to sleep. There was not enough room to lie down. There was also very little food and not enough drinking water. The sanitation buckets provided filled quickly and were not replaced for many hours. Diarrhea was rife. People fought for a place beside the two air vents. Nami's cramps were so violent she was certain her stomach was consuming itself, and her head pounded with a headache that wouldn't go away.

Several KAL 007 passengers who spoke Russian had tried to engage the guards in dialogue in an attempt to find out what was going on. These passengers had all been subsequently identified and severely beaten before being returned to the shipping containers, one with a broken arm. Soldiers with machine guns had then herded them from the shipping containers to the old Russian aircraft. The man with the broken arm had been seated beside Nami, groaning quietly, the sickly-sweet smell from his broken limb putrid beyond anything she had ever experienced. After several hours, the man had gone quiet, his skin a greenish color. When they landed, soldiers had carried him off, his body frozen by rigor mortis in a seated position, the look of agony set onto his face. Other bodies had been carried off the plane, too—Nami had counted five in all. She had no idea how they had died.

The large plane had landed in darkness. At the airfield, soldiers hurriedly packed them into trucks, which had brought them to this new marshaling point. Here—wherever *here* was—more soldiers pulled them bodily from the trucks, until they got the idea and jumped out under their own steam. It was daylight now. Nami estimated the time as being early mid-morning. She took lungfuls of air and pulled the clean smell of the sea down into her being. Out of the wind, the warmth of the sun on her face felt luxurious. She could almost imagine—

A soldier pushed her from behind so hard that she felt as if she'd sustained whiplash. A man in front of her received similar treatment. The passengers were being formed into lines. Guards with dogs ranged up and down the formation, the snarling animals occasionally goaded by their handlers to maul the stragglers. There were many soldiers. They'd been brought to a deserted collection of warehouse buildings and were being marched behind them. Nami's heart beat faster. What was going on? Many of the guards had machine guns . . .

The lines of prisoners walked out of the shade and back into the sunlight. Before them was a railway siding with two railway freight cars and more soldiers.

As the guards herded them toward the rolling stock, a large black limousine drove into the area and parked. The driver jumped out and opened the rear passenger door. A man climbed out, an officer. Nami recognized him, a pure hatred burning in her chest. He was the man who had supervised them when they had first landed. It was *he* who had arrested the crew of the 747 and, she guessed, had them shot. It was *he* who'd climbed up on the truck and proudly told them all that they were spies captured by the glorious Soviet Union. It was *he* who'd had the congressman dragged away. It was *he* who had made them suffer in squalid conditions. This was the man keeping her from her family, keeping her locked up like an animal. At that moment, Nami had never hated anyone as much as she hated this Colonel Korolenko and she vowed never to forget his face.

A man several places in front of her in the line-up suddenly charged at the colonel. He was running fast, tripping over train lines, and screaming, his arms and hands outstretched as if he intended to wrap them around the Soviet officer's throat and squeeze with all the strength he could muster.

Released by its handler, a huge black dog intercepted the man before he'd closed half the distance to the officer. It leapt at him and slammed him into the ground. Then it spun around and buried its jaws in the man's neck while he struggled.

The Russians didn't seem in too much of a hurry to pull the beast off. When they did, the man wasn't moving. A soldier, weapon at the ready, lifted his arm and dragged him partially off the train tracks. Blood spurted from the man's throat and neck, spraying the guard. With a major artery severed, the prisoner convulsed as his blood drained away. No one went to his aid.

Nami looked at Colonel Korolenko and saw him grinning.

September 11, 1983

Washington DC. Roy Garret was sure he didn't want to be here, especially on a Sunday, but he'd done as Clark had asked and come down. A young woman with a mouthful of braces and rubber bands handed him a button as he approached the crowded steps up to the front door of Constitution Hall. The button read 'Remember Flight 007', which she reiterated with a high-pitched, excited voice.

Reporters were everywhere, taking photos of the attendees. There were also other photographers present, who were not employed by the media but were equally inquisitive about the guest list assembling to commemorate the life of Congressman Larry McDonald.

Garret walked into the hall. It was almost a political convention, the walls and chairs hung with red white and blue streamers, bunting and rosettes. Banners read 'Down with Communism' and 'This Time We Will Not Forget'. The front stage was hung with flower garlands and the US Navy Band played 'Yankee Doodle Dandy' as people took their seats. The place was absolutely packed, the atmosphere charged.

Garret wandered around the side of the hall and eventually claimed a seat on the end of a row. Scanning the crowd, he saw it was a who's who of the ultra right—generals, admirals, prominent businessmen, politicians, the clergy, lobbyists.

Kathryn McDonald, her children beside her, was saying hello to various friends and supporters of Larry McDonald's cause, which, as far as Garret knew, was to prevent the companies owned by the Rockefeller family buying up the world. Or something like that. Kathryn McDonald had personally invited the President, who had found an excuse not to attend. A wise choice, thought Garret. There was something a little crackpot about the proceedings.

Garret lasted until someone giving a speech compared McDonald to Samson of biblical fame and 'Amens' were tossed from the seated crowd like hats at a graduation. He snuck out during a round of rapturous applause.

On the stairs, a thin woman in her Sunday best beneath a broad pink sunhat handed him a bumper sticker that said 'Honk if you hate massacres'.

'Remember Congressman McDonald,' she advised him earnestly, a Daughters of the American Revolution button pinned on breasts that sagged well below her belly button.

'I sure will,' he replied.

At the bottom of the stairs he dropped the bumper sticker in the trash and wondered how Congressman McDonald was getting along.

The martial music pounded through the speakers with such force that droplets of condensation caught in the seams of the metal doors vibrated in four-four time. The approach to information retrieval employed at the dacha was different in several fundamental ways from that practiced at the Lubyanka, though the end result was the same. Instead of sensory deprivation, sensory overload was the preferred route taken to keep the subject awake, the music pumped into the prisoner's cell through enormous speakers set into the roof. And it didn't let up, not for a minute. Night and day it played, until the subject's nerves were ragged and frayed and he was ultimately bludgeoned into submission.

Then there were the other inducements to keep a subject awake. Korolenko opened the judas hole and peeked in. It was gloomy in the cell, no need for bright lights here. Prisoner 98987 was standing in the small cell, head forward, chin on his chest. He held his arms out from his sides, as he was forced to do to prevent being sprayed with ice water from a hose. Hour after hour he was made to stand like that, on a raised platform molded into the concrete floor, an island in a pool of water so cold that white ice blocks bobbed in it.

'Not good,' said Colonel Ozerov over Korolenko's shoulder. 'A day and a half at the Lubyanka, and two days here. If not for the four and a half days wasted resolving the transportation issues, we might have broken him by now.'

'A few extra days won't matter,' said Korolenko with a shrug.

'No, except to one's professional pride. But he will break soon, perhaps in ten minutes, perhaps in another few hours. Once his will collapses and his mind accepts there are two choices, talk or sleep, and that one is the only route to the other, we won't be able to shut him up. No man can beat his own mind.'

'You should expect him to be tough,' said Korolenko. 'As you know from his biography, he was a doctor in the navy before he was a politician. They teach interrogation survival techniques in their armed forces. He'll have tools to help him resist. Combine these experiences with a doctor's knowledge of physiology . . .' Korolenko let the thought trail off.

'We'll see. I don't believe the US military is quite aware of the best interrogation methods. Torture for its own sake is quite a different beast from information retrieval. And, of course, sadists often conduct torture simply for the sexual pleasure it brings them. But we are not interested in inflicting pain, as you know. As for his survival knowledge, it could work against him. If he knows what lies ahead, his willpower may collapse soon and spectacularly. An imagination can be a soldier's worst enemy.'

Korolenko saw that Congressman McDonald was now wearing gray pajamas, which were damp from being sprayed. His face was turned away from the door. He shifted his weight on the raised pedestal and his naked toes dipped into the pool, touching an ice block. He shifted his weight again, to bring his bare skin away from the water.

'How long has it been now?' asked Korolenko.

Ozerov checked his watch. 'In this cell? Coming up to thirteen hours. The last time he tried to sleep was three hours ago.'

Korolenko went off, enjoyed a lengthy breakfast of bacon and sour milk cakes, and had conversations with several comrades at the dacha, none of whom knew of McDonald or that he was being held. Security was tight. A few hours later, he returned to the dacha's basement refreshed and ready to go to work. Ozerov was sitting outside the cell with a *Pravda* on his knee.

'What's the truth today?' asked Korolenko, playing on the meaning of the newspaper's title.

'That we are winning,' Ozerov said.

'And what are we winning?'

'Everything, apparently.'

'Good, as it should be.' Korolenko gave his old friend a grin. *Pravda* was rarely the bearer of bad tidings. 'Anything new?' He nodded at the metal door of McDonald's cell.

'He went for a swim half an hour ago, did a little shouting . . . Since then, all has been quiet. Take a look.'

Korolenko put his eye to the judas hole. McDonald's pajamas were wetter than the last time he'd looked. While he watched, the prisoner urinated, a bright yellow stream running over his white foot, a yellow delta over the raised platform, a yellow stain in the surrounding water. Excellent: dehydration and hypothermia were working their magic. McDonald couldn't last much longer without fresh water and sleep. He was more slouched now, stooped, and swaying slightly. His hands were out from his sides, but only a few inches. And then, suddenly, he twitched.

'I think it's starting,' Korolenko said over his shoulder.

From many years' experience, the colonel knew what was happening. The combination of lengthy standing and sleep deprivation had become an intense and overwhelming torment from which there was no escape. And because the pain was induced by McDonald's own mind, there was no one he could focus resentment upon, nothing that could be forged into a kind of mental bunker inside which he could take refuge. Pain was now the man's whole universe, with every sleep-deprived cell in his body begging for release. His extremities would be filled with fluids. His legs would be swollen, and even bearing his own weight would be agony. If the veins in his legs were in the least incompetent, perhaps blood clots would have formed, further adding to the swelling and the pain. At least his heart was strong—that much had been established in a preliminary medical. Beneath the pajamas, there would be lesions. Soon, they would begin to suppurate. The only thing keeping McDonald upright was fear of slipping back into the ice water, the sensation of which would be like sharpened knives carving into his super-sensitized skin.

McDonald twitched again, and cried out. The cry was directed at no one in his cell, but at something *within* him.

'The hallucinations have started,' Ozerov observed. 'I think he is almost ready.' He smiled warmly at Korolenko beside him. 'No one holds out. Not ever. It's just not possible.'

McDonald screamed again and flailed his arms. The action caused him to lose his balance. He staggered into the water and fell to his knees, only to jump up off balance and slam into a wall. Sobbing, he took several shuffling, uncertain steps to the raised platform. His legs buckled and he fell to the water again, screaming, thrashing his fists at invisible specters in the air around him, all control gone. The madness was temporary, at least at this stage. He would recover his senses, but now was the ideal moment.

'It's time,' said Ozerov.

He beckoned at a heavy, square-set woman at the end of the corridor in the uniform of a KGB sergeant. She came forward with two of her subordinates, squat, thick-shouldered men in black rubberized canvas greatcoats, surgical gloves and knee-high rubber boots. One of the men carried a canvas bag of various items over his shoulder. Korolenko and Ozerov stood back and let the team do their job.

The woman opened the cell door and the two men went in. They appeared moments later behind a wave of loud music and human stink, the soaked and manacled congressman shaking with cold between them, plastered with his own excrement, his eyes rolling in his head, babbling something nonsensical.

'This is going to be interesting,' said Korolenko as he and Ozerov walked behind the congressman, who had begun to urinate again as he was being dragged, leaving a bright yellow trail on the floor for the two officers to follow.

313

The new room was the size of four of the smaller individual cells combined, and the ceiling was higher. It contained a simple desk, several chairs for the interrogation team—which also included a KGB stenographer, in this instance an attractive, petite brunette who wore make-up more suitable for an evening at the Bolshoi Ballet—and a reel-to-reel tape recorder, its spools revolving slowly.

The team delivered McDonald clean and dry, in a fresh set of gray pajamas. He was chained to the wall behind a narrow shelf on which he was allowed to sit. His eyes were inflamed, the whites the color of red light globes framed in fluorescent red rims, the color accentuated by the pale whiteness of his skin and the almost two weeks of ragged salt and pepper beard on his cheeks, chin and neck.

As Korolenko sat beside the stenographer, McDonald began to sob, his face cracking into an expression of absolute torment.

'Why, why, why . . .' he said, over and over.

'Lawrence,' said Colonel Ozerov, 'would you like to sleep?'

'Yes . . . sleep.'

Korolenko noted that McDonald said the word 'sleep' as if it were water and he had just crossed a desert without a drop, his Adam's apple shooting up and down in his throat.

'I will let you sleep if you tell us what we want to know,' the colonel said.

McDonald closed his eyes and so Ozerov slapped him—not hard; he didn't need to. The lack of sleep had sharpened the congressman's senses to the point where the slightest touch felt like the lash of a whip. The red coals that his eyes had become shot wide open.

He mumbled, 'Must sleep first.'

'No, talk comes first. There is a warm pillow waiting for you, a soft mattress.'

The congressman hung his head and then lifted it.

'You are Lawrence Patton McDonald, US Congressman for the state of Georgia.'

'Yes.'

'Why were you traveling to Korea?'

Korolenko leaned back in his seat and found the most comfortable position. The initial interrogation—there would be many to come—would follow the classic path and last around an hour, during which the congressman would be asked low-stress questions to get him used to answering them rather than asking them. There would be minimal physical coercion—the threat of going back to the music and the ice water and the memory of the endless hours of wakeful torment would be enough to keep him cooperative. If McDonald was compliant, he would be rewarded with several hours of uninterrupted slumber, after which he would be given the choice of cooperating fully with Ozerov or returning to his sleep-deprivation cell for another session with the demons in his own mind. For most people, the memory of the agony of their previous experience—the edge of madness, a cliff from which they had very nearly jumped—was enough to guarantee full and complete cooperation.

Colonel Korolenko was privately impressed. The congressman had, indeed, been iron-willed. After the brief sleep, he had woken newly defiant. It took four hours in the sleep-deprivation cell to remind him of the torment that could stretch on indefinitely. But now McDonald was ready to open out like a flower. It was time to tear off the petals.

Ozerov sat in a chair facing the congressman, who also sat in a chair, his manacles secured to the wall behind him. The colonel glanced at the notes, prepared by Korolenko, on his lap and nodded at the stenographer.

'So, Congressman,' he began, 'you wish to be President of the United States?'

McDonald spoke slowly. He said, 'I wish to protect the Constitution of the United States and the Bill of Rights. That's the President's first job, that's what being President is all about.'

'Oh, I didn't know that. I thought your President's first job was to wage war wherever and with whomever he pleases. Is your Constitution under threat?'

'You should know,' McDonald said, his eyelids heavy.

'And you should know that you can call off this friendly talk at any

315

time, in which case you'll be returned to your cell. We believe in freedom of choice here.'

McDonald said nothing, but the reminder was patently sobering.

'I asked you whether your Constitution is under threat,' said Ozerov with studied patience.

'The Constitution is under threat from globalists.'

'Who are these globalists?'

'They want a one-world government so that the spoils can be divided and the dividends maximized. This will be called the New World Order. But before it can come about, a revolution must erupt and it must be universal.'

'We don't need another revolution in the Soviet Union. We have had ours.'

'In the 1988 presidential elections, globalists within the United States will field their candidate. It could be a banker like Rockefeller; it could be a public servant like George Shultz. More than likely the candidate will be the current Vice-President, George Herbert Walker Bush. If he wins that election, Bush will put events in train—events that will lead to this New World Order, or One World as it's also called.'

'What will this One World be?'

'Perhaps it will be the end of the Soviet Union.'

'The end of the Soviet Union?' Ozerov glanced at Korolenko. There was mirth in his eyes.

'That will be just the first step.'

'The first step to what?'

'Globalism.'

'The only revolution that could possibly sweep the world is Marxism–Leninism.'

'You say that because you have to. Religion is revolution, so is technology. What if there was a global plague? Or another global war? Or another great depression? What if something could lead to another global war? What if something could cause a social meltdown on a global scale that required a supergovernment to take control?'

'So you don't know what form this revolution will take?'

'No. But as President of the United States, I might have a chance of stopping it. And that's why I'm here, isn't it?'

'You are here because you are a spy.'

'This whole thing was put together by the CIA.'

Ozerov sat forward intently. It was what the KGB believed, too. 'Do you have proof of this?'

McDonald shook his head. 'Come on . . . I'm here because *you're* CIA, not Russian. You want me out of the way, the field cleared. What about all the other passengers on the plane, aside from those who came here with me? Are you going to line them up against a wall and shoot them, just so that you can keep me?'

Ozerov threw Korolenko a concerned glance.

'I'm afraid you are mistaken, Lawrence. This is not some plot and we are not CIA. You are in a dacha outside Moscow, I assure you. As for your fellow passengers, they will enjoy rich and fruitful lives within the glorious Soviet Union, discovering the simple joys of work.'

Korolenko made a hand movement that suggested a change of direction might be worthwhile.

'Tell me about your association with Hilaire du Berrier.'

'He's my friend.'

'Just your friend?'

'My visor.'

McDonald was slurring his speech and becoming difficult to understand.

'Your visor?'

'Advisor.'

'Du Berrier was your advisor.'

McDonald nodded, his head barely moving.

'What sort of advice would an operative of the former Office of Strategic Services be giving you?'

'Hilaire . . . in the OSS during the war. Came up against your NKVD.'

'Ah, yes, the NKVD, our old intelligence machine, forerunner of the KGB. Hilaire du Berrier helped you set up your Western Goals Foundation. Am I right?'

'Yes,' McDonald whispered.

'Western Goals, your own personal spy network. Let's talk about that.'

'Western Goals is a counterpoint to the Eastern Establishment.'

'I see.'

'Do you?' said McDonald, discovering within himself a small reserve of strength.

'No. Perhaps you should tell me. What might the Eastern Establishment be?'

'The Eastern Establishment, the Council on Foreign Relations, the Trilateral Commission, the Royal Institute of International Affairs, the Aspen Institute for Humanistic Studies, the Atlantic Institute—they're different, but they're all the same. They're the institutions at the core of the global conspiracy to control the world's wealth—it's happening right under the noses of the American people. If you really are Russians, it's happening right under your noses too. Western Goals is an antenna organization set up to be an early warning network, the intelligence arm of the John Birch Society.'

'Ah, yes, the John Birch Society. That would be the cabal of fascists of which you are the current president. Did Reinhard Gehlen help you and du Berrier in this?'

'Yes.'

'Tell me about him,' said Ozerov. 'Tell me about Gehlen.'

'Reinhard ran Hitler's espionage rings in Eastern Europe.'

'And?'

'The CIA recruited him after World War Two. He set up and ran the BND.' McDonald's lips barely moved.

'Speak up,' said Ozerov, slapping the prisoner's face.

The congressman's voice rose briefly. 'He ran the West German intelligence ring that's *still* running circles around your client, Stasi.' McDonald slumped back into an exhausted torpor and whispered, 'But you know all this.'

'Do not concern yourself with what we may or may not know.'

'My cousin George Patton and Reinhard became friends. There was a mutual respect.'

'Gehlen was a Nazi.'

'He was doing a job for his country.'

'Tell me about your cousin, Patton. There was a rumor that Patton wanted to attack Marshal Zhukov's divisions with the US Third Army, supplemented with several divisions of re-armed Waffen-SS. Is that true?'

'I wouldn't know. I was ten when the general was killed in the car accident.' His voice trailed off.

'And?'

'And I never asked Reinhard.'

'Why not?'

'He wouldn't have answered the question.'

Ozerov grunted. 'After he retired, Gehlen, along with a number of his spies, came to work for your Western Goals.'

McDonald hesitated. 'Yes.'

'Looking for telltale signs of your New World Order?'

'Yes.'

'So, where have you placed these early-warning assets?'

McDonald looked about the room languidly, as if searching in slow motion for a means of escape. There was none.

'Lawrence, Lawrence,' Ozerov prompted, 'you must tell me. There is no holding back. You know and I know that you will talk sooner or later. It would be better for you if it were sooner. Would you care to go back to your cell now?'

McDonald licked his lips, perspiration instantly blooming across his forehead.

'The US embassies in West Germany, Great Britain, France and Italy,' he said, his chin quivering, his mind recoiling from the thought of the four walls of his cell and the constant music. 'There are some others in the diplomatic corps in Washington.'

'Your State Department?'

McDonald nodded.

'You will speak your answers aloud for the tape recorder.'

'*Yes*, the US State Department.'

Ozerov got up from his chair and walked around the cell, signaling a change of pace.

'We have been informed that your staff refer to your office as "Hewak East",' he said, prompted by his notes. 'What is Hewak?'

'The House Un-American Activities Committee.'

'Ah, *HUAC*—your country's communist witch-hunt of the fifties. What has that to do with your office?'

'If you know the answer, why ask?'

'I want it stated. Do not attempt further evasion.'

'Supposedly I have the HUAC files. But I don't.'

'If you did have these files, you would know of many high-placed Soviet sympathizers throughout your society.'

'But, as I said, I don't have them.'

'I warned you about evasion, Lawrence.'

Ozerov stood and walked to the door. He opened it and the two boulder-shouldered thugs who had brought McDonald from his cell to the interrogation room rolled in. McDonald tried to climb away from them, back into the very brickwork behind him. Tears streamed from his eyes as they darted from thug to thug.

'Yes, yes, okay,' he said. 'I had the files. I . . .'

Ozerov nodded at the men and they turned and lumbered back out the door. Korolenko was impressed. His comrade had an impeccable sense of timing.

Ozerov picked up a notebook and pencil from the desk in front of the stenographer and handed it to McDonald. 'I want names,' he said.

'Names?'

'Of your agents; of every man and every woman you know who was acquainted with Gehlen; of every communist sympathizer on your list. I want to know who and I want to know where.'

McDonald hesitated.

'Then I want to hear about your experiences on the House Armed Services Committee—the weapons, the budgets, the plans.'

Congressman McDonald groaned and rolled his head.

'And the sooner you have told me everything I want to know, the sooner I will let you sleep for a week.'

September 16, 1983

NSA HQ, Fort Meade, Maryland. Garret had spent most of the night sitting up with Richard Burt and the team, going through press reports on the KAL 007 downing, and reviewing the many communiqués still being drafted and sent by embassies around the world to each other. More than two weeks after the downing, the US version of events was partially unraveling and several key aspects of the official line had had to be revised as more information came to light. The US State Department had eventually come around to admitting that the Russian interceptor had, in fact, fired warning cannon shots at the 747 prior to launching its missiles, though Burt himself had muddied those waters by suggesting that perhaps the Russian interceptor had fired them *at* KAL 007. More information had also surfaced about the involvement of the RC-135, though its actual role had been confused by a vast weight of conflicting information. There was also a growing chorus among journalists and pedants curious to know how it was possible for a modern civilian airliner to fly so far off track, unless the deviation was intentional. The undercurrent here, of course, was that it had been a CIA spy flight gone wrong, just as the Russians had said all along. Burt and his team had worked hard to imply that the individuals taking this line were merely spreading Russian communist propaganda and disinformation. And several journalists had had to be 'stomped on', as Burt had called it.

Fortunately, the overwhelming weight of opinion, both domestically and internationally, was still firmly in the United States administration's corner. And the opinion was that the Soviets had wantonly, brazenly and callously shot down a civilian airliner full of innocent people for the insignificant crime of accidentally flying a couple of hundred miles off course. The rest was just detail.

Case closed.

The debate had now moved on to the attempts made by South Korea and the relatives of 007's passengers to sue the Soviet Union for damages. The other question was how, exactly, the world should punish the Soviet Union for its antisocial behavior.

Garrett, making his way to the analysts section, nodding a good morning to a friendly face here and there, allowed himself a smile as he thought about this. The punishment would probably come down to a few banned Aeroflot flights and a little less Russian vodka sold by retailers. As for the grieving relatives hoping to fight it out with the USSR in the courts, it looked likely that they'd get nothing.

Case closed.

He noted the *Washington Post* on his desk as he placed his briefcase beside the filing cabinet and hung his coat on the back of his chair. KAL 007 was off the front page and the civil war in Lebanon was back on it. He found what he was looking for on page three. The headline read 'House Passes Defense Bill'. He scanned the article quickly. The $187.5 billion defense bill asked for by Ronald Reagan had been passed 266 to 152. Garret nodded as he read. The budget session in the House had followed a session the previous day where a resolution condemning the Soviet Union's actions over KAL 007 had been passed 416 to 0. The timing was perfect. Everyone was keyed up to send the Reds a message. The budget was a five percent increase on last year's defense funding, which had itself been a record expenditure. It was a great day for the free world. The President was going to get his MX missiles, money for the deployment of the Pershing II missiles throughout Europe, funding for the production of Bigeye binary nerve gas, the redesigned B-1 bomber, and financial assistance for various anti-communist forces such as the Contras in Nicaragua. With the mood in the House being what it was, no doubt the administration's options in El Salvador would also be freed up, and the President would get his wish to deploy troops to Lebanon for a further eighteen months.

Garret folded the paper. Case closed.

There was a soft tap on his partition.

'Special delivery,' said a female voice.

Garret recognized the voice. It belonged to one of the Middle East analysts by the name of Mary Peugeot. He looked up. Mary had nice legs, and today her skirt was above the knee. In her outstretched arms was a large box wrapped in gold paper with a gold ribbon around it.

'I was asked to pass this on to you,' she said. 'And it came with its own very good-looking secret service agent.'

Garret stared at the parcel, perhaps an instant too long.

'Mind if I put it down somewhere? It's heavy.'

'Yeah, sorry, Mary.'

Garret jumped up, took the parcel from her. She was right about it being heavy. There wasn't a lot of room in his cubicle, so he placed it on his chair.

'So, who's the admirer?' she asked.

'Damned if I know,' he replied.

'Are you going to open it or just look at it?'

Settling the point before Garret could answer, she passed him a pair of scissors.

He checked for a note.

'There isn't one,' said Mary. 'I looked.'

He cut the ribbon and peeled off the paper, exposing a plain brown box beneath. Opening the box revealed a dozen bottles of champagne. He took one out.

'Vintage Krug. Wow, that stuff's worth a mint,' said Mary.

A pale blue envelope had been wedged between a couple of bottles. Garret picked it out, opened the flap and removed the card. At the bottom was the familiar seal of the President of the United States of America. He read the card.

Dear Roy,

There have been times in our nation's history when fate has chosen a special citizen with unique insight. This is one such time and, according to my advisors, you are that citizen. A grateful nation thanks you. And, from one patriot to another, I personally thank you for all your hard work.

Ronald Reagan

The note was ambiguous. Garret wondered how much the President had been brought into the loop. More than likely, to protect him from possible fallout, he hadn't been.

'Well, don't keep me in suspense. Who's it from?' asked Mary.

'Sorry, that's classified,' Garret said, folding the note and slipping it into the inside pocket of his jacket over the back of his chair.

'Then what about sharing a bottle or two?'

'That I can do.'

'Shall I stop by your place after work?'

'Sure. You know where I live?'

Mary slid her thumb and forefinger down Garret's tie, well inside his personal space.

'As a matter of fact, I do.'

October 10, 1983

The Old Executive Building, Washington DC. 'Oh, Roy, you're early,' croaked Deirdre, the eternal cigarette burning between thin fingers stained the color of old rust. Her hair was a different shade of red than the last time he'd been in Clark's office, darker, a crimson color matched by her shade of lipstick.

'I suppose you've heard the news?' she rasped.

'No. What news?' Garret asked.

Her tone, the angle of her head and shape of her eyes said it wasn't *good* news. What had happened?

'Oh, I'm sorry. I thought you already knew. Hank will fill you in. He's in there.' She pointed at the door with one of her yellow-orange fingers.

Garret opened the door to the National Security Advisor's office.

'You think that's a good idea, sitting there like that?' he asked.

Hank was leaning way back in the Judge's chair, his feet on the Judge's table, tossing balls of paper into the Judge's waste bin under the window. A collection of paper balls were scattered around the base of the bin. Hank took his feet off the desk.

'He's not coming back,' he said.

'Who's not coming back? Des?'

'Oh yeah, Des. Well, he's *definitely* not coming back. He died two days ago on that hill in Vermont.'

'Oh.'

'Yeah, but it's not who I meant. It's the Judge. The President has asked him to consider the position of secretary of the interior.'

'What?' Garret was stunned. 'What happened?'

'I really don't know. The Judge has his enemies. Plenty of people in the administration resent his close friendship with Ronny. Maybe Shultz or Weinberger put two and two together on this KAL thing. A word or two in the right ear and suddenly the Judge becomes a serious liability.'

'You think people outside our circle know what happened?' asked Garret, a bottomless hole opening up in the pit of his stomach.

'We're not the only people who can open doors and pull strings around here. Blowing the whistle on 007? The messenger would get shot along with the administration *and* the President. Quite a few bureaucrats wouldn't fare so well, either. I assume you haven't heard anything?'

'No. I came over here to inform the Judge that the peace movement in Europe seems to have disintegrated. Our missiles are going to go in unopposed. They'll be in their deployment areas by Christmas. His strategy worked.'

'*Your* strategy, Roy.'

Garret didn't feel like patting himself on the back. 'What do you think is going to happen with Clark?'

'He won't accept the position, of course. He'll politely decline the President's offer, as he's supposed to, and cut himself adrift from Washington.'

'The second most powerful guy in town?'

'That's the point. He ain't no more.'

'So what happens now?'

'You're being moved to a more hands-on role,' said Hank. 'Up and out.'

'Where to?'

'Langley—the CIA. Bill Casey wants you. Look in the mirror and introduce yourself to the new assistant director.'

'You're kidding.'

'And the icing on the cake—I'm your new personal aide.'

October 11, 1983

Galati, Romania. They came for Nicolae Balcescu at 3 a.m., just as he rolled out of bed and put on his slippers, sleepily pondering how to make cakes sweet when there wasn't any sugar to put in them. The bakery was downstairs, its oven calling him. Four men did the job, two of them rushing through his bedroom door. The first man in pressed the black snout of a Tokarev hard against his forehead, while the second secured Balcescu's wife's cooperation and silence with a threat to pistol-whip her. Afina whimpered and meekly allowed the men to handcuff her, tape her mouth and blindfold her. The other two men took care of the girls. Nicolae knew they would be frightened, but there was nothing he could do or say that would change their abductors' minds.

The vehicle the secret police—the Securitate—put them in was a large delivery van for the state-owned department store; one of Nicolae's customers, as it happened. Perhaps the van had been chosen for specifically this reason. No one would think its presence in the street suspicious; not that anyone would dare to bring this to the authorities' attention if they were suspicious. Two of the men climbed with them into the back of the van and covered them with their weapons. He had seen one of the other men starting up his Dacia. Presumably, the remaining man would be driving the van. The fact that they were bringing his car along was troubling in a way Balcescu couldn't put his finger on.

His heart broke at the sight of his wife and two young daughters, their hands bound behind them, their eyes and mouths covered. For some reason he couldn't fathom, the men hadn't blindfolded him, though they'd secured his mouth shut with tape.

As the van got under way, Balcescu spent some time pondering what had managed to convince him that this day would never happen. Now, faced with the reality of their situation, this moment seemed perfectly inevitable. He had risked the lives of innocent people—people he loved more than anything on this earth—and he had lost.

Originally from Munich, and trained by Reinhard Gehlen, the master, Balcescu had arrived quietly in this Romanian city of Galati eighteen years ago. He had been secreted into its fabric by remnants of Gehlen's Iron Guard, the local fascist organization rampant until the end of World War Two, which held an abiding hatred for the communists. For all those eighteen years, he had heard nothing, seen nothing, and reported nothing. The inaction had made him complacent. He'd married, baked bread, produced two beautiful girls, become a sleeper tucked deep within the folds of Ceausescu's mad Romania.

He sat in the back of the vehicle looking at his family as it sped along. The blast from a nearby barge horn told him they were close to the river. What had happened? Someone had talked. So what would happen now? Obviously, he told himself, his captors would want other names, and would secure his cooperation by threatening his family. Torture would be involved.

The van slowed, came to a brief halt, turned hard to the right and rumbled over some bumps. It then came to a stop, the loud ratchet of the handbrake informing him that this was the end of the line for the moment. The back of the van opened. A hundred meters behind was another car, its lights off but its motor running, clouds of smoke rolling out of its exhaust pipe. Nicolae recognized it as his Dacia.

The men with the pistols didn't speak. They didn't have to. They guided Nicolae's wife and children toward the car, the Danube sliding past in the pale moonlight. One of the men opened the vehicle's doors—all of them. The others assisted Afina and the two girls inside. Nicolae was then brought around to the driver's door.

'Get in,' growled the man holding the door.

Why were they doing this? Nicolae Balcescu took a step forward, but not fast enough. The man grabbed him by the arm and pushed him impatiently into the seat behind the wheel. At this point, he realized that there were others with far more active profiles than his who would have been arrested first. Someone who knew a lot of names must have been captured and broken.

The gun in the hand beside Balcescu exploded and his wife's head was blown through the shattered window beside her. He was stunned. The weapon blasted twice more, the sound ringing as if the inside of his head was made from metal. His girls were slumped in the back seat, their short lives ended. And then Balcescu realized why they hadn't blindfolded him. They wanted him to *see*. The pistol would be placed in his hand afterward. He could see it all. A murder/suicide. He and his family would be found in this lonely, cold place beside the river in the early morning. There would be evidence of the van in the soft earth, footprints, the presence of others, but the police were compliant with the Securitate. Nicolae Balcescu—child-killer, wife-killer. These thugs didn't even want names of other agents. Why not? There was a reason.

Just as the bullet shattered his skull, the answer came to him. It was very simple. Because they already had them all.

Vidor Messinger waited for the film to finish rolling through the projector. It was a Wednesday night in Spandau, East Berlin, and tonight's showing was a popular regular—a love story between two valiant workers separated by the revolution, and a fight to the death with counter-revolutionary forces. The credits finished and all that was left were several meters of blank tape.

Before turning off the powerful projection light, he looked down onto the backs of the seats and saw two silhouettes, both men, halfway down the center section, sitting on the end of the row by the aisle. What were they waiting for? He shrugged, pulled an empty film storage tin from the stack and turned on the main theatre lights. The end of the film snaked through the rollers and wound onto the spool. He turned off the main switch and took another glance through the small glass pane out into the seating area. The men were gone. He could close up and—

There was a knock on the door.

Messinger released the lock and opened it an inch. The handle was ripped from his hand and two massive men in dark overcoats threw him back. Vidor was trapped, nowhere to run. He'd been careful, wily, but he could see in the darkness of their faces that they had him and the game was over. He had lost.

One of the men latched onto his shoulder, spun him around and locked his arms behind his back. Vidor was a small man. He was helpless, a moth caught by two sadists about to rip off his wings. The man facing him pulled something from a pocket and held it where it could be clearly seen—a capsule.

Messinger knew what it was. He tried to turn his head away but the man with the capsule grabbed his jaw and squeezed, a grip of steel. The small gelatin object was pushed between his front teeth and then the man holding his jaw forced it shut, crushing the capsule. The taste of bitter almonds filled Vidor's mouth and nose and invaded his throat. A wave of destruction swirled into his head and fused his brain. He lost control of his limbs. They began to shake. His heart was next. It swelled like a balloon filling with water and then burst in his chest. He slid to the floor, pulling down the film tins, dead before he reached it.

The train, the last of the evening, the one she always caught home from the museum, was running late. The carriage was empty as it rumbled through the darkened city, its buildings a solid black against the dark navy sky. Maria Rutkowski's home lay on the outskirts of Warsaw, where the city thinned and the rural landscape took over. Tired, she allowed her head to roll forward on her chest. There was plenty of time till the train arrived at her station.

The next thing she knew, she was being dragged off the seat by her ankles, held by a huge man in a black coat that reminded her of the midnight sky.

A second and third man walked behind her. One of them was shaking his finger, tsk-tsking. A roar filled her head. It was the wind and the noise of the train wheels and the rushing landscape. The man dragging her had opened the door.

Maria screamed and tried to twist and turn, but the big man in the midnight coat easily had her measure. The people who had coached her in West Germany, Gehlen's people, had told her she'd have a warning. They were wrong.

Maria Rutkowski managed to wrap her fingers around the bottom of the partition separating the passengers from the door between the carriages, her heart thumping, panic locking her muscles. The man immediately behind her raised his boot and brought the heel down on her fingers, pulping them. Maria screamed again, but the sound was lost in the deafening clatter of the train's wheels rattling over switch points.

The man holding her ankles heaved her out the door as a power pole flashed past, which took her head clean off above the ears.

BOOK THREE

February 2, 2012

Moscow, Russia. 'It's not what I expected. Appears friendly enough—like a big slice of carrot cake,' Ben commented on his first sight of the yellow and red Lubyanka. 'Doesn't look like an evil headquarters at all. Is that a hammer and sickle emblem over the clock up there on the top of the building?'

Akiko took several photos of the vast wedge-shaped 'square', the old KGB HQ at the top end of it, and then put the camera in her pocket and replaced her glove. 'Yes.'

'Awesome. It's like seeing a real swastika or something. Well, let's get this party started.' Ben's breath steamed in front of his face, which was framed by an open ski mask and a knitted woolen skullcap on his head.

They walked slowly up the sidewalk toward the building, holding up Muscovites behind them hurrying about their pre-work business. Two women overtook them, both wearing knee-high black leather boots with sharp stiletto heels. Akiko wondered how they managed it.

After hovering around zero, the overnight temperature had dropped suddenly to minus ten degrees Celsius, and there was a slight breeze to go with it. The sky was white-gray and low, occasional light snow flurries drifting across the open square. A steady stream of vehicles, blackened by successive dirty snow melts, surged and then stopped, and surged and then stopped again, along the road pocked with ice-filled holes.

Ben and Akiko darted through the traffic. The Lubyanka's front door lay ahead, fifty yards further along the sidewalk. A lone militiaman wearing blue camouflage all-weather gear and a fur hat with the flaps tied under his chin patrolled out front. Above the cop were two surveillance cameras, cantilevered out from the face of the building on short poles. Ben and Akiko approached like a couple of inquisitive tourists. The front door was small for such a large building. It said visitors weren't welcome, an impression augmented by the militiaman, who was short, stocky and frowning. He looked straight into Akiko's eyes, and then Ben's, as if they were guilty of something. It was a standoff. Ben broke it by turning away and walking straight through the Lubyanka's front door.

Open-mouthed, Akiko watched him disappear into the building. Then she did the only thing she could do and went through the door after him. She found him looking at various notices and curled posters taped onto drab, mustard-colored walls.

From a side door, a couple of short men in old beige parkas appeared. They stopped, looked Ben and Akiko up and down, then glanced at each other. The cop from out on the street suddenly burst in, sandwiching Akiko and Ben between himself and the men in beige.

'Who are you?' demanded the cop in loud, abusive Russian. 'What do you want here?'

Ben caught the tone, even if he didn't understand the words. 'Hang on,' he said, holding up one hand, open-palmed. He reached into his pocket with the other and pulled out a copy of *Lonely Planet, Russia*. 'Tourista, tourista.'

The men in the beige parkas turned them around immediately and herded them firmly out the narrow front doorway with assistance from the militiaman. Once Ben and Akiko were back on the sidewalk, the two men returned inside, leaving them with the cop.

'What do you want?' he asked, fingering the nightstick on his hip.

'The KGB museum,' said Akiko in Russian. 'We have a tour booked.'

'So you are Russian?'

'No, Japanese. My friend is American.'

'Passport. Him, too.'

'Here we go,' Akiko murmured to Ben in English. 'Do you have your passport photocopy?'

Ben removed a glove and produced it from an inside jacket pocket.

'*Nyet!*' the cop snapped when he saw the paperwork. 'I want the original.'

Akiko shook her head and told him it was back at the hotel. He grunted, annoyed, realizing that if he really wanted the original documents, he'd have to desert his post and escort them back to wherever their hotel was. He half-heartedly skimmed the papers and then flung them back.

'Go away. Is police building,' he said in English, gesturing at them to get moving.

'And the KGB torture museum?' Ben enquired pleasantly.

The cop ignored the question, turned his back as if they'd ceased to exist and resumed his position outside the door.

'Perhaps we could try the back entrance,' suggested Ben, smiling. 'Or is that one used only in the dead of night?'

'Why did you go in there?' Akiko asked, annoyed.

'Because you're not supposed to, obviously.'

'The communists have gone, but things can still happen here, things you wouldn't like.'

Ben flared. 'Shit, we don't even know how the hell we're going to achieve what we came here to do. So, until we get a lead, you can count on me pushing a button or two, okay?'

The street was not the place to argue. 'The museum is down the side,' she said, fuming, looking at her watch. 'And we're late.'

They retraced their steps in silence, both feeling the friction between them, then turned the corner and kept walking past the back of the building where it was dark and gloomier. The public was even less welcome here, the only access to the building via a heavy roller gate. A crushing sense of foreboding filled Akiko. What must it have been like being brought to this entrance, sandwiched between KGB thugs?

Fifty yards further along was a brightly lit supermarket. A squat woman in a dark green woolen suit with a blue camouflage militia

337

parka and the ubiquitous furry hat loitered in the adjacent entrance-way. This was still part of the Lubyanka complex. On the first two floors, Akiko had been told by the tour operator, were offices, confer-ence rooms and a club, all for ex-KGB personnel. The museum was on the third floor. Behind the female guard, near the elevator, was a man in a red ski jacket, black gloves and hat, clapping his hands together to keep warm. He seemed to be waiting for something.

'Are you with the tour company?' Akiko asked him.

'Yes, you must be Ms Sato?'

They introduced each other and Akiko handed him a voucher for the tour.

The guide's name was Evgeny Smirnov. 'Like the *wodka*,' the man said jauntily, handing them his card.

'A cheap imitation,' Ben whispered in Akiko's ear. 'The real stuff's spelled with a double f.'

They took an old squeaking elevator to the third floor, Smirnov talk-ing without a break. The elevator stopped with a jolt and opened onto a large, overheated, airless room full of glass cases and other exhib-its. They seemed to be the only visitors. They opened their jackets and removed their gloves while Smirnov launched into a story about how American spies were cleverly caught by the KGB. Akiko peered into cases displaying fake mustaches, cyanide capsules and concealed weapons while the guide continued with his story, explaining how the passports forged in the US might have looked authentic, but were held together with staples that didn't rust, unlike real Soviet staples. A drop of water on a staple left overnight, he concluded with triumph, was all it took to unmask the most convincing spy.

Akiko only half listened, waiting for the right moment to ask the question uppermost in her mind.

'This is the desk that belonged to Lavrenty Beria,' said Smirnov, moving on. 'Here the monster signed the death warrants of hundreds of thousands during Stalin's purges. And, ironically,' he said with good cheer, 'it was made in America. Sears, Roebuck!'

Akiko peered into a glass case where there was a letter scrawled in Russian, the words difficult to read.

'This was written to Stalin by a man sent to the gulags,' said an unfamiliar voice in passable Japanese behind her. 'The author is protesting his innocence. He wrote the letter in his own blood.'

Akiko glanced over her shoulder. The man was well fed and tall with ruddy cheeks overlaid with a lattice of broken spider veins. He wore a different drab green uniform from the police. There was a patch on his upper arm that included the Cyrillic initials 'FSB', the Federal Security Service, the organization that replaced the KGB.

'You speak Japanese well,' she told him.

'I spent half my life in the Soviet Far East,' he said with a dismissive wave of his hand. 'You pick these things up. I am Colonel Andrei, the deputy director here. What do you think of our little museum?'

'It is very interesting,' she said. 'How did you know that I was Japanese?'

'An educated guess. That, and only tourists visit here.'

Nearby, Akiko heard Ben say, 'So, all those people sent to the gulags; did the commies keep records?'

'Um . . . yes, they did,' replied the guide. 'Why are you asking?'

'My friend here lost her father in one of those purges,' Ben explained as he examined a fake tree stump full of telemetry instruments. 'Her mother emigrated to Japan. While we're sightseeing, we thought we might, you know, look him up. See what happened to the old guy.'

'Well, yes, there are records, but . . .'

'They were opened briefly in '91, but they have been sealed again,' said the colonel in English. Switching to Russian, he asked Akiko, 'Where did your mother live before emigrating?'

'Irkutsk.'

'Irkutsk. The Paris of Siberia. A beautiful place. You have been there?'

'No.'

'Tell me, your father. What year did he . . .'

'Disappear?'

'Yes.'

'Nineteen eighty-three.'

'Hmm . . . 1983. Was he a member of the Party?'

'I think so. Wasn't everyone back then?'

'Perhaps he supported the wrong faction. They were tumultuous times. Yuri Andropov was in power.'

'Yes.'

'Do you know when exactly in 1983? The month, the day?'

'Early in September is all I know.'

'Perhaps I could make some enquiries on your behalf.'

'Would you?'

'Tell me, where are you staying? Which hotel?'

'We're at the Ararat Park Hyatt.'

'Ah, a good choice. Would you mind writing down your names?' The colonel produced a notebook and pen and handed them to her.

Akiko caught the tour guide giving the colonel a sideways look.

'Well,' the officer said as he slipped the notebook inside his jacket, 'the first or second week of September, 1983. I will see what I can do. Please, enjoy the rest of your tour. A pleasure to meet you and your friend.'

Colonel Andrei gave her a nod and then walked off to an office, closing the door behind him.

The tour lasted another ten minutes, Smirnov rushing through the remainder of the exhibits. On the way down in the elevator, he was fidgeting with his clothes, uncharacteristically silent. As soon as the doors opened, he said, 'I hope that you find what you are looking for,' and then hurried off before Ben could hand him a tip.

'I saw you writing something down for the colonel,' Ben said as he watched Smirnov round the corner. 'What was that all about?'

'I gave him our names.'

'What? Are you kidding?'

'He said he would help.'

Ben pushed his hands into his gloves. 'Jesus . . . Colonel Andrei. The guy didn't give us *his* last name. Did you notice? According to Smirnov, before the guy was FSB he was KGB—Fifth Directorate. He said the colonel was one of those responsible for imprisonment and torture at the Lubyanka, among other places.'

Akiko felt sick.

'And let's say the offer to help is genuine, he's going to be looking for your father. Just tell me you didn't let the guy know where we're staying.'

She looked away.

'Aw, shit . . .'

Colonel Andrei waited for the Japanese woman and the American to leave before checking his contact book and dialing.

'Yes?' asked the voice on the line.

'Colonel Andrei Popov.'

'Colonel Popov! My old friend. It has been a long time. I heard you were still serving.'

'Yes. I am single-handedly keeping the motherland safe.'

'Ha! And how is Moscow treating you these days?'

'The city has been stormed by the bourgeoisie. There is nothing in their lives beyond money.'

'It is the same here in Leningrad,' the voice said, using the Soviet name for Saint Petersburg. 'It is time we got together again over some caviar and a bottle of *Novocherkasskaya* to talk about the old days, when life had meaning.'

'My favorite vodka. You have a good memory, General.'

'I will send you over a case immediately, for old times' sake. What else can I do for you, old friend?'

'Actually, it's what I can do for you. I just had a couple of visitors at the museum. You are still interested in keeping your finger on the pulse?'

'Of course.'

'I thought you might like to know. A Japanese woman. She was interested in the records. She said she lost her father. September 1983 was specifically mentioned. She is traveling with an American. I have their names and their hotel.'

'You are legendary, Comrade.'

The colonel passed on the details.

'You did the right thing. What did you tell them?'

'Nothing.'

'More than enough.'

'If they come back, I will let you know.'

The retired general ended the call and pocketed his cell phone.

'Something the matter?' asked Hank, sitting on the corner of a desk, patting a golden retriever on its head.

Valentin Korolenko wiped the frown off his face. 'That depends. Do you agree to my fee?' he asked.

'Two million euros. That's a lot of money.'

'Plus expenses,' Korolenko reminded him. 'I won't be able to do this job on my own.' He waited for a response, but got none. 'You terminated our previous agreement, Mr Buck, sent me the blank cigarette paper. It is about supply and demand in Russia now. You have a demand which only I can supply. My revised terms are more than reasonable. And I warn you, it will cost you far more if you walk away and come back later to restart the negotiations.'

Hank expelled a sigh.

'Why you are interested in these two?' Korolenko enquired.

'The sort of money you want comes with no questions asked.'

'Knowing something about them might help me find them.'

'They're looking for survivors from KAL 007.'

'And why might they be doing that when the world believes the plane crashed and everyone on board was killed?'

'Because some people refuse to accept the truth.'

Korolenko hadn't laughed for a very long time, but it shot out of him now as if he were throwing up. Eventually, he brought himself under control. Clearing his throat, he said, 'Well, back to my fee . . .'

Hank scratched the general's retriever behind its ears. 'Those "expenses" you mentioned. I take it they're your little helpers.'

'Grisha Soloyov and Vlahd Bykovski.'

'You've used them before, haven't you? They like to kill people.'

'They follow orders, especially ones accompanied by money.'

'Okay,' said Hank, 'we have an agreement. Two million euros, plus expenses. Half now and half when my two parties get on a plane bound for the States.'

'That is only fair. And all you want is for me to find them and keep them under surveillance?'

'I want to know what they do, where they go and who they meet.'

'There will be a further negotiation if the terms change.'

'I'd expect nothing less. If I need to communicate with you, we'll stay with our old channel—the Chesma.'

Korolenko nodded. He pulled out a couple of photos from the manila folder—one each of a Japanese woman and an American man—and turned them over. Their names were Akiko Sato and Ben Harbor, the names just provided to him by Popov. And they were staying at the Moscow Ararat Park Hyatt. This had to be the easiest money he'd ever make.

May 10, 1984

Labor Camp F07982, Siberia, the Far East. The air compressor was down. There'd been problems with this one before. A pocket of dirt was caught somewhere in the fuel system. The whole thing needed to be stripped down properly, but, through an interpreter, Nami understood that the machine had to be up and running as soon as possible. The Russian overseer wanted a quick fix rather than a permanent solution. So every few days each week, she had to remove the injectors one by one, taking this section of the mine tunnel offline while she worked in the dust and the pale light from her hard-hat lantern.

Nami had been dispatched to this camp with six other passengers from the airliner, a journey that had involved a train ride, three months in a disgusting holding camp with murderers and thieves, and then a long journey in a closed truck across frozen rivers and lakes, a rust hole in the floor of the truck the only window on the outside world.

The camp they eventually arrived at was mostly populated by North Koreans and was surrounded by mountains and thick forest. From what she could gather from the few who spoke a smattering of Japanese, the Koreans had been rounded up and sent here by their own government for reasons unknown. There were other Asian races here too: Mongolians and Chinese. The mine was state-owned and the camp inmates were slaves—no other word for it. The mine was worked day and night,

344

twelve hours on and twelve off, by inmates on rations that were mostly rice, potato, some indescribable vegetable matter, sour milk and hard, insect-infested black bread. Occasionally, there was vodka. Everyone received the same rations—male or female, young or old. Food was often stolen. People killed for it. Nami had been accused of stealing food once—falsely—and had paid the consequences. They had thrown her into a stinking concrete cell, an airless, slime-covered hole too small to stand up or lie straight in. Nami knew who had taken the food, but coming forward with the culprit's name would have signed her own death warrant at the hands of the guilty inmate's friends. And so she had taken the punishment: three weeks on filthy water and rice rations, without sunlight and with no human contact. She had lost a lot of weight, her hipbones almost pushing through the skin. And then two of her teeth dropped out on the day before her release back into the general population. The camp administration put her in the camp hospital for four days of recovery. They wanted her back in the mine.

There were deaths every other day: mine slips and cave-ins, accidents with the heavy machinery, exposure to the chemicals used to release the gold from the ore, disease, fights among the inmates for the few available women, general misadventure, and old age. The graveyard up on the side of a hill overlooking the camp was very large.

The camp's task was to mine the rock ore, extract the gold and meet some commissar's arbitrary quota. The mine's administration had first put Nami to work with the drill crew, one of the worst and most dangerous jobs, picking away at the seams of ore far below ground, operating heavy pneumatic machinery, the walls often trembling and groaning with the awful surrounding pressure. But then, one day, a drill broke and there was no one around to fix it. Using some initiative and a hitherto undiscovered understanding for things mechanical that turned out to be innate, Nami repaired it with tools scrounged from a nearby underground loader. Thereafter she was attached to engineering, and spent more time above ground than below it, which was a relief.

The men shuffled past Nami, ignoring her as she got down on her knees and opened the box of tools. The last man to leave was the overseer, who yelled at her to hurry. Once he was gone, Nami could feel the heavy

345

silence pressing down on her. It was hot in this tunnel several hundred meters below ground, the air close, compressed, as if by the millions of tonnes of rock above. Sweat trickled down her forehead and stung her eyes. Nami fixed the heavy socket wrench over the injector and tapped the end of the tool with another spanner, breaking the thread's seal. She wound it off until the injector came free. She pulled it out and placed it on a grease-stained patch of canvas that she'd laid over the rock floor.

The rock cracked behind her, accompanied by a slight tremble. She was used to the movement of the earth, so it didn't concern her overly. Nevertheless, she glanced over her shoulder in the direction of the sound. It was then that the two men attacked her, appearing from behind a mound of ore and rushing her. They pushed her down on the ground and pinned her there. One of the men hit her hard across the face, dazing her, taking away her fight. Both men stood and looked down at her as she lay there, moving slowly. Nami couldn't focus, her vision blurred by the blow. The men were miners, but she didn't recognize either of them.

They bent down and dragged her behind the load-haul-dump machine where the shadows were blackest. The bigger of the two began to pull open the buttons of his fly, while the other leaned over her and ripped open the front of her coveralls, exposing her. He smothered a breast with a dirty hand while the tall man bent over and jerked her coveralls off her shoulders and pulled them down below her knees. Nami tried to scream, but the dust choked her throat. She gagged and began to kick and struggle. She felt a hand between her legs, groping. The men were talking to each other, laughing. It was then that she realized the ring spanner was still in her hand. She closed her fingers around the shaft, her fist tight, her heart racing, and then swung it at the man on top of her chest with all the strength she could call on. *Thud.* The metal head buried itself in something hard, breaking through into softness below. She swung again as the other man tried to grab the tool. He missed and it smashed into his cheek. He screamed, stood up and ran away, holding his face. Nami dropped the spanner, the end of it smeared with something wet, and kicked the slumped body off her with her foot.

The camp police took Nami to the hut among the trees, opened the door and threw her inside. She had picked up enough Korean words to know that they called her a whore, and a few other things besides. She lay on the floor motionless, curled into a ball, until the door was locked shut. She pulled her coveralls back over a shoulder and noticed that her skin was smeared with blood and rock dust. One of her eyes was swollen almost shut.

The air in the hut smelled revolting, of dirt and pine sap mixed with a musty human funk—urine, sweat and other bodily fluids. The steady breeze through the pine trees outside made a sound like television white noise.

The floor beneath her was beaten earth with old rough-cut carpet not quite covering it. There were two small windows just under the ceiling, on opposite walls that were themselves made from rough-hewn logs. The striped shadows thrown by the sun coming through one of the windows told her they had bars on them. The hut was small, though bigger than the disgusting concrete cell she had recently experienced. She crawled onto the low cot, no more than bare slats of wood over a wood frame, and took in her surroundings. There wasn't much else that she hadn't already seen—two buckets, one for water, one for her own waste. There was no internal handle on the door. A metal plate was set in the door's center with a spyhole. An eye blinked in it and then the hole closed.

Nami tried her best to travel beyond her body, to take her mind elsewhere. She went on a springtime walk through the *hanami* displays in the Shinjuku Gyoen garden with Hatsuto and little Kimba. How Akiko's perfect face had opened with wonder that day when she saw the *sakura*, the cherry blossoms. It was just before her fourth birthday, a magical day. They had all wandered for hours hand in hand through the Shinjuku Gyoen, among a thousand trees exploding in soft pinks and whites, the lake speckled with blossoms like something from a traditional Sansui painting. As the memory faded, it left Nami with questions: Would she ever see Hatsuto or Akiko again? What were they doing right now? Was it a school day? How was Hatsuto managing without her? When would Akiko stop remembering her? When would Hatsuto take another wife?

She took the back of her lip between her front teeth and bit down on it hard so that her mouth filled with blood and the pain wiped away the tears forming in her eyes. Here, in this brutal place, weakness was despised, the weak feasted on by the strong.

It felt like April, or possibly May. There were wildflowers blooming among the trees and the bitter winter weather was a bad memory. The plane had come down on September 1, 1983, the previous year. That much Nami was sure of, but all certainty had ended that day. If her guesswork was right, she had been in the USSR for seven months. What did the people in Japan, Korea and the United States think had happened to them? What was going on in the world beyond this labor camp? Why had no one come for them?

Nami absently scratched her leg. When they'd thrown her in the cell, they'd told her that she was a troublemaker. They'd said she would be moved. Where would they move her to, she wondered as she scratched her ankle. Suddenly she was aware that her body was on fire with hundreds of bites. She looked at her hand and saw that the skin on the back of it, as well as up her arm, appeared to be moving. She held her hand out in front of her face, bringing it into focus, and saw that it was crawling with ticks.

☭

'Do you mind if I keep it for later?' asked Korolenko, regarding the box of Royal Habanos Colonel Ozerov was holding toward him across the desk.

'As long as you don't mind if I have one now. Helps with my appetite—suppresses it. There is a new cook here. She spoils milk.'

Korolenko leaned forward to take one and, through the window behind Ozerov, caught a glimpse of the Zavidovo dacha's beautiful manicured gardens in full spring bloom. 'Perhaps you should let her cook for your guests in the basement,' he said. 'Which reminds me, how is our congressman?'

'Used up. The doctors believe his mind is cracking. They all do eventually, as you know. I think we've managed to squeeze everything worthwhile from him, though, which is just as well.'

348

Korolenko ran the cigar under his nostrils. He breathed in the aroma, the rich, acrid smell of first-class tobacco leaves grown in the Cuban sunshine.

'I can tell you now that the First Directorate is well pleased,' Ozerov continued. 'McDonald proved to be a veritable treasure chest of information. We are now in the process of winding up many counter-revolutionary cadres operating within our sphere of influence—spies who thought they had escaped into anonymity; even some sleepers personally trained by Gehlen. We also have some interesting leads in the congressman's own world; individuals who might be prepared to work for a worthy cause.'

'The revolution of the proletariat?'

'Of course.'

'Oh, while I think of it, did you unearth the root of the One World conspiracy?'

Ozerov grinned. 'He says that the USSR will be finished by the end of the millennium.'

'And what will take its place?'

'The Chase Manhattan Bank.'

'Ha!' laughed Korolenko. 'What will you do with the congressman now?'

'There will be periods of lucidity. We will keep him for those. Oh, and I believe congratulations are in order, Comrade.'

'Is the word out already?'

'Yes, indeed it is. So when do we start calling you General?'

February 4, 2012

Moscow, Russia. Even though the hotel Ben and Akiko moved to was large, it was considered boutique. It was also half the cost of the Ararat and still expensive by any standard other than Moscow's. There was a knock on the door. Ben looked through the security peephole.

In a muffled voice, a young woman in hotel uniform said, 'Excuse me, please. Your paper, sir.'

Ben opened the door and exchanged the copy of the *Izvestiya* for some roubles. He took the paper and laid it out on the writing desk. As he turned the pages, scanning them, he said, 'Early to bed, early to rise, work real hard and advertise. Do you know who said that?'

Akiko shook her head.

'Me neither, but it sounds good.'

'There it is,' said Akiko.

'You want to check it?' Ben asked. 'I don't read Russian, either.'

Jerome Grundy had said it half-jokingly—'*Run an ad*'—but after their experience with the creepy ex-KGB guy at the museum, it had shot to the top of their list of ideas. In fact, it was their *only* idea.

Akiko read the ad aloud: '"Attention survivors of KAL 007. Contact Ben Harbor, Florida. Reward offered. Facebook."'

'Naïve, but hopefully effective. Shall we see what's been caught in our net?'

Akiko opened the laptop and waited for the connection. After a few moments, her face brightened. 'Yes, we've had responses.'

'Many?'

'A few.' As she read, her expectant look faded.

'What's up?' Ben asked.

'One man says he saw the plane in a dream. It was being carried to the planet Mars on the back of a flying saucer.'

'Hmm,' said Ben. 'Too much vodka, obviously. They all like that?'

'Another person says the plane crashed off Honshu, Japan, after being shot down by missiles launched by American fighter planes.'

'Right. How many responses did we get all up?'

'Twenty-two.'

'Anything sane?'

'They all want the reward before they talk to us. This is odd.'

'What is?'

'This one just says, "Montana Coffee, Kuznetsky Most, 7:11 a.m., February 4."'

'What's Montana Coffee?' Ben asked, leaning over Akiko's shoulder to look at her email.

'It's a local chain.'

'Is it an invitation to meet up?' he wondered.

Akiko shrugged. 'Don't know. It's almost eight.'

'If it is, we're late. What do you want to do?' Ben asked. 'Check it out?'

'Might as well. We can have breakfast there.'

'And nothing else even vaguely interesting has come in?'

'No.'

Ten minutes later they were walking up nearby Kuznetsky Most, heads bent into the driving wind and snow. The café was an oasis of warmth in the frigid conditions, its windows heavy with condensation and tobacco smoke. The place was crowded, but they managed to secure a table as some customers got up to leave. Ben stood in the queue at the counter to order them coffee, while Akiko hung up their gloves and jackets, then took advantage of the free WiFi and fired up the laptop.

'Anything new?' Ben asked when he returned, putting the coffee on the table and sitting beside her.

'Four new emails. They all say the same thing: don't we know the plane crashed and everyone on board was killed?'

They shifted their interest to the clientele, scanning the room. No one paid them the least interest. Customers came and went. The time passed slowly. At ten past eleven, Ben yawned and said, 'I can't drink any more coffee. I'm somewhere between having a seizure and falling asleep. Let's go.'

'Stay till eleven thirty,' Akiko said. Emails were still coming in, but all were either crank callers or reward hunters.

Ben shrugged. They had nowhere else to go. He didn't want to say it, but he could see them getting on the freedom bird and heading home within days. He found a Russian gossip magazine and flipped through it, killing time, looking up whenever the front door opened to let people come and go. At eleven thirty he stood and stretched. 'C'mon. This is bullshit.'

Akiko had no choice but to agree.

They headed back to the hotel, dispirited. Going up to their floor, Ben undid his coat and felt around in the pocket for the door key. He took it out, along with a business card from the café. He didn't remember collecting one. There was writing on the back in blue ink. Something startled him: the numbers 007.

'Hey—I just found this in my pocket.' He showed Akiko the card. 'Did you put it there?'

Akiko shook her head. 'No.'

The elevator stopped and they got out.

The writing was Russian. 'What's it say?' he asked.

Astonishment swept across Akiko's face. 'It says, "007. Sept 1, 4:07 a.m., 261 of 269 PAX landed Dolinsk-Sokol base, Sakhalinskaya. Kom-somolskaya, Koltsevaya line, 2:30 p.m., today."'

The Komsomolskaya metro station was a work of art: domed ceilings, revolutionary iconography and colorful mosaics. It was a large station twenty minutes from the center of Moscow and, from the size of it, obviously a transport hub. But at 2:30 on a Saturday afternoon, the foot traffic was steady without being a stampede. Whoever they were meeting here had chosen the venue and time with good reason.

Ben and Akiko took up a position in front of a tiled mural depicting a complicated scene showing happy workers of the revolution mining ore for the manufacture of machine guns to be used against the oppressors. At least, that was Ben's take on it. They had no idea of the identity of the person they were meeting here, though obviously he or she knew them.

Several likely contenders came and went—men of imposing bearing who vaguely reminded Ben and Akiko of Colonel Andrei back at the museum.

'My name is Sergei Glazkov,' came a rasping voice from behind Ben, startling him. 'And you are?'

Ben turned and saw a short, hunched man wearing a black puffy parka and the omnipresent furry hat Akiko had told him was called a *ushanka*. The man walked by them slowly without stopping or looking up. He was utterly plain in every way. A cigarette was wedged between the gloved fingers of his right hand. He took a drag and then spat on the ground.

'Tell us why we're here first,' Ben said.

Sergei stopped and, without looking at them, said, 'You believe in the power of advertisement. I am but a slave to its will.'

'What?'

'You ran advertisement—007. You have forgotten already? I am responding. We cannot stand here. Follow me. You have tickets for train?'

'Yes,' said Akiko.

'Follow me, not close. Wait till we are on train.'

Sergei took the escalator to another level and loitered on the platform, which was peppered here and there with travelers. A rush of air preceded the train, which decelerated with a screech and pulled to a stop. Sergei went in one door, Ben and Akiko in another at the far end of the carriage. Ben noted that several other passengers entered with them and the carriage was around a third full.

As the train pulled away, Sergei caught Ben's eye and gave a nod for him and Akiko to approach.

'Why are we on this train?' Akiko asked him.

'Train is safe. You can see who gets on, who gets off. And there is too much noise for listening device. Tell me why you want to know about the Korean airliner.'

'My father was on Korean Air Lines Flight 007,' Akiko said, continuing the small disinformation begun at the museum. 'We have studied the incident. We do not believe the plane crashed in the sea.'

'You are foolish to come here, to Russia.'

'And why's that?'

'People would kill to protect such a lie. And you run advertisement.' He grinned and shook his head at the audacity.

'Your turn,' said Ben, failing to see anything humorous. 'Who are you?'

'A former Soviet citizen.'

'How did you find us?' he asked. 'You weren't at the café.'

'I watch the café. You arrive after eight. No one follow you. You leave twenty-five minute to twelve. I follow you, but you not notice. You stop at traffic light. I brush past, put card in pocket. You are not spies.'

'No, we're not spies,' said Ben, a little bewildered.

'It is what I just said. So, you want to know about Korean plane?'

'Your note said there were 261 passengers,' Akiko said. 'What happened to the other eight?'

'Why not let this go?'

'Because my mother might still be alive.'

'You said your *father* on plane.' Sergei laughed. 'Now I am *extra* sure you are not spies.'

Akiko blushed.

The train slowed. Passengers stood and moved toward the doors. The Russian stopped talking until the train had resumed its journey.

'Two hundred and sixty-one passengers and crew survive the flight.'

'What happened to the others?' asked Ben.

'Missile strike kill them.'

'How do you know all this? How can we believe you?' Akiko asked.

'It is up to you whether you believe or not. I cannot prove this to you.'

'How do you know what happened to the plane and its passengers?' Ben said.

'In 1983, I was KGB—Fifth Directorate—at Lubyanka. What you would call sergeant. Hard to believe now, maybe, but then I was very popular with ladies. I have affair with KGB woman whose husband, another guard, witness interrogation of American. She tell me this. She tell me also he was politician.'

Akiko and Ben glanced at each other, the electricity that passed between them difficult to contain.

'There were other prisoners brought to prison at same time: pilot and crew, journalists, computer scientists—eighteen people. They arrive September 8. I know it was this date because it was my lover's birthday and her husband had to work. So we celebrate without him.' Sergei rewarded himself with a private smile at the memory.

'What happened to them?' Akiko asked.

'Pilot and crew are executed. The others are held in prison cells below ground. Politician is taken somewhere else—I don't know where.'

'What happened to the 243 passengers who *didn't* end up in the Lubyanka?' Ben enquired.

Sergei shook his head. 'This I do not know.'

'Where do you think they might have been sent?'

'There were labor camps. West of Khabarovsk, in the hills. It is said some still operate.'

The train slowed to a stop. People got on and off. Once the train was moving again, Ben said, 'The reward. You haven't asked about it.'

Sergei waved his hand. 'I am not caring for reward.'

'Then why talk to us?' Akiko asked.

'I work hard for revolution. I enlist in KGB. I am trained. I am good communist. And then Kremlin fools lose control. And we, the proletariat, give up everything. We give our lives for revolution and then we are betrayed, abandoned, forgotten. Then criminals move in; take everything—everything that was ours. They leave nothing. Not food, not job, nothing to believe, no future. But I am lucky. I have beautiful daughter. She marry rich Ukrainian car dealer. I do not need reward. You give me one thing I want.'

'What's that?' asked Ben.

'Revenge. Go to Khabarovsk. Look there.'

The train began to slow.

'I have told everything I know,' said Sergei. 'I get off here. You take train to next station, change platform, go back.'

The train stopped with a jolt, the doors slid open.

'Goodbye,' Sergei said. 'Perhaps I will see you again at café.'

'*Spasiba*,' said Akiko. Thank you.

'Thanks, buddy.'

Ben held out his hand and they shook.

Seconds later, the ex-KGB man was absorbed by the milling crowd on the station. A number of passengers pushed their way into the train. Akiko and Ben took the remaining seats.

'Do you believe all that?' Ben asked.

'Don't you?'

'He didn't want the reward. Makes a nice change. I'd like to believe he was genuine.'

'But you are not sure.'

'He got the dates right. The Soviets admitted to the shootdown on September 6. Jerome Grundy believes the high-value passengers would have been moved soon after. September 8 fits. The politician would be Lawrence McDonald. They held him for a while, and then shipped him off to some other more secret place to wring what they could out of him.' He nodded. 'It *feels* believable.'

'Yes.'

'If we're prepared to accept everything he said, it's more confirmation that the tape is real, that the plane landed, and that Curtis and Yuudai were on to something.'

Akiko wiped an eye.

'Are you okay?'

'My mother—she is alive. I know it.'

The train slowed again. They got out as instructed, walked through a set of arches and stood on the platform for the train heading back to Komsomolskaya.

Unnoticed by them was a man of average height and weight in a blue and white ski parka at the other end of the platform. When the train arrived, he waited until the two foreigners he was tailing took it before climbing on board himself.

Sergei changed trains at Krasnopresnenskaya, changed again at Chekhovskaya and exited the metro back at Kuznetsky Most. It was after 4:30 and getting dark. He stopped at a supermarket, bought some bread, dried fish and vodka for dinner, then walked the kilometer through heavy snow to his home, an apartment in the Plaza Mediterrano, an old Soviet building renovated by the bored wife of an oil baron. It was well after five when he arrived there, and dark. The light outside the building was poor, and the snow hadn't yet been shoveled off the sidewalk, so he didn't hear the footsteps coming up behind him until it was too late. His first awareness of another's presence was a tap on his shoulder and the word, '*Izvinitye*', excuse me.

As Sergei turned, an icicle about half a meter long, snapped off a neighboring eaves, was swung down into the base of his neck. The tip ripped through the collar of his parka, slashed his carotid artery and continued far into his windpipe where the tip broke off and began to melt. Sergei knew he was dead before his knees buckled. The killer took a snow shovel leaning against a wall and prodded the apartment's overhanging eaves, releasing an avalanche of ice stalactites, some of which skewered the corpse. He then hurried off, completely unaware of the presence of a witness.

February 6, 2012

Gainesville, Florida. 'Don't let the fact that I'm packing intimidate you,' said FBI Special Agent Miller Sherwood, glancing at the Glock 17 holstered beneath his armpit.

'Actually, Sherwood, it feels strangely reassuring,' Lana said, stroking his ego.

In fact, that Miller now carried a gun didn't so much intimidate her as make her downright nervous. There was a juvenile quality to Miller Sherwood. He was the type who'd stand in front of the mirror drawing his weapon on his own reflection until he was sure he had the right facial expression to go with the move. Sherwood had ended up receiving a commendation for his action at the El Paso shooting, instead of the dismissal Lana thought he deserved. His Pavlovian response to this, she suspected, would be to resolve everything with his weapon. Her boss, Sam Whittle, had said he was going to get her a partner who could break down doors. Well, he'd given her one who could do it with his head, and probably would.

From what she could gather, Sherwood didn't seem too pleased to be back on this case with her, either. There was more exciting work to be done with his new employer—counterterror, and so forth. Being repartnered with her at NSA was like taking one step forward and two back. But neither of them could argue with the umpire's decision, and doing so would make no difference to the outcome. They were stuck with each other for the duration.

And so it had been a long day on a road that, aside from taking them to Gainesville, had led nowhere. It started in Miami with an interview with Ben's attorney, Kayson Bourdain. Lana discovered that the lawyer had known Curtis Foxx personally, which was interesting enough. But until the reading of the will, he had apparently never met Ben. Bourdain said that he had no idea what was in safe deposit box number 007 in Orlando. A phone call to Nikki Harbor, Ben's mother, confirmed that she didn't know, either.

Tex Mitchell was the man Lana really wanted to catch up with. Mitchell, however, had disappeared after withdrawing $20,000 from his bank account and announcing to his staff that he was taking all accrued vacation time. After the business with the cell phones and his background exposed to NSA practices, Lana was sure he'd manage to stay below the NSA's radar until he was good and ready to surface. Nevertheless, she'd called Saul Kradich back at NSA HQ and given him Mitchell's license plate number to play with.

Lana and Sherwood were now sitting in a rental across the road from Grundy's, the bar in Gainsville that Ben had visited, Sherwood playing with the veins on top of his hand, pushing the blood back behind the valves with a pen. The day had turned nasty with cold, wet squalls sweeping across from the Gulf. It was a Monday evening, and most folks wouldn't be thinking about spending it out on the town. Two university types ducked into the bar to escape a wind gust that whipped up a sheet of water off the road and threw it onto the sidewalk.

'We expecting any trouble from this Jerome Grundy?' Sherwood asked, giving his veins a rest and returning to his notebook.

'No, no trouble,' Lana assured him. 'He was one of our assets during the Cold War. I briefed you on that already,' she prompted him. 'The Soviet expert?'

'Yeah. I remember now.'

Lana hoped so. 'Let's go.'

She opened her door, deployed an umbrella, and huddled under it as she jogged across the road, nimbly dodging traffic, Sherwood behind her. Entering the bar, she was enveloped by warm air laced with hops and malt.

Grundy's was close to empty. 'Achy Breaky Heart' played on the jukebox and Smackdown Wrestling occupied the flatscreen monitors around the bar. She recognized Jerome Grundy from photos supplied by Kradich. He was on his own behind the bar, leaning on his forearms, chatting to one of the few customers. It was a cozy place.

Grundy raised his eyebrows at her and asked, 'What can I get you?'

'A couple of Zeros, please,' she said.

He excused himself to the customer he was talking to, picked two glasses out of a tray, filled them with ice and then the Coke.

'Investigator Lana Englese, NSA,' she said, showing him her ID when he put the drinks on the counter in front of her.

'FBI Special Agent Miller Sherwood,' her partner said, also showing his credentials.

'The ears of the nation, with teeth,' Grundy said, glancing at Lana and then Sherwood. 'An interesting combination. If I'd known you were coming . . .'

'Nice place you have here,' she said.

'I like it,' he responded.

'Not that busy today.'

'It's a Monday.' He shrugged. 'Now, what can I do for you folks, besides the Cokes?'

'On the night of January 28,' said Sherwood, 'you had a visit from Ben Harbor. Mr Harbor is a person of interest to the Agency. Would you care to tell us what that was all about?'

'No, not particularly.'

'We were hoping for your cooperation, Mr Grundy,' said Lana.

'Why?' he asked bluntly.

'You worked for the government once, on the team. Mr Harbor hasn't done anything wrong; you haven't done anything wrong. I can't see why you *wouldn't* want to be helpful.'

'Because I left the employment of Uncle Sugar years ago. I'm not in the game any more, I own a bar.'

'And a very nice bar it is too, Mr Grundy,' said Sherwood, his elbows on the benchtop, leaning forward. 'Business looks a bit slow tonight.'

'Like I said, it's Monday.'

'How long have you had this place?'

'Long enough.'

'Ever had any trouble with your liquor license?'

'No.'

'Really? I heard the local PD is cracking down. I also heard you've been keeping this place open long after the laws say you should be closed. Kids are getting drunk. There have been . . . complaints.' Sherwood smiled, showing his teeth, one of which was broken.

Grundy looked at Lana, who shrugged. He sighed, knew when he was beaten. 'Ben wanted to know about the KGB, about forced labor camps, about the Lubyanka.'

'Do you know why he was interested in those things?' asked Lana, jumping through Sherwood's breach.

'He was interested in going to Russia—incarceration tourism, I think they call it.'

'Why?'

'Why what?'

'Mr Grundy, we know Ben Harbor is particularly interested in the incident involving a Korean Air Lines 747 shot down by the Soviet Air Force off Sakhalin Island in 1983.'

Grundy nodded. 'So . . . ?'

'Why did he come to see *you* about it?'

Grundy rubbed at the spotless bar with a cloth, his lips a tight seam.

'Complaints . . .' Sherwood reminded him.

Grundy rolled his eyes. 'Because he believed there may be survivors of the crash held in Russian labor camps. He believed I might be able to help narrow down the search.'

'Why did he know to come to you?' Sherwood asked. 'You and Harbor have a mutual friend?'

Grundy rubbed the benchtop. 'Tex Mitchell.'

Lana and Sherwood shared a glance.

'This belief in survivors being held in Russia,' asked Lana. 'Did Harbor say what had convinced him of this?'

'I have no idea.'

'Did he mention anything about a tape?'

'No, he did not.'

The crease that suddenly and momentarily appeared between Grundy's eyes informed Lana that she'd touched a nerve. 'Are you sure?' she pressed.

Sherwood raised an eyebrow at him.

'I can't tell you what I don't know, okay?' said Grundy, openly exasperated.

'Grundy, leaving your license aside for a moment, we're talking about a matter of national security, which means we can bring a whole suite of laws to bear, some of which hold the Bill of Rights at arm's length.' Lana didn't want to have to use threats, especially ones they couldn't enforce, but they were low on options.

'I still don't know anything about a tape. Like I said, these days all I know a lot about is drinks.'

'How about Tex Mitchell? You seen him lately?'

'No.'

'Know where we could find him?'

'Nope, no idea. Sorry.'

Lana stared at him. They weren't going to get any further.

'Thanks for minding my stuff, Jerry,' a woman called out, bouncing in through the front door. She was tall and slim with strawberry blonde hair cut in a bob. She ducked under the bar, pulled out a bag and headed back to the front door. Jerome gave her a brief wave and said, 'See you later, Tiff.'

'Who's Tiff?' Agent Sherwood enquired, animated at last.

Lana's face felt hot. She didn't need to ask, and they were starting to go round in circles. 'Thank you for your time, sir,' she said. She left some bills on the counter and walked out.

Her cell began to ring as she ran across the road to the car. She answered the call as she fumbled with the umbrella and the car door. 'Hello, Englese.'

'Lana? Saul Kradich.'

'Hey . . .'

'Where are you? The static's awful.'

'That's not static, it's rain. Hang on . . .' She closed the door and threw the soaked umbrella in the back seat. 'What's up?'

'You still in Florida?'

'Yeah, why?'

'You asked me to look out for the license plate on Tex Mitchell's car.'

'And?'

'Well, nothing's come up, and I mean *nothing*. Does he have a garage? If so, you might want to check inside it.'

Sherwood opened the door and let in a bucket of water.

'We did,' said Lana, annoyed. 'The vehicle's not there. He might have swapped plates on us.'

'Try enlisting the local PD and see what they come up with—get some boots on the street. The Feds have zip.'

'Thanks for the advice. That it?'

'No. Impatient today, aren't we?'

'Yes.'

'As you're still in the retirement state, there's something you might like to look into. There's a webzine I subscribe to called *e-Fuzz*. It specializes in high-end dweebs, of which, I guess, I'm one. The zine tackles complex computer and electronics problems. In the latest issue, just out, there's an article titled, "The Awesome Architecture of Analog Algorithms". The example used was the encryption algorithm for the Raytheon AN/SPS-32.'

'Saul, in *English*, please, if you don't mind.'

'The SPS-32 was the radar used by the Chosa Besshitsu station at Wakkanai in the early eighties. There's no by-line on the article, but *e-Fuzz*'s owner is a former NSA SIGINT spook by the name of Lucas Watts. Oh, and one more point worth mentioning: Watts flew with Tex Mitchell out of Shemya. These days he lives in Florida, a place called Port Charlotte.'

Lana's phone beeped.

'That'll be his address. I've just SMS-ed it to you.'

'Saul, that's great.'

'Here to help.'

'Before I go, one more thing.'

'Yeah?'

'I want to know who was read-in on KAL 007.'

'No can do.'

'What's it worth to you?'

'What's it worth to *you*?'

'What would you say if I told you I just recorded that proposition? Are you open to being bribed?'

'Oh, come on—that's not playing by the rules.'

'I want *everything* you can give me on 007—everything on the crash. I also want copies of any transcripts taken during the psych evaluations for Major Curtis Foxx—the actual transcriptions of the interviews, if you can get them. I want the ICAO report on the crash, as well as everything you can give me on the Chosa Besshitsu facility at Wakkanai. But most of all, I want to know who was read-in.'

'Jesus . . .'

'Here to help—didn't you just say that?'

'Did you really record my proposition?'

'Would you like me to play it back?'

'Alright . . . I'll see what I can do.'

February 7, 2012

Moscow, Russia. Akiko and Ben entered the elevator and she pressed '0' for ground. The doors closed, and then opened on the next floor down to let in another hotel guest, an elegant woman in her early fifties wearing a white-spotted *ushanka*, knee-length black leather coat and black high-heeled boots with gold buckles. Moscow chic. She leaned in front of Akiko and pressed a button.

'We get out at next floor,' she said unexpectedly, her voice Russian-accented, her singsong tone belying the directness of the command. Demonstrating that this was no idle request, she showed Akiko and then Ben the pearl handle of a compact pistol in her coat pocket. 'Do not play game with me,' she warned Ben. 'Bullet will beat man—always.'

Ben nodded, eyes wide. He had no idea what she thought he might do.

The elevator doors opened. 'There is guest sitting room around corner,' the woman said, indicating the direction with a tilt of her head. 'Go there.'

The hallway was empty of other guests and hotel staff, between the morning and lunchtime shifts.

Akiko led the way into the guest lounge.

'Sit,' the woman commanded.

Akiko and Ben sat.

'What do you want?' Ben asked.

The woman chose a chair with its back to the wall.

'You have meeting with my friend on train yesterday. His name is Sergei. He is killed afterward.'

'Oh!' gasped Akiko, her hand in front of her lips.

'Killed?' Ben echoed, stunned.

'What did you talk about?' the woman demanded.

'The Lub-Lubyanka,' Akiko stuttered.

'What did you want to know?'

'We asked him about prisoners.'

'What prisoners?'

'He told us about an American politician brought to the Lubyanka in 1983,' said Ben. 'We asked him about survivors of Korean Air Lines Flight 007.'

The woman shook her head, but seemed to relax a little. 'He tell me about your foolish advertisement and ask me to keep watch on his back. I see men follow you, and Sergei. I follow men who follow Sergei. I see Sergei killed.'

'Jesus,' Ben whispered.

'My friend want to help you. And now I honor his memory by telling you to go home, back to America.'

'We can't,' said Akiko.

'Why not?'

'We are looking for someone.'

'Who?'

'Someone taken prisoner.'

'Forget about this person. Also, your room is bugged with listening device.'

'What?' Akiko was shocked.

'What did the killer look like?' asked Ben. 'In case he comes after us.'

'Tall, thin, bald. His name is Vlahd Bykovski.'

'You know him?'

'He was my husband. Do not take elevator, use stairs. Stairs take longer than elevator. You do not want them to know that we have talked. Do not discuss things you do not want known in your room.' The woman stood. 'For health, leave Russia now.'

She turned and walked out without looking back. Somewhere down the hall, out of sight, a door opened and closed. Ben and Akiko continued to sit, overwhelmed.

Akiko moved first. Ben followed her down the stairs, through the foyer and into the street. It was snowing. Neither talked for a block and a half.

'Are we being followed?' Ben finally asked, glancing behind him but seeing nothing in the least suspicious.

'I don't know,' said Akiko. 'We should take her advice and leave.'

'And go home?'

'No, go to Khabarovsk.'

'Why did you kill him?' Valentin Korolenko asked. He gazed down onto the roof of the Bolshoi Theatre. A copy of the *Izvestiya* lay on the low coffee table, opened to a grainy, long-distance photo of a police cordon around the Plaza Mediterrano, where the body of retired FSB sergeant Sergei Glazkov had been found.

'The subjects were getting nowhere and then my ex-wife's lover volunteered to be their tour guide through the basement cells of the Lubyanka.'

'I know of your history with Glazkov, Vlahd Ivanovich. I am not paying you to settle old family scores.'

'If I hadn't killed him, who knows what he might have told them?'

'Nevertheless, you don't have carte blanche on my account to leave a trail of bodies from one end of the Rodino to another. How did Glazkov connect with our two tourists?'

'They placed an ad. Sergei answered it.'

'An advertisement?' Korolenko shook his head. 'Americans . . .'

He picked up the newspaper. The article said the police believed Sergei Glazkov's death to have been an unfortunate accident. It wasn't uncommon for falling icicles to cause death, and no witnesses had come forward to report any crime. Korolenko gave a mental shrug. Perhaps, as Bykovski was saying, the man was better off dead, at least for them.

'Where is Soloyov?' asked Korolenko.

'Grisha's following our targets.'

'Well then, perhaps you should rejoin him.'

☭

Lana pressed the button beneath the security camera. A green light came on.

'Lana Englese, NSA, and Special Agent Miller Sherwood, FBI, to see Mr Lucas Watts,' she said, holding their credentials up to the camera lens.

'Do you have an appointment?' asked a female voice through the speaker.

'Do we need one?' was Lana's response.

'Just a moment, please.'

The light went off. A moment later, there was a buzz and Lana pushed the gate open. The cinder path leading to the front steps of the house was almost the width of a driveway. The front door, also, was wide enough for three people abreast to walk through. It reminded her of the elephant pen at a zoo she once visited as a child.

They stood at the front door. There was another camera and buzzer. The light was green. They were being checked again. Lana turned her back to the camera and took in the surroundings. The front garden was expertly manicured grass. The flamingos were pure cheese. The thick screen of pines and the fence spoke of neatness and privacy issues, maybe even paranoia.

The door opened on a vast man stuffed into a motorized chair. His hair was short and greasy and his spectacles were on the verge of being pushed off his face by his cheeks.

'Good afternoon,' said Lana, holding up her ID. 'I'm Investigator Englese and this—'

'Yeah, I got it the first time,' said Watts. 'What do you want?'

'Can we come in?' she asked.

'Nope,' he said.

Behind Watts, Lana could see his nurse—attractive in a blonde

Swedish way; the voice on the security speaker. She looked well paid. From what the woman probably had to do, she'd have to be, Lana thought. The dimensions of Watts explained the modifications to his home. He'd obviously spent a small fortune remodeling. The webzine scene had to be lucrative.

'You. You're staring,' Watts snapped at Sherwood. 'What's to stare at? We won't be talking to *you*.'

Before her partner could retaliate, Lana said, 'Mr Watts, *e-Fuzz* is yours, am I right?'

'It certainly is.'

'It's carrying an article in the current issue that looks at the construction of analog algorithms.'

'That's correct.'

'The particular algorithm in the article was the one used to encrypt radar cross-sections detected by Raytheon AN/SPS-32 long-distance radars, one of which was located at Wakkanai on the Japanese Island of Hokkaido in 1983.'

'What of it? The algorithm was declassified years ago, and the US and its allies employed that radar system extensively for years. It's common. Or, I should say, it *was* common.'

'Mr Watts, you recently had a visit from an old buddy of yours—Mr Dallas Mitchell,' Lana said. 'He brought along some friends. They wanted you to decrypt a tape. You cracked it. Your article is proof of that. The United States government wants that tape back.'

'I don't know what you're talking about.'

'You do, and so do we. The NSA has taken you to court several times over the years. Now the laws are tougher, the penalties harsher. You can't win them all, Mr Watts. You've created a comfortable world for yourself here, sir. You wouldn't be so comfortable out of it.'

'Turn up with the police and a search warrant, Ms Englese. Then you can come in, have a look around for yourself. I don't have the tape, but, as you've observed, I've seen what's on it. Trust me, the United States does *not* want to take me to court on this one. Now, if there are no other questions?'

The interview was getting away from her. She asked the first question that popped into her head. 'Tex Mitchell. Where can we reach him? Do you know where he is?'

'I have no idea. Now, if you'll excuse me, this interview is concluded.'

The giant man reversed and disappeared into the gloom like a whale diving deep.

'Thank you for your time, sir,' Lana called after him, working hard to keep the frustration out of her voice.

The blonde woman reappeared and closed the door without looking at them.

Lana stood on the front steps and watched Sherwood walk down the path, uninterested. The tape . . . *I've seen what's on it. Trust me, the United States does not want to take me to court on this one.*

February 8, 2012

Khabarovsk, Siberia. The cab driver lifted his head with a sneering grunt, which Ben and Akiko assumed meant that he'd agreed to the fare. The taxi was a large Japanese people-mover with a crack in the windshield that ran the width of the glass. The driver smoked and wound his window down a few inches to spit.

They pulled out of the frozen airport parking lot in the shadow of a gray marble Soviet building. The road to the city took them past skeletal black trees and crumbling tenement apartment buildings with frozen washing hanging rigid from lines strung between the windows.

'I counted six tall, thin bald men on the plane who looked like killers,' Ben said. 'And one of them was the pilot.'

'Yes,' said Akiko with a smile. She sat beside him in the rear seat buried beneath half a dozen layers of clothing. 'I looked for him, too.'

'How far is it to the hotel?'

'The driver said ten minutes.'

Ben turned around and peered out the back window. There were cars behind them, but were they being *followed*? What are you expecting, he asked himself. He looked again. The vehicle behind them was a silver Toyota wagon. There were no apes in trench coats hanging out the windows with submachine guns. They were on the main road connecting the airport to the town, and another antiquated passenger jet had landed only minutes after theirs, packing out the arrivals hall. Ben told himself that the tension he felt was lack of sleep. It had been a red-eye flight and he was shattered. The back of his seat on the plane had separated from the frame, providing no support. It was an ancient aircraft, a real Cold War antique. The interior smelled like he imagined an old Times Square porn theatre might and the rubber matting in the toilet floor had stuck to the bottom of his shoes. The engines had made some strange sounds, too, which began when they were on the tarmac at Moscow's Sheremetyevo Airport, the fan blades grinding in their bearings as the frigid wind blew through them.

Khabarovsk bumped by out the window, its citizens mostly dressed in black with black hats, heads down, picking their way across the icy broken sidewalks. It gave the impression of a provincial town down on its luck. The buildings looked like their maintenance managers had been on strike for forty years. The rows of tenements were punctuated by houses made of wood, blackened like the trees by the ferocity of the elements, one-room homes each with a chimney exhaling a thin tendril of smoke, a last gasp.

'Does our hotel have a heated pool?' Ben asked as a shiver rippled through him.

Akiko was flicking through a guidebook. 'No, but it says here that hot water for the showers can mostly be expected.'

'Mostly?' he said. 'Reassuring.'

The cab driver took the road slowly, avoiding occasional patches of black ice. Eventually, the traffic behind them thinned out, and by the time they pulled into the access road to a building that looked like a block of iron slag with window slots, they were on their own.

'That's our hotel?' Ben asked.

'*Da, da*. Is hotel,' said the driver.

The cab pulled into a parking space beyond the front doors. The driver counted the notes Ben handed him. He then leaned forward, pulled the release on the trunk, sat back in his seat and lit another cigarette.

'The Russians haven't quite got this whole service-with-a-smile thing worked out, have they?' Ben said as he pulled their bags from the trunk.

He saw the corners of Akiko's eyes crinkle in acknowledgement as she took her pack's handle and lugged it to the doorway, an airlock with glass doors at both ends. They walked into a foyer empty of guests. Two bull-necked men in charcoal pants and cheap jackets stood inside the doorway like nightclub security expecting trouble.

Ben and Akiko walked to the reception desk, which was occupied by a woman in a red knitted sweater with red lipstick and badly tea-stained teeth. She ignored them for several minutes.

'Akiko Sato and Benjamin Harbor,' said Akiko eventually. 'We have a reservation.'

The woman checked her computer terminal before responding. 'Passports,' she said, making no eye contact, holding her hand out across the counter.

Ben and Akiko gave them to her.

'Two night?'

'Yes,' said Ben.

'Single bed?'

'Two twin beds—singles.'

'You have credit card?'

Ben held out his Visa, which she took, debited the first night's accommodation, and then put it back on the vinyl-topped counter with the receipt.

'Room 617. Give this to woman on sixth floor,' she said, handing him a card with the number 617 on it. 'She has key.'

While Ben dealt with reception, Akiko wandered over to a couple of stands containing tourist information pamphlets for various activities in the area, and picked her way through them.

'Do you have hot water for the showers?' Ben asked.

'Perhaps,' the woman said, with a facial expression that implied, 'You'll be lucky.'

The elevator was small and bounced on its cables.

'When the KGB was dissolved, the agents who didn't end up in the FSB must have gone into the hotel business,' Ben observed as he watched the buttons light up for each floor they passed.

The elevator ground to a stop and the door rattled open, revealing a woman seated at a counter, a board with keys hanging from it behind her. Ben presented her with the card and the woman exchanged it for a room key, then leaned forward and pointed down the hallway, jerking her hand back and forth in a manner that indicated their room was way down the far end.

The hallway was carpeted in red plush pile, the walls highly polished mock wood. Chandeliers lit the space at regular intervals. Room 617 was second last on the right. Ben opened the door. It was the light-weight type, veneer sandwiching old newspapers. He noted that the door lock and handle had been sawn out at some time in the past and replaced. The room inside was small with a musty smell; two narrow beds, one each against opposite walls.

'Be it ever so humble,' said Ben, and waited for Akiko to choose where she preferred to sleep.

He went to the window, unzipped his parka and pulled the nylon curtain aside. The windows were new and double-glazed and the room was pleasantly warm. The view was to the north and west, and took in a length of the Amur River, which was frozen solid, a wide ribbon of gray that cut through the mustard-colored winter scrub. Somewhere out there was a gulag, or the remains of one. Movement out on the river distracted him. Two individuals dressed in black were seated in the middle of the ice, hunched over a hole, hoping for dinner to take the bait. It had to be at least minus twenty out there.

Akiko peeled herself out of several layers of clothing and went to give the bathroom an inspection.

'There is no hot water,' she said as she came out a minute later, wiping her hands on a paper towel. 'Perhaps at night it gets hot.'

'Yeah. That was the word the woman downstairs used—"perhaps".'

'I found these downstairs,' Akiko said, splaying a selection of tourist brochures on the bed. 'It is early. We have the whole day. We must keep moving.'

Ben picked up one of the brochures, on the cover a glossy picture of a couple of quad bikes motoring through a snow-blanketed forest with an inset photo of a big cat captioned 'Rare Amur Leopard'. The main headline read 'Siberian Winter Safaris'.

The reality was somewhat less glossy than the brochure. They found the tour company located in a garage beneath one of the old Soviet apartment blocks a mile across town. The garage reeked of petrol and burnt grease. One of the quad bikes was stripped down; two twenty-something mechanics sitting beside the dismembered machine, smoking, spitting and passing a quarter bottle of vodka between them. Their pupils were as small as needle points. Akiko spoke to them in Russian. One of them blearily motioned behind his shoulder.

Akiko and Ben followed the direction into an adjacent garage where a middle-aged man was leaning back in a chair with his feet up on the desk reading a magazine, a half-naked teenage girl with pimples on the cover.

'Are you open for business?' Ben asked.

The man closed his magazine and took his feet off the desk. 'Yes, yes,' he said. 'American?'

'And Japanese,' Ben answered. 'We'd like to hire quad bikes.'

'Of course, yes,' the man said.

From this sudden overwhelming enthusiasm, Ben deduced that business had been far from brisk.

'We have wildlife tour, fishing tour, sightseeing tour. What kind of tour you like?'

'Do you give gulag tours?' Ben asked.

The man's smile flipped to a frown. 'Gulag?'

'My colleague and I are university professors writing a book on incarceration methods of the twentieth century,' Ben said, impressing himself with his own bullshit. 'No such book would be complete without a few chapters on gulags.'

The man didn't understand, so Akiko repeated the cover story in Russian. He seemed to buy it and started talking in Russian.

Akiko held up a hand and said, 'In English, please.'

'Okay, okay. This most unusual. You have permit?'

'Yes, of course,' said Ben. He reached inside his ski jacket and pulled out a wad of euros, counted out 500, and placed them on the man's table.

The man licked his lips.

'There'll be no need for a receipt,' Ben said.

The man pounced on the money and buried it deep into his pants pocket.

'There will be further cost for tour,' he cautioned.

'Naturally,' Ben replied. He felt Akiko squeeze his hand.

'The trip—it is not easy. When you want to go?'

It had just gone 8:15 a.m. 'Now,' Ben said.

'Now?'

'Now.'

The man mumbled to himself and then dashed about his office, pulling various folders from drawers. He tapped the keys on his computer keyboard, stood back and waited for the page to load.

'Hmm. Weather report. It will get colder in afternoon.'

'We love the cold,' Ben told him.

The man shrugged. 'Siberian cold is different.'

Ben shrugged back at him.

'Okay,' the man said. 'I am Oleg. I will be guide today. Excuse, please.' He picked up his cell phone and made a call.

'Food, supplies,' Akiko translated.

The order placed, Oleg pulled a map from one of the folders and laid it across his desk. The city of Khabarovsk sat toward the bottom left of the map, the Amur River and its tributaries snaking diagonally across the map from Khabarovsk up toward the top right.

'We are here,' Oleg said, pointing with a grease and tobacco stained forefinger. 'We go here.' He moved his finger a considerable distance from the city and tapped a range of hills set back from the river, out to the west.

'How far is that?' Ben asked.

'Three hours,' said Oleg. 'First part of journey easy. Second part, not so easy.'

'Were there many gulags around here?' Ben asked.

'One only.'

'No others in the area?'

'Yes, north. Much further. Too far for quad bike.'

'When do we leave?'

'Come back in hour. Bring warm clothing.'

Ben didn't feel like he was exactly dressed for Florida, but he and Akiko returned fifty minutes later in their warmest gear, each with a travel pack containing extra thermals, chemical warmers, space blankets, a thermos of hot tea, and chocolate bars. Two quad bikes stood abreast outside the garage, one of the young mechanics jumping on a footpump, adding air to a tire. Oleg was strapping gear into a trailer.

'Ah, you are here,' he said when he saw them, standing up and stretching his back. 'Who will drive?'

Ben and Akiko glanced at each other. Ben raised his hand.

'You have driven these before?'

'Never had the pleasure,' Ben replied.

'It is easy.' Oleg gave him a quick lesson. 'Brakes are here,' he said, squeezing the levers on the handlebars. 'Another brake here.' He pointed to a pedal in front of the left footpeg. 'This is accelerator.' He twisted the throttle grip on the right side of the handlebars. 'No gears. Is automatic. Easy to drive.'

He glanced at his watch, which prompted Ben to do likewise: 9:15 a.m. 'We go now,' said Oleg. 'Stay in my tracks on river. I will go slow until you are familiar with vehicle.'

'How thick is the ice on the river?' Ben asked.

'Trucks use river. We have no problem.'

The Russian pulled a ski mask from his pocket and pulled it over his head, followed by a full-face helmet, the visor replaced with ski goggles. Ben and Akiko picked up the helmets stuffed with ski masks and goggles sitting on the second bike's seat and did the same.

A few minutes later, they were motoring through the streets, heading generally down to the river. A boat ramp took them onto the ice, the metal nipples on the quad's snow tires scratching for grip on the steep incline until the gradient flattened out. They bounced over water quick-frozen in the shapes of wavelets, plastic bags and booze bottles embedded in them.

They accelerated out into the middle of the river where the ice was smoother, broken only where fishermen had cut blocks out of it with chainsaws. Oleg gave these fishing holes a wide berth and headed for the distant bridge that carried the tracks of the Trans-Siberian Railway across the Amur. Once beyond it, with Khabarovsk left far behind, the fishing holes disappeared and with them all traces of human habitation.

Their speed increased to sixty-five kilometers per hour and the wind began to find its way through the seams in Ben's clothing. Within minutes his face and neck were numb beneath the ski mask, a crust of ice formed around his nostrils. He kept his body rigidly locked in place behind the handlebars. Moving around gave the cold opportunities to find new paths to his skin.

They followed the river for an hour, sticking to the center. Eventually, Oleg stopped. Ben pulled up beside him. The Russian took the map from his jacket pocket and laid it across the tank. Ben and Akiko climbed off their quad as stiffly as if they'd been frozen in place. Both cracked chemical warmers and, after thawing their faces, stuffed them down inside their gloves and jackets. Ben squatted in front of the bike to harvest the warmth radiating off the idling motor. The frostiest temperatures he'd ever experienced were limited to those that blew down from the north during winter in the Keys—high fifties. All warnings about the Siberian version of cold had been an understatement.

'Here,' Ben heard Oleg say. He stood up as the Russian held a bottle toward him. 'Vodka.'

Ben shook his head and tried to speak, his jaw still frozen. 'Something hot—tea.'

'No, teeth frozen. Hot tea will crack them.'

Ben pictured the windshield in their cab from the airport. He accepted the bottle. The vodka was oily and cold, but it went down warm and spread through his body. He passed the bottle to Akiko, who took a swig.

'Much further?' Ben asked.

'Half an hour,' said Oleg.

'Good.'

'Then it will get more difficult.'

The Russian went to the trailer behind his quad, threw back an oilskin and pulled out a rifle that looked military. 'Bear and leopard,' he said when he saw the look of surprise in Ben's and Akiko's eyes.

Half an hour later, Akiko shouted over Ben's shoulder that she wished they were back on the river ice. Oleg had taken them off the trunk of the Amur and into a tributary at the foot of a set of high, forested hills. The tributary eventually became a frozen rocky creek that snaked and climbed through the hills. The all-wheel-drive quad handled the terrain reasonably well. Oleg kept the going slow, picking his way up the creek bed. Eventually they had to leave it and strike a path through the pines, motoring up inclines that threatened to overturn their vehicles.

Ben was starting to sweat. He wrestled with the quad, mimicking Oleg's riding style, standing up on the footpegs. Akiko stayed close, also up on the pegs, her arms wrapped tightly around his waist. They stopped on a ridge line with a clear view of the river far below. Oleg got off his bike and walked stiffly to the trailer.

'Food,' he said, finding a plastic container. He pulled back the lid and offered around the contents—squares of something deep-fried.

'What is it?' Akiko asked, taking one.

'Lard,' Oleg replied.

'Did you say lard?' Ben looked at the yellow square between his gloved fingers.

'Yes. Is special recipe. Fat soak in sour milk, cover in dough and fry.' Oleg took a whole slice in his mouth and went back in for more.

Ben took a small bite. The flavor was dense, salty and sour, and he could taste animal in the roof of his mouth. It was disgusting, but he guessed fat cooked in fat was probably the sort of sustenance you'd need to survive a vicious Siberian winter. And, in fact, now that they had stopped, the cold was again creeping over him, gnawing on his bones. He ate the rest of the slice.

A distant movement caught Oleg's attention. He put down the tray, picked up a set of military binoculars and trained them on the river far below.

A moment later, he passed the glasses to Ben and asked, 'You know these people?'

Ben brought into view a four-wheel-drive vehicle towing a trailer with two skidoos mounted on it. Was there a tall, thin bald man behind the wheel?

'No.' He passed the glasses to Akiko.

'Hunters. Perhaps they want bear,' Oleg concluded.

The four-wheel drive had left the Amur and was probing the riverbank for a trail up through the trees.

'How far now?' Ben asked, turning to Oleg.

'Half an hour.'

The trail worsened, becoming steeper, rockier, with drifts of snow hiding holes and fallen trees. They dipped down into a valley and climbed again, both quads having to be dug out on two occasions with trenching tools. Eventually, they made a third ridge line and Oleg stopped, Ben pulling up beside him. Out of the trees and unshielded by the valley, the wind was up and it had teeth.

The Russian handed the binoculars to Akiko and pointed down into the valley. 'There.'

With his naked eye, Ben could see a very large patch of rectangular ground in the forest below, obviously cleared and reorganized by human hand. A road joined it to a vast wasteland area of dead earth, acres of poisoned forest, huge tailings cones and man-made ponds covered in ice slicks.

Akiko gave him the binoculars. 'There is nothing left,' she said, her voice edged with bitterness.

'What did they mine here?' asked Ben.

'Gold,' Oleg replied.

'Where are the shafts?'

'Further up into the valley.'

They took the descent down through the trees slowly, the tires pushing waves of snow in front of them. Eventually, after another short climb, they motored into the remains of what, according to Oleg, was once Labor Camp F07982.

'This is all remaining of camp,' the Russian said.

Ben and Akiko stepped off the quad and walked through what was now no more than a cold and distant memory. This was the barracks area where, according to Oleg, the inmates were housed and fed. Part of the external wire boundary fence remained in one corner, attached to a leaning tower where guards armed with machine guns would have once kept watch. Now there was nothing to watch, except for perhaps the final collapse of a doorframe here, a brick chimney stack there.

'What happened to this place?' Akiko asked.

'The communists fell,' said Oleg with a shrug.

'The people held here—what was their crime?' Ben lifted the binoculars and surveyed the area again, looking for signs of life.

'They were Koreans. Their government sent them here to work—a goodwill gesture.'

Ben grunted. 'I'm sure the workers felt honored. Where did they go? Home?'

'Some went. Others stayed.'

'Where?'

'There is a village nearby.'

Ben heard Akiko's breath catch in her throat.

'Maybe we should go take a look there?' she suggested.

'You want to make photograph for book?' Oleg asked, his rifle slung over his shoulder.

'Yes.' Ben took a camera from his backpack and began snapping photos. There were appearances to keep up. 'Who took away the camp, removed the buildings?'

'Villagers use for firewood,' said Oleg. He was walking around, toeing at the thin layer of ice and snow on the ground.

'We'd like to talk with some of the former prisoners—get the human perspective,' said Ben.

The Russian shot him a look of uncertainty. He wasn't happy about the idea. 'There are FSB in village. They do not welcome visitors.'

'We'll pay extra.'

'Hundred euros.'

'Deal.'

'Okay.' Oleg still didn't seem happy about it.

'We'll settle up when we get back to Khabarovsk.'

'*Da*,' their guide replied, scanning the sky.

Thin wisps of high cirrus clouds were arcing down from the

northwest. It was after midday; soon the sun would fall behind the hill and the chill factor would increase.

'How many people were here?' Akiko asked.

'Over many years, thousands.'

'Men and women?'

'Yes, both.'

She walked over to an area that must have been a huge shed, the earth covered by a cracked and broken slab riddled with concrete cancer.

Oleg took a mouthful of vodka from the bottle as he walked and passed it to Ben, who also had a belt. Akiko declined the offer with a wave of her hand.

'Did they find much gold?' Ben asked.

'Not enough,' Oleg replied.

'How did they get it out? They use the same route we just took?'

'Mules. There was different path. Landslide close it.'

The Russian walked over to his quad bike and climbed on. 'We run out of time,' he said. 'We go now.'

'I found this,' Akiko said when she was back on the seat behind Ben. She reached around and opened her gloved hand. In her palm was a brass belt buckle embossed with a hammer and sickle.

It was a short ride to the village, uneven rows of dwellings tossed onto the side of the hill below the tree line. The homes were like the black wood homes they'd seen in Khabarovsk, only smaller and meaner, and each was accompanied by a miniature backyard corraling stacked firewood and scavenged, rusting, unrecognizable machinery. No lights shone from any windows. There were no power lines, no satellite dishes to be seen, and no vehicles. Movement—a black shape hunched against the cold huddled down a narrow pathway and disappeared into one of the buildings. It could have been a medieval village eking out an existence. The poverty line was something it might aspire to.

Occasional wind gusts swept up the valley, blowing clouds of dry snow into shapes that reminded Ben of giant jellyfish. Oleg led the way through the village. He pulled up in the lee of one of the larger buildings and directed Ben to park close beside him. The Russian went to the trailer, lifted out a tarpaulin, shook it, and then threw it over both machines.

'You want to meet people. We go to bar,' said Oleg.

The bar was a brick building Ben and Akiko hadn't noticed. It was lit, a portable Honda generator humming away outside.

'Old commissar building,' Oleg explained as he opened the door.

☭

A wall of human odor and alcohol sweat rushed toward them with the force of a body block. They walked into a room lit by several bare bulbs and a promotional sign for a brand of Russian vodka. More than twenty people sat at low tables. Some talked quietly among themselves. Most spoke only to the drinks in their hands, slumped forward on their tables. Heads that were sober enough to register their presence turned toward them with hooded, exhausted eyes.

'Drink?' Oleg asked.

Ben nodded.

Their guide went off to place the order with the barkeep, a short, stocky man wearing a filthy apron.

'No women here,' Akiko whispered to Ben.

'I noticed. Coyote Ugly it ain't.'

Akiko took off a glove and unzipped the front of her parka. From an inside pocket she retrieved a small scrapbook and took out a photo, a copy of the one on the altar in her home back in Tokyo, and held it in front of a drunk attempting to pour himself a drink. The man ignored her and the photo, circling his dirty glass with the lip of the empty bottle. The glass sat in a puddle of clear liquid that dribbled away off the edge of the table.

Akiko surveyed the room, then walked over to a table occupied by a man on his own who was writing in a journal. She sat opposite him. The man glanced up.

Ben took the remaining chair. 'Do you mind?' he asked.

The man, in his mid-thirties, was wearing a new North Face ski jacket. He mumbled something in Russian and went back to his writing.

'Hello,' Akiko said, speaking in Russian.

'Yes?' he said, looking up again.

'Do you mind if I ask you a question?'

'Why do you want to ask me a question?'

'Do you live here?'

'No. My family did. My grandfather died here.'

'Were they Korean?'

'Yes.'

'What are you writing?'

'I'm a journalist documenting this place—researching my family history. And you? Why have you come here?'

'I'm searching for my mother.'

'And she was held here?'

'I'm not sure. We were told that there was a good chance she would have been sent to a camp in this area.' Akiko showed him the photo. 'Her name was Nami.'

He gave it a cursory glance. 'She was pretty. Looks like you.' He went back to his journal.

'She is Japanese.'

He looked up, eyes widened. 'Japanese!'

The door opened and an older thick-set man lumbered in, brushing light snow from his bare brown head.

The journalist stiffened. 'FSB,' he mouthed.

He closed his book, stood and walked out of the bar without looking back.

Akiko scoped the room. There was no one else conscious enough to show the photo to.

Oleg returned with three shot glasses and a half bottle of vodka. 'Did something happen?' he asked Akiko in Russian.

'This is my mother,' Akiko replied in English, passing him the photo. 'I think she was held here.'

Oleg slid the photo off the table and out of sight. '*Vih shumashetshi?* Are you crazy?' he whispered. 'Follow me now.'

He got up from the table and moved quickly to the door, just as the journalist had done moments earlier. Outside, he handed back the photograph and said, 'You come to find her?'

'Yes.'

'You are not from the university,' he accused.

384

'No,' she said as Ben joined them.

'I should charge you more for lying to me.'

'We've given you enough already.'

'What were you hoping for?' Oleg asked, speaking Russian, his anger flushing his cheeks livid. 'The people here, they are all trying to forget, not remember. I wondered why you paid me so much, why such a big hurry. This is a fool's errand, and a dangerous one.' He switched to English to include Ben. 'We leave.'

'You okay?' Ben asked Akiko, clearly sensing her anxiety. 'What's up?'

'Nothing,' she said.

They walked through the refrozen slush, their boots crunching the ice, back to the quad bikes. Angry and frustrated, Akiko had nothing to say.

Oleg flicked back the tarp and handed out the helmets without saying a word. As they climbed onto the machines, a man stepped from the shadows—the journalist. He glanced around nervously and beckoned Akiko. She got off the quad and hurried over to him. He pulled her into the shadows.

'We must talk quickly,' he said. 'There were foreign nationals, besides North Koreans, held here. Seven people were brought. All were Asian— South Koreans, Japanese, Taiwanese. There was something about a spy plane. It caused a stir in the camp.'

The news electrified Akiko. 'How do you know?'

'I heard my grandfather talking to my father.'

'When? What year?'

'I was ten. That would make it 1983. That's all I know.'

Excitement surged through her. 'Are any of them still here?'

'No. All were dispersed before the Soviets fell.'

'Do you know where they were sent?'

'The rumor was to another camp—somewhere north of Ulan-Ude.'

The cover offered by the tree line was good. They were watching from the dark into the light, with an unobstructed view of the back of the village. Vlahd Bykovski lowered his glasses.

'What do you think?' he asked.

Grisha Soloyov, his eyeball nestled against the rubber cup of the telescopic sight, moved the crosshairs from one head to the other, and settled them in the middle of the Japanese woman's face when she reappeared. The tip of his finger massaged the front of the trigger guard.

'I think Comrade Korolenko is going as soft as milk cakes. Two bullets would end it here. The line of sight is perfect. *Pak. Pak,*' he said, mimicking the sound of the suppressed Nikonov 'Abakan' assault rifle, its sling wrapped around his right arm to brace it. 'Half a day trudging through the Siberian snow and we have nothing to show for it.'

'We are being paid by the hour. Rushing this will cost us good money.'

'What do you think they have found down there, apart from human waste?'

'I know as much as you. What I *would* like to know, however, is as much as their *guide.*'

Soloyov pulled his eye from the sight and grinned at his partner. 'Yes, me too.'

April 6, 1986

Lefortovo Prison, Moscow. The guard and two Fifth Directorate transport officers accompanied General Korolenko down the dank corridor, past the anonymity of a hundred closed concrete and steel doors bleeding rust stains, homes to murderers, arsonists and other common criminals. The sound of Korolenko's polished boot heels cracked and echoed off the walls like hammer strikes. There was no need for silence. The prisoners in this wing were here to rot. The state required nothing further from them other than their eventual deaths.

As he walked, Korolenko reflected on his first meeting with prisoner 98987. The arrival of the Korean plane had proved to be a bonanza for his career and a living hell for the congressman, who had spent the years since in a box no bigger than the general's closet. During that time, McDonald had endured having every moment of his adult life dissected, probed and documented.

Korolenko's interest in the American had waned once he'd been broken and emptied of everything of worth. The interrogation had stopped some time ago, after the man's mind had gone, blown like an overloaded fuse. Apparently, these days the congressman had a ten-minute memory.

'Walk out of the room, return eleven minutes later, and 98987 will see you as a complete stranger,' the prison commandant had told Korolenko recently when the general had called.

So Lawrence McDonald's mind was mush. Korolenko had come to see it for himself a month ago and it was true. The congressman hadn't recognized him. They had talked in Russian about prison food, the comfort of the mattress, the fleas. Korolenko had then stepped out for twenty minutes before re-entering the six walls of McDonald's world and it was clear that the American didn't recall a single detail of their earlier meeting. That a man could be cored of his whole life had seemed to Korolenko a hell worse than any torture.

It was then that the general had made up his mind to release the American. Mikhail Gorbachev, the new Premier, was backing up his talk for change and renewal with action, and this madness was even reaching into the KGB. Charity had nothing to do with it, Korolenko assured himself. Setting a few harmless prisoners free would look agreeable to his superiors in the Politburo. He could be a man of the future as much as anyone.

And so, it had been arranged.

The guard paused outside one of the iron doors and reached for his keys. A card with the familiar number 98987 was held in a slot. Korolenko stopped the guard and the man stepped back from the door. Korolenko leaned forward and peered through the judas hole. He was startled to see a bloodshot eye as cold as a bird's staring back at him. A lid slid over the orb and the eye moved back into the recesses of the cell.

Korolenko motioned at the guard to open the door. The key rattled heavily in the lock and turned with a rusty grind. Korolenko ducked his head and walked in, by which time Congressman McDonald was seated on his bunk with his knees drawn up under his chin, rocking slowly. Korolenko was amazed at what a few short years had done to the American. He was thin now, his muscles wasted and his joints swollen with misuse. Clumps of his hair had fallen out and patches of gray scalp showed through the close-cropped white bristle that remained. His face had shrunk, too, all the fat gone from cheeks that had taken on the green pallor of the long-term inmate. His own children probably wouldn't recognize him, Korolenko thought.

McDonald looked up and, in Russian, said, 'What do you want? I cannot be disturbed.'

'Today you're going on a trip,' said Korolenko.

'I don't know you. Get out.'

'You want to see the sun, don't you?'

'I don't know. Why would I want to see it?'

'I am setting you free, Lawrence.'

'Free? What's free? I don't want to be free.' The man looked around his cell, his head darting as his eyes flicked from one corner to the next.

'You'll like Kazakhstan. There is a little village. You can sit in the sun and spend your last years chasing women, eating and drinking.'

Terror filled the congressman's face. Korolenko realized all of a sudden that freedom—even the little freedom an old forced-labor camp town in the desert plains of Kazakhstan might provide—was the last thing the man wanted. But there was nothing Korolenko could do, not now. The papers had been submitted and the wheels were in motion. He nodded at the transport detail to prepare the prisoner. They stepped forward and Congressman McDonald began to kick and scream, his mind unable to cope with the enormous emptiness brought on by the prospect of the complete unknown.

February 9, 2012

Khabarovsk, Siberia. 'Get up.'

Half conscious, Ben thought the demand and the pushing were part of a dream that he wasn't aware he was having. Exhaustion won and he slipped back into a comatose sleep, his body worn out from the previous day's trek to the gulag.

'Come on, damn you . . . get up!'

The pushing became slaps and suddenly Ben knew the voice wasn't in his subconscious. There was a stranger in the room.

'Jesus,' he said, snapping out of the fog of sleep. The lights flicked on, hurting his eyes.

The woman stepped back from his bed and threw something at him. His clothes.

'Get dressed.' She turned to Akiko. 'You, too.'

'W-what . . . ?' Akiko stammered, pushing herself up and out of bed, confused.

'You must get up. There is something you must see with your own eyes.'

'Hey . . .' Recognition dawned on Ben. It was the woman from the hotel in Moscow. 'What the hell are you doing in our room? Get out before I throw you out.'

'That would be unwise. Now, hurry. I want to show you something.

Perhaps then you will understand why you must leave.'

'Lady, we're going nowhere until you tell us what's going on. And you'd damn well better hurry.' Ben was out of bed, his hands clenched into fists by his sides. 'I meant it when I said I'd throw you out.'

'And I meant it when I said that would be a mistake.'

The woman's vehicle was a 7 Series Beemer that smelled of leather, walnut and the showroom. A new luxury rental. Ben leaned forward between the woman and Akiko, who was riding in the front passenger seat.

'What did you say your name was?' he asked.

The Beemer rumbled and bumped across a set of tram tracks no longer embedded in the road and then turned left. Ben was sure this part of town looked familiar.

'I did not say. My name is Luydmila Pozlov. I told you in Moscow that I was married to Vlahd Bykovski, the pig who killed Sergei, my friend. Bykovski is the man I warned about—tall, thin and bald, remember? He is FSB. He is also sociopath. He will kill you while he thinks about what to have for lunch. His partner, Grisha Soloyov—he is worse. Bykovski and Sergei were Fifth Directorate guards at Lubyanka prison. I was in First Directorate—counterintelligence.'

Luydmila moved the Beemer to the side of the road as two cop cars came up behind them, sirens and lights blazing.

'You and Sergei were having an affair,' said Ben, watching the cops speed past, 'and this Bykovski didn't like it.'

'*Da.*'

'Are you telling us that we've walked into some kind of fatal love-revenge story? Because, you know, that puts me back on familiar ground.'

'Shut up,' Luydmila snapped.

She turned hard right, tires squealing, into a street and slowed. A police vehicle half blocked the road. A man in uniform with a torch waved at them to stop. Down the far end was a collection of cop cars and fire engines, the night pierced with their flashing blue, red and yellow lights. Luydmila pulled to the curb.

'What is going on?' Akiko asked.

'Hey, I know where we are,' said Ben. 'Down there—isn't that where Siberian Winter Safaris is?'

'Not any more,' said Luydmila. 'Bykovski and Soloyov, they murdered your guide, the man who took you to old labor camp yesterday. They torture first, pour petrol down his throat. Then they lit him.'

'They w-what?' Ben stammered.

Luydmila lowered the window to speak with the cop. They exchanged a few words and then she backed up the car and did a U-turn.

Another cop car sped past, on its way to the crime scene.

'Your guide lived in apartment building above the garage. They took him downstairs. They torture to get information—about you.'

Ben was stunned. He wanted to say something but nothing came out.

'My friend Sergei was killed helping you, and now this man is dead because of you. More people will die unless you leave, and I think now you will both die. I have brought you here to show you. This will happen to you. It will be bad. You must leave.'

'No!' Akiko snapped at her. 'We're here for my mother. She was on that Korean plane. We will find her and *then* we will leave.'

Ben was now familiar with this tone in Akiko's voice. He had decided that she was probably the most stubborn person he'd ever met.

'Flight 007. Still you do not understand,' Luydmila said with a sneer, throwing her head back. 'And neither did Soviet intelligence service until it was too late. Your government wanted this. They wanted zero option—no one was supposed to live. Everyone was supposed to die to embarrass Soviets. Aircraft was not meant to land, but it did. It was meant to crash. And that is secret that must not be known. Do you not comprehend? It would embarrass your government, my government.'

'I don't believe it,' said Ben.

'You don't believe your government would lie to you?'

'They wouldn't have sent 269 people to their deaths. That's just cold-blooded murder.'

'You are naïve fool. Governments have always killed their own people for good of country. That is what governments do. Between them, Lenin and Stalin kill 35 millions of Russians for this reason. What is one plane full of people?'

'My country is different,' said Ben.

Luydmila laughed mirthlessly and shook her head as she turned the car toward their hotel.

'Sergei, your friend,' said Akiko, 'he died helping us. And so did Oleg. If we give up, they died for nothing.'

'That is foolish. When you are also dead, what will it matter? Who will care? Sergei? Guide? They are not caring. Not now.'

Luydmila stopped just beyond the lights flooding the hotel's forecourt. She took a large envelope from the door pocket beside her, removed a handful of photographs and passed them around. 'This is Bykovski and this is Soloyov. They work for this man.'

'I thought you said they were FSB,' said Ben.

'Russia has become expensive. They have two jobs.'

'So who's the old guy?' Ben asked.

'His name is Valentin Korolenko.'

Ben picked up the photo and angled it toward the ambient light.

'Korolenko is KGB and then FSB,' she continued. 'In KGB he is Fifth Directorate. He retire as general in charge of all foreign national prisoners in USSR. He keep this position in Russian Federation after Soviet world collapse. When Korean 747 land on Sakhalin Island, Korolenko is KGB officer in charge of prisoner distribution.'

'Jesus,' said Ben.

'I think someone pay him to stop you. Korolenko and his men Bykovski and Soloyov are assets.'

'Who would that someone be?' Ben asked.

'This I do not know.'

A business card fluttered from the envelope onto Akiko's lap. 'What is "Fidelity"?' she asked, examining it.

'That is my company. I uncover husbands who cheat. There is much cheating in new Russia.'

'You're a private detective?' asked Ben.

'Yes.'

'We will hire you,' said Akiko, checking with Ben for his opinion. He nodded.

'If Bykovski knows I help you, he will kill you for pleasure.'

'According to you, he's going to kill us anyway,' Ben said. 'We've got nothing to lose.'

'I could not help Sergei.' Her voice was subdued. 'Do you also want to end up with back full of ice daggers?'

'They took you by surprise, there was nothing you could do. But you can help us. We're in this country operating alone. We need an insider.'

'You need to go home.'

'As we said, that's not an option for us.'

'Take photographs.' She leaned across Akiko and pulled the latch, opening the door.

Ben and Akiko gathered up the pictures and got out of the car.

'What would your guide have told them before he died?' Luydmila asked through the window. 'What did he know?'

'He knew that we were going to Ulan-Ude,' Akiko said.

'What is in Ulan-Ude?'

'Another camp,' said Ben.

'You want to grow old? Catch plane home,' said Luydmila. Her window rolled up and she drove off.

October 3, 1990

Paris, France. General Korolenko sat in a public park by the River Seine and waited. The air was cool but not yet cold, especially for a man used to Siberian winters. Few leaves remained on the trees, but some golden stalwarts were still attached to twigs and branches. Across the square, breakfast was being served and the aromas of brioche and café au lait tantalized his senses. So this was Paris. It was soft, but nonetheless pleasant, and reminded him somewhat of Leningrad. He watched the Parisians going about their day, heading to work, oblivious to the global struggles. What would it be like to be so blissfully unaware, so untouched by world events? Would a life spent in ignorance be better, or worse?

At home, in Moscow, the world was crumbling, falling down around everyone's ears, while that fool Gorbachev systematically dismantled everything, throwing open the doors and letting in the decay. There was nowhere to hide, unless you had American dollars. No one was being paid. Toilet paper was worth more than roubles. The KGB was tumbling, the Red Army in disarray. The world Korolenko knew was rushing to its own destruction.

The money had been shoved under the door of his apartment in a fat envelope: $50,000 together with the open-ended round-trip airline ticket to Paris on Air France. The people who had done that were brazen. If something like that had happened even a year ago, Korolenko would have fully expected to have been arrested, interrogated and shot. But now the First Directorate was more worried about the future than the present. There was no security guard on the door in the lobby, and his was a building set aside especially for high-ranking Party members. A note came with the money. On it was written a date and a time. Brazen didn't do this justice. It was utter lunacy, a sign of the times.

Korolenko watched a man walk slowly into the park. He tossed dried breadcrumbs on the grass from a bag in his hand. Birds flew down and swarmed at his feet. He finally emptied the bag and took a seat beside the general.

'I loathe pigeons,' the man said. 'Just take a look at the statue. Covered head to toe in shit.'

Korolenko glanced at the standing bronze figure in the center of the park, an eighteenth-century man carrying an armful of books. A local scholar, he assumed, the deeds that had earned him a place in this park lost to history.

'Are you wearing a wire?' the man asked.

'Do you wish to check?'

'What do you think?'

Ordinarily, Korolenko would have had a man beaten for impertinence like this. But he was hoping that the money he'd received was just the beginning, and he didn't want to jeopardize it. He stood up, removed his coat, lifted his shirt out of the top of his pants and turned around slowly.

'You pass,' said the man. His face was pointed and pinched and reminded Korolenko of a ferret. He wore sunglasses. It wasn't sunny.

The man spoke into his shirtsleeve and then said, 'Sit, General, you're making me nervous.'

'Why am I here?'

'To take a meeting a couple of thousand of your red Ivan buddies would kill for to take your place.'

A second man walked into the park. Korolenko recognized him immediately. He was stunned. It was the assistant director of the CIA.

The man with the sunglasses stood, walked some distance away and appeared to patrol the park's entrance.

'Major General Korolenko of the Fifth Directorate of the Komitet Gosudarstvennoi Bezopasnosti,' Garret said in Russian. 'It's a pleasure to meet you.'

'And you, Assistant Director Garret.'

'Good. As we know each other, there's no need to exchange business cards.'

'You have a Leningrad accent,' said Korolenko.

'I'll take that as a compliment.'

The general took a deep breath and exhaled to steady his nerves. What was this all about?

'You have your money, obviously. I recommend that you open an account with a bank in Berne. Hank over there can provide you with the name of a good one. Stuffing envelopes of cash under your door comes with attendant risks.'

'Which brings me naturally to my first question. Why would you want to pay me money?'

'You have something we want, of course.'

'Whatever it is, what makes you think that I would give it to you?'

'Because your country's sinking into a quagmire, General. Your only security will be to have a certain amount of, shall we say, liquidity.'

'You seem certain of yourself, Assistant Director.'

'It comes with the job, if you do the job well enough.'

Garret glanced across at Hank, who was speaking into his sleeve again. The two men made eye contact and Garret received a nod.

'General,' Garret continued, 'you are the man in charge of all foreign national prisoners?'

'You know this already.'

'I can make you a rich man if you're prepared to continue doing your job.'

'That was my intention regardless, to keep working for the good of the Soviet Union.'

'The wealth aspect is a problem though, isn't it, General? All the perks and special considerations you've come to expect as one of the elite are going to dry up, if they haven't already. When was the last time you were paid? The USSR will cease to exist within the foreseeable future. Give it six months, a year at most. It has already begun.'

Korolenko chose not to respond.

'How secure are your prisoners?'

'They're not going anywhere.'

'When the USSR falls, what will happen to all your foreign national prisoners held in the Ukraine, Kazakhstan and Turkmenistan? What will happen when all these 'stans turn their backs on Moscow?'

'That won't happen.'

'Open the barn doors and all your horses will run.'

Korolenko was intrigued. 'Which foreign nationals in particular, Assistant Director?'

'The ones recovered when a certain 747 was forced down.'

Korolenko worked hard to keep the surprise out of his face. He wanted to swallow and he could feel the vein pulsing in his temple.

'What 747?' he asked.

'There was more than one?'

'It crashed into the Sea of Japan and everyone on board was lost.'

'You can be a rich man, General, or not. The choice is yours.'

Korolenko hadn't survived a lifetime in the KGB not to have learned when to take and when to give. The man called Hank was circling the park's entrance, scanning the overlooking apartments.

'When did you know?' Korolenko finally asked.

'More than twenty low-level agents were killed within the Eastern Bloc from October to December in 1983. Your client intelligence services cleaned out all the sleepers. There was only one common link.'

Korolenko knew instantly who Garret was talking about. 'Congressman McDonald.'

'You might as well have printed an announcement in TASS.'

Korolenko managed to keep a lid on his anger. Those stupid Tartars in the First Directorate had caught Andropov's paranoia, and in the process they'd shown the CIA their hand.

'So the CIA has known the truth almost from the start, and yet you did almost nothing about it.'

'Did nothing? General, we did *everything* in our power to go along with it. Taking down KAL 007 was like shooting yourselves in the foot. You helped us win the war.'

And suddenly Korolenko saw it all clearly. 'It was planned.'

'What was planned?'

'The plane wasn't sent into Soviet skies to gather intelligence, but to change world opinion.'

'A suicide mission? For public relations purposes? Well, if that were true, no one could claim we didn't have commitment.'

Korolenko was shocked.

'The Soviet Union will be gone within a year, two at most, and the United States will be your country's friend. Friends look after each other. And we'll pay a lot of money in order to cement a very special *personal* friendship with you.'

Korolenko watched the pigeons strutting around in circles, the larger ones bullying the smaller birds for any remaining crumbs. The world was moving in a new direction. In many important ways, McDonald had been right about his so-called One World conspiracy.

'Your President Bush is going to war in the Gulf. He is an oilman. I don't think the Muslims there will welcome him.'

'I don't think they have much choice.'

'Is this the start of a new world order?'

'Maybe, General, maybe. Things are happening pretty fast on this President's watch—the Berlin Wall coming down, the rise of democracy in your neck of the woods, the end of wars of adventure . . .'

The words 'a new world order' clearly meant nothing to the CIA assistant director. Korolenko grunted. The world was indeed changing and here was an opportunity to profit from it. The irony of this capitalist way of thinking wasn't lost on him.

'How much money would you pay? And what would I be required to do?'

'You would receive a bonus payment of another $50,000 simply for coming on board. And then, every year for the foreseeable future, you'd receive $300,000 indexed to the US rate of inflation. This would be paid into your Swiss bank account on the proviso that your prisoners remain safely tucked away. As I said, we're going to pay you to keep doing what you've been doing. We're not asking you to spy on your country. We're not asking you to compromise your integrity. But what we are asking you to do is in Russia's interest.'

'And America's.'

'Of course, General. This isn't Adopt an Orphan Week. What we're asking is in both our national interests, Moscow's and Washington's. Both sides would be extremely embarrassed if these ex-passengers suddenly turned up. They would make liars out of all of us, but especially of the Soviet Union, of Russia.'

'When will you need an answer, Assistant Director?'

Garret glanced at his watch. 'I leave the park and you sort out the contact and billing arrangements with Hank over there. Or you leave here with an uncertain future. Choice is yours.'

February 9, 2012

NSA HQ, Fort Meade, Maryland. Lana didn't particularly want to share with Sherwood, but partners is partners. She leaned against the wall with her arms folded while he reviewed her written report sent off to Whittle and, through him, Hank Buck at the CIA. He made no comment on it and moved on to the additional material on her HP PC, kneading one of his biceps as he paged down through the transcripts of Curtis Foxx's psych evaluations.

'The guy was clearly a basket case,' he concluded.

'He didn't start out that way. The intercept with KAL 007 drove him too far.'

'What's to say he wasn't already on the slippery slope prior to 007?'

'Because his first date with a psychologist is September 8, 1983, a week after the downing.'

'Like I said, he could have been predisposed.'

'Here's a guy who comes top of everything. He aces every aspect of training, gets every commendation in the book, wins medals, rescues people from certain death. Then, within a week of the 007 incident, he can no longer fly, or wants to fly, and he's in a deep and meaningful with hard liquor.'

'It's not clear. Half these shrink reports have been redacted. On a few of these pages, all that's left are ands and buts.'

'You don't think that says anything?'

'The censorship? Jesus, if we looked for a conspiracy every time the censor drew his marker . . .'

Sherwood was right and Lana knew it. Many of the documents they accessed had whole chapters and sections blacked out. Standard procedure.

'What *I'd* like to know,' Sherwood said into the silence, 'is how any of this is bringing us closer to finding that tape?'

'It's bringing me closer to having an understanding. You said it yourself, Miller: KAL 007 happened so long ago. Why all the continuing cloak and dagger? I'd like to know why, too. A lot of people thought it was a CIA mission that went wrong.'

'Who cares if it was? Intelligence cluster fucks happen every day of the week.'

'269 people died. You're a sensitive flower, aren't you?'

'Let me remind you, we're not paid to know why. In this instance, we're being paid to *find*.'

Lana cocked her head to the side. 'You've got buddies in the CIA, don't you?'

'Yeah, so . . . ?'

'Ever heard of a Mr Hank Buck?'

'Do you have any idea how many people are employed by the CIA?'

'No.'

'Me neither. And anyway, I believe the number's classified.'

'So that's a no, you don't know him?'

'That's a no.'

Lana's phone rang. The screen told her the call was from Saul Kradich.

'Saul,' she said, picking up.

'I've found a couple of things that might interest you. Wanna come up?'

'I've got Agent Sherwood with me,' she said, giving her partner a smile.

'You know, Lana, people judge you by the company you keep. Come on up anyway.'

402

Kradich swiveled in his seat as they walked in. 'So, Sherwood,' he said. 'Nice to see you. Is that a holster under your armpit or a wet patch?'

'Still wearing that stupid hat, I see,' Sherwood replied.

Lana ignored the alpha male crap and sat down. 'Hi, Saul. What you got?'

'I sent you a bunch of stuff from the Chosa Besshitsu radar facility at Wakkanai. Any of it useful?'

'Interesting for background, but nothing particularly significant—unless I missed it.'

'I kept the search between September and October 1983—to keep it tight with the 007 event. I didn't want to bury you with megabytes of files. But I've been tooling around, doing some random sampling, and this popped up.'

He leaned forward and tapped the control screen. Up on the wall appeared a decrypted facsimile from a colonel commanding the 6920th Electronic Security Squadron.

'Can you make it out?' asked Kradich when he saw Lana squinting at the panels.

'Having trouble. Can you enlarge?'

Kradich tapped his panel and the fax filled the wall.

She read the message aloud. '"Lieutenant Colonel Moore advises that encrypted recording from low-level array for 830901-181030Z-185030Z has been reported unaccounted for."' Lana's mouth dropped open.

'It's your missing tape,' said Kradich. 'The night of the shootdown and then the time—thirty minutes from 18:10 GMT to 18:50 GMT. The 6920th Electronic Security Squadron is letting the NSA know that the tape is gone.'

Lana peered at the scanned sheet of paper. The fax had been sent on 20 September, 1983. There was a signature at the bottom of the decryption, acknowledging receipt. 'Who signed for it? Who belongs to that scrawl on the bottom of the paper?'

'Oh, this is the bit you're really gonna love,' said Kradich, tapping his panel.

Sample signatures appeared onscreen, a name beneath each. All of the signatures matched the one on the fax.

'Shit . . .' Lana murmured. 'Is that *the* Roy Garret?'

'The one and only governor of New Mexico and presidential hopeful.'

'Sergeant Yuudai Suzuki was the radar operator on duty the night the plane was shot down fifty miles away,' said Lana, thinking aloud, her suspicion confirmed. 'He saw what really happened and co-opted the tape.'

'And what *really* happened?' asked Sherwood.

'KAL 007 didn't crash and break up with all passengers and crew killed, but landed or ditched safely.'

'Oh, of course,' sneered Sherwood. 'That's the only possible logical outcome.'

'It's one explanation for why everything about KAL 007 is still classified,' Kradich reasoned. 'There must've been people in the NSA back then who knew the truth. There were sixty-one US citizens aboard that plane. If they weren't killed, they were taken captive and held prisoner.'

Lucas Watts' words came back to Lana: *I've seen what's on it. Trust me, you don't want to take me to court.* 'What about Governor Garret? Would he have known?'

'I don't know for sure, but I think it's a reasonable assumption that he would have. You could always ask him,' Kradich replied.

'And how are you going to do that without it leaking to the media? This is a national security issue, for Christ's sakes.' Sherwood stood and paced the room. 'Aside from the fact that you're wading into the political arena, you'd be killing our careers.'

'Most sensible thing I've ever heard you say,' Kradich agreed.

'Any luck getting into the KAL 007 compartment?' Lana asked.

'No.' Kradich was emphatic. 'Even if I wanted to spend the rest of my life in prison—which I don't—I can't even *find* the compartment, much less get access, because I have no idea what it's called. There's no central reference database for info like that. What you're asking for is way beyond top secret.'

'Relax, Saul,' said Lana. 'We'll just have to look in another direction is all.'

Kradich gave her a wan smile. 'Did any of the other stuff I sent you help?'

'The psych evaluations for Curtis Foxx were interesting. The fate of 007 really busted him up. We don't know why exactly, because most of the sessions were blacked out, but it had something to do with a Criticom. Do you know much about them?'

'What was his problem with it?'

'According to Foxx, they sent one off while flying a mission, but never received a reply.'

'Was it sent in the early morning hours of September 1?'

'That bit is helpfully blacked out,' said Sherwood. 'Could have been any night.'

'But I think we can safely assume it *was* the night 007 was shot down,' Lana countered.

'You can't *assume* shit, Lana! Y'know, the trouble here is that you have an outcome in mind and you're just looking for evidence to support it, even if you have to manufacture it.'

'Is that what you really think?'

'This Ben Harbor guy really crawled under your skin and laid some eggs, didn't he?'

'Oh, now that's a nasty metaphor, Sherwood,' Kradich interjected. 'You just made me feel sick.'

Special Agent Sherwood folded his arms across his chest and slouched back in his chair. He shook his head slowly a couple of times, like a man tuning himself out.

'If you want to move on from this case, Miller, I'll agree to it,' said Lana.

'Suits me,' Sherwood replied.

'A Criticom,' said Kradich, ignoring the tension, 'was a back channel commanders could use to communicate with the National Command Authority.'

'As in the President?'

'Yeah, him—Ronny Reagan in this instance. A Criticom allowed the man on the spot to tell the boss exactly what was going on. It was a nuclear war failsafe of sorts, bypassing any potential filter that might creep in as intelligence traveled up through the chain of command.'

'And what was supposed to happen in response to it?'

'Criticoms were structured to reach the President within minutes of being sent. In a critical emergency situation, receiving it the next day would have been too late.'

'Okay. That's interesting. So you'd only send a Criticom if you saw a dire event taking shape, or to prevent one from happening.'

'It was a protocol devised to prevent an unnecessary nuclear war.'

'So let's speculate that you see a civilian 747 heading toward the secret Soviet submarine base at Petropavlovsk, and you think the Russians might mistake it for an unidentified military aircraft. Might that prompt you to send a Criticom?'

Kradich nodded. 'It's possible.'

'A message like that is going to come through the NSA here at Fort Meade.'

'Yes.'

'Would it have been logged?'

'I see where you're going.'

'And the President's response would have come back the same way, wouldn't it?'

'I'm on it,' said Kradich.

'You're in some deep shit here, Lana, and you're not wearing the shoes for it.'

'Thanks for your support, Miller.'

'That's exactly what I'm doing, Lana. I'm supporting you by being level-headed. I'm trying to stop you ruining your career, or worse, and for what? Something that happened in another millennium. Half the country wasn't even born when this went down.'

'That's just the point, Miller. It has *never* stopped happening to all the families and relatives of the people who were on that plane. No one has had any real closure.'

Sherwood shook his head. Lana could see that they were on opposite sides with no chance of meeting in the middle.

'Easier than I thought,' said Kradich, looking up at the wall where a scanned document appeared. One line was highlighted green with an electronic marker. 'The Criticoms themselves are still classified but looks like their arrival status has slipped under the radar. The code for a Criticom is CP-1-3. That's command protocol one—the highest group—and three is the third highest status within the group. I'd say CP-1-1 would be "Run, they've dropped the bomb". According to the log, a CP-1-3 came in on September 1, 1983 at 16:07 GMT. From memory, KAL 007 got its tail waxed at around 18:26 GMT. So that CP-1-3 has to be your friend Curtis Foxx telling the President the shit is about to hit the nuclear fan.'

'He got no reply,' said Lana, searching the log.

'Doesn't look like it.'

'So Curtis Foxx, the commander of Arctic 16, believes he has a possible nuclear war on his hands as he sees KAL 007 heading off toward Petropavlovsk. He sends off a Criticom, and the President doesn't respond.'

'Hmm . . .' Kradich rubbed his chin. It didn't seem right.

'And President Reagan ignored the Criticom—which is unlikely. Most probably he never received it. Where was the Criticom going?'

'From the destination code here on the log, it went to the White House. That was standard procedure.'

Lana almost smiled. She'd spent the last couple of days becoming an expert on KAL 007. 'But President Reagan wasn't *at* the White House on the morning of September 1, 1983.'

'Where was he?'

'Holidaying with Nancy at their ranch in Santa Barbara. The State Department made him cut his vacation short, come back to Washington and deal with the 007 crisis.'

'The fact that he was over in California shouldn't have mattered. He still should have received it.'

'So they deliberately bypassed President Reagan. He had no idea,' said Lana.

'Who did? Who's "they"?' asked Kradich.

'Garret, National Security Advisor Clark, and probably Meese and Casey. Clark and Meese were with the President in Santa Barbara. I wonder if it was their idea for the President to take a vacation at that time.'

'Like I said, Lana, you're just seeing what you want to see,' said Sherwood.

'Ah, the beast wakes,' quipped Kradich.

'You're looking for a conspiracy here, but all you're seeing is human error.'

'Just walking the trail, Sherwood.'

'I'd call it chasing your tail.'

Lana ignored the comment. 'Who has this facility booked this afternoon?'

'Another analyst—North African sector. Why?'

'Some kind of diary would be kept for the use of these rooms, wouldn't it?'

'Yep.'

'Would that schedule be classified?'

'No, though what they do in here will be.' Kradich's face cracked into a grin. 'You *are* good at this. Give me a minute.'

Lana sat back and watched Kradich work the control panel, while up on the laser wall the massive processing power at his fingertips wound back time.

'Here's the log for 1983, August 31/September 1 . . . Oh, shit,' he said.

The signature hadn't changed much in all these years.

'Roy Garret. He was in GF1,' said Lana, examining the familiar scrawl. 'What was GF1?'

'This is VIB2—virtual investigation booth number two. Back then they were called global facilities. GF1 was probably the main facility. They didn't have the immediate grunt that we have, but in a GF you could monitor the world from a variety of feeds.'

'That Criticom sent by Curtis Foxx out over the Bering Sea, alerting the President to the looming catastrophe—could Roy Garret have seen that, perhaps given it a push along to the White House?'

'Jesus, Lana. Enough,' warned Sherwood.

'It's possible,' said Kradich. 'But I can't tell you whether that's something he actually did.'

Up on the screen, Kradich opened the governor of New Mexico's website. The home page showed the presidential hopeful standing in front of a collection of people, old and young, black, white and Hispanic. The slogan overarching the gathering read "Roy Garret. For all America". Garret looked presidential, thought Lana. Tall, a full head of hair tending to silver, tan skin, wrinkles that hinted at a sense of humor, and lines in his forehead that suggested a capacity for concern, compassion and a love of hard work.

'He sure looks the part,' said Kradich as he clicked through various screens, drilling into the site.

'Wait!' said Lana urgently. 'Can you go back?'

'To what?' asked Kradich.

'A few pages back. They loaded fast—I thought I saw something.'

'Sure.'

'There!' said Lana. The photo was titled 'Roy Garret's Family'. Lana read the caption aloud: '"Some of the hardworking people who are helping to make my candidacy for this most high office possible".' She pointed. 'It's him.'

'Who?' Kradich asked.

'There, just behind Garret. It's the guy I met with Whittle. We're on this 007 investigation because of him. That's Hank Buck.'

February 10, 2012

New Mexico Governor's Mansion, Santa Fe. 'That's what I'm talking 'bout,' said Felix Ackerman, slapping the latest poll results on Roy Garret's desk, his chins vibrating with excitement. 'It's a complete turnaround. Instead of being two points behind, as you were ten days ago, you're now two points *ahead* of Chevalier in the most-preferred President stakes. I just got off the phone from the senior analyst at Gallup and he believes a broader cross-section of the electoral colleges are getting behind you. He says not to quote him but he thinks this turnaround could be a trend.'

'At last, some good news,' said Hank, unbuttoning his jacket, sitting on the couch and crossing one leg over the other. 'The dirt we dished on Chevalier and his crackhead nephew paid off.'

Garret allowed a grin to sweep the almost perpetual scowl off his face.

'The only minor dark cloud in all of this,' Ackerman continued, 'is that some unkind members of Chevalier's staff are saying that *we* dredged up this story and leaked it to the press.'

'Aww . . . how could they think such a thing?' said Hank, pouting.

The press had been hungry for new angles on the Democratic candidates. All he'd done was feed the beast. As Garret had demanded, he'd simply peeled off the top of the Louisiana senator's life, dug around, and found a skeleton. And he hadn't needed to dig all that deep to find it. Armed with the details, Ackerman had outlined them in an email, which was sent anonymously to a New York current affairs radio program looking to improve its ratings. Once started, the brush fire had gone multimedia and now the flames were searing Chevalier's reputation. Maybe the senator wasn't the fair-minded liberal with staunch family values that he'd led the American people to believe he was after all.

'Is this going to come back and bite us?' Garret enquired.

'I don't think so,' Ackerman claimed with a smugness that said, 'Not a chance'. 'Not everyone in the press wants another bleeding heart in the White House. Guys like Chevalier don't make for very exciting headlines. The upshot is, Governor, that, according to the polls, if the election was held this week, you would go to bed on Sunday night as the forty-fifth President of the United States of America.' Ackerman mopped his neck with a splotchy beige handkerchief. 'You've got a press conference in an hour. I recommend that you be gracious in this hour of your adversary's distress.'

'Can't we be even a little smug?' asked Hank.

'Definitely not. Hey, it's news time. You want to see what kind of treatment Chevalier's getting from the networks now that the story's broken?'

'Abso-fucking-lutely,' said Garret.

Ackerman aimed the remote at the flatscreen on the wall. The picture flashed on. The timing was perfect: Senator Chevalier appeared to be under siege from a media mob, cornered while trying to get into his vehicle. An aide held the door open. The voice of the news anchor could be heard over the picture: ' . . . cross live to Senator Chevalier to get his reaction'.

'Senator,' said a reporter at the scene, 'were you aware that your nephew had committed suicide while out on bail?'

'No, I was not. In fact, I only just heard the news myself this morning. My nephew had chosen for some years to distance himself from the family. Even his father, my brother, was not aware of his son's state of mind.'

411

'Your brother has said that you refused to provide the boy with legal representation when he needed it most. Don't you feel at least partly responsible for his death?' the reporter persisted.

Another question was fired at Chevalier before he could answer. 'Senator, the Gallup poll has you trailing Governor Garret for the first time in quite a while. Do you think that America has already judged you?'

'And found you wanting . . .' added Hank.

Senator Chevalier held up his hands in an attempt to calm things down. Garret thought he looked drawn, worried. He should be. His campaign was on the verge of being fed into the shredder, even if his nephew was a bum. Hank had dredged it all up. By the time he was ten, the deceased had a juvenile record for shoplifting. At age twelve he was in the gangs with a reputation for violence. He was selling drugs before his thirteenth birthday—crack and crystal meth—and stealing cars by his fourteenth. By the time the kid was nineteen, he'd spent five of the previous ten years in some kind of correctional facility. He'd been completely disowned by his family, having stolen from them for years to pay for one habit or another. His timely suicide, barely days after the media had learned that Chevalier had personally intervened to deny the young man access to legal services provided by his centers, was just one of those breaks that was good luck for Garret's campaign and luck of the other kind for Chevalier. Sometimes Fate worked for you, and sometimes she sucked. At the time of his death—he'd jumped off a freeway overpass in front of a truck—according to a witness in the police report, Chevalier's nephew had appeared to be high on something. Maybe the kid thought he'd fly, Garret mused.

'First,' Chevalier said, 'let me say that my nephew's death has hit his family hard. Despite his brief, troubled life, he was the son of a mother and father who loved him. He also had family support whenever he asked for it. I personally tried on many occasions to help the boy, but the kind of help I offered—a detox program for drug dependency—was the sort he wasn't prepared to take. I loved that boy, despite his troubles. He was my family. I was there when he was born, so the news of his tragic and untimely death breaks my heart. Many American families face grief for a variety of reasons. Today, it's my family who grieves. I ask that you please give me a little private time to commune with his mother and father and God.'

'Grieving?' Hank snorted. 'I read the kid's sheet. I'd say his parents are high-fiving at his demise.'

'You've gotta admire the way the bastard handled it though,' Ackerman commented, motioning at the flatscreen. 'I almost feel sorry for him.'

'Why?' asked Garret.

'He's good.' Ackerman added hurriedly. 'But you're better.'

The reporters rushed at Chevalier with more questions. He put up his hands again, this time to signal that he wasn't going to answer them.

'Senator, the Gallup poll . . .' a voice beyond the view of the camera enquired, breaking through a moment of relative quiet.

'The only poll that matters is the one on election day,' Chevalier said as he ducked out of sight into his car and the aide slammed the door shut. The crowd of reporters surged forward into the wake of the departing vehicle. Garret aimed the remote at the flatscreen and turned it off.

'Excellent, excellent,' said Ackerman. 'I'm going to have a few words with our press secretary. Tonight's press conference is important. I don't want any surprises. I'll be back in a moment.' He bounded through the door excitedly and closed it behind him.

'Looking good, boss,' said Hank, whose stomach had been churning for the best part of two weeks since the NSA debriefing. 'Let's hope nothing comes along to snatch defeat from the jaws of victory.'

'Is there something I should know?' Garret asked, catching a certain tone in Hank's voice.

Hank leaned forward and placed a rolled-up copy of Investigator Lana Englese's progress report on his desk.

'Read this,' he said. 'I'll let you be the judge.'

December 6, 1990

Forced Labor Camp ZJa5756. Two military helicopters banked low over the outskirts of the settlement and landed on ground cleared of forest beyond the last of the black wood huts. Soon after, four men with the slouch of long-term prisoners accompanied by four armed guards and an officer ambled into the center of the main square, a rectangle of crushed rock and sawdust put down to control the mud when the spring thaw eventually came. They stood in front of the small bronze bust of Lenin, which was raised above head height on a column of stone, and looked around, waiting for something. Nami, grinding the sled across the frozen conglomerate of ice and granite chips, allowed herself furtive glances past her shoulder at the men gathered in front of Lenin's cold gaze.

Two men, the settlement's KGB guards, walked into the square and smartly saluted the officer, who had his back to Nami. It seemed to her a familiar back, as was the tilt of the man's head, though she couldn't place the familiarity. She put the feeling out of her mind and continued on her way. Her shift was due to start in twenty minutes and she still had to get home with the wood piled on her sled, light the kitchen fire, and kick her lazy husband out of his vodka stupor.

Nami snuck another glimpse. New prisoners. They must be important to have arrived by helicopter with an officer to escort them. Perhaps they were political prisoners, Party members fallen from favor—there were plenty of those here already. She wondered what these new men had done, or not done, or thought, or not thought. There was no right or wrong in the Soviet Union, she had decided. Just the powerful and the powerless.

One of the prisoners, a man with long white hair, coughed, coughed some more, then bent over with his hand over his face, hacking into it. He turned away from the guards as he coughed. The fit finished as Nami reached the edge of the square and the corner of a black timber house. The man took his hand away from his face as he stood up and Nami's heart nearly jumped into her throat. She pulled the sled past the edge of the hut and leaned against it, her chest heaving as she hyperventilated. It was *him*. It was the doctor from the plane, the American politician. They had brought him *here*.

Nami wanted to take another look, to make absolutely certain, but first she had to fight her fear of discovery. An inquisitive nature was not an admired quality among the camp's inmates, or their KGB guards. Other inmates were shuffling through the square, ignored by the new arrivals. Nami decided that she would risk it and make another crossing. She held her breath, turned her sled around and walked out into the open. But the prisoners were no longer there. Her disappointment was intense. They must have been taken somewhere by their guards, guided by one of the camp's KGB men. However, the officer with the familiar back was still standing around, talking to the remaining KGB man, enjoying himself, laughing.

The sense of familiarity grew as she watched him, sneaking furtive glances. Then Nami realized that she was invisible to the men. Emboldened by the discovery, she circled around them, but the officer seemed to move, keeping his back to her. It was only when she reached the other side of the square that the man suddenly turned toward her. They looked at each other for what seemed like a minute, but was probably less than a second. There was no recognition whatsoever in his eyes; Nami was utterly invisible to him, made of glass, and he saw through her as if looking through a window pane. Nami wondered if she was already dead, killed by this man, the man she recognized instantly.

His was a face she would never forget. The picture of a man standing on a truck appeared in her mind, along with his words: '*I am Colonel Valentin Korolenko. I am an officer in the Komitet Gosudarstvennoi Bezopasnosti. You may know of this as the KGB.*'

Lingering in the square had caused Nami to be ten minutes late for her shift, an offense that earned her various threats of retribution. The intimidation was hollow, though, and she knew it. Her camp husband had a still, and his homemade vodka made him second in importance to the KGB stooges who were the camp's overseers and his regular customers. Nami drifted through the day, lost in thought as she drove the rig, shuttling between the hillside being logged and the mill by the river. Seeing the Soviet officer and the American doctor after all these years triggered a flood of memories that she had managed to keep suppressed, because they were memories that had caused her much grief. Akiko was four years old when Nami had said goodbye to her in the Anchorage departure lounge. Now, Nami had a baby boy with her distiller husband; he was two, half the age little Kimba had been when Nami boarded KAL 007. She had remarried to survive. Her Russian husband was reasonably kind, and rarely beat her. She had learned which moods to avoid and life had settled into a secure routine. Nami wondered whether Hatsuto had also remarried, and whether he still remembered her.

The day dragged on. Where would the new prisoners be housed? How soon would she be able to engineer an excuse that would enable her to talk to the American? New arrivals were popular for a time. They sometimes brought news of the world beyond. Here in this camp, there were no radios, no newspapers, no roads in or out until the river froze in the winter months. Civilization, the world beyond, was a dream. Nami gave herself a mental shake. She would have to be careful. If the authorities were aware that she and the American knew each other, one or both of them would be moved. And Nami had been moved several times to different camps since she had been taken prisoner. The moves were the hardest to take: new rules, new isolation, a reminder that she meant nothing to anyone in this ghastly human wasteland.

It was dark by the time Nami finally pulled into the mill with a full load of logs on her rig. They had to be taken off with a crane and stacked by the road. She turned into the bay, pulled on the handbrake, and climbed down from the cab onto the frozen ground. The evening was cold with a biting wind. There was snow in the air. She wrapped her coat tightly about her to keep out the chill and watched the steel jaws of the crane close around a log on her rig. The machine lifted it out carelessly, bouncing and nudging the truck. The load swung over the logs already stacked and was lowered into place. But the crane operator released the log too late and it rolled backward off the stack with a series of heavy thumps that came up through the ground. An overseer came along with a flashlight, shone his light up into the crane's control cabin and threw abuse at the operator. The door of the cabin opened and a hand waved back with a gesture of apology. The man was probably drunk, thought Nami, and more than likely on her husband's liquor.

The jaws of the crane swung back, slower this time, more carefully, and picked up a log that was larger and heavier than the last. The crane's diesel motor gunned with the effort required to lift this load. The log came up, jaws clamped around it, and the operator swung it across to the stack. But he judged it poorly again, this time letting it go early. The log crashed onto the stack and bounced down the front. And then, suddenly, all the logs were on the move, tumbling over each other. The stack was collapsing. It happened fast. There was nowhere for Nami to go. The truck behind her and the lethal tumbling loads bouncing toward her blocked the only escape routes. She was dead. She knew it seconds before a massive weight struck her in the chest. There was no panic, just a sense of inevitable calm. And, in an instant, the world went black, an infinite and all-consuming nothingness where consciousness and pain were equally impossible.

February 11, 2012

Siberian Far East. The Trans-Siberian train rocked eastward toward Moscow through mile after slow mile of emptiness, the monotony of snow, ice and pine trees broken only by tunnels that plunged passengers instantly into complete and claustrophobic blackness.

Ben lay on his bunk as he had done for the past thirty hours, lost in his own thoughts, and stared unseeing at the passing taiga through unwashed windows made semi-opaque by successive layers of dust. Akiko lay on her bunk on the other side of the cabin, gazing in the opposite direction, out through the cabin doorway, across the narrow hallway and through an equally dirty window at scenery uniformly cold and bland.

'What do you think the chances are that we'll see a Siberian snow leopard?' Ben asked idly, sweating in the ninety-degree heat set by the carriage attendant, or *provodnitsa*—a tall, heavy-set woman who wore orange lipstick below a black mustache.

'There are not many left,' said Akiko, yawning.

Ben wondered why the snow leopard question had meandered into his brain, and then remembered seeing the photo on the cover of the brochure for Siberian Winter Safaris. The thought led him to their guide, Oleg, who was now dead, burned from the inside out. What sort of people were these?

'Do you believe what Luydmila said about the zero option?' asked Akiko.

Ben realized that his question about the tiger must have seeded similar thoughts in Akiko's mind.

'No, I don't. You can't cover up shit like that.'

'But the tape is proof that it happened. People *knew*, but the world was told a different story. Yuudai knew, your father knew. Perhaps that was why he went . . .'

'Went nuts?'

'No, I was going to say that it was the reason he left your family. Isn't it possible that he left because he knew staying would be dangerous to you and your mother? That is what a hero would do, and Curtis was a hero. He would sacrifice his own happiness to ensure your safety, wouldn't he?'

Akiko's words formed into a solid lump at the base of Ben's throat. He swallowed, but couldn't remove it. *What kind of man leaves his one-year-old son and never comes back?* 'I don't know,' he said. 'I'll never know.'

'But it makes sense,' she said softly. 'If American intelligence knew that the plane landed and knew there were survivors, the greatest fear of the people hoping to hide the truth would have been 007's captain returning to America to tell his story. Your father also knew the truth. He was friends with Yuudai, but he was bound by an oath of secrecy.'

'"I will be prouder still if you embrace the truth,"' Ben said.

'"Spend it wisely and in pursuit of the truth."'

'We're in a lot of danger here, Akiko,' said Ben, stating the obvious. 'I think I've only just realized how much. If possible, we're going to have to be more careful.'

'Yes,' Akiko said.

They retreated again into their own thoughts.

'She is alive, and she is here,' Akiko said eventually. 'I know she is here.'

'A lot can happen in twenty-nine years.'

'I would know it if she was dead.'

Ben nodded. They were here to give an impossible task their best shot. It was too late to deny Akiko hope.

Akiko resumed her position on the bunk, her head more or less below the window through which Ben watched Siberia slowly pass by. She picked up a magazine, flipped through it and then put it down.

'When do we get into Ulan-Ude?' Ben asked.

'One thirty in the afternoon Moscow time; eight thirty in the morning Ulan-Ude time,' said Akiko, referring to the Trans-Siberian Railway's odd hangover from the Soviet era when the world ran on Moscow time.

'I'll just lie here then,' said Ben, his eyelids heavy with a combination of heat, boredom and lack of movement.

'Ben! Ben! It's *him*! Wake up! Wake up,' Akiko hissed.

Ben woke with Akiko leaning over him, shaking his shoulders, her nails digging into his skin, her face a mask of fear.

'Who? What?' he asked, confused with sleep.

'*Him*! The man in the photo. The man Luydmila called Soloyov. He just walked past. I saw his eyes. He looked in, came to check on us.'

'Which way was he headed?' he asked.

'There!' She pointed.

Ben was up and out of the cabin in a second. He raced down the narrow hallway, blocked by other passengers stretching their legs, gazing out the dirty windows, or going to the urn to get hot water for the discount traveler's staples—instant noodles and tea. There was no sign of the man. Ben heard the door open and close at the far end of the carriage, letting in the sudden clatter of steel train wheels smashing over railway track joints. Someone had left this carriage, moving to the next one. He squeezed past the *provodnitsa*, who was delivering some unspeakable train food from the dining car to one of the passengers, and made a dash for the door. He slipped through into the next carriage. It was identical to the one he'd just left in every way, passengers loitering in the hallway in their socks, swaying gently with the movement of the train.

A burst of track noise told him the door at the far end of the carriage had opened and then closed. And suddenly the world was plunged into utter blackness, as if a hood had been thrown over his head. The train had entered another tunnel. Ben couldn't move without becoming totally disoriented, so he braced himself against a window and waited it out. He wondered what he was going to do. One of the passengers standing in the hallway lit a cigarette with a lighter and kept the flame burning. The train left the tunnel and light returned. There was no way he could catch the man, if indeed it was the guy in the photo. Soloyov could have entered one of the cabins in this carriage or the next, or the one after that, and he couldn't check every cabin in the train. Defeated, Ben turned and made his way back to their cabin.

When he got there, Akiko was gone. He panicked.

'Kiko!' he called down the hallway. Some of the passengers turned wearily to look at him, wondering what all the anxiety was about. 'Akiko!'

The door between carriages opened behind him. Ben spun around and raced to it. He went through the door moments after it closed and caught a father and his young daughter on the other side, stepping over the metal plate above the frozen tracks below. Ben gave the man a weak smile and closed the door. He turned in time to see Akiko coming out of the communal bathroom, dabbing her face with a towel.

Ben's relief was instant.

'Did you catch him?' she asked.

'No.'

'Are you okay?'

'Yes. I thought . . . I thought something might have happened to you.'

'Oh, I am sorry.'

They walked back to their cabin. Once inside, Ben said, 'Thinking about it, it wouldn't be a good idea for those guys to know we're on to them. We want them to think they've got us just where they want us. If they were going to do us harm on this train, they probably would have done it by now.'

'Why kill Sergei and Oleg?'

'I don't know. Luydmila said Sergei was killed because those guys had a history with him. And she believed Oleg was tortured to obtain information he might have had about us. All he could have told them was that we're looking for your mother and that we were headed for Ulan-Ude. And now they're on this train, keeping an eye on us.'

'Waiting,' said Akiko.

'Yeah, but for what?'

☭

'Seriously, don't you go anywhere without that hat?' Lana asked as she took a seat. 'You got some kind of horrible scalp disease or something?'

Kradich ignored the questions. 'You look awesome, but I was kind of hoping that with legs like yours you'd be wearing a short skirt.' He puckered his lips. 'Haven't you forgotten something?'

Lana leaned across the table, kissed him quickly and then whispered in his ear, 'Don't push it, buddy boy.'

The waiter came over, asked how they were doing, and handed out menus. Lana asked for mineral water and a few minutes in which to interrogate the wine list. The waiter bowed slightly and said, 'Certainly, madam,' before walking off to service another table.

Both Lana and Kradich were getting paranoid about this case. In a town as small as Washington, and especially where FBI Special Agent Miller Sherwood was concerned, they felt there had to be a reason for seeing each other outside of usual office hours. Having a burgeoning relationship was Kradich's idea. Despite his ulterior motives, Lana went along with it—there was no easier cover story.

'I had a look at every page on Garret's website and there's no mention of Buck, and only the one photo,' she said, getting down to business. 'I googled him. He's mentioned in the odd news article as being the governor's security advisor.'

Kradich scoped the reasonably full restaurant. 'Perhaps Garret just likes having the guy around—they're both ex-Company. And Buck's been with the governor a very long time.'

'Back to my first question,' said Lana. 'How did you go? Find anything? Or are we here under false pretenses?' She leaned forward and adjusted his collar for appearance's sake.

'Did I find anything on our Mr Buck? No, nothing of consequence. I can tell you that he was in the Green Berets in Vietnam, but, unusually, his service records have been sealed. I can't get to them. And I can't dig into his CIA career, either, because that's classified, too, along with every other CIA personnel file, I might add. Interestingly, though, I did discover that Hank Buck worked for the office of the National Security Advisor for about a year. From November '82 to October '83.'

'Then he worked for Bill Clark,' she said.

'Back then, Buck was a middleweight. He worked specifically for a guy called Des Bilson, Clark's senior aide, who died from AIDS before anyone really knew what it was. Buck's employment records from those days—which aren't classified and are in the public record—have him leaving the office of the National Security Advisor the day Clark resigns. I've got nothing more on him. He never married, has no family. He's a bit of a mystery.'

'Okay,' said Lana, disappointed.

'But I do have something interesting. Shouldn't we order first?'

'No.'

'I think I've found confirmation that 007 really did land on Sakhalin.'

'You're kidding.'

'No. I started with the assumption that it landed at one of the Soviet bases on the island and that most, if not all, of the passengers and crew survived. In that scenario, one passenger in particular would have gotten Ivan all excited.'

'Lawrence McDonald.'

'Exactly. So I went through all that declassified stuff I sent you on the congressman—the files on his so-called "Western Goals" intelligence network, the Reinhard Gehlen/Du Berrier/George Patton connection and so forth. And it got me thinking . . . If the Soviets got their hands on a man like that, there'd be consequences. What do you think you might see a few months down the track?'

'Once they'd broken him?'

'Yeah, and I don't think there's any doubt that they *would* have broken him. Along with the torture, they'd have told him that the world believed everyone on board KAL 007 was dead. There would have been absolutely no hope of a prisoner exchange. You can bet the KGB would've shown McDonald pictures of his own funeral and probably an obituary or two just to drive home the hopelessness of his position.'

Kradich picked up the menu, opened it and used it to shield a sheet of paper, which he removed from his inside coat pocket. He placed it in the menu, closed it and handed it to Lana.

'Handwritten, in pencil,' she observed when she opened the heavy leather-bound folder and scanned the sheet.

'You want to keep it secret, these days you go low tech. Besides, I could hardly expect you to eat a thumb drive.'

Lana glanced up at him.

'You think I'm joking. I'm not. Once you've had a good look at what's on that paper, do what you have to do to get rid of it. Ketchup works, I'm told, though if it were me I'd try washing it down with a lusty cabernet sauvignon.'

Lana was intrigued. Kradich's neat handwriting showed a numbered list of twenty-seven names, all of which looked foreign. 'Who are these people?' she asked.

'They're dead people. They all died within four months of the crash of 007.'

'I'm sorry, am I missing something?' Lana asked. 'I don't recognize any of these names.'

'They're agents, anti-Soviet. They're not ours, not directly anyway. They lived in various Eastern Bloc countries—Czechoslovakia, Poland, East Germany, Romania. Perhaps it's a coincidence, but I doubt it. Every single name on that sheet had a connection with Gehlen, either when he was the Nazi spymaster in the east, or when he was the boss of the West German BND intelligence service. Most of those names belonged to people who were personally trained by him. Agents.'

'Jesus . . .' Lana said as the connection became apparent to her. 'Jesus—McDonald gave them up.' Then: 'There were 268 people besides McDonald on that airliner. Are you saying they were all held or executed so that the Soviets wouldn't have to return the congressman?'

Kradich summoned the waiter.

'I think that list of dead agents might be one of the items you'd find in the compartment you're not read-in on,' he said. 'I also think we both know who *is* read-in on it.'

'The man who could be the next President of the United States,' Lana whispered.

February 12, 2012

Ulan-Ude, Buryatiya region, Siberia. The platform was crowded with people waiting to board the train, accompanied by suitcases, boxes, crates, hessian sacks straining at their seams, and various other unidentifiable goods stacked and ready to load. They jostled with those waiting to welcome the newly arrived, who themselves were collecting cargo being passed down to them from the train. Meanwhile, snow was falling, fat flakes that drifted and swirled on the wind, whipping across railway tracks and ties embedded in ice. Ben and Akiko moved quickly through the crowds, stepping through snow up to their calves, encased in layers of clothing and trying to stay warm, hoping not to bump into the men in the photos, avoiding eye contact.

They left the area of the train station without delay and found a hotel after ten minutes of careful walking along cracked, icy sidewalks, located behind an odd, pyramid-shaped shopping center. A couple of low-browed thugs held the entrance door open for them as they approached.

After grabbing a few hotel cards and fulfilling the usual financial and immigration requirements at reception with a surly woman who wore her hair in a sixties beehive, they dumped their bags in their room and went for a walk in the freezing cold. A couple of old and dirty snowplows roared past, one behind the other, pushing the ice, snow and gravel slush toward the gutter.

'The guidebook says there are a couple of good tourist information centers here,' Ben yelled over the traffic noise. 'I think we should just go to both and ask about gulags in the area.'

'What?' yelled Akiko, shaking her head, indicating that she couldn't hear.

Ben made a gesture that said 'Forget it, follow me' and walked down the hill toward the underpass that took the local traffic snarl, banked up behind more snowplows, under the railway lines.

'I don't know about you,' he said into Akiko's ear when they were away from the road, 'but I could use a few shots of vodka, and maybe some of that deep-fried lard.'

Akiko, falling snowflakes melting on her cheeks, gave him a wan smile, put her head down and kept walking.

The first of the tourist offices was located on the ground floor of another hotel. They went inside and peeled off layers of clothing, instantly starting to sweat in the steaming, overheated foyer. The office was small, dark and covered with posters for places like Australia's Great Barrier Reef, the Bahamas and Fiji, probably, Ben decided, to keep the staff's minds off reality. He spoke to a middle-aged woman sitting at a desk, knitting.

'Excuse me, do you speak English?'

She shook her head, nodded at a narrow doorway and then called out something. A young Mongol woman with a chubby, perfectly round face and narrow black eyes came out.

'Yes, can I help you?' she asked in surprisingly unaccented English.

'Can we come into your office?' Ben asked, not wanting to broadcast their plans.

'Please,' she said, standing aside and holding the door open.

Akiko hesitated, then went in first. '*Spasiba*,' she said.

'You're welcome,' the Mongol woman replied. 'Please, sit. How can I help you?'

The office was small and dark, the desk littered with papers and dominated by an old PC desktop cluttered with folders bearing Cyrillic names. More posters of summery island escapes plastered the wall, along with a large political map of Russia.

'We are college professors,' Akiko began, going into their spiel, delivering the now familiar lie.

'Gulags?' the woman said, frowning, once Akiko had finished. 'I wouldn't know. Let me call my mother. She has been here her whole life.'

Akiko sat back as the woman dialed out on her cell phone, and started talking into it in a language that wasn't Russian. After a few minutes of conversation that ended with, 'Uh-huh . . . uh-huh . . . uh-huh . . . uh-huh,' the woman put down her cell and said, 'I'm sorry. There were labor camps to the north of Ulan-Ude many years ago, but they were abandoned.'

'Are there any towns in the area where the gulags used to be?' Ben asked.

'There are small settlements, I'm sure.' From the top drawer of her desk she pulled out a map of the area around Ulan-Ude. 'My mother said that up here, along this river, there were rumors. Two camps. Sometimes the KGB would come to Ulan-Ude and drink. When people drink, they talk.'

'Could someone take us to this area?'

The woman shook her head. 'I don't think so. It is too cold, too much snow. Also, my mother says many Russians today do not want to know what happened back then. Do you understand?'

'Yes,' said Akiko.

'We'll pay whatever it takes,' Ben said.

'I can ask around for you. What would you pay?'

'What would be fair?'

She smiled. 'This is Russia—whatever you are prepared to pay is fair. Where are you staying?'

Akiko hesitated, then gave her a card from their hotel.

'What's your name?' Ben asked.

'Irina.'

'I'm Ben, and this is Akiko.'

They took a card and thanked her and went back to the foyer. Through its smoked brown windows, they could see that it had stopped snowing. But from the lean on the people walking around outside, the wind was up, blowing fiercely. It would be bitingly cold.

'The other place isn't far,' said Ben, adjusting his clothing before they took on the weather. 'Just across the road. Here.' He handed Akiko the guidebook, his gloved finger on the spot.

Moments later they were scudding along the street, the wind behind them. They found the tourist center, but the door was locked shut. There was a notice pinned to it.

'Closed until Tuesday,' said Akiko.

It was Sunday.

'Terrific.'

Ben glanced across the road. A massive bronze head of Lenin, the size of a two-story house and mounted on huge blocks of granite, stared impassively cross-eyed in their direction, impervious to the cold. Snow had collected on his bald head, eyebrows, the tops of his ears and the bridge of his nose. A gust of wind blew a swirling veil of snow around his chin.

'Let's go,' Ben said.

They made their way back past Irina's tourist office and headed down the hill toward the river. Ben found a supermarket on the way and bought a bottle of vodka like a good Russian, developing a taste for it.

A plaza opened out at the bottom of the hill between two rows of buildings that provided shelter from the wind. Buskers, vendors selling sweet cakes and pastries, and merchants with stalls of winter clothes, old CDs, underwear and kitchen staples had gathered in the lee of the buildings out of the worst of the weather in the hope of attracting shoppers.

'You wouldn't believe it's fifteen below,' said Ben.

Akiko answered with a smile and flipped the fur-lined hood back from her face. At the far end of the plaza, an old Russian Ortho-dox church with a gold dome caught a faint gleam of sunlight and, beacon-like, magnified it. They wandered through the market toward the church, taking a few moments to act like tourists in a country far different from their own.

Akiko's cell rang. 'Hello,' she said, answering it. 'Yes, it's Akiko.' She turned away to improve the signal. 'Oh . . . No sooner . . . ? Yes, we will

429

take it. A deposit? Can we come by this afternoon? *Spasiba. Dasvidanya.*'
Thank you. Goodbye.

'What's up?' Ben asked.

'Irina has found someone who will take us, but not until Tuesday.'

'What is it with Tuesday?'

'They say the weather is going to get worse tomorrow. It will cost around 500 euros.'

'Tour operators don't seem to cross the street for less in this country. I guess we don't have much choice.'

'That's why I agreed,' Akiko said as they stopped to let a snowplow rumble past, its ancient rusted front bucket pushing a rolling ball of dirty snow. Once past them, it pulled to the side of the road. The operator jumped down and strode off with a day pack over his shoulder, his shift over.

Ben and Akiko crossed the road and arrived at the church. It was in the middle of restoration work, one side encased in scaffolding. The walled grounds were full of concrete moldings, tiles, stacked lumber, steel reinforcing rods and other building materials, much of it covered by recent snowfalls. The church was still open for business, though, and a busload of worshipers was getting ready to leave, several zealots kneeling in the snow at the main entrance gate, crossing themselves.

'I would like to go in and have a look,' said Akiko.

'I might wait around outside and drink some of this vodka. Purely for medicinal purposes, of course.'

'I'll be quick.'

'No need to hurry. I bought a pint and a half.'

Akiko walked through the gate, up to the main door and went inside. She skirted a tourist stall selling various religious icons, books and postcards, and took a seat. On the opposite wall was the reason for the church's popularity: an ancient painting depicting Jesus and various saints robed in rich greens and reds, surrounded by gold. In front of it, an old lady was on her knees on the bare stone floor, her head bent in prayer. She stopped muttering, struggled arthritically to her feet, and waddled off.

After a few minutes of quiet solitary contemplation out of the snow and the wind, saying a prayer in her head to her *kami*, Akiko went over and lit a candle. She returned to the main door, dropped some loose change into a donations bucket, then pushed the door open and let in a wind-blown flurry of snow. The door closed behind her and Akiko hurried to the gate. She got halfway there before realizing that she'd left the *Lonely Planet* guide on the seat in the church. She turned and went back for it. The woman manning the tourist stall inside the church scowled at her with brown milky eyes. Akiko found the book where she thought she'd left it, on the seat. She picked it up and walked to the main door, which opened just as she put her hand on it. A man was standing in front of her, about to come in. They looked at each other. He hesitated. Akiko recognized him. This was the man in the photo. The man on the train. The man called Soloyov. Murderer. Torturer.

Akiko fought to keep the recognition out of her face, fought the desire to run. She looked down and took a step past him. She heard the door click shut behind her. She took another step, her heart racing. The man was behind her. Suddenly a gloved hand was over her mouth. She flinched and her knees collapsed beneath her, but an arm slipped inside the crook of her elbow and she was almost lifted off the ground as he marched her forward. Akiko tried to scream, but the gloved hand tightened around her mouth and she tasted sweat and leather and smelled burnt tobacco.

He pulled her head back and said, 'Scream and I will kill you.' The whisper was hoarse and alcohol-stained. 'Struggle and I will kill you. Move forward, go to your right.'

The Russian steered her in the direction he wanted her to take. He was maneuvering her behind the church. Akiko's wide eyes flashed from side to side, searching for help. They were alone but for the drone of the snowplows at work somewhere beyond her view.

The man pulled something from his pocket. 'I am going to take my hand away. Do not make a sound. If you do, I will kill you. Nod if you understand this.'

Akiko was paralyzed with fear. It was almost impossible to move her head, but she managed.

The hand came away from her mouth, as did the arm locking hers behind her back. In an instant, something was around her throat, a thin wire. It sliced into the delicate skin beneath her chin. Tears welled in her eyes.

'For your own safety, move only when I tell you,' he warned her.

He pulled a cell phone from his pocket and dialed one-handed. 'Vlahd, they know about us . . . Yes, the Japanese woman and her boyfriend,' he said in Russian. 'We have lost our cover . . . I ran into her going into the church. She knew me. I have her . . . Yes . . . yes . . . We are behind the church. I will take her across to the river . . . Korolenko will understand. In the field, things don't always go as planned . . . Find the American. Wait . . .'

The Russian rotated his fist, tightening the wire so that it bit into Akiko's throat. In English, he asked, 'Where is your friend?'

Her eyes darted with terror. *Ben, run . . .*

'He is somewhere near,' Soloyov said into the phone. 'Once you have found him, bring him. If he won't come, kill him.'

Akiko's heart thumped against her ribcage.

Grisha Soloyov ended the call.

'We are going to walk through that gate up ahead,' he told Akiko, switching again to English, turning her toward an archway in the wall where there was an old rusted gate askew on ancient hinges. 'We are going to meet your companion down at the river. He is waiting for you. If you do as I say, you will not be harmed.'

As much as Akiko was able to function, she realized the man wasn't aware that she spoke Russian. She also realized with complete certainty that he was going to murder her.

The vodka was good. It tasted peppery and went down easily, flooding his stomach with a comfort that chased away the chill. Ben regarded the bottle. 'Liquid Russian culture,' he said aloud. This was the kind of culture he could get into. What was there to look at inside a church anyway. Pews? He took another swig and figured he had ten minutes to kill while he waited for Akiko, perhaps less. The church was deserted now. The busload of worshipers had departed, headed to another cold stone building most probably. Akiko was the sole remaining visitor.

Ben walked behind the church to have a look at the river. A narrow bridge spanned it. He went across and looked over the bridge on both sides. The river was by no means a big one and it was completely iced over but for a narrow trickle of running water in the middle of the flow where the ice was thinnest. The banks were littered with thousands of empty booze bottles and beer cans, and away in the distance, up river, there were small groups of young people standing around in the cold, drinking, urinating, kissing.

As Ben turned back to the church, he saw two people coming out a side gate in the surrounding wall. It took him a moment to register the picture for what it was: Akiko, and a man wearing a black *ushanka* behind her. Her hands were raised, like she was trying to balance, and she was walking carefully, delicately poised as she maneuvered through the gateway. Something was wrong. For one thing, she appeared to be sobbing. For another, there was a bright red stain on the shoulder of her white parka. Was that blood? The man pushed her forward, both his hands up behind her neck. An instant later Ben pegged the guy. He was one of the men in the pictures Luydmila had shown them, the man Akiko said she'd seen on the train—Grisha Soloyov. He had captured her, and now he was taking her somewhere.

Ben threw himself into the ice and snow, shielded from view by the bridge's solid concrete handrail, and crawled forward on his elbows and knees to the end of the bridge closest to the church. He peered around the concrete railing. The man behind her was pushing Akiko across the road to the riverbank.

'Shit, shit, shit . . .' Ben whispered, steam from his breath rising in front of his face. What the fuck am I supposed to do?

He took another peek around the end of the bridge. Both the man and Akiko had their backs to him. A few steps later they disappeared from view, down the riverbank.

'Shit,' Ben said again, his palms sweating, his mind racing but not coming up with any solutions. He crouched, looking left and right, hoping to see something or someone that could help. But there was nothing and no one.

He stood up to get a better view of the situation. He could no longer see Akiko or the man with her, but from the higher vantage point he spotted another man within the walled church grounds. He was walking around, choosing each step carefully, and there was a black shape in one of his hands. *Jesus Christ*—a pistol with a long, fat barrel on the dangerous end. A silencer. The man was walking slowly among the piles of building materials, looking for something. At that moment, Ben realized that the man with the gun was looking for him.

He clamped his eyes shut for a few long seconds. What to do? What to do? He had no idea. But he did know that if he didn't act, and fast, Akiko would be dead within minutes. The man in the church grounds had a weapon. Ben couldn't turn his back on him to try to rescue Akiko. He had to try to neutralize the threat at his rear first—that much he was sure of.

Running at a crouch across the road, Ben timed it while the man had his back to him. He entered the grounds on his hands and knees and dived for cover. He worked his way quickly around a loose pile of bricks and leapt behind a stack of wood beams. He went to move again, to try and get behind the Russian killer, but his foot tangled in a coil of wire, one end of which was attached to a couple of the beams. His momentum brought several of them crashing to the ground. *Jesus!* Ben knew instantly that he'd just told the man with the gun exactly where to come looking.

Ben moved fast. He took cover behind a couple of pallets containing roof tiles. He was sure he hadn't been seen by Bykovski. He noticed the snow kicked up by his feet. *Damnit!* He'd just laid a nice trail to follow.

Hurried footsteps crunching through nearby ice caught Ben's attention. A heavily accented voice called out, 'We have your friend. We just want to talk with you. Make it easy for us and yourself. Stand up. You don't need to hide.'

Part of Ben wanted to do as the Russian suggested. Was he just imagining the situation? Surely this was all a mistake. No one was going to get killed here. Not him, not Akiko. But another part of him knew this was just his desire for the nightmare to be over. Ben wondered what this man had said to Oleg before he and his partner murdered him. And, of course, the man carried a silenced handgun for a reason.

Ben noticed there were other tracks in the fresh snow, probably made by the Russian as he'd searched on an earlier pass. He moved again, following these as quietly and as quickly as he dared. After twenty yards or so, he took a divergent path away from them. He would make the bastard choose which trail to follow. He came to rest behind a collection of stacked toilets, removed his gloves and hurriedly searched his pockets for something he could use. His fingers found some loose change, the bottle of vodka, a cell phone and half a packet of gum. He concluded that there was only one thing he could do—bury himself beneath his coat under the snow. And hope.

Vlahd Bykovski heard the scuffle of movement, but the sound insulation provided by the snow coupled with the maze created by all the building materials made it impossible to know with any certainty the location of the source. Bykovski didn't expect the American to stand up so that he could shoot him. But he did expect him to freeze with indecision and fear so that he could move in and shoot him. Korolenko would understand that the American and the Japanese woman had to die. Grisha said the Japanese woman had identified him. Bykovski wondered how they had known that he and Soloyov were following them. There had to be a connection they had missed, an informant. He put the questions out of his head to better concentrate on the job at hand. The church grounds wouldn't stay empty for long. If someone came along before he could finish the job, the American would escape. They had the Japanese woman, but she was only half the problem. Perhaps she would reveal their mystery connection before she died so that all the loose ends could be tidied up.

A cell phone suddenly chimed among the building materials reasonably close by. Bykovski grinned. The American really is an amateur, he thought as he hurried in the direction of the ringing.

He approached the sound from the back, circling a large snow-covered collection of cement sacks. When he came around the far side, he shook his head at what he saw. The American was hiding beneath his coat, which he'd managed to cover with snow he'd spooned over himself with a piece of broken plywood. Stupidly, though, the soles of his shoes were poking out from the bottom of the mound. And, of course, his phone was ringing. It stopped. The Russian made a clucking sound with his mouth as he shook his head with amusement at the amateurism. The phone started ringing again somewhere under that snow. A persistent caller, thought Bykovski. A relative? His landlord? An airline confirming flights?

He lifted the pistol and—*phut, phut, phut*—fired three rounds at close range into the mound between the shoes. The phone kept ringing. The mound didn't otherwise make a sound, or move. This was strange. It wasn't—

Ben swung the short length of concrete-reinforcing steel like a baseball bat, putting all his 220 pounds of weight behind the swing. The Russian's eyes were wide with a mixture of horror and surprise. The end of the rod connected with the side of his exposed neck, below the ear. Ben felt the crunching vibration of the man's shattered vertebrae reverberate up through the steel and into his frozen fingers. With his neck broken, Bykovski's eyes went wide and his head tilted to one side as the pistol dropped from his hand. His knees buckled an instant later and he collapsed like a house of cards exposed to a sudden draft.

Ben heaved for breath over the body, trying to come to terms with what had just happened, his teeth chattering with cold. His bare, pink feet were achingly numb, as were his hands. He pulled his coat out of the snow, and sat on one of the toilets, massaging his freezing feet before putting his socks and shoes back on. As he blew on his fingers to get some feeling back into them, the alarm on his cell phone rang again. He reached over and picked it up. Turning it off, he put it in his pocket, feeling nauseous. A dead man whom he had killed lay in the snow nearby. It didn't matter that the man had wanted to kill him. Ben had never killed a man, had never even seen a dead body before. It was a day of firsts. He had to hurry. He had to kill again.

☭

'You know who I am,' the man said into her ear, the wire tight around her neck. 'Why do you know this?'

Akiko was too frightened to move in case the wire sliced deeper into her skin. The man released the pressure, but left the wire around her neck. One end, she noticed, was wrapped around a wood toggle, so that he could hold it without cutting his own hand. This told her the weapon was one he carried on him. He had killed with it before. He reached inside his coat and pulled out a pistol. It was small, smaller than his hand. He cocked it and then pointed it at her from beside his waist, into the base of her spine, so that it remained concealed from possible witnesses. The air was still and quiet but for the ever-present noise of the snowplows scraping the streets.

'Do not run. From this distance, even a gun like this is deadly. Understand?'

Akiko gave him a nod. The gun was not as personal or as gruesome to her mind as the garrote. The immediate shock of the confrontation and capture was wearing off. Her brain was starting to work. Her own survival instincts told her that to have any chance of seeing another day, she had to clear her mind of the fear paralyzing her.

'Give me your passport—no copies. And your credit cards and wallet. Drop them on the ground.'

Akiko reached inside her parka and took the packet hanging from a string around her neck. She dropped it onto the snow beside her feet. The man bent, picked it up. He glanced at the passport through the clear plastic window and then put it in his side coat pocket.

'Answer my question or I will shoot you now. Who told you about us? How did you recognize me? You have three seconds to answer. Three . . . two . . .'

'A woman told us,' Akiko blurted, her mind racing, trying to find something that would prolong her life without endangering someone else's.

437

'Which woman?'

'I don't know her name. You and your friend killed someone in Khabarovsk. There were witnesses.'

Two teenagers, no more than boys, appeared over the top of the river-bank nearby. They clambered down the slope and shared a bottle of something in a bag between them, not far from Akiko and the man threatening her.

'Hey, you two gay boys,' the man called out to them in Russian. 'Fuck off somewhere else. I have paid good money for this whore. Can't you see I'm busy?'

The boys sneered at him. One of them flipped him the bird, but they moved off anyway and disappeared under the bridge.

'What witnesses?' he continued in English. 'I don't believe you.'

'The police interviewed us. We were the tour operator's last customers. They showed us photographs. I recognized you and your partner from them.'

The man smiled. In other circumstances, Akiko would have called it a friendly smile.

A snowplow came down the access road a hundred meters away, pushing the snow in a wave-like curl off the incline and into the water. The truck's presence distracted Soloyov. He switched the pistol to his left hand to keep it hidden. The vehicle stopped and appeared ready to make a U-turn that would take it back up the access road.

'Now I know that you are lying,' Soloyov continued. 'I am the police—FSB—and I know those Khabarovsk idiots are still running around dragging their cocks in the snow. You will tell me the truth or you will die where you stand. Your body will be thrown in the river. They won't find you until the spring thaw.'

'They have your names. You are Grisha Soloyov. The other man is Vlahd Bykovski.'

That Akiko knew the names of him and his partner appeared to make the man nervous. He licked his lips and looked to his right, distracted by a roaring sound.

The bucket of the snowplow smashed into the Russian. It scooped him up in a ball of snow and carried him away. As the dirty truck flashed past, Akiko saw Ben up behind the wheel, the cords in his neck stretched tight as cables, his mouth open, screaming a war cry, the sound drowned out by the howl of the diesel engine. The snowplow's wheels locked up, but the vehicle continued to skid forward on the snow, heading for the bridge. Seconds later it crashed into the base of one of the abutments in a shower of powdered snow. Steam blew like a geyser from under the vehicle's buckled hood.

The driver's door swung open and Ben toppled out, landing heavily on the snow. He picked himself up and staggered forward to look at the front of the truck, to check the bucket. When Akiko reached him, his face was calm, though spittle flecked his lips. He was swaying slightly, unsteady on his feet. She looked down on a body sandwiched between the bucket and the concrete abutment. Broken limbs stuck up from the top edge of the bucket. They twitched and quivered briefly.

'Thank you,' she said.

'You're okay?'

'Yes.'

Ben turned to look at her and saw the garrote still around her neck. 'Jesus,' he said, in no more than a whisper. He unwound the wire carefully, Akiko not making a sound. When he'd finished, she hugged him and then went to the body and located the coat pocket with her passport pouch.

'Get his ID,' Ben said.

Akiko checked the Russian's other pockets and came up with a wallet and a matching black leather credentials case. There was a shield inside it. 'Grisha Soloyov. FSB—Russian Security Police,' she read aloud.

'So I'm a cop killer. Great.'

The Luydmila woman had been telling the truth. Snow had started to fall again. Ben blew some warmth into his naked fingertips.

'We'll put you in the water,' Akiko said, addressing the broken corpse. 'They won't find you till the spring thaw.'

Ben wiped his eyes and looked up and down the riverbank. The nearest people were maybe 600 yards further up river, on the far side of the bridge. He climbed back into the truck and managed to reverse it a couple of yards before the engine finally died, overheated. No longer pressed against the bridge pylon, the body slid away from the bucket. Ben climbed down from the vehicle. The Russian's sightless eyes stared into nothingness, a deep depression in the side of his skull, his arms and legs assuming impossible positions. There was no blood.

Ben stuffed the garrote inside the corpse's jacket, grabbed the collar and dragged the body down toward the water. He picked up speed when he reached the ice and used the gathering momentum to swing the body in an arc. The dead Russian slid out to the edge of the ice and then disappeared, rolling languidly into the running water with a minimal splash. The river would take the body downstream, depositing it under an ice sheet once the current slowed. Ben fell to his knees and threw up.

Once the stomach convulsions had stopped, he walked back up the bank toward Akiko, one heavy step at a time, overwhelmed by tiredness and stress. More than anything, he wanted to sleep, just to shut his eyes and drift off to oblivion.

'What about the truck?' Akiko asked.

'With luck the police will think it was taken for a joy ride. We need to get away from here before we're seen. There's blood on your parka. Can you turn it inside out?'

'Yes, good idea,' she said, taking it off.

Ben took another look at the vicious slices made by the wire into her neck.

'You need antiseptic on these cuts.'

'I have something in my bag. Where is the other man?'

'Dead.'

Akiko regretted asking the question. She'd known the answer instinctively.

'We need to leave Russia,' she said. 'Forget our search. It's too dangerous for us here now. We should have listened.'

'We were just protecting ourselves. It was self-defense.'

'We killed police.'

'*I* killed police.'

440

'With an accessory.'

A horn sounded above them. They looked up and saw a familiar face. It was Luydmila and she was leaning far out over the bridge's handrail.

'Come! Hurry!' she called down to them.

Ben and Akiko looked at each other. They quickly searched the truck and the riverbank. Akiko picked up the *Lonely Planet* and they scrambled up a trail cut in the snow on the steep section of bank beside the bridge. They dived in the back of the car as it started to move.

Luydmila glanced in the rear-vision mirror. 'They are both dead—Bykovski and Soloyov?'

Ben gave her a nod.

'Then you saved me the trouble. I owe you.'

'Where are we going?' he asked.

'I have found someone who will take you to gulag, if you still want to go.'

'We are leaving Russia,' Akiko said.

'Do not decide now. You are in shock.'

'We should go to the police,' said Ben.

'No, you should get as far from here as you can—and as quickly as possible.'

Luydmila swerved down a street into a busy bus terminus and parked the vehicle between two others.

'Hurry. We must change cars.'

'Why?' Ben asked.

'Because this one is stolen.'

They got out and followed her as she hurried down a narrow connecting street behind the terminus, which opened up into a wider secondary road. She pulled out an alarm remote, aimed it at a new model Mercedes Benz and its indicator lights flashed.

'You will come and stay with me,' she said as they got in.

'What about our luggage?' Ben asked.

'Forget luggage. You have your passport, money?'

'Yes,' said Ben. 'Why?'

'You cannot go back to hotel.'

'Why not?' Akiko asked.

'Because police from Khabarovsk wish to speak with you about Oleg's murder. The two mechanics who worked for him told police that Oleg was angry and agitated when he returned from your trip with him. It is only matter of time before Khabarovsk police learn of your hotel booking through tourist police and send Ulan-Ude police to interview you. The questions will be difficult and they are eager to make arrest. You would be easy target for this. '

'Jesus,' said Ben from behind his hands, which were pressed against his face.

February 13, 2012

Ulan-Ude, Siberia. Yellow police tape across the main entrance and the smaller side gate made a crime scene of the church and its grounds, though the forensics team was concentrating on the immediate area around the dead officer. Reconstruction workers had raised the alarm just after sunrise. Crows had found the frozen body much earlier, removing its eyeballs, tongue and lips. Korolenko looked down on his friend and former comrade-at-arms and seethed with anger. Bykovski's neck had been broken; his head sat at a ridiculous angle on his neck, the exposed teeth and empty eye sockets combining in a strange deathly grin, as if the corpse could recognize some humorous irony in this grisly end.

A preliminary judgement logged the time of death as being around 4 p.m. the previous day. There were no reliable witnesses, though an old lady who attended the tourist stall within the church recalled a female visitor at roughly the time of death, but she was uncertain about this, as well as being partially blind with cataracts.

Another crime scene had been established around the snowplow crashed into the base of the bridge over the river no more than 100 meters from the church. Two young male witnesses had come forward and given detectives details of what seemed likely to be a second murder. Their story was confusing and contradictory, except on the points that a man had been hit by the snowplow and his body dumped in the river. A compact Czech Republic CZ 2075 pistol had been recovered from the snow collected in the snowplow's bucket. Police divers were on the way to search the river for this second body.

Korolenko had had an old FSB comrade in Moscow phone through his bona fides to the Ulan-Ude police, giving him access to the detectives handling the crime scene. They gave him a reluctant on-site brief in the churchyard. It appeared to Korolenko that they knew almost nothing, other than Bykovski's name and that he was a plain-clothes officer in the FSB who had once worked for the now retired general they were talking to. They wanted to know if Korolenko was aware of any motive for what appeared likely to be a double murder. Korolenko said that he didn't, which they didn't believe. When pressed on this point, Korolenko declined to cooperate further, delivering the sidestep the FSB always gave local police when it suited them—that there were national security issues at stake. In fact, Korolenko was inclined toward filling in some of the blanks for the detectives and providing them with the identities of the two people he strongly suspected of the killings, but decided against it. The knowledge would spark a province-wide manhunt for the American and the Japanese woman and that would not suit his purposes.

The detectives finished their briefing and, through gritted teeth, politely said good morning. Korolenko left the church and walked back toward the center of town. So, the two people that Mr Buck had informed him were ordinary citizens had somehow managed to dispatch two experienced killers. Were the American and his Japanese friend more than he'd been led to believe?

His cell rang, a Moscow number. It was the tourist police, a call he'd been expecting, providing him with the current address logged for the passports belonging to Ben Harbor and Akiko Sato. A few minutes later, Korolenko arrived at the Hotel Sagaan Morin. He brushed the snow from his jacket and *ushanka* before walking through the door manned by security.

A middle-aged woman with heavy make-up and two metal front teeth sat behind reception. He showed her his FSB shield, which weaved its magic, the woman's demeanor switching from bored and slightly resentful to helpful and respectfully fearful. He asked her name. It was Evgeniya. According to Evgeniya, the two foreigners were the hotel's only guests and, as far as she knew, they were still in their room.

One of the security men went up to confirm this while Korolenko stood in reception, gazing out the windows at the blizzarding snow with his hands behind his back, impatiently rocking on the balls of his feet. It wouldn't be long before the Ulan-Ude and Khabarovsk police talked to each other and, like himself, turned to the tourist police.

The security man returned with the news that the guests' beds hadn't been slept in, but all their baggage was still in the room. Everyone was puzzled by the discovery, including Korolenko, albeit for different reasons. Were the American and the Japanese woman also at the bottom of the river, he wondered. He asked whether the guests had received any calls or messages. Evgeniya checked under the counter and came up with an envelope. Inside was a message signed by a woman called Irina. It read: 'Tentative travel arrangements have been made on your behalf. Please call.'

Korolenko pocketed the letter, said good day to the woman with the metal teeth. A few minutes later he had the phone numbers for the travel agents in Ulan-Ude, which he called one after the other until he got the answer he wanted. A police car with its lights flashing rushed past. He watched it turn into the forecourt of the Hotel Saagan Morin. Korolenko hurried in the opposite direction, the GPS on his phone taking him to the Buryat-Intour for a talk with Irina.

☭

Ben and Akiko had both slept fifteen hours, waking just after dawn. Luydmila was already up and speaking on the phone when Ben hauled himself off the sofabed. She concluded the call and put the phone down.

'What's happening?' he asked as he stood and scratched his stomach.

'The police have no leads. The crime in Khabarovsk has not yet been linked to what happened yesterday, but it will not be long until it is.'

Ben pulled up a chair. It wasn't that he'd forgotten, he'd just refused to believe the pictures that kept playing across his mind in the twilight of consciousness before waking.

'I think you have surprised yourself,' Luydmila told him.

That's an understatement, Ben thought. He sat slumped, his head hanging forward.

'You must get past this. The men you killed have killed many themselves. They were killers with badges. They tried to kill you and Akiko. You did what you had to do, which was to kill them first. Give yourself pat on back.'

'You could get a job in hotel reception with that attitude,' he said.

Luydmila smiled, lifted his parka, which was draped across a chair. She held it up and showed Ben the three bullet holes in its back.

'You were lucky.'

She passed him a plastic zip-lock bag containing a flattened pellet of lead. 'I picked up your coat to move it and this fell out.'

Ben squinted at the gray slug. He exhaled heavily. Whether it had been in self-defense or not, ending another man's life was so far beyond his everyday experience, it was almost impossible for him to comprehend that he was capable of such an act. This Ben was utterly foreign to his self-image, as if there was someone else living inside his skin, acting on his behalf. Yet while this person was foreign to him, he was also strangely familiar.

'I also found this.' Luydmila placed a handgun on the table.

Ben stared at it. It was black with wood grips, darkened with years of sweat. It had an extra-long barrel.

'You recognize it?'

'Yes,' said Ben. 'I wasn't aware I'd picked it up.'

'It is Makarov, much modified. An old Soviet weapon favored by Spetsnatz—Special Forces. The magazine holds ten rounds. Three have been fired. Of course, the bullet I found in your coat comes from this gun.'

Ben stared at the pistol.

'And where do you come from?' he asked.

'From Moscow.'

'That's not what I mean and you know it. You keep . . . I don't know . . . you keep just turning up.'

'You employed me back in Khabarovsk.'

'I remember you telling us to go home before you drove away.'

'You offered me job. I decide to accept, at least for short while. I didn't want you getting caught up with police. They are not always so understanding, especially to foreigners.'

'We don't know your rates.'

'I am sure you can afford them—don't worry.' Luydmila changed the subject. 'I went to shop and bought new underwear and thermals for you and Akiko.' She indicated a parcel on the table. 'I guessed your size.'

A door opened and Akiko appeared, wrapped in a blanket, sleep in her tangled hair.

'Good morning,' said Luydmila.

'Hey,' Ben said.

'Have breakfast,' Luydmila told them. 'We leave in one hour.'

The truck smelled of wet dog and was covered in dog hair. The man driving had a big nose, heavy jaw and jowls to match. He looked like a dog and smoked a cigarette that smelled of fresh shit. His name was Marat and he spoke no English, apparently. He drove too fast for the conditions, the van sliding precariously around every corner. Somehow, though, he managed to catch the slides before they amplified and hit anything.

Luydmila sat in the front, beside Marat, chatting easily with him. They laughed occasionally.

Ben and Akiko sat behind them on wooden boxes. Their backs rested against steel mesh that kept dogs caged in the back when they needed to be transported somewhere.

The windows were heavy with condensation. Ben wiped away a patch, but there was nothing to see outside except for snow and ice. Occasional dark shapes wrapped in mist flashed past—homes made from the black wood. Eventually, even those gradually gave way to trees. He glanced at Akiko, who gave him a nervous smile. It could have just been a smile. But it could also have been an admission that their continuing quest had brought them nothing but an introduction to death and to the darkness hidden within their own natures. Failure and despair were creeping into the spaces once occupied by optimism. It was a smile that said, 'What the hell were we thinking?' Nevertheless, they'd agreed to have a final throw of the dice. Ben gave Akiko a rub on her knee, Gore-Tex against Gore-Tex, a sound like sandpaper against wood.

After an hour's drive, the van bumped over some rough ground and came to a stop. Dogs barked and yelped somewhere close by.

Luydmila turned around and said, 'We're here.'

'Where's "here"?' Ben asked.

'This is where Marat keeps his dogs. It is also where we part company.'

'You are not coming with us?' Akiko asked.

'No. I hate dogs,' Luydmila replied.

'Was there no other way to do this?' Ben asked.

'No. The weather is getting worse. I could find no one else to take you until at least Tuesday.'

'Where are you going now?' asked Akiko.

'One of Marat's sons will give me a ride back to Ulan-Ude. From there, I am going back to Moscow.'

'We should pay you,' said Akiko.

'I have address from passport. I will send invoice,' Luydmila replied. 'You speak Russian. Marat is Mongol but he also speak Russian. He is charging you 500 euros for this trip.'

'Of course he is,' said Ben.

'The old gulags are half a day's journey from here, perhaps more. I wish you good luck.'

'Thank you,' said Akiko. She leaned forward and the two women embraced.

☭

'There have been developments,' said Korolenko, his voice coming through the earpieces along with an echo and a half-second delay.

Governor Garret poured himself another Glenfiddich and felt the Gulfstream bank smoothly to the southwest, headed for Santa Fe. Ackerman, three campaign strategists and two consulting journalists were hunkered down up the front of the aircraft, planning the next media event, well out of earshot.

'What developments?' Hank asked, pulling a curtain across the aisle.

'Your friends negated my associates.'

'Providing you're taking the standard precautions, General, you can give it to us straight up,' said Garret. His private jet was swept for bugs twice daily and the 'standard precautions' referred to a random public telephone line at the Russian's end.

'My men have been killed,' said Korolenko.

'We're talking about Bykovski and Soloyov?' Hank asked.

'Yes.'

'Killed by which friends?' Garret continued, puzzled.

'The Japanese woman and the American.'

Hank, disbelieving, glanced at Garret.

'What happened?' asked the governor.

'There was some kind of shootout.'

'The subjects have no military, paramilitary, police experience or training,' said Hank. 'The American is a civilian pilot and the Japanese woman is a teacher. Something else must have happened.'

'Perhaps, but *I* have military and police training and experience and both are telling *me* that things aren't what they seem with these two. They are now wanted by the police at Ulan-Ude for questioning about these killings.'

'Where are they now?' Garret enquired, looking for a solution.

'On their way to a labor camp. It is twenty-five below zero, it is snowing, and still they are on the move. You would have to admit that they are very determined for a tourist pilot and a schoolteacher. I should tell you that they are also wanted by the local police in Khabarovsk in connection with a murder there.'

'Did they kill someone else besides your men?' Hank asked.

'That is what the police there believe.'

'Why do I have the feeling that you're not giving us everything?' said Hank.

'The operation is on the verge of spinning out of my control, unless you think having them rot in a Siberian prison suits your purposes.'

'Fuck,' Garret muttered. The last thing they wanted to give Harbor and Sato was a US State Department official, a lectern and a room full of journalists, which he saw as the inevitable outcome of an arrest.

'I do not think these two are going to stop until they have achieved their objective,' the general said.

'Is their objective achievable?' Garret enquired, his gut churning.

'There is always a risk. With Soloyov and Bykovski dead, they are moving beyond my scope to micromanage this situation.'

'You don't have other people?'

'Yes, but they are not as reliable or discreet.'

'I sense a recommendation on the way,' said Hank.

'You told me that you hoped they would return home convinced that their quest was a worthless endeavor. I think now is the time to reconsider whether they come home at all.'

A small amount of long-distance static drummed through the speakers. Garret considered his options. The Englese woman over at the NSA hadn't managed to produce the missing tape. It was still out there. Perhaps if Harbor and the Japanese woman were dead and buried, the tape would suffer the same fate. There was a lot at stake—too much to risk. Garret gave Hank an imperceptible nod.

Hank agreed. It was the right decision.

'If it presents itself, General, take the zero option,' he said. 'You understand me?'

'Yes, I understand.'

The line was cut from the Russian end. Hank concluded the call from theirs.

'It's not just those two in Russia, Roy,' said Hank. 'They have connections here. We're going to need to close those down, too.'

'How many?' Garret asked.

'Less than half a dozen—four, maybe five.'

Garret upended the drink and let the Glenfiddich curl around his tongue. 'This goes back to that RC-135, Hank. It was a mistake.'

'You want to say I told you so?'

'I believe I just did.' Garret breathed deeply and longed for another scotch. He could sense the presence of chaos and it was closing in. 'This stops now, Hank. Is Korolenko up to the job, because I'm wondering.'

'Maybe he's getting past it.'

'We need a result here, Hank. You get on a plane and hold our Russian friend's Zimmer frame. Do you have a reliable backup on home soil?'

'It can be arranged.'

'Then do what you have to do.'

The snow and the cold weren't nearly as bad as the wind, which sliced through the seams in Akiko's clothing and ate into her skin like acid. Marat kept the dogs going to keep them warm, stopping only occasionally to feed them chunks of raw meat. Akiko reclined on the forward part of the sled beneath an ancient goose-down rug, Marat standing on the back of the sled behind her, steering and driving the team of eight Siberian huskies with a fine whip that curled out over the dogs like a trout fly cast over a white river. Behind them, on a second sled, was another of Marat's sons, Anatoly, transporting Ben. The teams had barked and yelped for the first hour of the journey, but now they were running through a track in a pine forest, the branches laden with snow, and the only sound was their breathing, the *shush* of sled skis over the fresh powdered snow, and Marat's voice reassuring the dogs that they were doing a good job. It was a strange dream-like sensation being pulled along with the familiar accompaniment of an engine replaced with panting.

The wind stopped for a time, but then started again as they exited a valley, a shrieking banshee of a gale that whipped the tops of the pines back and forth, deposited frozen branches across their path and threw a blinding whirlwind of powdered snow into their faces.

Akiko counted three brief stops in a journey that seemed to last days, but was in fact less than five hours. Eventually, the dogs pulled into a small village of black huts on the edge of the forest in the dying moments of daylight, the smell of wood fires in the air. While Anatoly attended to the dogs, Marat took them to a crowded bar where they drank vodka with shaking hands and chattering teeth and breathed the acrid smell of dozens of Russian cigarettes and warm unwashed bodies. He then showed them to a room in the roof of the bar where there was a single large bed. Akiko and Ben climbed in without thinking about it, their bodies shattered by the cold. They fell asleep before their heads touched their rolled-up parkas.

'You got anything yet on our Mr Buck?' Lana asked Kradich over the speakerphone.

'Zip. His records are sealed up tighter than a fish's butt, and that's watertight. That suggests to me he was involved in black ops. I even called Governor Garret's campaign office for the heck of it and asked for a bio. He doesn't have one.'

The fact that they knew nothing about this guy only served to light a fire under Lana's curiosity. 'Keep at it,' she said. 'What about Garret?'

'According to his people, he's a great patriot who has dedicated his life to the service of his country.'

'So nothing solid on him, either.'

'I can tell you where he was born, went to school, college, university and so forth.'

'I was thinking ... Garret was an NSA analyst. What was his specialty?'

'He was in European—Soviet Relations.'

'See if you can dig up some papers he wrote.'

'You want to see if he was any good?'

'Call it professional curiosity.'

'A lot of the stuff from that era has since been declassified. You can get it yourself from NSA records.'

'Okay.'

'Garret wasn't the reason I called you,' said Kradich. 'Something's

452

turned up on Harbor and Sato. I've been dipping into FSB comms. They're wanted for murder.'

'What?'

'Yeah, at a place called Ulan-Ude, out in the middle of Siberia.'

'Who are they supposed to have killed?'

'I've sent you a link to the photos.'

Lana found it and clicked. Two photos came up: male Caucasians, both in their early fifties, broad Slavic faces, brutal faces.

'Who are they?' she asked.

'The one with dark hair is Vlahd Bykovski and his buddy is Grisha Soloyov. Both career FSB, based in Moscow.'

'Ben and Akiko killed cops?'

'That's the rumor.'

'What were they doing out in Siberia?'

'Good question. At the very least, they were getting bumped off by Ben and Kiko—allegedly. Bykovski was run over by a snowplow. The other guy had his neck broken. We intercepted a little police radio traffic. Seems Ben and Akiko have headed into the badlands and the local sheriff has sent a posse after them. I'd say their arrest is imminent.'

February 15, 2012

Somewhere north of Ulan-Ude, Siberia. Ben made his way down a rickety wood staircase into the bar, Akiko close behind. The room stank of ingrained alcohol, sweat and tobacco smoke. An elderly woman with concave cheeks and toothless gums hailed their arrival. She walked out of the room and came back moments later with a plate of black bread, cheese and sour milk cakes, put a bottle on the table with two glasses, and started sweeping the floor with a birch broom.

'Vodka?' Ben asked.

Akiko poured herself a glass and sipped it. 'No, water.'

'I didn't think they did that stuff around here.'

'How are you feeling?'

'I was going to ask you the same.' Ben examined her neck. If anything, the cuts and bruising seemed worse.

'I'm a little sore,' she said, moving her head from side to side, checking the level of discomfort. 'The cuts were clean. No infection. And I think the cold helped.' She drank some water. 'You can see my wounds, but I can't see yours.'

'I . . .' Ben choked. He was about to say that he was fine when the emotion suddenly welled up and overwhelmed him. The truth was that he'd been having problems. He kept seeing the frightened disbelief in the eyes of the man whose neck he'd broken, and hearing the sound the snowplow bucket made when he hit the other man—a dull, crunching, bone-breaking thud. Sleep provided the only relief. What scared him most was that those eyes would soon haunt him there as well.

He felt Akiko's arms around him. They held each other in a motionless embrace for a full minute, an eternity, aware of each other's heartbeat, their breathing.

Akiko released him.

'Sorry . . .' he said, wiping his eyes with the back of his sleeve.

'What for?'

Ben shook his head.

'You did what you had to do. Like your father would have done.'

Ben understood what she meant. There was a moment when he had felt an awful responsibility for Akiko, and he'd taken other lives to protect her. He hadn't been given a choice, or rather, he had been given a stark choice: to do what he knew in a split second had to be done, or be responsible for letting her die. In that instant, Ben had been given a window into the reality of Curtis Foxx's world, and his choices. Curtis had done what he'd had to do, which was to leave his wife and child. The alternative was to put them at terrible risk from potentially malevolent forces that wouldn't have cared about collateral damage. Curtis had given his life for theirs, endured a slow and lonely death that crept up on him over the years, knowing that his son was growing daily and that he would never see him, have a relationship with him. And all the while the awful truth of KAL 007 burned into him while he honored the promise he'd made to his country—to keep its terrible secret. And suddenly Ben loved his father, a man he never knew on the one hand, but knew instinctively on the other, just as if he had grown up with him in his life.

He felt Akiko's hand on his shoulder. 'I've had enough,' she said. 'We were never going to win. My mother probably died years ago. It was a foolish thing to come to Russia and expect to find her.'

Ben didn't know what to say. Even if he was ready to call it quits, it wasn't as if they could just leave, and they both knew it. There was the murder of Oleg back at Khabarovsk, and the two killers left in the snows of Ulan-Ude. With Luydmila's help, Ben and Akiko had managed to get away, but sooner or later they would have to hand their passports to someone behind a hotel reception counter or at a passport control point and a red flag would be raised with the tourist police against their names.

Ben went over to the window. 'The weather's lifting.' There was a patch of blue sky, people moving around, a few dogs and a . . . 'Hey,' he exclaimed, 'what's *that* doing here?'

A large green and white helicopter was perched on a plateau of raised ground at the highest point of the settlement, its main rotor blades drooping. A man in a red parka was on top of the machine checking the rotor heads and sweeping away the loose snow.

'Can you read the writing on the side?' he asked.

Akiko joined him at the window. 'It says, "European Softwood and Lumber Company".'

The village was too poor to have a helicopter at its disposal. There didn't appear to be any hangar facilities up there, which explained why it was sitting out in the open during the storm.

'Maybe it put down to get out of the weather,' Ben suggested.

The door opened and Marat strode in.

'Oh, you're awake,' he said in Russian. 'I've found someone for you to talk with.'

Akiko passed this on to Ben, who stuffed bread into his pockets and the cakes in his mouth and followed them out.

The wind had died completely, which made the bitter sub-zero temperature bearable. The sun burst through the patch of blue moving slowly across the sky, warmed their faces and caused them to squint. They shuffled down a narrow path behind Marat, through calf-deep snow between the black weather-beaten huts, and into a kind of general store containing a selection of goods from food items to basic hardware. The store was empty but for a man who was probably younger than he looked, because he looked about 100. His face was covered in liver spots and he was bent over double and leaned on a cane. He looked up at them sideways, his head turned at an odd angle.

'These are the two I told you about,' said Marat in Russian. 'This is Akiko.'

'Good morning,' the old man said.

'Good morning,' Akiko replied.

'You are looking for foreign national prisoners, I hear.'

'Yes.'

'I am one of those.'

'You are from North Korea?'

'Yes. I was brought here as a young man.'

'I believe my mother was a prisoner in a camp, possibly in this area.'

'Do you have any idea which camp? There were several around here. I spent most of my life in Labor Camp ZJa5756. It was nearby, over the hill behind the village, but they pulled it down and resettled us.'

'No, no idea.'

'What was her crime?'

'No crime. She was a passenger on a plane that was shot down.'

'A plane crash?'

'Possibly.'

'I knew a woman who was held at the camp. I heard that she had survived such an incident, though it might have been a train crash. Or a car crash. Sometimes my mind wanders and I find it hard to remember. Tell me, are you Korean?'

'No, Japanese.'

'Hmm . . . too bad. I seem to remember that this woman was Korean. It was such a long time ago. I have tried to forget, but it comes back, though often the memory changes, the details merge.'

Akiko nodded. Perhaps this was just an old man whose mind had gone.

'Did you say that she was Japanese? Where are you from?'

'Japan.'

'It was a long time ago. I was driving a crane. I was drunk. I made a fatal mistake.'

Akiko felt the man's eyes searching her face. He held up a bony finger and pointed at her, the tip trembling. It was as if he recalled her from somewhere, but then the certainty drifted away and his hand dropped back onto the handle of the cane.

'What happened?' Akiko pressed him.

'I told you, I made a mistake. I had been drinking. Yes, I was drunk. The log dropped from the crane when I tried to place it on the stack. She was killed, you know, crushed. I killed her. She was Korean. No, she was a Mongol.'

'What's happening?' asked Ben. 'What's he saying?'

'I don't know,' said Akiko. 'It is difficult. His memory wanders. He is too old.'

'Or maybe he's had a little too much of the local firewater,' Ben suggested.

'You remind me of her,' the man said. 'What's your name? Hers was Nami.'

'What?' That name! Her mother's. Hearing it jolted her. 'What did you say?'

'She was a Mongol. Yes, I'm sure of it—a foreign national. But I killed her.'

'What was her name?' asked Akiko, holding the man's thin arms, her fingers squeezing his bones.

'What's going on?' Ben asked.

Marat burst through the door. 'Follow me. Now! The police—they have come to arrest you.'

Before Akiko or Ben could react, a large Mongol swinging a length of steel chain came through the back door. An instant later, a second man came through the front door, wielding a lump of wood like a club, blocking any chance of escape.

The man with the chain shouted at Akiko and kept shouting. She put her hands above her head, as did Marat. Ben mimicked them. The old man cowered back against a row of farming tools and plumbing supplies. The two men approached Ben carefully, nervously, as if expecting some form of retaliation, the way people approach a wild and dangerous animal. They yelled at him and the one with the chain darted in and swung it across Ben's stomach. He sank to the floor and yelled, 'What do they want?'

'Your hands, put them behind your back,' Akiko said.

Ben did as he was told and felt duct tape being wound around his wrists. Akiko received the same treatment, as did Marat.

'We are so sorry,' Akiko told their guide.

Marat said something that earned him a sharp whack across the shoulders with the club.

'They are not police,' Akiko hurriedly told Ben as they were marched across the village. The two men herded them toward a small, two-story brick building that had seen better days, whole chunks of stucco dropping off here and there.

'Then what are they?' Ben asked. 'Concerned citizens?'

'Sons of ex-prisoners,' she whispered. 'It came over the radio—two westerners wanted by police for three murders. Marat heard them talking about this in the village. The police are arriving this afternoon to take us into custody.'

The man without the chain barked at her, warning her to keep her mouth shut.

Once inside the old building, they were led down a flight of stairs. The two men put Ben up against a wall and searched him, taking his passport, wallet, wristwatch, belt and shoes. They then pushed him into a small room sealed with a heavy rusting steel door and banged it shut. There were several such doors. Ben heard two more slamming, one each for Akiko and Marat. He examined his surroundings. The walls were brick and mortar, both crumbling in places with rising damp. They were probably once food or grain stores, he thought, rather than prison cells. There was nothing to sit on, shit in, or wash with. There were no windows. The air was heavy with a damp, musty smell and a black creeping mold occupied most of the walls and floor.

After ten minutes of silence, during which the only sound was his own breathing, he heard Akiko's voice call his name, followed by the clang of the chain thrashing against her door and a man shouting at her. Ben sat on the floor and drew up his knees, but the floor was cold and within another twenty minutes he was pacing, just to keep warm. And then he saw the eyes. They were surprised eyes, the life slipping from them as the swinging length of steel reinforcing rod turned the man's vertebrae and the spinal cord within to mush. The eyes lost focus, dulling, the head rolling to one side as the body simultaneously crumpled to the snow. There was also the man he had killed with the snowplow and the feeling of triumph that came with the moment, the exultation turning almost instantly into a ball of anguish and disgust that ate away at his insides. He had killed. Twice.

Ben heard Akiko's voice again, muffled by the walls. She was talking to someone. Whatever happened, he had to get her out of Russia. She hadn't killed anyone. She was the victim. His victim, just like the men he had killed.

A key suddenly rattled in the lock and the door flew open. It was Marat and his son, Anatoly. Akiko and the Korean man from the store hovered behind them. The Mongols who'd locked them up were nowhere to be seen.

'Where are our jailers?'

'Drunk,' Akiko said, handing Ben his passport, shoes and other items. There was no money in his wallet. 'They are congratulating themselves.'

'So the old guy sprang us?' Ben asked as he hurriedly dressed.

'Yes.'

'He's going to get in trouble. Why's he on our side?'

'Because I remind him of Nami.'

'What?!'

There was no time to talk about it. Marat whistled softly, urgently, and gestured at them to follow him and Anatoly up the stairs.

They regrouped in the shadow of the building's brick columns and surveyed the open, snow-covered ground between them and the black huts clustered in random fashion more than fifty yards away. It was mid-afternoon. The sun had retreated, veiled behind a layer of light gray cloud that had lifted somewhat. They squinted into the glare. A few people dressed in black shuffled through the snow here and there, ignoring them.

Marat and Anatoly discussed the options with Akiko, who translated them for Ben.

'The dogs and sleds are over there to the right, around the back of the hut on the edge of the square,' she said, pointing it out. 'The sleds are packed and ready to go. Marat and his son will go now and hitch the dogs. We will follow in two minutes.'

'Where are we going?'

'Mongolia. Marat is going to get us across. He knows people.'

'Okay,' Ben acknowledged with a nod. Half a plan was better than none.

Marat and Anatoly were already on the move, sauntering across the square like they had all the time in the world.

Ben glanced back over his shoulder to make an observation about this to Akiko, but she was no longer behind him. She was saying good-bye to the old Korean who'd come to their aid. As he watched, she bowed and then kissed the man on the cheek. He pulled out a piece of cloth and wiped his eyes with it. Akiko wiped her eyes with the backs of her gloved hands. Ben wondered what he knew about Nami. The Korean turned and shuffled off without looking back, across the square in the opposite direction from Marat and Anatoly.

'I'll tell you later,' Akiko said, answering the look on Ben's face when she rejoined him. 'We need to go.'

Ben followed her into the glare, bursting with questions. They walked slowly, forcing themselves to appear casual, mimicking their guides' example. They passed an old couple walking together, neither of whom looked up, choosing instead to watch their feet push through the snow.

The dogs were barking as they neared the black hut. Marat was talking to them in a hushed voice, trying to keep them calm. The animals yelped with excitement, keen to go. Akiko and Ben rounded the edge of the building and saw the sleds lined up. Marat was rubbing one dog's head between its gray pointed ears, while Anatoly checked the harnesses. Neither Ben nor Akiko needed to be told what to do and assumed their positions on the sleds. Marat and his son jumped on behind them. The dogs took the strain at the sound of Marat's voice. With the snap of the whip, they surged forward. The police from Ulan-Ude could arrive at any moment.

Marat turned the dogs toward the higher ground behind the

461

settlement. The animals bounded in their harnesses, straining with the effort required to drag their loads up the hill. It was likely that the police would take the same trail Marat and Anatoly had used yesterday, which would bring them into the lower part of the settlement. The dogs kept close to the huts, avoiding the cleared ground between the buildings and the trees. After 100 meters or so, Marat guided the dogs across toward the cover of the trees. Spread out below were the black roofs of the settlement and something that caught Ben's eye, the sun flashing off its polished green and white paint scheme. The helicopter. He could see the pilots in their seats, headsets on, running through checklists. He pushed himself up off the sled to get a better view, which caused a rail to dig into the snow as the sled turned and it toppled suddenly onto its side. Anatoly helped Ben haul himself out of the dry powder and then they both righted the sled. Ben grabbed his pack and found what he was looking for, a voice in his head telling him that this was the right thing to do. He lifted his legs high, awkwardly, trying to run to Akiko through snow that was thigh deep.

'Get your things,' he told her, breathing heavily with effort.

'What?'

'Get your backpack and let's go. Thank Marat and Anatoly for us.'

'What are you—'

'Akiko. Do it now. We're going to take *that*.' He gestured down the hill at the helicopter.

Akiko explained the situation to Marat, who shook his head dubiously.

Ben and Akiko were fugitives, so Ben was doing them a favor, but from the looks on their faces, he could see that the Mongols thought he was crazy. He shook both father's and son's hands and started galloping and stumbling down the hill, lifting his knees high out of the fine, dry snow. Akiko followed.

They approached the helicopter from behind.

'Go knock on the door there,' Ben said, indicating the right-hand front door. 'Quickly.'

A whine suddenly electrified the air and a shadow passed slowly overhead as the helicopter's main rotor began to turn.

'What will I say?'

'I don't know. Ask them if they've seen Rudolf the red-nosed reindeer. Whatever you say, give them a big smile. Don't spook them. Go now.'

The tail rotor was spinning faster.

'Hurry,' he said.

Akiko walked forward, uncertain about what she was doing or why. She glanced back at Ben and saw him duck under the long tail boom and disappear from view. She walked to the door as instructed and knocked on the window. The pilot turned toward her and clearly got a fright, not expecting to see anyone standing there, his eyes momentarily wide. Akiko gave him a smile and a wave, which made him relax a little. The man reached overhead, flicked a switch or two, and then leaned forward, turned something on the front instrument panel and the motor died. The window slid down and he angrily told her in Russian to stand clear of the aircraft.

Ben appeared on the other side of the helicopter. He tapped the window beside the other pilot with something that startled Akiko. Both men turned toward the direction of the sound and instantly put their gloved hands above their heads as they saw the barrel of a silenced Makarov pointing at them.

'Akiko!' Ben called. 'Come here!'

She ran around in front of the chopper's stubby nose.

Ben again tapped the pilot's window and gestured at him to lower it.

'Tell them to undo their seat harnesses one-handed. Tell them to do it slowly,' Ben told Akiko. 'No sudden movements.'

She repeated his instructions. Both men reluctantly tripped the release for their shoulder and lap restraints.

Ben glanced at the main door for the aft cabin. Keeping the gun pointed at the temple of the co-pilot, he said, 'I want the other guy to open the door. And tell him that if he doesn't do it nicely, I'll blow his friend's head off.'

Akiko let the man know.

Marat whistled from the higher ground above the helicopter. Ben glanced up toward him. He'd stepped out from the tree line, the dogs and sleds hidden, and was frantically gesturing at something going on in the village. Ben turned and saw three police 4x4s and a quad bike roll out of the trees 500 meters below them.

'Akiko, I want them out of the chopper one at a time. And tell them to keep their hands above their heads. First one to drop them will regret it.'

She snapped at the pilots in Russian.

'Come over here and stand behind me,' he told her. 'I don't want these guys getting clever and taking you hostage.'

Akiko moved several paces to her right so that Ben was between her and the pilots. She looked down at the village and saw the police vehicles motor into the square near the building in which they'd been imprisoned.

'Ben,' she said urgently.

'I know.'

He kept his focus on the two Russians as they jumped down from the belly of the chopper onto the snow.

'Helmets off,' he said, gesturing at them with the Makarov. 'Put 'em in the chopper. Slowly . . .'

They understood without having to get it translated.

Akiko watched as the two big Mongols who had locked them up ran toward the police. A hurried conference ensued as the two parties met, and then the police vehicles and the quad took off, racing out of the square.

'Akiko, get them to walk down toward the village.'

The two Russians were grumbling. One of them put his hands down and took a step toward Ben. Ben fired off two shots at the man's feet. *Phut. Phut.* The rounds missed the man's toes by less than an inch, kicking up the snow. The shots stampeded them. They turned and fled down the hill before Akiko had opened her mouth.

'Get in—hurry,' Ben said. 'Take the right-hand seat.'

Akiko ran to the open door and stepped up into the chopper, Ben just behind her. He shoved the Makarov in the front of his parka and grabbed the helmets on the way through. He stepped over the center console and squeezed himself into the left-hand seat, his eyes taking in the instrument panel, overhead and center consoles. He handed Akiko a helmet and donned the other. He'd never flown a Bell 412 before, but how different could it be from a JetRanger?

'Jesus,' he muttered. Very different, when all the instruments and switches were captioned in Russian.

He flicked the switch on the overhead panel and the BATT indicator for engine one jumped into the green. Plenty of juice there, and the fuel load stood at more than three quarters. Ben bypassed the normal pre-flight checks and went into what he hoped would be the starting procedure. Noting that the three switches for fuel transfer, boost and valve were already in the on position for engine one, he stabbed the button for engine start. He was gratified by a deep whine that ground up through the airframe and the foot pedals as the Pratt & Whitney turbofan spooled up. A blade of the main rotor swung by overhead, and the spinning masses began to make themselves felt, rocking the aircraft gently from side to side in the familiar manner. Fuel pressures, normal; engine and transmission pressures, normal. Ben hoped he was doing this right. It might be rash taking shortcuts, especially with unfamiliar machinery, but it was even more dangerous hanging around here. So, with seventy percent turbine speed showing, Ben switched over to generator power and repeated the start-up procedure for engine two. He held his breath. Nothing happened for a couple of seconds, but then the whine from engine number two made itself heard. Relieved, he took a moment to glance over the instrument panel and down towards the village. The quad was occasionally getting bogged in the thicker snow around the outskirts of the settlement, but it was still making ground, climbing steadily. The rifle slung around the driver's shoulder was now clearly visible, and the police 4x4s were clawing up the hill toward them. The pilots were running and falling down the slope, making good headway, waving their arms.

The engine and transmission temperatures weren't within their normal operating limits, but Ben had no choice. He gave Akiko what he hoped was a reassuring smile. The altimeter told him that they were at 1900 feet, a couple of knots of breeze coming from the left. There were power and transmission settings he should know before attempting to fly this aircraft, but there simply wasn't time to check the performance charts in the flight manual, which was probably in Russian anyway. It was seat-of-the-pants time. Ben selected 100 percent power and pulled up on the collective, which steepened the angle of attack of the main rotor blades, causing them to bite into the airflow. The 412, a medium-lift chopper, workhorse of mining, emergency rescue, coast guard, hospital and firefighters, leapt off the snow. Ben caught it as the nose reared up, and adjusted collective, stick and tail rotor pedals to keep it in a hover.

A neat hole appeared in the plexiglass windshield in front of Akiko, the round exiting through the quilted vinyl-covered metal above Ben's head. He didn't need any more prompting and thrust the stick forward. The nose dropped and the chopper surged ahead. Ben lowered the nose further as the ground fell away, so that the chopper accelerated faster, gravity giving it a kick along. With eighty knots showing on the air speed indicator, he pulled back on the stick. The 412 climbed and banked sharply, the main rotors flogging the dense cold air, the jet engines snarling. Within moments, the roofs of the black huts shooting by beneath the chopper's skids gave way to the tops of snow-laden trees.

Ben took them up to 3000 feet, 1000 feet of clearance above the higher peaks, and headed due west. He showed Akiko where to plug the jacks for the headset in her helmet into the aircraft's radio/intercom. She then leaned forward and put her gloved finger against the hole in the windshield directly in front of her.

The round had penetrated the fuselage just above Ben's head on its way out. There were probably other shots fired. Ben hoped none of them had hit anything important. He surveyed the gauges; they all showed normal settings.

'Have a look for any maps,' he said. 'There'll be a pocket in the door, or they'll be jammed down beside your seat.'

The problem was this: where to now? They were wanted by the police and were deep inside what had become enemy territory. Mongolia was south, but then so was Ulan-Ude. Ben checked the navigation suite. The aircraft wasn't a recent model, but it had been fitted with some new avionics. He found what he was hoping for in the center floor console—a GPS navigation system. Firing it up, he adjusted its option settings and changed the display language to English.

'Lake Baikal,' he said. 'Remember that from the briefing before we left? You can see it on the horizon directly ahead. There were camps on its foreshore.'

'She's dead.'

'What? Who's dead? Nami?'

'The Korean back there, the old man I was saying goodbye to, he believes he killed a foreign national by the name of Nami.'

Ben looked at her, incredulous. 'Couldn't that be a coincidence? Is Nami a common name?'

'In Japan, yes. He said I reminded him of her. She had survived a crash. He thought it could have been a plane crash. There are too many coincidences.'

Ben recalled the odd manner in which the man had pointed at Akiko. It was as if he was seeing a ghost. 'And he's sure he killed her?'

'There was an accident. He said it was his fault. They took her to hospital and he never saw her again. She lost an arm. There were rumors that she died of her injuries.'

Ben wondered whether knowing what had happened to her mother would help Akiko come to terms with her loss.

'The old man told me that now he had met Nami's daughter, her soul would stop tormenting him.'

Ben knew what the old guy meant. 'What do you want to do, Akiko?'

'Go to Mongolia. We are finished here.'

Ben took a deep breath. He felt relieved and yet defeated at the same time. They had found Akiko's mother, but the one place they couldn't bring her back from was the grave.

'You're sure?' he asked her.

'Yes. Marat was going to take us to a place called Ulaanbataar in Mongolia.'

Ben found the city on the GPS. It was around 300 miles south of their current position. The 412 had a healthy range and there was more than enough fuel.

'Any luck with those maps?' he asked.

'Why do you need maps? You have that.' She nodded at the GPS.

'I'm hoping a map will show us if there's any military airspace around here.' It would be worth avoiding, he thought, given that they were a couple of murder suspects in a stolen chopper with its transponder turned off.

Akiko went back to her search while Ben turned on the VHF radio and checked the preset frequencies. There was a brief, distant exchange between Russian voices in his headset. He dialed in the international emergency frequency of 121.5 MHz.

The sharply defined shoreline of Lake Baikal was fast approaching, its wintry surface a flat expanse of snow-covered ice that glowed pink in the afternoon sunlight. He took the chopper down to within 200 feet of the lake's elevation and maintained their course due west. The skies were clear and there was nothing coming through his headset other than the sound of his own breathing. Flying felt reassuring, a constant, a few minutes of Zen-like peace. He looked at Akiko. Her face was green. A solid row of hills rising 1500 feet above the lake's shoreline approached. Ben climbed, the main rotor chopping at the frozen air.

A burst of chatter came through the headsets. It was close. Ben looked around at the empty sky. A Russian fighter suddenly appeared from nowhere off the right-hand side of the chopper. Missiles hung from the pylons beneath its wings.

'Shit,' Ben said. Where the hell did that come from?

The fighter was a big aircraft with twin fins and a blue camouflage scheme. Ben didn't know anything about Russian fighters, but it looked like an F-15. It was a MiG, perhaps, or a Sukhoi. The pilot was clearly visible in the bubble canopy, signaling at him aggressively, pointing down. The fighter had its flaps and gear down, and the nose was riding high, close to stalling. The pilot was fighting to keep it in the air at this low speed. It accelerated ahead of them and rocked its wings, then broke to the right. The instruction was clear: they had been intercepted.

'What does he want?' Akiko asked, fear in her voice. 'Is he going to shoot us down?'

'He wants us to follow. If we don't, *then* he'll shoot us down.'

He didn't have to remind her about KAL 007. If he was thinking about it, Akiko would be, too.

'Then we should follow.'

'And what happens when we land?'

As Ben saw it, they really had only one answer.

'Hang on,' he said.

He pulled back on the stick, pushed the collective to the floor and the chopper dropped out of the sky like an anvil pushed off a cliff. The rotors thrashed at the air and a sickening shudder hammered up through the helicopter's airframe. They sped nose first for a jumble of smashed rocks and broken scree at the base of the cliff. The vertical face shot past in a shuddering blur. Just when it seemed that death was imminent, Ben hauled up on the collective and pulled back on the stick. Akiko dry-retched as the 412 clawed out of the dive and scribed a tight, banked turn away from the vertical cliff face and headed back toward the ice of Lake Baikal. Ben kept the turn going, straightening out only when the towering hills that edged the lake's shoreline lay directly in their path, and headed for a narrow, wooded ravine. He had no time to reassure Akiko that the uncomfortable feeling of being turned inside out by the G-forces was quite normal.

A thousand feet above them, and half a mile away, the fighter executed a tight turn and bled off height. Its pilot knew exactly where they were. The Russian was coming back for them, his voice loud in the headset.

Ben kept to the ravine and watched the fighter until he lost it some-where behind them. By his calculation, they had probably five seconds to live if the pilot's ground controller had given him the order to fire one of those missiles. He counted them off in his head. *Five, four, three, two, one* . . . But there was no explosion, no fireball, no final moments of falling. A jet roar filled the chopper's interior and the fighter ambled slowly overhead, the pilot rocking its wings. And then its afterburners lit with a blue-white fire, the sharp nose came up and the plane accelerated vertically, shrinking within seconds to a black dot that became lost in the wisps of high-altitude early evening cloud.

'Why didn't the pilot fire on us? What did he say?' Ben asked Akiko. Her face was turned away from him. 'Akiko . . .'

She held out her hand toward him, palm open, as if to say, 'Leave me alone . . .'. Her body shuddered, racked by another heave. Airsickness. Ben knew she'd be next to useless for a while, even after they landed.

He set the chopper on a gentle climb until they had the altitude to clear the ridge, and then doubled back to the edge of the lake. They were still faced with their original problem: where to go? The GPS gave their position as being about 35 kilometers northeast of a small town called Listvyanka on the lake's southwestern foreshore. A cluster of lights off to his right caught his attention. According to the GPS, there were no other towns on this side of the lake, and yet here was a small settlement tucked into a narrow valley a kilometer back from the lake's foreshore. The village solved their immediate problem. Night flying was out of the question. It was too risky. Ben banked the 412 toward the light. A few minutes later, he'd landed without incident on the only available open ground, the solid ice of a frozen river, a hundred meters from a collection of black huts.

Ben completed the helicopter's shutdown and gave Akiko a few moments to catch her breath. She nodded at him when she was ready and he helped her into the aircraft's back seats where there was more room.

'Where are we?' she asked, her voice weak.

'Good question. According to the map, this place doesn't exist.'

Akiko groaned, her eyes closed.

Ben looked out through the plexiglass. No movement on the embankments on either side of the chopper. Night was falling. He found a torch and several spare parkas in a locker.

'Lie down,' he told Akiko. 'We're going to stay put for the night.'

Akiko gladly slumped sideways, exhausted from the airsickness, and stretched out along the row of seats. Ben covered her with the parkas. He checked the embankments again. No movement. Strange. The village was obviously occupied, but no one had come to investigate their noisy arrival.

February 16, 2012

NSA HQ, Fort Meade, Maryland. Lana had to admit it—Garret was good. His papers were succinct, intuitive and, given the benefit of hindsight, accurate. The unclassified material that predated 1985 had yet to be digitized and was only available on microfiche, which made it difficult to access in the sense that it couldn't be removed from the NSA reference center, but at least it was freely available. And even though the censor's black pen was active throughout the papers, the clarity of Garret's strategic thinking was impressive.

Lana yawned. She'd been reading since 4 a.m. If the material wasn't so riveting, revealing a world no longer in existence, she'd have given it up by now and gone down to the cafeteria for breakfast. She moved the display to an overview with Garret's name on it, penned in June 1983, about a Soviet operation called RYAN, which suggested Yuri Andropov believed the US was on the verge of launching a pre-emptive nuclear strike on the USSR. Lana had had no idea that the world had come so close at that time to being obliterated in a thermonuclear firestorm. The ailing Russian Premier was obviously paranoid and desperate, and outmaneuvered by the Reagan administration on many fronts. The one place where Moscow seemed to have the ascendancy over the United States was in its relationship with the general populace of Europe. Garret had written a number of papers on this in general, and on the flourishing European anti-US peace movement. Fueling the fire was the imbalance of missiles in the region. The Soviets had intermediate-range missiles aimed at Western Europe and NATO's answer—the deployment of Pershings and cruise missiles in West Germany, England and Italy—was being strongly resisted by the peaceniks.

A clock on the wall told Lana that it was almost time to call it quits. She checked the catalog and skipped forward to September 1983 and a piece Garret had written on the collapse of the Western European peace movement, which he attributed in no small part to the shooting down of KAL 007, the only paper Garret had written where the Korean airliner had been specifically noted. The tone of this analysis was gloating, almost self-congratulatory, and unlike his other papers. In several places throughout, Garret quoted an earlier paper he'd authored. Its first mention was in a footnote, where it was referenced as '"Engineering the Collapse of West European Opposition to US IRBMs": Roy Garret/European–Soviet Relations/12.22.82', and thereafter as 'ECWEOUSIRBM:RG/ESR/12.22.82'. Interesting title, thought Lana. She didn't remember seeing this paper indexed, which was confirmed when she went back through the catalog. Cross-checking the NSA's general reference, she found that the analysis ECWEOUSIRBM:RG/ESR/12.22.82 was still classified top secret. So, before closing down, she sent Kradich a request asking him whether it was possible to dig this paper up from another source. She then packed up and headed to her office via a quick breakfast of coffee and a slice of raisin toast.

Her cell phone rang as she sat down behind her keyboard with the remains of the toast on a napkin. The number wasn't familiar, but she answered it anyway.

'Englese,' she said.

'Since when did the NSA engage in murder?' said the male voice, full of disgust. 'This is going to blow up in your face, Englese.'

'Who is this?' she asked. 'How did you get this number?'

'You wrote it down on the business card you gave me.'

Dallas Mitchell. 'Is that you, Tex?'

'Have you got someone after me, too?'

Lana was on the edge of her seat.

'Don't bother tracing this call,' he said. 'I'm on a disposable and I won't be on it long enough.'

'What murders? What are you talking about?'

'Lucas Watts and Jerome Grundy—both dead, Englese, and there's no one else but you in the picture.'

Her mind raced. Watts and Grundy, murdered? Panic settled on her.

'Tex, you need to believe me when I tell you I have *no* idea what's going on. Give me ten minutes and I'll ring you back.'

'No way. I'm gone.'

'You have to trust me. Ten minutes.'

She didn't wait for a response and ended the call, her palms sweating. It took two minutes to confirm that Lucas Watts was dead. Local homicide's preliminary report was that it was accidental: Watts had been electrocuted when a two-liter bottle of Pepsi was spilt into a nest of electrical cords and his home's circuit-breakers had malfunctioned. Grundy had been killed in a hit and run at 3 a.m. one day ago. Lana's scalp prickled. She took a business card from her bag and dialed the number.

'McBride, Sweeney, Sweetman & Bourdain, attorneys at law,' said the woman's voice on the line. It was a timid voice, a quiver in it.

'Can I speak with Kayson Bourdain, please.'

Silence.

'Hello?' Lana asked.

'Are you a client of Mr Bourdain's?'

'This is Lana Englese from the National Security Agency. Mr Bourdain was assisting us with an investigation.'

'I'm sorry . . . Mr Bourdain drowned in his swimming pool last night.'

Lana put the handset back on the cradle. 'Oh my god . . .' she whispered. She lifted the handset again and dialed. The phone rang until the message bank kicked in with a woman's voice.

'Hey, you've lucked out. We're not in right now, but leave your name and number after the tone and we'll get back to you, promise.' Beep.

Lana got up and paced while she placed another call.

'Special Agent Sherwood,' said the voice.

'Miller. Get the Bureau's chopper. I'm coming to you.'

'What's going on?'

'Just get it. This is priority one, cancel-all-leave, number-one fucking urgent. I'll tell you about it on the way. I'll be there in fifteen.' She grabbed her coat and ran down the corridor to the elevators.

Lana reached her vehicle in record time. She hit the redial against Tex Mitchell's number once she cleared the boom and accelerated into the traffic with a shriek of tire rubber. The phone rang eight times. 'C'mon . . . c'mon . . . pick up, pick up.' On the ninth ring, he answered.

'Englese, there's nothing you can tell me that –'

'Tex, I wrote a report,' she said, breathing hard. 'It was about the tape—the missing tape. It was an analysis of what I believed was on it and the people who knew about it. It detailed the interviews with Lucas Watts and Jerome Grundy. Ben and Curtis's attorney, Kayson Bourdain, was mentioned. I just called Bourdain's, office. He died last night, drowned.'

'Shit . . .'

'There's one other person on the list besides you. I just called and the phone went to voice mail.'

'Who?'

'Nikki Harbor. Ben's mother.'

The FBI MD-530 'Little Bird' picked up both Lana and Special Agent Sherwood from CIA, Langley, where he happened to be in the middle of an inter-agency training program. The pilot put his foot to the floor, or whatever pilots do to make helicopters go fast. Lana had called ahead to the Norfolk police and notified the Norfolk FBI Field Office. She hoped the response would be commensurate with her demand to haul ass. And, indeed, a call was patched through when they'd been in the air barely five minutes. Police on the scene informed her that the Harbor residence was vacant, the back door left ajar. There were no signs of a struggle inside. Everything seemed in order. False alarm.

'What about the open back door? Who walks out of their home

these days and leaves it unlocked?' Lana asked Sherwood as the chopper continued its high-speed run.

'I don't think that's reason enough to mobilize all law enforcement on the eastern seaboard, do you? So they forgot to close the damn door when they went out for lunch. What do you want the FBI to do about it?' said Sherwood, pissed.

'I guess they should stand down,' she said.

'And what about us?'

'We're almost there. I'd like to take a look for myself.'

'I think we should turn back, Lana. We've just wasted a lot of man-hours, not to mention squandered the priority on this aircraft. I'm starting off on the wrong foot here with the Bureau and I—'

Lana hid her exasperation. 'Like I told you, Miller, we've got three murders, all linked to that report.'

'Three *accidents*, Lana. And look at what you're suggesting.'

'What I'm suggesting is that the investigation into the missing Wakkanai radar tape was instigated by an ex-CIA operative, the right-hand man of possibly our next President who is himself an ex-NSA analyst, and that both of them appear to have had something to do with the downing of the Korean airliner and the subsequent cover-up. Maybe they're still covering it up.'

Sherwood almost laughed. 'This case had you spooked from the beginning.'

'Trust me, Miller, we *have* to do this.'

'And I suppose women's intuition is a reliable investigation tool?'

'Look, if you turn around now, you're going to look stupid.'

'Yeah, that about sums up how I'm feeling.'

'I say we follow through, look around, ask questions, finish the job—be professional.'

Sherwood shook his head, folded his massive arms and shifted his attention to the built-up landscape slipping by beneath them.

An agent from the FBI Field Office, Norfolk, met them at the front door to Nikki's and Frank's house. It was a big, stately old place, freshly painted white, with soaring columns over the front portico and a cinder driveway edged by ancient, overhanging moss-covered trees that presented like an arboreal guard of honor. The local PD had left about an hour before and the FBI agent from the Norfolk FO was anxious to do something other than baby-sit an empty house. He delivered the debrief, which was a personalized version of the one they'd received en route: that no one was home, there was nothing suspicious, and thanks for spoiling my fucking day.

Lana shrugged off the rebuke and began an external examination of the home. Sherwood took it on the chin and sighed deeply as he watched his fellow FBI agent drive off in a burst of aggravated wheelspin.

The Harbors had money; that much was evident. Lana walked around the back of the house. There were footprints all over the rear steps. She walked up the steps, snapping a rubber glove onto her hand. The many bootmarks suggested that there were going to be police prints all over the door knob, but that didn't mean she had to add hers. She twisted it—the door was still ajar—and pushed it open. She tested the door, opening and closing it. The frame was slightly sprung, warped with moisture. To close it properly the door had to be pulled shut hard. Had the door been properly closed, she noted, it would have locked. She wondered whether it was just something the Harbors had simply forgotten to do. The garage, which was open, was a short walk from the back door. If they were going somewhere, it was probably the route they would have taken—out the back door and down to the garage.

Lana entered what appeared to be a rear sitting room. The furniture was antique and expensive. She moved through into the kitchen, which was ultra-modern with white marble benchtops, dark wood cupboards and brushed stainless steel everywhere else, including the large ice-through-the-door fridge. There was an intricate scale model of a nineteenth-century clipper in a glass case on a sideboard, and a framed collection of half a dozen seaman's knots on the wall behind it. There were also pictures of a serious-looking ocean-going yacht on the walls, several of which featured an attractive middle-aged woman in a wide-brimmed white hat sitting in various poses on the back of the boat—Ben's mother, Nikki, Lana presumed. There was no food left out on the island. Lana felt the side of the electric kettle. The water inside was only a handful of degrees above room temperature. It had been used, but hours ago. Inside the fridge there was plenty of food. Closing the door, she noticed more photos of the yacht. It was named *Safe Harbor*. Cute, she thought.

Moving through the home, she found nothing in the least amiss. Nikki kept a tight ship. She went up the central staircase and put her head in the bedrooms. All beds were made. There was a small pile of clothes on the floor in the main bedroom—a man's shorts, undershorts, socks, knitted shirt. Frank Harbor's, she figured, wondering if his habit of dumping his dirty laundry on the floor might be something that got under Nikki's skin. She went back downstairs, through the kitchen, out the back door. And then it hit her—*Safe Harbor*! She raced back inside, examined the photos of the boat on the fridge door and found what she was looking for, held there by a cracker biscuit magnet. Behind *Safe Harbor* was a sign that read 'Hampton Marina'.

'Don't you get it, Miller?' she said as they exited the drive. 'Someone came looking for them, but Nikki and Frank weren't home. When that someone left, they didn't pull the door hard enough to close it properly—the kind of idiosyncrasy you're only aware of when you live in a house.'

'Really.' He looked at her, unimpressed.

Directory assistance gave Lana an address for Hampton Marina. She keyed it into the vehicle's Navman so that Sherwood would know where to go.

Next, she placed a call. 'Hello, Norfolk PD? This is Investigator Lana Englese from the National Security Agency. I'm with FBI Special Agent Miller Sherwood and . . . Sure, I'll hold.' Lana got twenty-odd seconds of an old ELO track piped down the line before another voice took over. She repeated the introduction. 'Earlier today,' she continued, 'a couple of uniforms looked over a place for us belonging to . . . Yeah, that's the one. We now have reason to believe there could be a possible hostage situation at . . . Uh-huh, uh-huh. Look, *everyone's* busy, Sergeant.'

Lana held the phone out from her ear and looked at it angrily. 'The asshole just hung up on me.'

'Yep,' said Sherwood, underwhelming her with support. 'And I think you'll probably get the same reaction from our FO here.'

'Just fucking step on it, Miller, would you?'

Hampton Marina was an upmarket parking lot dredged out of the mud for the playthings of multimillionaires. It presented as a sea of white hulls and rigging floating on gray, oily water. As Englese and Sherwood stepped onto the marina, a young guy in a runabout with 'Hampton Marina' written on the side pulled up at a nearby service pontoon. He jumped out, hoisted a fuel tank off the pontoon and placed it in the runabout before jumping back in.

'Excuse me,' Lana called out. The guy looked up and she held her credentials out at him, even though he was too far away to read them. 'Investigator Englese, National Security Agency. Can you tell me where I can find a boat called *Safe Harbor*?'

'Yeah, you're after Frank?'

She nodded. 'You seen him this morning?'

'Nope. But I've been busy. You're looking for an Azimut 68S.'

'What's that?'

'Red hull, white superstructure. Seventy foot long. Tidy little unit. Keep walking straight ahead, take your second left and you'll find it out on the end.'

'Thanks.'

'No problem. Frank's, er, not in any trouble is he, ma'am?' he called out.

'Oh, I don't think so.'

'He's one of the good guys.' The boathand gave them a wave and went back to stowing the fuel tank.

It was a warm and humid day, with a blue sky, relentless sun and puffs of steamy cloud. Lana's shirt was sticking to her. She waved a fly away from her face and picked up the pace.

The marina seemed largely deserted, but it was a Thursday so that figured. It was around lunchtime, which meant that even the crews paid by the rich owners were off somewhere else, on a break. The boats themselves were still, sitting in gray water free of ripples or movement.

'Jesus, there's a lot of money tied up here,' said Sherwood, stating the obvious.

A boat that looked similar to the one in the photos back at Nikki's and Frank's home came into view. And impressive though she was, among the company at this marina, she was nothing special.

'You bring your Sig, Miller?' Lana asked.

'Nope, switched to the Glock 22—more stopping power.'

'Whatever. You bring it?'

'Hell, I sleep with it,' he replied.

The boat's white stern was presented to the walkway, *Safe Harbor* written on the side of the hull in large gold script outlined in white. The cruiser appeared to be as empty of people as any other boat at the marina, except for one small detail—occasional pressure ripples emanated from the hull, indicating movement aboard. Lana pointed them out to Sherwood and then held a finger against her lips. She was about to step down into the boat when Sherwood stopped her, an arm across her chest like a boom. He reached inside his jacket and pulled out the Glock. He checked its magazine as a matter of standard procedure, and confirmed that the safety was on. Removing his shoes and socks, Sherwood lowered his 250 pounds onto *Safe Harbor's* stern without making a sound. The seventy-foot boat was big enough that it accepted his weight without raising the bow. Lana came aboard after him. The teak decking was warm underfoot. It was then that she heard a faint, muffled thump. She stopped.

'You hear that?' she whispered.

Sherwood cocked his head as if to say, 'Hear what?'

The tender boat had just motored past and its wash rocked the moored boats so that there was the gentle slapping of hull against water and lanyard against mast. Somewhere else, a radio played.

She shrugged and they kept moving.

Sherwood walked at a crouch into the bridge area of the boat, his weapon raised in the standard two-handed grip. The area was clear. He led the way forward into a kind of sitting/dining room trimmed in white leather, chrome and teak. A bar and a huge flatscreen television dominated. They went down a flight of stairs into the boat's sleeping quarters. Lana opened the door on what was the main bedroom. Empty.

Sherwood checked the kitchen. 'Clear,' he whispered as he backed out of it.

A muffled thump came through one of the walls.

'You heard it that time, right?' Lana whispered.

Sherwood nodded. He pointed up. Lana agreed. They backtracked their way upstairs to the television room and out into the sunshine. There was no place for anyone to hide.

They heard the thump again. It was coming from somewhere below them.

'Engine room,' Sherwood mouthed.

There was a trapdoor beneath his feet. He heaved it up and jumped down into the darkness.

Lana went down the ladder after him. Her eyes had trouble adjusting to the twilight of the cramped space below decks. Sherwood was leaning over a dark shape lying between the massive twin engines. A moment later, she recognized what the shape was—two bodies. Her partner stood back and let her through. The bodies were gagged with duct tape, their hands secured behind their backs with lock-ties. From the photos in their home, Lana knew for certain they were Nikki and Frank. She crouched and peeled off the tape. Nikki's eyes were wide with terror. There was blood smeared against the white fiberglass walls. Frank had been hit on the head with something blunt.

'Bomb,' Nikki gasped.

'Where?' Lana asked.

'Propane cylinder for the stove. Frank . . .'

'Who put you and your husband down here?' Lana asked as she quickly checked Frank's pulse. It was strong. 'Your husband's going to be fine, Mrs Harbor.'

The available light flickered, as if something had passed in front of it. Two loud bangs followed and a crushing weight fell on Lana, knocking her down on top of Nikki and Frank. It was Sherwood. His warm blood gushed over her from a wound in his throat. He'd been shot. The way his body quivered, Lana knew that he was dead. It had happened so fast, she couldn't believe it. Sherwood was dead. *Jesus Christ!*

A shape was coming down the ladder, the killer. Sherwood's weight was squashing the life out of her. There was something hard pressing into her hand. She ran her fingers around it to identify it. The moving shape was silhouetted by the light above and behind it, ultimately blocking it.

'Maybe it would be easier if I just put a bullet in you?' said a man's voice, hoarse and full of gravel.

Lana lifted up the object in her hand and squeezed it three times. Three deafening explosions rang in her ears. Her wild, unaimed fire was exchanged and she felt Sherwood's body quake on top of her, absorbing the energy of the returned gunfire. The shape leapt up the ladder and the trapdoor slammed shut, plunging the room into darkness that was total and complete.

Another shot was fired, somewhere close outside, and a loud thud sounded through the fiberglass ceiling above Lana's head. A few seconds later, the trapdoor opened and a flashlight beam swept aside the darkness.

'Englese, you down here?' A male voice, a different one, familiar.

'There's a bomb,' she said.

'Where?'

The man came down the ladder.

'Look for a propane cylinder. It's down here somewhere.'

The flashlight beam hunted through the engine room.

'Yep, got it. I think it's secured. There's a remote detonator, but the guy holding it isn't going to be pressing any buttons, trust me.'

'My partner . . .' Lana wheezed. 'He's dead. Help me.'

Beneath her, Nikki groaned under the weight of both Lana and Sherwood pressing down on her.

A face in shadow appeared above Lana. He shone the beam on himself.

'Tex!' she said, not quite believing her eyes.

'I couldn't get over here any faster.'

He got his hands under Sherwood's armpits and shifted his body to the side, freeing Lana.

The sound of police sirens drawing close penetrated the hull.

Tex helped Lana up, and then he cut away the lock-ties from Nikki's and Frank's hands and feet and helped Nikki up into a seated position.

'Hey, it's been a long time, hasn't it?' he said to her.

'Tex . . .'

'Let's have a look at your husband.'

He focused the beam on Frank's head. There was a nasty wound on the crown of his head, and he grunted as Lana and Tex sat him up.

'Frank,' Nikki said, embracing him. She turned toward Lana. 'I don't know who you are, but . . .' The words choked in her throat. 'I'm so sorry about your partner. He's dead, isn't he?'

'Yes.'

'He gave his life for us. He was a brave man.'

'Yes, he was.'

'I want to see everyone's hands,' yelled a young female voice above them. The local PD had arrived. 'Put 'em where I can see 'em. Into the light! Now!'

'This is NSA Investigator Englese,' Lana called back, waving her ID where it would be seen. 'We have an officer down and a freed hostage who requires medical assistance. We need an ambulance. *Now!*'

She threw her ID holder up onto the deck.

A few minutes later, they were topside in the sunshine. Frank was still semiconscious and being attended to by paramedics. Agents from the Norfolk FBI FO were also on hand, their casual attitude evaporated as they secured the crime scene and paid their respects to their fallen colleague.

'Do you know who this is?' Tex asked as he lifted the towel away from the dead killer's face. The man was in his sixties and hadn't carried an ID.

'No. It's not who I thought it would be,' said Lana.

'And who did you think it would be?'

'A former CIA spook by the name of Henry Buck.'

February 16, 2012

Lake Baikal, Siberia. Frozen condensation on the chopper's plexiglass windows made them as transparent as steel plate. It was gray outside, half an hour before sunrise. Ben woke Akiko, who moved stiffly under his hand. The aircraft's interior was as cold as a tomb.

'Sleep well?' he asked her.

She raised herself up on an elbow, her hair squashed into an awkward shape.

'Let's see if we can rustle up some breakfast out there.'

Ben opened a door and climbed down onto a thick ice sheet that was a river eight months of the year. The air was cold, dry and still. Something caught his attention up on the embankment. Three pink shapes—children dressed for the chill in puffy parkas. He waved at them and they turned and ran away. A couple of stocky old women armed with lit hurricane lanterns stepped forward to take their place. They wore frowns to go with their black and gray shawls and black *ushankas*. They stared at Ben and the helicopter from the embankment as if about to pronounce punishment. Ben waved and gave them his best smile before showing Akiko how to climb down. He held her hand, taking her weight.

'You might have to reassure these people about our intentions,' he said. 'They don't seem that friendly. Maybe European Lumber and Softwood has a bad reputation around here.'

'What *are* our intentions?' Akiko leaned against the side of the helicopter, sleepy and cold.

'I don't know . . . a few shots of vodka, some lard. The usual.'

'Then what?' Akiko asked, her eyes closed.

'The nearest town is twenty kilometers that way,' he said, hooking a thumb back over his shoulder. 'We can't stay here long. The fighter pilot will have given the authorities our location. We can wait here for the inevitable police vehicles, or we can give it a go.'

'Give what a go?'

'Mongolia, in the chopper. We've got the fuel. We stay low, avoid population centers . . .'

'You don't sound confident.'

'More confident about that than I am about taking our chances on the ground. Which reminds me. What did the pilot in that fighter say?'

'I don't know. I didn't catch it. I was being sick. What shall I tell them about why we're here?'

'Tell them the truth if you like—that we'd have been shot out of the sky if we hadn't landed.'

☭

Ben and Akiko made their way up the embankment toward the old women. More people had joined them.

'What do you want here?' said a thin white man in Russian. He was dressed in shades of black and had a weeping red nose and blue veins in his temples.

'We've had problems,' Akiko told him. 'Can we get some food? We have money.'

The man turned away from them and conducted a hurried conference with the people gathered, looking for a consensus.

'Yes. You can go to the church,' he said. 'I am the priest here, but you must leave as soon as you can. The authorities do not like strangers.'

'What's he saying?' Ben asked.

'We can stay,' Akiko told him.

'Good.' Ben smiled at the unwelcoming committee.

'What's the name of your village?' Akiko asked.

'We don't have a name,' the priest said. 'We have a number: TS17170.'

'You're a camp?'

The priest had said as much as he was going to. 'Go with Rozalina. She works for me.'

Rozalina was wide and squat with cruelly bowed legs. She beckoned at Akiko and Ben to follow her.

'Do you know where we're going?' Ben asked as they fell into line behind her.

Akiko gave him an overview of the arrangements as the crowd parted to let them through. Rozalina trudged slowly uphill through the snow, toward the small black homes. The sun was up but it would be several hours before it climbed above the hills behind the village. Every hut seemed to have a fire going, blue smoke streaming from many chimneys. The village was small—no more than 100 or so huts—and most were no bigger than a single room. There were no vehicles of any kind in evidence and no overhead electrical wires or satellite dishes. Like all of the small settlements they'd visited, this one was positioned on the side of a hill, facing away from the prevailing weather, protected from the worst of it by the hills and the trees, which had been cleared right back from the settlement's perimeter.

Ben stopped to look at a young boy sitting on a doorstep, mucus running from his nose and down his top lip. He was gnawing at something yellow in his hands.

'What's he eating?' Ben asked.

'Smoked fish.'

'I think I've lost my appetite.'

The boy smiled up at them as the door behind him opened and a woman came out, carrying a tub. She ignored Ben, Akiko and Rozalina and walked with a pronounced limp to a neat stack of chopped wood in what was the backyard, a small enclosure that also held assorted nondescript scrap metal. The woman set the tub on the snow beside the chopped wood, bundled some logs into it and then hoisted the weight back onto her hip. It was only then that she glanced up at the strangers stopped by her fence.

Akiko stared at her and the woman stared straight back. And then she dropped the tub in the snow and hobbled inside, dragging the child with her and slamming the door behind them.

'Friendly,' said Ben.

Akiko rushed to the door and pounded on it. '*Okaasan! Okaasan!*'

'Hey, Akiko,' Ben called out. 'What's up?'

'*Okaasan!*'

He walked over to her, the Russian woman shouting behind them, and grabbed her shoulders. 'What is it?' She was shaking. 'What's going on?'

'It's her . . . *Okaasan*,' Akiko said, the sobs catching in her throat.

'Who?'

'*Okaasan*—my mother!'

'That was Nami?' Ben asked, stunned.

☭

The door opened again and the older woman stood framed by the darkness behind her, tears streaking her face, the cold burning red circles on her cheeks. Her mouth was down-turned with anguish. The woman sure looked familiar, Ben thought. Akiko took a step forward and the two women held each other in a gentle embrace, crying on each other's shoulders.

Ben stood open-mouthed, the realization dawning on him. They'd found Nami. She was alive. Fate had brought them to the woman's doorstep in the middle of this bitter emptiness.

He sat down on a rusting fuel drum, overcome by the enormity of their discovery. If he hadn't known it before, he knew it now. KAL 007 was a sham. A survivor had been found when there weren't supposed to be any. And that meant 269 innocent people had lost their lives, not through death but through abandonment, sacrificed for reasons he couldn't fathom. They had simply been left for dead, buried by lies.

He glanced up in time to see Nami push Akiko back beyond the doorstep and slam the door shut between them.

February 17, 2012

NSA HQ, Fort Meade, Maryland. 'Who is he?' Lana asked, cradling the receiver under her chin as she tapped away at the report.

'His name is, or, I should say, *was* Arlo Locke. He was sixty-four,' said Saul Kradich.

'A little old to be a contract killer, don't you think?'

'I don't believe those guys have the usual retirement plans. There was a tattoo on his upper arm—arrows crossed over a dagger. He was a Green Beret. I checked him out thoroughly. Army specialist Arlo Locke was a CIA recruit for an operation called Phoenix. Heard of it?'

'An assassination program during the Vietnam War targeting suspected VC sympathizers.'

'You got it. He was recruited from a unit whose ranking NCO was your buddy Hank Buck.'

'You're kidding . . .'

'That's where the trail to Buck's military history begins and ends, which tells me he was also probably in Phoenix, but someone had every vestige of his records pulled.'

'Someone with plenty of elevation in the Company who also knew his way around NSA, perhaps?'

'If you mean someone like Roy Garret—yes, that's how I'd read it. It's pretty weird. I can't find *anything* about Buck's military service aside from what I just told you. It's like the guy never existed. I've got something else for you. Guess.'

'I've got no time to play twenty questions, Saul.'

'Okay, okay . . . You know that paper you asked me to trace? The one titled "Engineering the Collapse of West European Opposition to US IRBMs" et cetera and so forth?'

'You found it?' she asked, her fingers poised over the computer keys.

'I found it, but can you at least feed my ego a little by asking me *how* I found it?'

Lana sighed, playing along for the sake of cooperation. 'How'd you find it, Saul?'

'Well, it wasn't easy. You're lucky I want to sleep with you, otherwise I'd have given up.'

'Kradich . . .'

'I couldn't find it anywhere, not by the usual means. And then I got a call from the medical examiner about Locke and I found a lead about Buck through a back door. That got me thinking. Many of the other analyzes Garret wrote all had Ed Meese, William Casey, Bill Clark and Des Bilson on the circular. Turns out Bilson donated his archives to the Library of Congress when he died. Guess what I found among his records.'

'You *are* a genius. I mean that.'

'But will it get me laid? Never mind, I think I know the answer. I'm sending the hard copy down to you.'

'And it's worth reading?'

'In a word, fuckyeah.'

☭

Nami lay awake and listened to her husband in the darkness, every breath causing his chest to rattle like old bones hanging in the breeze. The day she had dared not think about for years had arrived.

At first, survival had depended on keeping alive a connection with her old life. She had dreamed of Akiko and Hatsuto and the cherry blossoms. But as the years slipped by, she had given away hope, cut it loose, and accepted her fate.

She remembered Akiko as the little girl at the airport. Now her daughter had come to find her. And somehow, among the vastness of this twilight life, she had succeeded.

Nami's husband's breath caught in his chest. He would be dead soon, she knew. And there were many others she cared for in this village. Too many to leave behind. Little Kimba would find it difficult to understand.

☭

Akiko had spent the day camped in front of Nami's house. Her mother wouldn't come out and so Akiko had refused to leave. She couldn't, not now. She had to speak with Nami. The priest had relented, allowing them to stay overnight. Then, he said, if they refused to leave, he would make a formal protest to the authorities in Listvyanka.

Once the shadows had lengthened and night had marched down the hills, Akiko had had no choice but to retreat to the church.

She sat on the edge of the cot in the dark and rocked back and forth, her arms around her drawn-up knees, trying to recall every smell, every memory, every story connected with Nami. The holes in her memory made her both angry and sad. The sheer loss she felt was like a black and empty sea in the center of her being. How *dare* they! Her mother was now an old woman. The years had been ripped from her and she was old. But there was strength within her. Nami had survived. And, from the embrace and the shared tears, Akiko knew that during all the lost years Nami had not forgotten her.

February 18, 2012

*Resettlement community TS17170, Siberia.*It was still dark when Akiko lit a candle and went looking for Ben. Rozalina had made him a bed on the floor at the back of the church, where the frozen air rushed up through the cracks in the worn boards. He was already dressed when she found him, sitting on one of the prayer benches, his head in his hands, his teeth chattering.

'How are you?' she asked.

'Cold. Be surprised. How about you?'

'We need to get Nami and leave here.'

'I know, but you don't think it's a bit early?'

'Let's go.'

'That would be a "no" then.'

Akiko opened the door and the frozen inrush of air blew out the candle. There was a lightening in the eastern sky, while overhead the stars were still shimmering with cold. Occasional people-shaped smudges of darkness could be seen moving about against the ghost-white backdrop of the snow.

'So, what's the plan?' Ben enquired. 'Just knock on the door and ask Nami if she'd like to go back home to Japan?'

'Yes.'

The morning was thick with a freezing white mist that sucked the sound out of the air, deadening their footfalls in the powdered snow. Akiko walked fast, with purpose.

When they arrived at Nami's home, Ben stopped at the back fence while Akiko kept going to the door. She hesitated, and then tapped on the door with a block of wood. She knocked again. And again. Finally, the door opened and Nami came out with the familiar tub and walked past her to the stacked firewood.

'We came here to Russia to find you,' said Akiko behind her.

'Please, can you speak Russian? I cannot remember Japanese.'

'Of course, yes.'

'I don't have time,' Nami said, looking back at the closed door. 'My husband wants his hot water.'

'You are married?'

'A woman can't survive here without a man. My husband has been a good provider and protector. I've had three children, but they are grown up.'

'What about the boy I saw?'

'A grandchild.' Nami dropped some small logs into the tub.

'I have thought about you every day,' said Akiko.

'Yes, me too, little Kimba.'

Akiko's chin dented at the mention of her childhood pet name.

'Can you tell me . . . How is Hatsuto?' Nami asked.

'He died some years ago. When he lost you, it broke his spirit.'

Nami stopped what she was doing and lowered her head. The mist was now suffused by the gray pre-dawn light, providing enough illumination for Akiko to see that Nami's lips were trembling.

'We met a man in another camp who said you were killed in an accident,' Akiko continued. 'He told me that you had lost an arm.'

'No, it was a leg,' said Nami. 'I was close to death. Afterwards, I was sent here. I have to go now.'

'Leave with us,' Akiko said.

'I can't.'

'Why not?'

'My life is here now.'

'But you *have* to come.'

'Why?'

Akiko couldn't get the words out. This was an outcome she hadn't expected.

'You are grown up,' said Nami. 'You have a husband. And he is very handsome.' She looked past Akiko toward Ben, who was idly dusting snow from the top of the fence post, beyond earshot.

'He is not my husband. His name is Benjamin. His father was also a victim of 007.'

'A passenger? Perhaps I knew him.'

'No, not a passenger. There were many more victims besides those who were aboard.'

'It happened so long ago. Everyone has forgotten.'

'No, you're wrong. The authorities said your plane crashed into the sea and everyone was killed. But they searched and found nothing.'

'And people believed this?' She snorted. 'I wondered why no one came to look for us.'

'The Russians, the Americans, our own people—they all lied. We came to Russia to find the truth.'

'You can't change what has happened. You can't make it right.'

'But if you come back with us, the truth will win.'

'Truth?' Nami said, shaking her head. 'There are only perspectives.' She removed the glove from her hand and put it on her daughter's cheek. 'My place is here. I belong here.'

Akiko saw her cracked and broken nails, felt the warmth of her mother's fingers against her skin, and the tears again welled into her eyes.

'Don't cry, little Kimba. I have made a life. It just wasn't the one I expected.'

An old man appeared in the doorway of Nami's home. He was a Russian, short and fat with a crimson vodka nose.

'Who are you?' he shouted in a quavering voice thick with phlegm. 'What do you want? Go away!' He leaned on the doorway as if the effort of getting there had exhausted him. 'Are these people another of your charities, Anastaysia? Come inside now before I beat you!'

'I'm coming,' Nami said.

'Anastaysia?'

'I have not been Nami for many years.'

'He beats you?'

'Not for many years also.'

'Why did he call us "charities"?'

'I look after people who can't look after themselves. They will die if I leave.'

'Kiko,' Ben called to her. 'What's happening?'

'They do not like strangers in this village, Akiko,' said Nami. 'You and your friend must go. I'm sorry.'

She lifted the tub onto her hip and limped to the door of her house. Her husband held the door open for her and then closed it with a bang as she disappeared inside.

'What's happening?' Ben asked.

'She won't come with us.'

'What? Why not?'

'I'll tell you later.'

'Hang on . . . We have no *proof* that Nami exists. Nothing! We don't even have a damn camera.' A thought occurred to him. 'If we could get a little of her hair, you know, DNA testing could—'

'It's over,' Akiko said as she walked down the hill, barely able to speak.

☭

Ben followed her downhill, his mind racing. They'd come all this way and, against the odds, they'd found Akiko's mother. And for what? With her, they could prove what had really happened to KAL 007. The news would bring closure to so many lives, answer so many questions. Curtis had sacrificed his life for this. Without her . . . Why the hell *wouldn't* she want to come back? What sort of life did Nami have here in this god-forsaken frozen shit hole that she *wouldn't* be desperate to leave it?

As they made their way to the helicopter, Ben could see the disappointment clinging to Akiko like the fog wrapping around her.

They passed the last of the huts and the 412 came into view. Ben stopped. So did Akiko. It was just as they'd left it the day before, except for one significant difference—now it was surrounded by army-style, khaki-green vehicles and armed troops in the same winter blue-on-blue camouflage scheme of the fighter jet.

There was a movement beside him and two armed soldiers stepped around the side of the hut. They shouted and raced toward them. Akiko put her hands on her head. Ben followed her lead, his heart rate soaring.

There was some frantic activity among the Russians around the chopper when they saw that Ben and Akiko had been detained. There was someone inside the machine—Ben could see the movement through the chopper's perspex windshield, even though it was frosted with snow. The figure jumped out of the machine on the far side and received a report from a subordinate.

The Russians beside Ben were talking to him, making gestures with their weapons that he didn't comprehend.

'We can put our hands down,' said Akiko, lowering hers warily.

Ben's short, tense breaths steamed in front of his face.

The person from the chopper came into plain view and waved at them. 'You two are most difficult to keep up with,' said the officer with a grin as she made her way up the hill, lifting her feet high out of the deep snow.

'Jesus,' said Ben. 'Is no one in this fucking country who they say they are?'

It was Luydmila, only now she was some kind of military officer.

'Why did you not follow fighter jet yesterday? It would have been easier for all concerned. I was waiting for you at base.'

'The pilot wasn't going to shoot us down?' Ben asked.

Grinning, she said, 'If he did, he would have been sent to Siberia.'

'So what are you? Army? Air force?'

'I am FSB. These three gold stars on each shoulder mean I am colonel.'

Two more green military vehicles drove up along the frozen river, one of them tooting its horn. The lead vehicle skidded to a halt and the passenger door opened. A young uniformed soldier raced up the hill toward the colonel when a fellow soldier pointed out where she was. He arrived in front of her, snapped to attention and saluted, puffing clouds of vapor, and gave his report. Colonel Luydmila Pozlov quietly gave her orders to a subordinate, who then barked at the soldiers in their vicinity.

Ben and Akiko found themselves being hurried toward the nearest hut while the unit deployed. Inside the hut it was cramped, dark and smelled of boiled potato, alcohol and dirt.

'I think you need to tell us what's going on,' said Ben.

'Korolenko—the man in the photo I showed you, the man who ran Soloyov and Bykovski—it is he who wants to kill you. This much you know—I have already told you. We had information that Korolenko is here. Or, I should say, somewhere out there.' Luydmila made a gesture that implied a 360-degree arc. 'My men have just located abandoned FSB vehicles, confirming it. They are nearby.'

'He's FSB and you are FSB?' Akiko asked, unable to hide her confusion.

'As in any large organisation, there are factions.' The colonel shrugged. 'There are people like Korolenko who want a return to the old ways, and there are others like me.'

'And what do you want?' Ben asked.

'A final changing of guard.'

A muffled noise came from outside, and the door opened. An armed soldier brought Nami into the room and then took the colonel aside for a private word.

'This woman wanted to know where you are being taken,' said Pozlov when the soldier had finished his report. 'Do you know her?'

Ben and Akiko glanced at each other, both uncertain now about how much they could trust Luydmila.

The colonel read their concern.

'I am on your side,' she said with a hint of exasperation. 'I think I have proved myself ally, yes?'

Akiko went to Nami and put her arm around her.

'Your mother?' Luydmila asked Akiko.

'Yes.'

'So you located the person you were searching for?'

Akiko gave her a nod.

'I commend you, but it would have been better if you had not.' The colonel took a moment to think through the situation. She then lifted her eyes and peered through the thinning mist at the wooded hills on the far side of the river. 'Korolenko will be aware that you have found her also. As KGB Fifth Directorate commanding officer in charge of foreign national prisoners, he would have had her transferred here. And he must know that this is his last chance to keep his actions over the years a secret. He will be desperate.'

'How desperate?' asked Ben.

'I have deployed my men to search the surrounding area to ensure that you don't find out. In the meantime, perhaps you should give me your clothes.'

☭

There was a clear line of sight through the trees to the settlement on the other side of the valley. While the visibility was currently questionable, the fog would lift sooner or later.

'Are you comfortable?' Korolenko asked.

'The reassuring pressure of a telescopic sight's cup against my eye, all joints locked and frozen in place, lying in my own chilled urine . . . Why wouldn't I be?' The shooter stroked the trigger guard of the SV-98 sniper rifle with his index finger to ensure he still had movement in the only piece of his anatomy that he cared about at this time. 'What do you estimate the wind?'

'Half a knot right to left.'

The shooter wondered why he'd bothered asking. At this distance, the deflection of the round's trajectory would be minuscule. 'What's going on beyond the chopper?'

Korolenko moved the binoculars to a view of the huts above the river. 'Occasional sightings of Colonel Pozlov's men. Nothing to indicate urgency. And you are sure that you can take three targets with confidence?'

'One male, two females. Standing still or running. From this distance and in these conditions . . . Providing the visibility doesn't deteriorate? No problem.'

The shooter shifted his view to the chopper itself. It reminded him of the old UH-1—the Huey. It made him feel vaguely nostalgic. 'I've been thinking . . . I could take out the rotor head when the chopper's about adjacent to our position here. It'll turn on its side and hit the ground hard. A fuel fire would almost certainly result. Might be a better plan.'

'I will leave the practical details to you,' said Korolenko. 'You're the expert.'

'Yes, I am.'

The shooter wasn't familiar with the Russian SV-98 sniper rifle, though he had taken the time to sight the weapon in the previous afternoon when they were still at Babushka, the town on the far side of the lake. Nevertheless, the rifle didn't feel right. The proportions and the weight were unfamiliar. It was a reasonable piece of equipment, but what he wouldn't give for an M107. A single .50 caliber round from an M107 pumped into that chopper's engine would turn its insides into metal slurry. He could wait until it had 500 feet of altitude before taking the shot. There'd be no survivors. Job done. And watching that big old bird spiral into the ground would be a spectacle.

'Okay, there is movement,' said Korolenko.

'Where?'

The magnification of the telescopic sight was easily powerful enough to pick out even the dust on the rivets in the chopper's aluminum skin. But with the magnification came a narrow field of vision. The bigger picture was the responsibility of the spotter who in this instance was Korolenko.

'Fifty feet high, fifty feet to the right,' the Russian said.

'Keep me informed,' the sniper whispered, nuzzling the rifle's stock against his cheek.

'I have Colonel Pozlov, the subjects, plus four providing escort. They are walking to the chopper. You will have them in less than thirty seconds.'

The shooter waited, concentrating on his breathing. Three clean shots coming up. Bodies, arms and legs filled the circle of his telescopic sight—five in uniform, three civilians. Of the civilians, one was male and tall, two were of slight build. They were all layered up with clothing against the cold, including their heads.

'I can confirm the identity of the three civilians. They are our subjects,' Korolenko whispered. 'You are cleared to fire.'

The shooter moved the crosshairs from the colonel to the male civilian, and slid his finger off the guard and onto the metal fang of the trigger itself. He let it take the weight of the firing mechanism, applying pressure to it gradually and then maintaining it at about three pounds of pressure. Another half a pound, an exhaled breath, and the rifle would jump on its bipod, the stock punching into the muscle above his collarbone.

'Oh, yeah,' he whispered as the targets moved into a slightly better position. 'Come to papa . . .'

He waited, willing the heads of his victims to bunch into a tighter group. The male target turned toward the chopper, giving him a good look at his face.

'Hey, wait a minute,' said the shooter, realizing that something was wrong. 'The male civilian here isn't supposed to be Asian. But this guy is—'

Sudden automatic rifle fire exploded behind them. The unexpected noise made the shooter start and the rifle jumped, thumping into his shoulder. He'd inadvertently squeezed the trigger. The round kicked up a small flare of snow on the hill behind the head of the male target. And now people were running everywhere. He couldn't get off another shot. More automatic fire. There was shouting. Korolenko was on his feet. They were instantly surrounded by FSB men who charged into the clearing, shouting, pushing. One of them kicked the rifle off its bipod.

'What the fuck,' said the shooter, getting to his knees.

An FSB soldier with a signaling pistol fired it into the air. A red flare soared out over the trees, away from the helicopter and the settlement below.

'Order your men to drop their weapons,' the shooter yelled at Korolenko.

'These are not my men. It won't do any good.'

'Where are your men? Order them to counterattack.'

'They won't.'

Colonel Pozlov strode into the area, snapping out orders. Four soldiers raced forward and searched the two captured men, while two more secured the weapons and ammunition. Ben, Akiko and Nami were escorted into the area.

'Colonel, how nice to see you,' said Korolenko, standing. 'I'm sure we can come to some arrangement here, don't you think?'

'Your two friends Bykovski and Soloyov killed a friend of mine, *retired* General Korolenko. There will be no arrangements—not with me—though I am sure someone will be happy to make them for you at Lefortovo.' The truth of what she had just said seemed to give the colonel pause. 'And that, perhaps, is a problem.'

Pozlov stepped across to one of her men, relieved him of his rifle, shouldered the weapon and fired it into Korolenko's solar plexus at point-blank range. The full metal jacket went through him as if he were no more substantial than the mist still blanketing ravines among the hills.

Korolenko looked down at the black smoking hole in his coat like a man checking a spot on his tie, and brushed it with a gloved hand. Blood began pouring down the back of his pants and quickly pooled in the snow around the heels of his boots. He appeared to want to speak, but no words came out. He fell forward into the snow face first, his hands by his sides.

Nami walked up to the body and spat on it, shaking with rage, her hands clenched into fists beside her face.

The colonel turned to Ben. 'My debt to you is now paid in full. Do not come back to Russia,' she warned him. 'We might not be so friendly toward you next time.'

She circled the sniper. 'And who might you be?'

'I don't speak Russian, lady,' the man said in a steady voice, defiant.

'You may call me Colonel. American?'

'Eat my dick, *Colonel*.'

'Passport,' Pozlov snapped.

The foreigner just smiled at her. Pozlov motioned to a subordinate who pulled the American to his feet and searched him. A moment later, the colonel had the document she wanted.

'I see you are a diplomat,' she said. 'An American.'

The man shrugged as the colonel flicked through the pages.

'Mr Henry L. Buck.' Her eyes flicked to Hank. 'Tell me, why are you shooting at people in my country with a sniper rifle?'

The American smiled again.

'What was your relationship to Korolenko?'

Hank gave her nothing.

'There are many questions and I think you have all the answers.'

'Let me guess. You have ways of making me talk,' said Hank.

It was Colonel Pozlov's turn to smile.

☭

The entire settlement turned out to watch the departure, the silent crowd lining the top of the embankment and looking down on the chopper, the FSB contingent, Ben and Akiko. It seemed that they were enjoying more entertainment than they'd experienced in a very long time.

Ben was done pre-flighting the chopper. He'd been provided with lat and long coordinates for the nearest Russian Air Force base as well as clearances to take off and land. Colonel Pozlov was going to come along for the ride and smooth the way for a rapid departure from Russia.

His countryman, Hank Buck, was sitting handcuffed in the back of one of the khaki vehicles. The man was to be taken back to Moscow by the colonel's subordinates for debriefing, before being released to the US embassy. The laws he'd broken included attempted murder, being in possession of a banned weapon, and consorting with a personal enemy of Colonel Pozlov's. She said that there would be a report released to Buck's people at the embassy, as well as to Reuters in the event that the US State Department attempted to hush things up. The man would have a hell of a lot of explaining to do, and Ben was looking forward to hearing what he might know.

'We've got a good break in the weather,' Ben said to Pozlov. 'We should use it.'

☭

Akiko searched the crowd on the embankment. An old woman made her way to the front and then walked down to meet her daughter.

'We are going now, Mother.'

'Let me hold you one more time, Akiko,' Nami said.

The two women embraced and Akiko whispered, 'Please change your mind. Come back with us.'

Nami took her hand. 'I want to, but there are sick people here who would have no one else.'

'But you must.'

'Little Kimba . . . I can't.'

Akiko looked into Nami's eyes and saw that her mother was resolute. 'Then I will come back here to you,' she whispered.

The two women embraced again.

'Could you please do me a favor?' Nami asked.

'Of course, Mother.'

Nami turned toward the crowd and gestured at someone to join her. An old man. He was frail with a weather-beaten, unshaved face, dressed in shades of black like everyone else in the village. A worn black *ushanka* was pushed down on his head. He stepped forward and made his way down the bank, crabbing carefully sideways in the loose snow. When he drew near, Nami took hold of his arm and gave it a reassuring squeeze. The man's eyes slid left and right. He seemed confused and frightened as if he didn't know where he was.

'Could you please take this man with you, back to America?' she asked.

Akiko looked the man up and down. 'Yes, if that is your wish. Who is he?'

'His name is McDonald. Congressman Lawrence McDonald.'

February 19, 2012

Sheraton Hotel, Seventh Avenue, New York City, New York. Roy Garret realized where he was. This was the very hotel where the flight crew—Captain Chun Byung-in, First Officer Sohn Dong-hwin and Flight Engineer Kim Eui-dong—had begun their long journey all those years ago. He wondered what had jolted his memory. They certainly hadn't conducted the briefing in the Presidential Suite up here on the twenty-first floor. He tried to recall that day as he took another mouthful of Glenfiddich and looked down on Seventh Avenue. A child had been hit by a cab, as he remembered, its mother dropping her shopping in the middle of the road and running to the kid. The memory was so vivid, it was like it had happened yesterday rather than twenty-nine years ago.

The evening's press conference at Radio City had been canceled by him. He'd given Felix Ackerman no reason for the cancelation. The man would find out soon enough. And when he did, Ackerman would be gone. Why hang around when the game was lost?

Garret sank into a chair and poured himself another glass of the fine scotch, spilling some over his hand. The bottle slipped from his grasp and fell beside the chair onto the carpet, its contents escaping with a *glug, glug, glug.*

The noise coming from the adjoining room told him that the secret service types were watching television. Had the story hit CNN yet? It would, and before the night was over, because two hours earlier an excited contact from his CIA days working in the US embassy in Moscow had called him with an astonishing story. The Japanese embassy had just informed the US mission that a man with no identification papers had walked in claiming to be Congressman Larry McDonald, a man who had supposedly been lost when the former Soviet Union had shot down the Korean 747 he was a passenger on nearly thirty years ago. It was the one that went down off Sakhalin Island. The news, when he heard it, had caused Garret to take a seat. The man claiming to be this congressman was accompanied by a female Japanese national and a US citizen who both backed this assertion. The Russians were also holding a man traveling on a US diplomatic passport, arrested for the attempted murder of the aforementioned US citizen and Japanese national. That man's name was Henry Buck.

Garret stared unseeing out the window at the lights of Seventh Avenue as a creeping headache swept over his brain like a fast-approaching storm front. The tumbler on his belly tipped and poured scotch all over his shirt.

The front door to the suite opened and Felix Ackerman burst past the secret service agent holding the knob. Garret saw the man's reflection in the window in front of him. He didn't need to see the color of Ackerman's face to know that he was livid.

'What the fuck is all this shit about Buck trying to shoot people with a fucking sniper's rifle in the middle of goddamn Siberia?' his campaign manager wanted to know.

Garret tried to raise his hand, but it remained in his lap, oddly heavy. It was the strangest sensation.

'And what the hell has it got to do with this looney tune who claims to be a long-lost fucking congressman? And how are you personally involved in this bullshit?'

Panic flashed through Garret's mind. He couldn't swallow, or blink. What in God's name was going on? He screamed, but all that came out of his throat was a dry croak.

'Governor? Are you okay?' Ackerman was suddenly on his haunches, peering into his face.

Garret tried to move his head, but couldn't. Oh, shit, he thought.

Ackerman waved his hand in front of Garret's bloodshot eyes.

'Boss, what's the matter?'

Garret managed to twitch a finger. Aside from breathing, which was becoming increasingly shallow, that was all the movement he could manage. He also realized that he could feel nothing at all and that his body weighed a hundred tons or more.

'Help!' Ackerman cried out. 'Help! Call an ambulance.'

Garret heard noises he associated with others racing into the room, but he couldn't turn his head to look.

Epilogue

Chena Lake, Fairbanks, Alaska. 'You made it,' said Ben, taking
Lana's hand and kissing her on the cheek.

'Thanks for asking me.'

'You deserve to be here. He would have wanted it.'

Lana hoped that Ben hadn't observed that she was blushing. It was
the kiss, his closeness. There was something about this guy . . .

She cleared her throat and said, by way of diversion, 'You might like
to read this.'

'What is it?'

'Something Governor Garret wrote a long time ago, about how to
win public support for government strategic interests. You're not supposed to know it exists, but the cat's well and truly out of the bag on
this one, so, you know . . . It'll explain a lot.'

'Thanks, I will. You didn't send a copy to the media?'

Ben resisted the temptation to tear the envelope open and read it
on the spot. Instead, he folded it in half and stuffed the paper down
the front of his backpack. According to various media, Garret was
lying in a hospital bed attached to tubes and various machines as the
result of a massive stroke, which, by coincidence, struck him around
the time the revelations about what really happened to KAL 007 and
its passengers were breaking. His frontal lobes were apparently mostly

unaffected. The *New York Times* had described his state as like being 'held prisoner within a body cast from solid lead'. As far as Ben was concerned, a hell like that couldn't have happened to a more deserving guy.

'No,' said Lana, 'but I thought about it. They need to work for it. Perhaps there's another copy out there somewhere. Or maybe they'll convince someone that it's in the national interest to open the NSA's compartment on KAL 007. I'm sure they'd find that document in there, along with a lot of other interesting stuff.'

'What'll you do now?' Ben asked. 'I heard you were gonna pack it in with the feds.'

'Yeah. I was thinking about horticulture. Plant trees, do something really useful.'

'You're kidding.'

'As a matter of fact I am—kidding.'

'What then?'

'Gonna head for the front lines. I was thinking FBI—anti-terror maybe. Get out of the back room.'

'Were you close to your ex-partner?'

'We had an understanding, but "close" isn't a word I'd have used. We got along fine sometimes, and other times we didn't. But his heart was in the right place. You couldn't fault Sherwood's commitment. He was the kind of guy who'd have been first out of the trenches knowing there was a machine gun zeroed on his position. I don't think he ever believed that he'd be killed in the line of duty, right up to the moment he died.'

'He have a wife, kids?'

'No. He had a home gym.'

A flight of birds flew overhead, squawking, fighting for something in midair that one of them had pulled from the lake's foreshore.

'What about you?' Lana asked as she looked right and then left, judging a break in the minimal traffic.

'Going back to Key West. My airplane's missing me.'

Lana smiled.

Across the road, in a park with swings, Akiko and Tex were waiting. They waved, and Ben returned it.

'How do you think it's all going to play out?' Ben asked.

'Now that the media's got its hooks in the story, things are going to move fast. There's a lot of pressure on Washington to lean on Russia and make them cough up as many of the passengers who might still be alive. There were very young children on that plane. I imagine there are Russians out there who are going to find out they're American, or Japanese, or one of a dozen other nationalities.'

'How about Garret? What's going to happen to him?' Ben asked.

'I don't know, but even if he wasn't on life support, I doubt that he'd win his party's nomination. And, of course, the Republicans are already claiming that it was all a Russian plot and their predecessors in the Reagan administration had nothing to do with it.'

'They'll never get away with it.'

'Oh, I don't know. There are people out there who'll tell you the holocaust was cooked up.'

Various experts had been called upon to claim that Lawrence McDonald was an impostor, but a simple DNA test comparing his genetic profile with that of his surviving children had cleared up the issue. Paternity was unequivocal. A lot of work had also gone into the discrediting of Yuudai's Wakkanai radar tape, which dissolved when McDonald's identity was confirmed. Ben had turned the tape over to CNN. He did it, he said, to honor the memory of Lucas Watts and Jerome Grundy. With the tape's authenticity established beyond doubt, they would have approved.

The governments of the thirteen nations other than the US who had lost citizens in the conspiracy of KAL 007 were all demanding that the records of the old KGB, and the newer FSB, be scoured for evidence of the whereabouts of their missing citizens. Litigation was under way and class actions had been launched against the incumbent governments of both the United States and Russia.

'Hey,' said Ben as they met the others.

'Hey yourself,' said Tex.

Akiko, Ben, Tex and Lana all exchanged hugs.

'Okay,' said Ben. 'We ready to do this?'

Akiko nodded. 'How are your mother and father?'

'Staying indoors. There are at least thirty news cameras and I don't know how many journalists camped outside their front door.'

'But they're alright?'

'They're fine, all things considered, though Frank's wearing a bandage on his head the size of a turban.'

'I had a bit of a scout around,' said Tex. 'There's a good place down here, where the grass ends. Or we could hire a boat.'

The sun was out, but the breeze was icy.

'No, this is good,' Ben decided.

They all walked down to the water's edge. Ben placed his backpack on the ground and pulled out the urn.

'Here you are, Curtis. Last stop, Chena Lake.'

He removed the top from the stainless-steel container. He didn't know what to say. Something religious wasn't on the cards. Curtis had been plain about that. Ben had been hoping that the right words would just occur to him. But now that the moment had arrived, his mind was a blank. And then, suddenly, he knew. It was a short speech, but it said everything that needed to be said.

'I embraced the truth, Dad. And I hope . . . I hope you're as proud of me as I am of you.'

Ben tipped up the urn and the falling ashes, caught by the breeze, scattered across the cold lake waters.

Author's note

Fact: In the early morning hours of September 1, 1983, Korean Air Lines Flight 007 flew more than 200 miles off course and headed for prohibited, heavily defended Soviet airspace.

Fact: Before this happened, a US RC-135 reconnaissance plane maneuvered so close to the 747 in the Soviet buffer zone over the Bering Sea that Russian air defense radar operators saw the blips of the two aircraft merge on their screens, confusing their identities.

Fact: After overflying some of the most sensitive military regions in Russia, Korean Air Lines Flight 007 was intercepted by a Soviet SU-15 over the Sea of Japan off Sakhalin Island. The fighter fired two missiles at the airliner and reported that at least one of the missiles had struck home.

Fact: A commercial airliner weighing close to half a million pounds hitting the water will leave a slick of floating debris a couple of miles wide. Yet despite a concerted air and sea search conducted by the navies of several nations—the biggest in history up to that time—no significant wreckage of KAL 007 was found. Two bodies, unidentifiable, were eventually recovered.

Fact: The Japanese Defense Agency first began searching the seas southeast of the island of Hokkaido because a report made by KAL 007 moments *after* the missile strikes positioned the airliner out along Romeo 20, 200 miles south of where experts believe it really was.

Fact: Within hours of the downing, a report attributed to the CIA claimed the aircraft had landed safely on Sakhalin Island. The CIA soon after denied that it had made the report.

Fact: Congressman Lawrence Patton McDonald was aboard KAL 007.

Fact: After years of denial by the Russians that they had the plane's black boxes, in 1992, Boris Yeltsin turned up with the plane's black boxes at a press conference, but they contained no tapes. He produced the tapes themselves at a press conference a year later. Subsequent examination of the tapes by a range of experts raised more issues than they resolved.

Was KAL 007 on a CIA mission? Why didn't the RC-135 send a warning to the 747's flight crew that it was headed for serious grief? What happened to the bodies? And the wreckage? If the plane landed on Sakhalin Island or, as another theory postulates, ditched safely in the Tartar Strait, where are the passengers today?

These and so many other questions require answers.

What really happened to KAL 007? It's time we knew.

Writing *The Zero Option* required a tonne of research. I had intended to supply a bibliography and webography for readers interested in checking my facts or doing a little research of their own. However, there has recently been a lot of good work put into the Wikipedia entry on Korean Air Lines Flight 007 and much of the source material I used you'll find a reference to there.

Another great overall resource containing a wealth of relevant material on the fate of KAL 007 is www.rescue007.com. Bert Schlossberg, whose father-in-law was a passenger aboard the Korean airliner on the night it was lost, manages this site.

There are many people I'd like to thank for helping me out with what became, I have to admit, something of an obsession. First on the list is Lieutenant Colonel Mike 'Panda' Pandolfo, USAF, who provided support of the technical and moral variety and almost on a daily basis.

I'd also like to thank Colonel 'Woody' Woodward, USAF (Ret.) for the many discussions we had sorting through what might and might not have happened to KAL 007.

Thanks also to my agent, Kathleen Anderson, who went above and beyond with editing and creative direction.

Thanks to Trisha, Mike, Richard, Andrew, Joe and Ed Elbert, all of whom read earlier drafts and provided notes and comments.

I'd like to thank Rob Mac for living the writer's dream and for giving me the courage to do a little of the same.

I'd also like to thank all the dedicated folks at Pan Macmillan, but especially my new publisher, Rod Morrison, for believing in the book, my new senior editor, Emma Rafferty, for doing such a sensitive job on the manuscript, and my new copy editor, Nicola O'Shea, for loving this story.

And finally, I'd like to thank my wife Sam, who suffered through endless recountings of the facts surrounding 007 over the two and a half years it took to research, plan and write this book. No doubt she counted herself among the victims.

David Rollins
April, 2009

OTHER FICTION AVAILABLE FROM PAN MACMILLAN

Grant Hyde
Lords of the Pacific

In the tradition of Wilbur Smith and Patrick O'Brian comes an epic South Seas adventure.

The year is 1793 and having suffered at the hands of Tonga's evil King Tui'pulotu for too long, the Island Nations of the South Pacific are poised on the brink of civil war.

When two heroic young warriors, Sevesi and Kiki, dare to challenge the King's absolute power, they incur his wrath, and only narrowly escape with their lives. The pair flee north, seeking sanctuary with the rebel tribes of Ha'apai. But instead of finding a safe haven, they are accused of being spies . . .

Meanwhile, as the British and French continue their relentless quest to colonise the South Pacific, one of their ships is hijacked and strays off course, inadvertently dragging both Empires into the greatest tribal war the Pacific has ever known.

As cultures collide, blood is shed, wrongs are righted and unlikely friendships are forged. Yet again, the British and French sorely underestimate the volatility and strength of their foes and the question remains: who will emerge as Lords of the Pacific?

Lords of the Pacific is a spellbinding tale of love, revenge and war set in one of the world's last great frontiers.

Greig Beck
Beneath the Dark Ice

When a plane crashes into the Antarctic ice, exposing a massive cave beneath, a rescue and research team is dispatched.

Twenty-four hours later, all contact is lost.

Captain Alex Hunter and his highly trained squad of commandos are fast tracked to the hot zone to find out what went wrong – and to follow up the detection of a vast underground reservoir. Accompanying the team is an assortment of researchers, including petrobiologist Aimee Weir. If the unidentified substance proves to be an energy source, every country in the world will want to know about it, some would even kill for it.

Once inserted into the cave system, they don't find any survivors – not even a trace of their bodies. Primeval hieroglyphs hint at an ancient civilisation, and an ancient, terrifying danger. Within hours, one of the party will die.

Soldiers we are not alone. Prepare to go hot.

To bring his team out alive, Alex will need every one of his mysterious abilities beneath the dark ice.

AVAILABLE AUGUST 2009

Tony Park
Ivory

Alex Tremain is a pirate in trouble.

The two women in his life – his financial adviser and his mechanic – have left him. He's facing a mounting tide of debt and his crew of modern-day buccaneers is getting restless. What Alex really wants is to re-open his parents' five-star hotel on the Island of Dreams, off the coast of Mozambique.

But a chance raid on a ship sets the Chinese triads after him and, to add to his woes, corporate lawyer Jane Humphries lands, literally, in his lap. Another woman is the last thing Captain Tremain needs right now – especially one whose lover is a ruthless shipping magnate.

Before he knows it, Alex is embroiled in two separate and equally risky pursuits – one takes him to South Africa's Kruger National Park and will pay enough for him to re-open his hotel, and the other involves the love of a lifetime. Can Alex pull off this one last heist and walk away with both prizes?